Raiding Forces Series

DESERT PATROL

by

Phil Ward

Published by Military Publishers LLC
Austin, Texas
www.raidingforces.com

Distributed by Military Publishers LLC

For ordering information or special discounts for bulk purchases, please contact Military Publishers LLC at 8871 Tallwood, Austin, TX 78759, 512.346.2132.

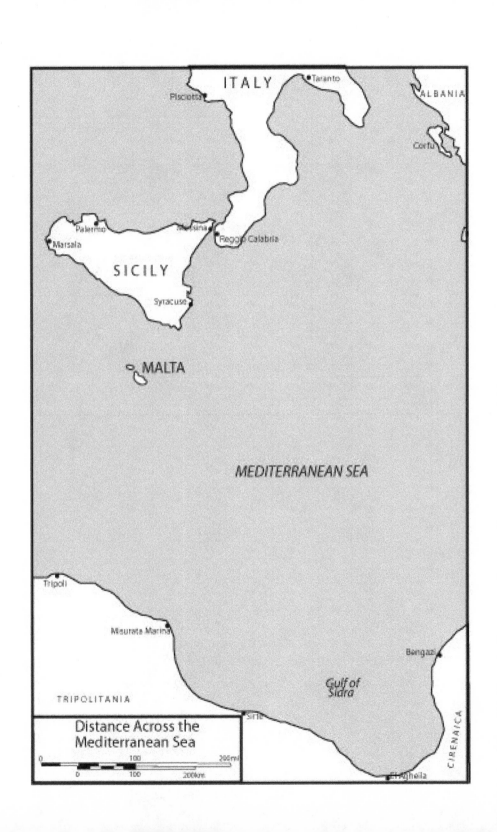

ITALY

Taranto

Pisciotta

ALBANIA

Corfu

Palermo

Messina

Marsala

Reggio Calabria

SICILY

Syracuse

MALTA

MEDITERRANEAN SEA

Tripoli

Misurata Marina

Bengazi

Gulf of
Sidra

TRIPOLITANIA

Sirte

CIRENAICA

Distance Across the
Mediterranean Sea

| 0 | 100 | 200mi |
| 0 | 100 | 200km |

El Agheila

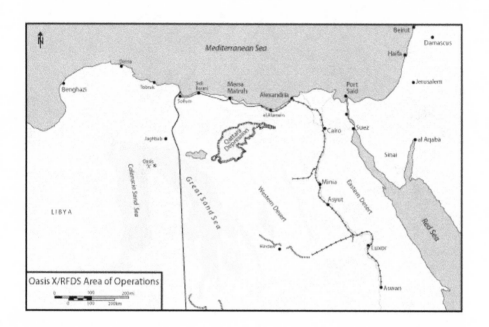

Dedication

DEDICATED TO THE LATE LT. GOV. BOB BULLOCK...

MY FATHER-IN-LAW

Upon graduation from Officer Candidate School, by tradition a new Second Lieutenant has to buy his first salute from the OCS Company First Sergeant...slipping a freshly-minted dollar bill—folded just so and pressed by an iron—to him with the left hand. Trying not to appear physically ill, the First Sergeant then renders the first salute – it being duly paid for.

I was 19 years old and two days late to Ranger School when mine was purchased. The First Sergeant broke tradition and actually spoke to me. He said, "Lt. Ward, can I give you some advice?"

"Absolutely, Top."

"Sir...don't fuck up and don't step on your dick."

A quick check to see if he was putting me on revealed the old soldier was as serious as a fire-breathing dragon.

"Roger, that."

Fast forward 25 years. I had married the best-looking girl in Texas. Her father was the most powerful and feared politician in the state (the State History Museum in Austin is named after him.) One day when the Senate was in session, he told the only female senator, "You'd stand a better chance of getting your bills passed if you wore more lipstick and shorter dresses."

Words cannot do justice to the firestorm of public indignation that resulted. The political correctness police were outraged, women's groups were calling for him to resign and the press was having the most fun it had had in years.

I wrote my father-in-law a letter.

I told him the story about my first salute and the advice my dollar bought. I concluded by saying, "Bob, I've been trying to follow my OCS First Sergeant's guidance ever since, but until I heard what you said about the lipstick and short dresses, it never dawned on me that it was physically possible to do both the things he warned against at the same time."

The phone rang. It was Bob. He said, "I got your note."

Gone but not forgotten.

"GOD BLESS TEXAS"

Randal's Rules for Raiding

Rule 1:   The first rule is there ain't no rules.

Rule 2:   Keep it short and simple.

Rule 3:   It never hurts to cheat.

Rule 4:   Right man, right job.

Rule 5:   Plan missions backward (know how to get home).

Rule 6:   It's good to have a Plan B.

Rule 7:   Expect the unexpected.

Intelligence Note Number 1

The year 1941 was the worst in British modern history. France had fallen. Russia was an ally of Nazi Germany. The United States was neutral.

Intelligence Note Number 2

In the Middle East Command, Tobruk was under siege. The Africa Korps was on the Egyptian border preparing to invade. Crete was standing by to be invaded by German Airborne Forces. In Greece, the British Expeditionary Force had been evacuated by sea in a mini-Dunkirk. Malta was under siege. And in Iraq, the Golden Square had launched a coup d'état.

Intelligence Note Number 3

Without warning, Iraqi Forces surrounded and laid siege to the isolated, peacetime flying school at RAF Habbaniya. Nazi Germany indicated it would supply the 22nd Air-Landing Division, plus provide a Luftwaffe Mission, to help the Golden Square drive the British out of their country.

Intelligence Note Number 4

The Iraqi Petroleum Company and the Anglo-Persian Oil Company provided Great Britain with all of her non-American oil.* If Germany controlled Iraq, then it would also control Iran.

American oil supplies were vulnerable because the oil had to be shipped by sea in tankers subject to U-boat attack.

Intelligence Note Number 5

Fighting on five fronts, Field Marshal Sir Archibald Wavell did not want another battle in Iraq to deal with. He advised negotiation. Communications were so poor that he did not know the Anglo-Iraqi war had been going on for two days and that the besieged cantonment at RAF Habbaniya was giving a good account of itself.

Intelligence Note Number 6

Iraq lay almost on the dividing line between Middle East Command and India Command. Prime Minister Churchill decided to relieve Field Marshal Wavell for lack of aggressiveness, but that was not possible at the moment. The PM ordered responsibility for operations in Iraq transferred to General Claude Auchinleck of India Command. However, the changeover would take a few weeks to implement.

Intelligence Note Number 7

Deputy Führer Rudolf Walter Hess flew solo—in an ME-110 fitted with long-distance fuel tanks—to Scotland, where he parachuted out. Hess was there to negotiate a separate peace treaty between Great Britain and Germany. There was only one condition: England had to pull out of Iraq.

Intelligence Note Number 8

RAF Habbaniya was down to one days' rations for the 9,000 civilians trapped on the station.

1

WOLF'S TEETH

"ARE YOU PREPARED TO RECEIVE A WARNING ORDER?" Major John Randal, DSO, MC asked. It was not really a question. No answer was expected.

Captain Valentine Fabian, Captain John Smith, Squadron Leader John Page, Squadron Leader Paddy Wilcox, DSO, OBE, MC, DFC, Squadron Leader Tony Dudgeon, Lieutenant Pamala Plum-Martin, OBE, Lieutenant Roy Kidd, Lieutenant Kit Wilson and Mr. Zargo were sitting in folding chairs in the small private briefing area of Maj. Randal's red-and-white-striped Command Post tent. The formal statement alerted them that a mission was imminent and that they would be playing key roles in it.

Tension ratcheted up.

"SITUATION…"

Colonel Ouvry Roberts came in the back of the tent accompanied by a tall, broad-shouldered civilian in a cream-colored suit, wearing round, steel-rimmed glasses.

"Colonel," Maj. Randal said, "this is a classified briefing."

"Quite right, Major. I think in this case we can make an exception."

"Sir…"

"Jimmy has been touring the Middle East on official business and arrived here at RAF Habbaniya this morning in the capacity of a neutral observer," Col. Roberts said. "Among other things, he is a captain in the United States Marine Corps.

"I am confident you can count on his complete discretion."

Sqn. Ldr. Wilcox made eye contact with Maj. Randal and gave him a small nod.

Maj. Randal said, "SITUATION: The rebel Iraqi Army in division strength occupies the escarpment between RAF Habbaniya and the lake two miles distant. The rebels have been subjected to intensive bombing, an aggressive night-raiding program and a psychological warfare campaign that caused the Golden Square to have to replace the 4th Infantry Brigade because their troops quit fighting. They had to bring in a fresh artillery brigade after only two days of action.

"MISSION: Tonight at 0200 hours, Strike Force will conduct a raid on the village of Sin-el-Dhibban – the Wolf's Teeth – to show the enemy that we are capable of ground offensive operations in force at a time and place of our choosing."

Maj. Randal flipped the cloth covering over the back of the tripod holding a diagram map of the objective.

"EXECUTION: Capt. Smith, No. 4 Levies Company, will move down the road to attack the right flank of Wolf's Teeth with his Levies Company. Capt. Fabian, A Company, King's Own Royal Rifles, guided by Mr. Zargo's Z Patrol, will scale the escarpment, infiltrate around the left flank and attack simultaneously with No. 4."

"Sqn. Ldr. Page will follow Capt. Smith's company with No. 1 Armored Car Company (ACC). Once contact is made, the armored cars will pass through No. 4 Levies Company and spearhead the final assault.

"Five minutes prior to the main attack, Lt. Roy Kidd will land his patrol from the lake, move overland and conduct a demonstration to the rear of Wolf's Teeth.

"All three Strike Force companies will attack on signal and consolidate on the objective. Once Wolf's Teeth has been secured, we will return to RAF

Habbaniya. Order of return march will be Levies, King's Own and No. 1 ACC.

"CONCEPT OF THE OPERATION: Murder, Inc. will supply guides to lead the companies to their Final Objective Lines.

"Sqn. Ldr. Wilcox, flying a Gordon bomber, and Lt. Plum-Martin in her Seagull, will each drop 250-pound bombs on Wolf's Teeth at 0200 hours, which will be the signal for A Company, King's Own and No. 4 Company, Levies, to launch the ground assault. No. 1 ACC will pass through No. 4 and drive home the final attack.

"Sqn. Ldr. Dudgeon will lead an element of Oxford bombers flying from the airfield to carry out suppression missions in the event the Iraqi artillery attempts to engage. Sqn. Ldr. Dudgeon's flight will also interdict any mechanized or infantry reinforcements, should they attempt to respond to counter the Strike Force raid.

"Lt. Wilson will support the withdrawal phase with the two 4.5 guns that have been ornaments outside Air Headquarters. The cannons have been serviced and certified for action by his fitters.

"This is a raid of short duration. Execute it with speed and violence of action. Consolidate on the objective. Be prepared to pull out and return to base on command.

"Tomorrow at 1000 hours, Major Ted Everett will launch a follow-up three-company attack on Wolf's Teeth, with B Company of the King's Own under command of Captain Clayton, and C Company commanded by Major Gibbons. No. 1 ACC will be attached.

"Maj. Everett's mission is to mop up the remaining Iraqis — drive 'em out of Wolf's Teeth.

"COMMAND AND SIGNAL: I command the Strike Force raid. The chain of command is Capt. Fabian, Capt. Smith, and then Sqn. Ldr. Page. The Operations Order is scheduled for 1400 hours. Line of Departure time is 0115 hours for the King's Own, 0130 for the Levies. No. 1 ACC will follow the Levies Company across the LD.

"The signal to attack will be the airstrike on the objective at 0200 hours.

"The signal to withdraw will be three green flares.

"ADMINISTRATION AND LOGISTICS: Make sure every man has a double basic load of ammunition with one magazine loaded, all tracers for the initial assault, and four frag grenades.

"Questions?"

***

VERONICA PAIGE AND HER DAUGHTER MANDY came into the Command Post (CP) tent when the Warning Order was concluded. After everyone cleared out, Major John Randal sat perched on the edge of his desk.

"Take your blouse off, Major," Veronica commanded.

Maj. Randal started unbuttoning his faded green jungle jacket. He noted that Jimmy had not left the tent.

Getting the jacket off was not easy. Maj. Randal was wrapped in bandages from his armpits to the bottom of his ribs – some of which were probably cracked. He grimaced in pain.

Mandy started cutting through the bandages with a pair of scissors. Maj. Randal was black and blue, with brilliant patches of violet, dark purple and green mixed in. Jimmy's eyes squinted when he saw the scars. An experienced African big game hunter, he knew they were too large to be a leopard...lion?

Maj. Randal said, "United States Marines."

"James J. Roosevelt," Captain Roosevelt said.

"Really," Maj. Randal said.

"My *father*, President Franklin D. Roosevelt, sent me on an around-the-world tour to let certain interested parties know that it will only be a matter of time before the U.S. enters the war. I am out here on the final leg of my tour doing exactly that."

"Welcome to scenic Habbaniya," said Maj. Randal.

"You are on my short list of people to talk to," Capt. Roosevelt said. "James Taylor told me this was where I would find you."

"James Taylor?"

Capt. Roosevelt looked at Maj. Randal, "I flew in with him this morning. Baldie said you would probably play it this way – *Frogspawn.*"

Maj. Randal lit a cigarette with his battered Zippo lighter with the crossed sabers of the U.S. 26th Cavalry Regiment on the front.

Veronica had wrapped a clean bandage around his chest and was tying it off.

"Finish up, Mrs. Paige," Maj. Randal ordered. "You're not a doctor."

"Nor a veterinarian," Veronica said. "Mandy, make the Major soak one hour in the pool starting right now, then re-wrap him with fresh bandages."

"Yes, mother," Mandy said. "I am going to go change into my swimsuit. Be ready for the pool when I get back, John. Do not give me a hard time."

"On your way out," Maj. Randal said, "tell Flanigan no one comes in here."

When they were alone, Capt. Roosevelt said, "After I conclude my business in the Middle East, my next assignment will be in the office of the Coordinator of Information. Colonel "Wild Bill" Donovan's my new boss. He tried to see you when he was out here a few months ago but you were behind the lines in Abyssinia."

"Fighting 69th," Maj. Randal said, "Medal of Honor?"

"That's him," Capt. Roosevelt said. "He asked me to evaluate British Commando training and operations, with an eye to setting up Marine Battalions dedicated to raiding in the future. Your name came up as being an authority on small-scale raiding. In addition, Baldie says you're the most experienced guerrilla commander in Africa.

"Both raiding and guerrilla operations are of great interest to Col. Donovan."

"I see," said Maj. Randal, which meant he did not have a clue what Capt. Roosevelt was talking about.

"The Colonel asked me to advise you that when the U.S. enters the war, he intends to offer you a job."

"And what might that be?"

"I have no idea," Capt. Roosevelt said. "It is my understanding that Col. Donovan is working out a joint operating agreement with one of the British intelligence agencies, where the U.K. and the U.S. will cooperate on certain activities both overt and covert. Would you be interested in something of that nature – direct action?"

"Captain," Maj. Randal said, "the Iraqi Army can stroll down that ridge they're sitting on and overrun this base in five minutes any time they decide to get up and do it. I'm not thinking any farther out than that."

"You are not opposed to the idea then, in principle – I can report to the Colonel?"

"If the United States comes in, Col. Donovan can count on me to serve where needed," Maj. Randal said. "Best check back later though. There're ten thousand bad guys out there on that hill and we're planning to make 'em really mad tonight."

"Yes, you are," Capt. Roosevelt said. "A bold plan – some might call it a suicide mission."

"When I arrived, Habbaniya had four days' rations for the civilians," Maj. Randal said. "*This* is day four."

"Read your book *Jump on Bella*," Capt. Roosevelt said. "Didn't know what to expect when I finally got around to meeting you, Major. Never imagined I'd find the legendary commander of the Strategic Raiding Forces being bullied by a couple of women."

"Yeah," Maj. Randal said, "a disappointment, wasn't it?"

***

MAJOR JOHN RANDAL WAS SOAKING IN THE SHALLOW end of the pool, which was said to be the best in the Royal Air Force. He was in a lot of pain. Mandy was sunning on a lounge chair, reading a three-month-old movie star magazine.

Intermittently, an incoming artillery round detonated somewhere on the base. Most were aimed at one decoy installation or another, all designed by 15-year-old magician "The Great Teddy," and so doing very little material damage. The explosions had become commonplace.

Unless, that is, one landed close by.

Mr. Zargo was giving Captain James J. Roosevelt a tour of the Strike Force and its auxiliary operations.

Captain Valentine Fabian, Captain John Smith and Squadron Leader John Page were at their company command posts issuing Warning Orders to their platoon leaders – the two Strike Force infantry companies had both been reconstituted back to their original table of organization for the raid.

Squadron Leader Paddy Wilcox and Lieutenant Pamala Plum-Martin were making preparations for the night's mission. The Gordon bomber was flown down and landed on the stretch of road Lt. Plum-Martin used for her nocturnal operations in the Seagull. After it was covered up by field-expedient camouflage netting developed by "The Great Teddy" out of fishing nets, Sqn. Ldr. Wilcox entertained himself counting the patched-up bullet holes and shrapnel splinters in the airplane.

He gave up when the number reached 72.

Maj. Randal was lying on the steps in the shallow end of the pool, soaking his battered ribs while reading a pocket-sized training pamphlet authored by a Col. G.A. Wade, MC, titled *"FIGHTING PATROL TRAINING."*

The Colonel listed six of what he described as "CHARACTERISTICS": Determination, Skill, Ability, Instinctive Reaction, Simple Movements and Confidence.

'These are the six principal characteristics that we should aim to produce in our fighting patrols.'

Maj. Randal thought that sounded good.

Determination to attack any enemy quickly and bloodthirstily.

Skill in handling weapons.

Ability to move quietly, inconspicuously and *quickly* across the landscape.

Instinctive reaction to attack.

Power to carry out simple, well-synchronized pincer and other movements.

Confidence in the Patrol Leaders.

Maj. Randal went back and re-read the list of "characteristics" and verified that they did not match the second "six principal characteristics" – Hmmmm?

Nevertheless, *Fighting Patrol Training* was a neat little handbook with a wealth of good advice for how to prepare for and conduct a fighting patrol. Maj. Randal thought it would be an excellent tool for training patrol leaders.

Col. Wade was clearly keen to get at the enemy. His introduction to the art of training 'Fighting Patrol Leaders' on the flyleaf concluded with, "And then, when the Great Moment comes for you to lead your fighting patrol against the invading Huns, KEEP YOUR MEN TOGETHER, KEEP UP MOMENTUM, and you will find yourself enjoying the FINEST SPORT ON EARTH!"

No invading Huns here, but Maj. Randal thought the Colonel's advice was tailor-made for the night's raid on Wolf's Teeth – concentrate Strike Force's companies and drive hard on the objective, fast.

Overhead, a single Wellington bomber had detached itself from a formation of five on their way to bomb the Iraqi airfield at Fallujah. It did a flyover of the converted polo pitch/golf course airstrip at about 1000 feet. Three tiny specks detached from the aircraft, parachutes billowing out, looking like swimming octopuses as their static lines deployed them. The crack of each individual canopy popping open was distinct.

Mandy looked up and shaded her eyes with her hand. "Wonder who would be mad enough to parachute into a place surrounded by homicidal Iraqis?"

"You're tanning while standing by to be overrun by 'em," Maj. Randal said, going back to his reading. "And you think someone else isn't playing with a full deck?"

Presently a staff car pulled up at the gate to the Officer's Club.

Captain the Lady Jane Seaborn, Royal Marine Lana Turner and Royal Marine Rita Hayworth stepped out.

Maj. Randal said to Mandy, "Here comes trouble."

"Lady Jane?"

"Affirmative."

"Wow, she's even better-looking than people claimed," Mandy said.

"Nefertiti," Maj. Randal said. "Force N was named after Lady Jane." Which was not true.

"The Egyptian queen married to the Pharaoh Akhenaten," Mandy said. "Nefertiti translates as 'the beautiful one has arrived'."

"You tell Lady Jane I said that."

Mandy said, "You just did."

2

THE RAID

MAJOR JOHN RANDAL ISSUED THE OPERATIONS ORDER for the raid on Wolf's Teeth. Upon completion, all parties immediately departed to their individual headquarters and issued their own orders to their subordinate commands. Company commanders to platoon commanders, platoon commanders to squad leaders; then at the designated time, a full company operations order was issued to the troops.

Ammunition was drawn, weapons checked, radios calibrated, rehearsals conducted, inspections made and a million minor details worked out.

Time simply vanished. There is never enough time before a mission to do everything that needs to be done. All three companies were still making last-minute preparations as they moved up to the Line of Departure (LD). It is a given that a commander, once assigned an LD time, will cross it to the second no matter what – ready or not.

Strike Force personnel had been running around all afternoon like their hair was on fire. Now the troops were marching. Lead elements were already on the LD.

Excitement was in the air. Strike Force was on the move. There was going to be a fight.

Squadron Leader Paddy Wilcox and Lieutenant Pamala Plum-Martin took off from their improvised airstrip. Simultaneously, Squadron Leader Tony Dudgeon and one other pilot took off from the airfield.

Two miles away, Brandy Seaborn and Lieutenant Penelope Honeycutt-Parker were landing Lieutenant Roy Kidd and his patrol behind the Iraqi lines. The Lake Patrol's mission was to slip ashore and infiltrate Wolf's Teeth from the rear. Tonight, every trooper was armed with a .45 Thompson submachine gun or a Bergmann 9mm MP-18. At 0155 hours, the men were scheduled to open up on the unsuspecting village, firing all tracers.

Lt. Kidd was charged with creating a diversion, which was in fact a feint. The idea was to surprise and distract the Iraq battalion occupying the village. The intent was for the rebels to shift their attention to the unexpected attack from their rear, away from where the actual assault would go in.

Then the Iraqis were going to be hit with an airstrike, followed up immediately by a full-scale two-company infantry assault by A Company, King's Own and No. 4 Company, Levies, with fixed bayonets. Finally, No.1 Armored Car Company (ACC) would pass through the riflemen and exploit the objective.

Lieutenant Kit Wilson, Royal Artillery, was moving the two newly refurbished 4.5 howitzers into battery with the aid of a tractor from the airfield. The guns were going to cover the withdrawal phase of the raid and then be in position to support Major Ted Everett's dawn attack. It was hoped that the guns, besides doing execution, would have a demoralizing effect on the rebels.

From London, where he was home on leave, Raiding Forces' happy psychological warrior, Captain Hawthorne Merryweather, broadcast a segment on the BBC nightly news about specially-fitted Lancaster transports flying in heavy artillery to besieged RAF Habbaniya. It was a lie, of course – psychological warfare – but the Iraqis had no way of knowing that.

He signed off with a direct threat to the Iraqi troops on the escarpment.

"BEWARE THE ORANGE SQUIRRELS!"

Captain Richard Sorrels arranged for his provisional mortar battery to lay in triple the normal supply of mortar rounds expended per night. Once the raid began, the mortar battery was tasked with firing a 'seal' mission. The plan was to saturate the area between Wolf's Tooth and the rest of the Iraqi positions with a constant barrage to discourage the rebels from sending reinforcements.

All of the Levies' bunkers, running the length of RAF Habbaniya opposite the escarpment, were on stand-by to engage the Iraqi positions directly across from their position with intensive machine gun fire, beginning when the aerial bombs went off at 0200 hours. With any luck, this would confuse the rebels as to what was actually taking place. RAF Habbaniya might be preparing to launch an attack somewhere else...who was to know?

If it worked, by the time the Iraqis sorted out what was happening, the raid would be over.

The plan was the best Maj. Randal could craft under the circumstances. The scheme of maneuver was worked out in detail on the sandtable in the Operations Center. Capt. Fabian, Capt. Smith and Sqn. Ldr. Page had spent hours studying the problem before presenting their solutions to him.

Maj. Randal realized that there were a lot of *ifs*, *maybes* and *hopefullys*. However, he knew rolling the dice is an element of every operation. If a commander is skilled in the military arts, knows his enemy and possesses a lucky star, he can offset the chance aspect with planning, speed and violent execution – usually.

Maj. Randal eliminated complicated movement, simplified some of the proposed tactics and limited dependence on radio communications. Signals were visual – phase lines, flares, bombs exploding...things that people could see or hear.

The KISS principle was in full force and effect.

Strike Force troops thought of themselves as veterans by now, but Maj. Randal was mindful that tonight was the first time any of them had ever participated in a battalion-sized combat operation, much less one carried out in the dark against a superior enemy. It could all go wrong.

***

STRIKE FORCE WAS CLOSED UP ON A CUT in the wire at bunker No. 10 – the Line of Departure. No. 4 Company Levies, wearing their Australian-style slouch hats with one side pinned up, moved out right on time. There was the muffled rattle of equipment and boots crunching on sand but not much other sound.

The Assyrians were followed out by No. 1 Armored Car Company, RAF. The Rolls Royce Silver Spirits traveled in a trail formation. To cover the sound of their engines, Squadron Leader Tony Dudgeon and his wingman were buzzing the Iraqi advance positions directly opposite along the Main Line of Resistance (MLR) in their Oxford bombers.

Major John Randal's Strike Force HQ element moved next. It consisted of a single Dodge open-topped ammunition carrier borrowed from the RAF. Flanigan was at the wheel. King was manning the radio. He would double as machine gunner on the pedestal-mounted .303 Vickers K.

At the last minute, Captain James J. Roosevelt showed up in a sterile uniform – no rank or any identifying insignia…wearing a pair of high-topped tennis shoes and lace-up leggings. He was carrying a .45 Thompson submachine gun, in direct contradiction of his neutral observer status, and a large canvas magazine pouch. Without a word, he climbed in the back of the carrier.

"Let's go," Maj. Randal ordered, clenching one of his last Italian cigarillos from Force N in his teeth – unlit. He was in more pain than he wanted anyone to know, barely able to walk. Most movement hurt. A head first (almost) parachute landing fall had taken its toll.

Captain the Lady Jane Seaborn and Mandy wrapped his ribs extra tight for the raid – under normal circumstances he would be in hospital, or at the very least restricted to light duty. Almost worth getting dinged up, Maj. Randal thought, to have those two as his nurses. Unfortunately, he had not had time to enjoy it.

The minute the carrier started to roll, all his pain went away. Strike Force was going out 300 men against 10,000. Maj. Randal knew this was a venture without any guarantees.

Everything depended on execution.

And for the moment, that was out of his control. Now the fate of the operation lay in the hands of his three company commanders and their young platoon leaders, none of whom had ever done anything like this before – except in training. And even then, not live fire.

The moon was down and it was pitch-dark. The Dodge bumped along. Maj. Randal was in the dream state he clicked into on missions – an out-of-body sensation of being up high and looking down on the column, watching events unfold. That was going to go away on contact with the rebels…he knew.

Strike Force had only a short distance to travel – 1,000 yards. Wolf's Teeth was near the bend in the Euphrates. Out of the dark, the figure of Mr. Zargo came into view.

"This is the release point for the King's Own," Mr. Zargo said when the carrier pulled up next to him.

"Hold up, Flanigan," Maj. Randal ordered.

"We made a reconnaissance of the route to the objective," Mr. Zargo said. "Joker and Queen will guide the King's Own in. As expected, there is a gap between Wolf's Teeth and the left flank of the Iraqi MLR.

"The rebels are in the village asleep.

"Ace and Jack will lead the Levies to their Final Objective Phase Line. I will pick up No. 1 ACC to make sure they do not lose contact with No. 4 Company."

The lead platoon of A Company, King's Own, came up. Joker appeared, and after a brief conversation with the platoon leader, he led them out. A Company executed a column left, moving up the escarpment, platoons in trail. The troops looked determined as they crunched by the carrier.

Captain Valentine Fabian arrived with his command party.

"Keep 'em closed up," Maj. Randal said. "Joker and Queen will guide you to your Release Point."

"Sir!" Capt. Fabian said, absorbed in running his company and not in any mood for extraneous conversation – he knew the plan.

"Take it to 'em, Fabian," Maj. Randal ordered. "See you on the objective."

The King's Own filed by, bayonets fixed on their Lee-Enfield Mark IIIs. Soon the rear platoon disappeared into the dark, moving up the escarpment.

No. 1 ACC motored past, closing up on the tail of No. 4 Company, Levies.

"OK, Flanigan," Maj. Randal said, "run me up to Captain Smith."

The lime-green hands on the Rolex said 0150 hours. For once Maj. Randal did not have to wonder what Lady Jane was doing. She was in the Seagull orbiting overhead with Mandy and Lieutenant Pamala Plum-Martin, getting ready to bomb Wolf's Teeth into the Stone Ages.

Lieutenant Roy Kidd and his Lake Patrol were in position. They were closed up on a four-gun Iraqi artillery battery located to the rear of Wolf's Teeth village. His orders were to create a diversion but this target was too juicy to pass up.

He intended to take it down.

When the hands on his watch read 0155 hours, Lt. Kidd initiated his 'diversion' by emptying the full 32-round snail magazine of his Bergmann 9mm MP-18, loaded as specified with all tracers, directly into the rebel gun battery. The men in his patrol were all firing before the first shell casing from his submachine gun hit the ground. The cone of fire from the combined automatic weapons converging on the rebel guns was spectacular.

Normally, tracer is loaded one per every six rounds. All armies pretty much do it the same way, so when a solid wall of tracers streaked into their positions, the rebel artillery men – once they came awake – thought they were being attacked by a regiment, if not an entire division of blood-crazed Englishmen.

Having been trained by British officers, the Iraqi battery commander knew what was coming next – an assault with cold steel.

The CO set the example for his troops – he decamped in the direction of Baghdad. His artillerymen were not far behind.

In Wolf's Teeth village, the firing awakened the Iraqi infantry battalion commander, who was asleep in the village chief's house. He was shocked to come under attack from a direction *opposite* of where the British were trapped in RAF Habbaniya. The rebel Colonel immediately ordered a realignment of his troops to assume defensive positions to repel an assault from their rear.

Shifting his men required two things: First, the men had to be shaken out of their beds. Second, the soldiers had to relocate to new positions no one had ever planned to use prior to tonight. And that required a confusing troop movement – in the dark, under fire.

The rebel CO did not hesitate. He was not taking any chances – with his personal safety at stake. Two of his three companies were ordered to redeploy.

The two companies of sleepy, scared Iraqi troops were in the process of complying when the Gordon, piloted by Squadron Leader Paddy Wilcox with Jim Taylor in the co-pilot's seat, and the Seagull, flown by Lt. Plum-Martin with Lady Jane and Mandy onboard, arrived overhead. Bombs screamed down.

Wolf's Teeth village exploded under the weight of 1,000 pounds of high explosives.

A Company, King's Own and No. 4 Company, Levies, stood up and went in – guns blazing, bayonets fixed. The men all had one magazine loaded with tracers. Each man fired off a round from his Lee-Enfield every time his left foot hit the ground… walking fire.

To Maj. Randal, it looked like the troops were conducting a parade ground exercise – except that it had *never* gone this well during rehearsals, not ever.

Two companies of disciplined men firing tracers steadily in the dark as they advance, bayonets fixed, is an awe-inspiring sight. Particularly if you are on the receiving end, and have just been bombed by unseen aircraft that may be coming back to make a second attack run.

Squadron Leader Page was waiting for No. 4 Company to make contact and pause. That was his signal to pass through the infantry with the armored cars of No. 1 ACC to drive home the attack.

The men in the slouch hats never broke stride.

"Take two platoons and get around behind 'em," Maj. Randal ordered Sqn. Ldr. Page over the radio. "Put yourself between the village and the bridge – set up a blocking force."

Sqn. Ldr. Page was off like a shot.

"Follow me," Maj. Randal ordered the remaining armored car platoon commander. "Flanigan, let's go downtown… lock and load, King."

King stood up in the back, grabbed hold of the pedestal-mounted Vickers K.303 machine gun and racked a round into the chamber as the policeman switched on the siren he had installed on the carrier. Flanigan put the pedal down. Behind them the six Silver Spirits turned on their sirens and the charge was on.

Flanigan fishtailed onto the road leading into the village, tires spitting gravel. He was driving flat out. Maj. Randal had to hold on to keep from being thrown from the bouncing vehicle. They were headed straight at the Wolf's Teeth.

"Holy…," neutral observer Capt. Roosevelt shouted.

King opened with the .303 Vickers K machine gun. Iraqis were fleeing in all directions. The merc was triggering short bursts, doing terrible execution.

Maj. Randal began firing his 9mm Beretta MAB-38 at fleeting targets one-handed while holding on with the other hand, trying to keep from being thrown out of the carrier. Probably not hitting much, but he hoped he was giving the bad guys something to be concerned about.

It was a wild ride.

Sirens were screaming, machine guns blazing, bullets cracking, men shouting curses and grenades going off. Mass confusion reigned; the situation was fluid. In the distance, the fluttering thunder of the "seal mission" mortar barrage raining down sounded like a minor earthquake. The 250-pound bombs Sqn. Ldr. Tony Dudgeon and his wingman were dropping to suppress the Iraqis artillery created brilliant flashes that lit up the skyline.

The carrier careened around a corner and King opened on a group of rebels assembled beside the street. The Iraqis were chopped down as Flanigan raced up. As they rolled past, the merc tossed a grenade over his shoulder.

Capt. Roosevelt was blazing away with his Thompson submachine gun.

Once in the tiny village, the armored cars sped through the handful of streets, machine-gunning anything that moved. The King's Own reached Wolf's Teeth, followed shortly by No. 4 Company. Nothing could stand in their way tonight and the Iraqi rebels were certainly not trying to.

When the infantry came in with their bayonets, the rebels threw down their weapons and began surrendering *en masse*.

Lt. Kidd arrived, "Sir, we captured a 4-gun battery of howitzers."

"Round up rebel trucks and start towing the guns back to RAF Habbaniya," Maj. Randal ordered.

"Roger, sir."

"Get Fabian and Smith on the horn," Maj. Randal said to King. "I need situation reports and I need 'em now."

"Capt. Fabian, sir."

"Secure the objective 12 to 6," Maj. Randal ordered after listening to an elated young captain who had just won his first firefight. "Bridge is twelve o'clock. Be prepared to pull out on my command."

"Roger."

"Capt. Smith," King announced.

Maj. Randal took the handset, "Secure the village 6 to 12 – twelve being the bridge. Stand by to pull out on my command."

"Sqn. Ldr. Page, Major."

Maj. Randal took the handset, "Go."

"We have captured over 200 rebels," Sqn. Ldr. Page reported. "I have the battalion commander, his entire staff, four Crossley armored cars and some other vehicles."

"Bring 'em in," Maj. Randal ordered. "I want to move out in five minutes. Don't bother with consolidation."

"Wilco – moving now."

The platoon commander of the No. 1 ACC who had charged Wolf's Teeth drove up. He reported the platoon had close to a hundred prisoners.

"Send two of your armored cars to support Lt. Kidd," Maj. Randal ordered. "Make it snappy – I want those guns. We're pulling out in zero five."

"Sir!"

"Take charge of all the prisoners here in the village, Roy," Maj. Randal said as Lt. Kidd was leaving. "Get 'em started back to the cantonment now. Time for us to get the hell out of Dodge."

"Can I have a rifle platoon as support, sir?"

"King," Maj. Randal said, "round up a platoon from Capt. Smith."

"Wilco."

The lead elements of No. 1 ACC started trickling in, shepherding their prisoners. The Iraqis looked totally dejected – no fight left in them. For these soldiers, the war was over and they clearly thought that this was a good thing.

Lt. Kidd passed by with the captured howitzers in tow. Driving the rebel trucks proved to be no problem. They were Bedfords provided to the Iraqi Army by their British trainers. The two armored cars split off and fell in, flanking the growing file of prisoners marching back to Habbaniya.

No. 4 Company had platoons spread out on both sides of the column of POWs. Capt. Fabian's A Company folded back, bringing up the rear. Machine gunners on the No. 1 ACC cars eyed the rebels with their fingers on the triggers.

Because of all the prisoners, the planned order of the return march was scratched.

There was no need for Lieutenant Kit Wilson to fire his refurbished cannons in support of the withdrawal. He could save that little surprise for tomorrow's attack.

There had never been any time to put up the flares signaling the withdrawal – the situation had developed too quickly. No one had foreseen the Iraqis capitulating the minute the Strike Force showed up – not in a single one of the multitude of scenarios they had planned for.

The Dodge carrier was last out of Wolf's Teeth, traveling with the King's Own rear security element. Flanigan drove at the rear of the column while Maj. Randal dismounted and walked along with the platoon commander. King shadowed him carrying the Strike Force radio strapped on his back and his Bergmann 9mm MP-18 at the ready.

Capt. Roosevelt walked along with Maj. Randal, cradling his red hot Thompson submachine gun.

"That's some unorthodox footgear you're wearing, Jimmy," Maj. Randal said.

"Flat feet... can't wear shoes or boots."

"The Marines let officers in with flat feet?"

"The Marines will take almost anyone these days," Captain Roosevelt said, "whose daddy is the serving President of the United States."

Strangely, the Iraqi Army up on the escarpment made no attempt to interfere with the movement even though they could clearly see it – flares were up all along their MLR.

The POWs marched along as meekly as a flock of sheep. The prisoners peeled off at the airfield where they were going to be held. When a good count of the captured rebels was made, the final tally came to 409 Iraqi officers and men.

Strike Force causalities were minimal: three men wounded – none seriously. Maj. Randal had been more than a little worried about the operation. It had never crossed his mind that the Iraqis would implode, all run away or surrender. Military actions never go as planned. Tonight was a rare fine thing.

Lady Jane, Mandy, Rita and Lana were waiting at Bunker No. 10 when Maj. Randal finally limped up to the cut in the wire. The pain had kicked back in on the return march as the adrenalin from the raid began to wear off. It had only been a walk of half a mile but for a time he had thought he might have to get back in Flanigan's carrier.

"John," Mandy said, clearly exasperated, "the troops are saying you were a mad man out there tonight. Why do you have to be so reckless?"

"Would you lighten up," Maj. Randal said as he took out his battered Zippo and lit the thin cigar. "King and Flanigan were there. Jimmy too…what the hell you worrying about?"

"Worry?" Lady Jane flashed her patented heart attack smile – he could see it in the dark. "Why would we worry…you *are* a professional."

It was as if they had never been apart. Not for a minute. When Lady Jane was anywhere in the area, Maj. Randal felt like his IQ went down.

Tonight was no exception.

SITUATION REPORT NUMBER 1

6 May 1941

From: Officer Commanding Middle East Command to Prime Minister Winston Churchill.

On day five of the siege of RAF Habbaniya at 1000 hours, B and D Company of the 1st Battalion, King's Own Royal Rifles, supported by No. 1 Armored Company, RAF, attacked the Iraqi village known as the Wolf's Teeth. The fighting was fierce. The Iraqis had reoccupied the position in force, following the successful raid carried out by the Strike Force the night previous that had resulted in 409 prisoners taken.

The Golden Square ordered up massive reinforcements from Baghdad. The relief column arrived as all three brigades of the rebel forces occupying the escarpment above the Royal Air Force base decided that they'd had enough and began withdrawing in disorder.

The fleeing column ran headlong into the reinforcing column traveling down the single highway to RAF Habbaniya. Because the desert had been flooded, both columns were roadbound.

A massive traffic jam resulted.

The RAF caught the Iraqis when they were ensnarled. Pilots flew nonstop for six hours—bombing, strafing, landing, rearming and returning to the attack—turning the road to Baghdad into a highway of death.

The siege of RAF Habbaniya is lifted.

3

CAIRO

MAJOR JOHN RANDAL WAS RIDING IN THE BACK of the Shepard'S Hotel limousine. Captain the Lady Jane Seaborn was aware that he was in pain from damaged ribs. She knew just the thing to take his mind off his injury – shopping.

They had flown in from RAF Habbaniya last night, along with Lieutenant Roy Kidd and his batman Pan, King, and four men from the Strike Force who had volunteered for Raiding Forces and had been selected to enter training. Brandy Seaborn, Lieutenant Penelope Honeycutt-Parker, Red and Mandy were also on board the Hudson.

Squadron Leader Paddy Wilcox and James "Baldie" Taylor had flown back out again. They were going back to RAF Habbaniya to recover the elephant-skin suitcases containing the Iranian Air Marshal's secret stash of gold and deliver them to an undisclosed location. No mention was made of the bag of diamonds found on his yacht.

As the Hudson winged over Lake Habbaniya with the gold on board, an explosion occurred in the middle of the lake...the Iranian Air Marshal's yacht, used as a clandestine base for the Lake Patrol, had gone up in a massive fireball.

"Geez, that's too bad," Baldie said to Sqn. Ldr. Wilcox.

Today Maj. Randal and Lady Jane were taking Mandy to be outfitted in her Royal Marine uniform. Then she would be flying out to England to attend No. 1 Parachute School (Short Course) – the Royal Navy's WAVE officer's training school, there being no Women's Royal Marine OTS – and possibly some other courses offered by one or the other of the clandestine services.

"I cannot believe you did not say it, John," Mandy said, unhappy that Maj. Randal had not said, 'Let's get the hell out of Dodge.' "Lady Jane's heard you, Brandy and Parker both say they have, even Rita and Lana, but not me."

"Say…?"

"I was in the plane," Mandy said, "on the mission the one time you chose not to."

"What?"

"Oh, never mind…"

Red flashing lights came on behind them. Maj. Randal glanced over his shoulder and saw a Cairo Police Department car had swung in behind them. The driver pulled over. In less than a minute there was a tapping on the window.

Captain A.W. "Sammy" Sansom bent down to look into the limousine. He was the last person on planet Earth that Maj. Randal wanted to see today.

"Lady Jane, I apologize for the inconvenience," the Chief of the Cairo Counterintelligence Division said. "May I borrow Maj. Randal for a half hour or so. Promise to have him back all in one piece as quickly as possible. Duty calls."

"Certainly, Captain. We shall be…"

"I am aware of your destination, ma'am," Capt. Sansom said. "Won't take long, on my word."

"Give my regards to R.J." Lady Jane said.

As he climbed into the police car Maj. Randal said, "This better be good."

"The Brigadier would like a word with you," Capt. Sansom said.

"Brigadier…?"

"Raymond Maunsell," Capt. Sansom said. "My boss, the head of Security Intelligence Middle East (SIME)…likes to be called 'R.J.'"

"Banged yourself up a little, huh… some vacation you went on."

"Yeah," Maj. Randal said. "Met a friend of yours – Zargo."

"Tough guy type," Capt. Sansom said. "Scarface. Killed his last employer?"

"That would be him."

"Don't know anyone by that name or description."

"That's what he said about you."

"I met a friend of yours too, Major." Capt. Sansom said, "Rocky…unsure whether she should be locked up for indecent exposure or have the Kit Kat Club hire her to replace the dancer you shot."

***

BRIGADIER RAYMOND J. MAUNSELL INVITED MAJOR JOHN Randal into his private office. He was the senior MI-5 officer in the Middle East. R.J., as he preferred to be called, was a close associate of Colonel Dudley Clarke.

In the Middle East, things were often not what they appeared. Lines of responsibility were blurred. An officer might have one job but be doing another. An agency might have one name in London and a completely different one in Cairo.

R.J. was involved with more than counterintelligence.

"Major, I realize you are on your leave after spending a considerable part of the last year behind the lines in Abyssinia and the last few days in Habbaniya," Brig. Maunsell said. "I shall be brief."

The Brigadier did not mention that he had a complete dossier on his desk from his man in Habbaniya on Maj. Randal's Strike Force operations. The document was impressive. It read like fiction.

"I understand Sir Terry gave you a briefing on A-Force and the role you were slated to play in it when you first arrived out here."

"Only that Raiding Forces was to work for Col. Clarke," Major Randal said. "We never had a chance to go into details."

"Dudley is temporarily out of the country," Brig. Maunsell said. "He asked me to fill you in on a part of what he has in mind for Raiding Forces when you got back to Cairo – if you made it back.

"Wanted you have the opportunity to plan how to task-organize your command while you are standing by the next few weeks, waiting for your troops to return from their furlough."

"Good," Maj. Randal said.

"Naturally, we are not having this conversation," Brig. Maunsell said. "Everything I am going to say is classified Most Secret, Need to Know. No one other than James Taylor, Squadron Leader Wilcox and Captain the Lady Jane Seaborn, who will be acting as your liaison to General Headquarters (GHQ) and to Force-A, have a Need to Know at this point in time."

"I understand, Brigadier." In effect, Maj. Randal knew he was being issued a Warning Order, although the Chief of SIME did not actually say so...he clicked on.

"Call me R.J."

"Roger that, R.J."

"The Middle East Command is in the final stages of pulling our troops out of Greece, in yet another embarrassing Dunkirk," Brig. Maunsell said. "Crete is standing by to be invaded by German Forces. Malta is besieged under constant aerial bombardment surrounded by a U-boat blockade. We are still chasing the Duke of Aosta in a remote mountain corner of Abyssinia. And the Golden Square has to be dealt with, which is a sticky problem complicated by the Vichy French in Syria recently having allowed German aircraft landing rights en route to support the Iranian rebels...something we cannot stand for."

Brig. Maunsell took a Player's out of his elegant monogrammed silver case and offered the open case to Maj. Randal. "The German General

Rommel has driven down out of Libya across Egypt, sliced through our army, and trapped our troops in Tobruk...outclassed our generals.

"The biggest threat is Rommel. His Afrika Korps appeared on the scene at a time when our Desert Force had been frittered away in penny packets to Greece, Crete, and Abyssinia, etc. – caught us spread thin on the ground.

"Dudley always planned for Raiding Forces to be attached to A-Force – or at least be available to carry out missions from time to time.

"As you are already aware, Col. Clarke has aspired to develop an airborne capability in the Middle East for ages – but events keep intervening to prevent that from becoming a reality, like you disappearing into Abyssinia.

"Now, with Rommel on the scene and you back in Egypt, an urgent need has developed for a man with your special talent, Major."

"What might that be, R.J.?" Maj. Randal said, taking out his old, much-traveled U.S. 26th Cavalry Regiment Zippo to light their cigarettes.

"Irregular, unorthodox warfare," Brig. Maunsell said, "like the operations you have been conducting in Abyssinia."

"Take a look at the map. Rommel will obtain the bulk of his supplies by sea up here in Tripoli and/or these other Libyan ports. A lesser amount will be flown in to airfields on the coast. Now, his panzers have raced all the way down here to Tobruk. What say you, Randal?"

"The man has to bring everything with him," Maj. Randal said, studying the map. "Beans, bullets, fuel...a long, exposed line of communications. One flank open to the Western Desert and the other to the Mediterranean Sea."

"Exactly," Brig. Maunsell said.

"No way the Germans can protect the entire length of it," Maj. Randal said.

"The coastal corridor is 18 to 34 miles wide," Brig. Maunsell said. "Rommel's only hard-topped road runs down it...the Via Balbia. As you pointed out, the northern flank is wide open to unexplored, impassable desert – terrain that is harsh and unforgiving."

"Raiding Forces should be able to arrive unannounced and unexpected almost anywhere from out of the desert by land – hit and run, disappear back into the vastness. Then do it again somewhere else," Maj. Randal said.

"From the Mediterranean side, we can carry out quick in-and-out pin-prick Commando raids along the coast at points of our choosing.

"Originally, Dudley's idea," Brig. Maunsell said, "was for Raiding Forces to operate against enemy landing grounds, railroads, rolling stock, road networks, bridges, supply depots, rear-area headquarters, landline communications and the like.

"Now, with Rommel's Afrika Korps running loose, a more strategic mission has presented itself – stop fuel from reaching the panzers on the tip of his armored spear.

"Your Raiding Forces needs to be capable of deep penetration missions 1,500 miles or more into enemy territory – operate against Tripoli itself. Go after Petroleum, Oil and Lubrication (POL) facilities with 10-ton fuel tanker trucks taking precedence. Fuel is Rommel's Achilles heel."

"What about all those other targets, R.J.?" Maj. Randal said. "They'll be out there."

"Pinch off his POL and Rommel's Afrika Korps will be left twisting in the breeze," Brig. Maunsell said.

"Rommel's 10-ton fuel transports are worth their weight in gold. Afrika Korps only has a limited number of them and they are difficult to replace.

"Go after the other targets once you establish a raiding program against the fuel carriers…we shall draw up a priority list for you at the appropriate time. Make plans to put your first desert patrol in the field within the next six weeks.

"Transports that heavy will be road-bound," Maj. Randal said, "we'll know where to find 'em."

"Enemy convoys on the Via Balbia travel with heavily-armed security elements," Brig. Maunsell said. "How do you anticipate coping with that contingency, Major?"

"I'm going to ignore it."

*****

AFTER THE MEETING, CAPTAIN A.W. "SAMMY" SANSOM agreed to an unusual request Major John Randal made, without seeming surprised or asking any questions.

Then Maj. Randal had him drive to Shepard's Hotel. He went inside to retrieve something from his room. Back in the car, the policeman took him to link up with Captain the Lady Jane Seaborn and Mandy.

The two women were finishing with the tailor when Maj. Randal arrived. The next stop on their itinerary was Wesley-Richards. The custom gun makers did a brisk business even in wartime. Hand-built sporting shotguns were much in demand by the sporting set of GHQ staff crowding Cairo.

When they walked in, the Wesley-Richards employees responded as if the queen had arrived. The showroom personnel lined up to greet them, as was normal when going places with Lady Jane…she received royal treatment. The three were immediately escorted into a private gunroom paneled in dark wood with pile green carpet. Heavy leather couches, deep leather chairs and gun racks lined the walls.

Lady Jane was right at home in the exclusive gun store. Her father had been an avid big game hunter. The smell of cigars, leather and gun oil was among her earliest memories.

Maj. Randal surrendered his pair of 1911 Colt .38 Supers, the 9mm Browning P-35 and his High-Standard .22 Military Model D. The manager whisked the weapons into a back workroom where the master gunsmiths resided. Lady Jane had commissioned best grade walnut stocks for the weapons before she had flown home after returning from Abyssinia.

Now today they were being fitted. The ivory grips had served their purpose well…to make Maj. Randal look like a *tillik sau*, a 'big shot', to the Abyssinian natives in his guerrilla army. Now they were to be retired in favor of best grade walnut.

"Major," the manager said, "are you quite certain you do not require checkering, sir? Lady Jane specified plain, oil finished. Most of our clients imagine it provides for superior purchase."

"Negative," Maj. Randal said. "Smooth."

"As you wish, sir," the manager said. "Only a short wait. We need to do some minor hand fitting. Would any of you care for something to drink?"

A clerk tapped on the door, "Maj. Randal, a gentleman to see you, sir."

"Send him in."

Lady Jane said, "Expecting someone, John?"

"Roger that," Maj. Randal said. "A little business…take a minute."

An unsavory-looking Egyptian in an ill-fitting linen suit was ushered into the private showing room.

He did not introduce himself.

"Capt. Sansom said you required my services, Major?"

Lady Jane and Mandy took one look at the man, and then retreated to the corner of the room. They began leafing through large, illustrated volumes of engraving patterns. The two of them would find something to shop for if you dropped them out in the middle of the Great Sand Sea.

"You a car thief?" Maj. Randal said, taking out a cigarette.

"Do you desire an automobile?" the Egyptian said in a fawning tone. "I shall be delighted to make the arrangements for a small remuneration."

"I need 15 Dodge trucks," Maj. Randal said. "Same model the Long Range Desert Group uses."

"Sir, the LRDG drives 30-cwt Chevrolets," the Egyptian said. "At least, that was what used to be parked in front of their headquarters at Abassia Barracks – no longer stationed there."

"Chevrolets, then," Maj. Randal said. "Warehouse the trucks for me until I call for 'em."

"So many trucks will be expensive," the Egyptian said, cutting straight to the money and not dancing around it. "Naturally, since you are a friend of Captain Sansom…"

Maj. Randal produced a gold Patek Philippe watch from out of his pocket, last worn when he impersonated the Chief of the Iraqui Secret Security Police on the mission to rescue Red. The Egyptian's eyes bulged at the sight of the glittering diamonds and the heavy gold bracelet. Little beads of sweat popped out on his forehead.

"Expect your vehicles within the next two weeks, sir."

Maj. Randal slipped the watch back in his pocket. "I may have a few other items for you to pick up later…get it done and I'll throw in a gold wrist chain on the deal."

"Your wish is my command…a pleasure, Major," the Egyptian said. "How shall I get in touch, sir?"

"Go through Sansom," Maj. Randal said. "He's good at finding people."

When the 'best car thief in Cairo' departed, Lady Jane came over and slid next to him on the leather couch. Maj. Randal relaxed; she was the only beautiful woman to ever have a calming effect on him.

After RAF Habbaniya, the idea of being able to stand down – even for a minute – seemed very, very strange.

It felt good.

They were laughing about something when the manager brought out the pistols. He laid them on a green velvet pad on the glass top of the coffee table by the couch.

"Do these stocks meet your satisfaction, Major?"

They did…understated elegance, dark and deadly.

4

PHANTOM

MAJOR JOHN RANDAL AND CAPTAIN THE LADY JANE Seaborn took Mandy to the airport in the Shepard's Hotel limousine. She was wearing her brand-new Royal Marine uniform. One of the engraved 7.65 Sauer 38-H pistols Maj. Randal had given her was belted around her waist. The other was in her purse.

Royal Marine Mandy Paige was off on an adventure.

"I shall try to be there when you graduate from WAVE officer training," Lady Jane said. "The course is eight weeks, and then you go to No. 1 Parachute School. The short course is five days. Plan on me making your jumps with you. After that, we have to decide what to do with you next."

"I want to come straight back here to work with you, Lady Jane," RM Paige said. "Someone has to take care of John, and you may not always be available."

"Wonderful," Lady Jane said. "I shall make you my personal assistant, Mandy."

Maj. Randal lit a cigarette and stared out at the flight line. He was not big on goodbyes. About the time he got attached to someone they went away—sometimes permanently.

Red walked up. She was on the same flight. BOAC wanted a first-hand report on the condition of their station on Lake Habbaniya. It was a major aerial crossroads between the UK and India and thus of strategic importance.

The company wanted to get back in operation at the lake as quickly as possible.

Maj. Randal took her off to one side. "Lose the Baby Colt .22 and put this in your purse, Red," he said discreetly, slipping her the profusely engraved Walther PPK 7.65 found in the safe on the Iraqi Air Marshal's yacht.

"Why, thank you, John," Red said, turning on her fabulous Clipper Girl charm. "What a thoughtful present."

"Nice job at Habbaniya," Maj. Randal said. "You can work with me any time, Red."

Boarding began. RM Paige got misty-eyed. She hugged Maj. Randal, crushing his battered ribs. "Do try not to be so reckless while I am gone."

"Love her," Lady Jane said when they were back in the limousine. The glass was shut so they could have a private conversation without the driver overhearing.

"Yeah, well, you may have trouble getting Mandy a security clearance," Maj. Randal said. "Had a boyfriend who was a fighter pilot in the Regia Aeronautica stationed in Abyssinia …thinks I might have shot him."

"She was teasing you, John," Lady Jane laughed. "That *is* what happens though, when one goes off to school in Switzerland—meet all kinds of interesting people on the ski slopes."

"Are you up to speed on what Raiding Forces is slated to do with A-Force?" Maj. Randal asked, changing the subject.

"Only that the plan is for you to work with Dudley on certain projects," Lady Jane said. "Not assigned or attached….at least officially.

"I serve as the liaison between you two."

"We're going to operate like the LRDG. Except where they're primarily strategic reconnaissance nowadays, we're to raid Rommel's lines of communications as far as Tripoli. Deep-desert work is a specialist skill, Lady Jane."

"Yes, it is," Lady Jane said. "You have been entrusted with a vital assignment."

"I'm going to need help getting Raiding Forces organized, equipped and trained for it," Maj. Randal said. "I don't know anything about operating in the desert."

"We shall need to proceed carefully," Lady Jane said. "Dudley and Colonel Ralph Bagnold, the founder of the LRDG, do not get along. Dudley wanted to employ the LRDG for A-Force deception projects, but Ralph refused to cooperate. Both men are military empire builders.

"Each tends to view the other as a professional threat."

"That's not good," Maj. Randal said.

"We definitely shall want Ralph's advice," Lady Jane said. "I know his sister, Lady Enid—the novelist. She wrote my favorite book: *National Velvet.* Simply have to play down our A-Force connection to have any hope of his cooperation."

"I see," said Maj. Randal, which meant he did not.

"What you require," Lady said, "is a prewar desert explorer as your advisor. Someone who is at home out in the blue. Brandy will know the exact right man to recruit."

"Brandy?"

"Absolutely," Lady said. "In 1935 Bagnold was a serving Royal Signals officer allowed to spend most of his time out here on desert exploration. He was awarded a Gold Medal by the Royal Geological Society, but no money. To finance his expeditions, he permitted wealthy adventurous patrons to accompany his desert forays and charged them twenty British Pounds Sterling per mile traveled.

"Brandy and Parker went—spent six months in search of the legendary Lost Oasis of Zerzura."

"Did they find it?" Maj. Randal said, not quite sure he believed her.

"Still lost."

***

MAJOR JOHN RANDAL WALKED INTO THE LONG BAR in ShepArd's
Hotel. It was a famous watering hole. Local legend had it that if you were in
the bar long enough you would eventually encounter every officer you ever
served with.

The bartender, a Swiss named Joe, was the most knowledgeable source
on the British Order of Battle in the Middle East. He could tell you the exact
location of every unit—something the Operations Division at Grey Pillars,
the Middle East GHQ, was not always able to do.

Captain A. W. "Sammy" Sansom had confided to Maj. Randal that he
suspected Joe was a Nazi spy.

Joe caught Maj. Randal's eye.

"Sir Terry left this for you, Major," he said, handing over a sealed
envelope.

"When was he in here?"

"Three days ago," Joe said. "Resumed command of the Lancelot
Lancers from his brother who is in hospital."

"Where can I find Terry?"

"The Lancers are making a forced march to Haifa—linking up with
Habforce."

"Habforce?"

"Fourth Brigade of the 1st Cavalry Division—commanded by Maj. Gen.
J. G. W Clark," Joe said. "Driving on RAF Habbaniya to relieve you, Major.
Why they call it Habforce."

"We relieved ourselves," Maj. Randal said.

Sure enough, as advertised, when he glanced down the crowded bar,
Maj. Randal saw a young major he thought he recognized. There was a black
square patch on his sleeve with a white P in the middle. The "P" stood for
Phantom.

The officer stood up and walked down the bar to introduce himself.

"Clive Adair," he said. "We only met briefly. I was with Jack Merritt in Abyssinia...a captain then, commanding his Phantom Detachment. We were there the night you jumped in and blew up the elevated Italian tramline."

"Phantom?" Maj. Randal said. "Thought you men went back to the UK."

"Since we were already out here," Major Clive Adair said, "the powers that be at Regiment decided to form a new Phantom squadron by amalgamating the eight patrols supporting your Force N. I was promoted and put in command.

"Only no one at GHQ here in Cairo knows quite what to do with a spare Phantom Squadron.

"And there is concern about our ability to be able to communicate directly with our Battle Headquarters in London. The idea of Phantom transmitting directly to the UK unedited messages which are not approved by the staff makes people at Grey Pillars see blood red over their pink gins."

"I can see how it might," Maj. Randal said. "Why don't we find a table, Clive? I'd like to hear your story in private."

"GHQ Liaison Regiment, better known as Phantom," Maj. Adair said, when they relocated to a spot in a corner, "is a Most Secret unit that does not actually do much of anything that is actually a secret. Colonel Hopkinson, our commander, believes that if we call ourselves 'secret', then the regiment will have an easier time obtaining the men and equipment we ask for—so everything I tell you is classified, even if it has no real reason to be."

"Roger," Maj. Randal said.

"Phantom's mission statement is simple," Maj. Adair said. "We liaise with all paramount-friendly HQs, report on the location of the units they command, make an independent assessment of the senior Allied commanders and report back to our Regimental Battle HQ by long-range radio.

"The regiment has a liaison component, a signaling component and mechanized reconnaissance component to gather information on the location of friendly and enemy forces."

"The recon element is new news," Maj. Randal said. "Always thought you were a long-range signals outfit."

"You are not alone," Maj. Adair said. "Phantom is a highly mobile, multitasked regiment cloaked in mystery. Our insistence on secrecy is a double-edged sword—people do not understand our capabilities. Signaling, the best known of our skills, is the least of what we do."

Maj. Randal said, "Tell me about your command, Clive."

"My squadron, consisting of eight officer's patrols of six men each, equipped with No. 9 and No. 11 radio sets, is self-contained and completely mechanized. A mobile headquarters troop was dispatched to Egypt from Regiment to round out our establishment.

"Normally, Phantom squadrons consist of eight officers and eighty men. Mine currently has ten officers but only fifty-three other ranks…hoping to recruit locally to make up the shortfall.

"We are stationed on a three-acre patch of sand outside of Cairo at Camp Mena in tents."

"What are your plans?" Maj. Randal asked.

"No idea," Maj. Adair said. "The flap going on about this fellow Rommel has Grey Pillars in an uproar. No one has time for us. GHQ has no idea how to employ a unit like Phantom—enrolled us in a Signals Training School.

"Royal Signals see us as a competitor, which we are not.

"The rumor is N Squadron may be broken up and dispersed to various armored brigade headquarters to augment their existing signals people . . . still up in the air."

"How many of your men are jump qualified?"

"Everyone except the HQ troop. All the patrol members are. Went through Mad Dog's parachute training program when we first arrived in-country.

"Expected to spend my time in Kenya partying with the fast set at the Muthaiga Club. Nasty surprise, that—jumping out of airplanes."

"How would you like a job?" Maj. Randal asked.

"What kind of a job?"

"Classified," Maj. Randal said. "'Need to Know'—and you don't have any need to know unless you volunteer."

"Jack Merritt thinks you walk on water," Maj. Adair said. "The Phantom personnel assigned to your Force N HQ element are of a like mind.

"Can you arrange for the transfer?"

"As of right now," Maj. Randal said, "N Squadron, Phantom Regiment, is assigned to Raiding Forces, Middle East. Anybody asks who authorized it, say 'that's classified 'Need to Know' and *you* don't have the need.'"

"Will that work? Is it official?"

"What's the worst that could happen?" Maj. Randal said.

"Nothing more draconian than breaking up the squadron," Maj. Adair said. "I'm in. What do we do next?"

"Tell the commandant of the signals school that you have been alerted for a clandestine mission—wrap up your training."

"Completed the course yesterday," Maj. Adair said. "The troops are on a two-day pass; that's why I am in town."

"Outstanding," Maj. Randal said. "I'm here at Shepard's temporarily. Stay in touch, Clive. Your N Squadron's getting ready to disappear—turn into real phantoms."

"No one will ever miss us."

***

THE NOTE INSIDE OF THE SEALED ENVELOPE SAID:

John…

Returned to Cairo early. Unable to locate you. A flap at some place called RAF Habbaniya. The Lancelot Lancers ordered to ride to the rescue. My brother stricken with hives upon discovering FM Wavell rated the odds of success at only 50/50. I've rejoined the regiment in command.

Terry

PS: Met Rocky…wants you to call her.

PPS: Lady Jane will cut you dead if you do.

5

HIJACKED

BRANDY SEABORN WAS LYING OUT BY THE POOL. She was honey gold from head to toe. Major John Randal thought her one of the best-looking women he had ever seen in his life—and he had grown up in southern California.

Maj. Randal did not know her exact age, not that it was a secret or that he cared. Ever since high school, when his English student teacher had been the reigning Miss UCLA, he had been attracted to older women.

Shortly after he formed the Small-Scale Raiding Company, forerunner of Strategic Raiding Forces, Brandy had invited Maj. Randal (then Captain Randal) to dinner at the Bradford Hotel in London. Acting, she said, as the Seaborn family "designated hitter" to inform him that the family approved of his developing relationship with Lady Jane.

The Seaborns—one of the powerful group of families called the "Six Hundred," who controlled England through their great wealth, extensive land holdings, school ties and political connections—did not have to make the gesture.

Of course, at that point, Lady Jane was thought to be a widow. It was before Maj. Randal had rescued her presumed-dead Royal Navy husband on the first MI-9 (Escape) mission into Enemy Occupied France.

Since the dinner that night, Maj. Randal and Brandy had been especially close friends.

"Hello, handsome," Brandy said. She knew exactly what effect she had on him.

"So you and Parker are desert rats," Maj. Randal said, sitting down in a lawn chair next to her lounge. "Searchers after the Lost Oasis of Zerzura."

"How did you hear about that, John?"

"What do you know about celestial navigation, Brandy?"

"Father taught me around the time I learned to ride a horse…which was before I could walk," Brandy laughed. "One of the perils the daughter of an admiral who does not have a son has to cope with: learning seamanship. I know quite a lot of knots.

"Why do you ask?"

"Navigation at sea much different than navigation in the desert?"

"No," Brandy said, intrigued. "What is this about, John?"

"Hard to learn?"

"Depends," Brandy said. "It is not the same thing as map reading. As you know, land navigation using a lensatic compass and a map is an art as well as a science— celestial navigation is pure mathematics.

"Once you master the basic discipline you have to practice; it's a perishable skill."

"Could you teach me?"

"Do you think you would be able to concentrate," Brandy laughed, "if I tried?"

Maj. Randal said, "We need to talk."

***

CAPTAIN THE LADY JANE SEABORN STEPPED OUT of the Shepard's limousine, accompanied by Rita and Lana, as Major John Randal was walking out the door of the hotel.

On Lady Jane's Sam Brown belt, to the right of the buckle in front, was a tan leather Bloods-made holster for a full-sized 1911 Model Colt .38 Super. The flap was cut away so the entire grip was exposed, holster mounted high on the belt and raked for easy access. Her Colt .38 Super was sporting a pair of Maj. Randal's recently-retired ivory grips.

There was no mistaking them: "RAIDING FORCES" was carved in high relief.

"More shopping?" Maj. Randal said, deciding not to notice her hijacking of his pistol grips. Lady Jane had a history of doing things like that. Rita and Lana used to work for him too.

"Inspecting real estate properties," Lady Jane said. "Found exactly what we require, John."

"What might that be?"

"A villa in a private compound twenty-five miles out of town," Lady Jane said. "Completely isolated, might as well be on the far side of the moon... perfect for Raiding Forces. A hush-hush outfit has no business having its barracks here in Cairo."

"You are right about that."

"Care to ride out and see for yourself, John?"

"I would," Maj. Randal said. "Let's do it."

In the limousine, Lady Jane said, "Ralph Bagnold is no longer with the LRDG. He chose to give up his combat command for promotion to full colonel and the red tabs of a staff officer. Straightaway he made an attempt to take control of A-Force—have Dudley Clarke report to him at GHQ.

"Like I mentioned, an empire builder."

"I see," Maj. Randal said."

"What Col. Bagnold did not realize," Lady Jane said, "and this is Most Secret—no one has a need to know, *including* the two of us—Dudley was already manipulating the LRDG surreptitiously.

"For several months now, the group has been performing missions devised by A-Force. Dudley has GHQ Intelligence issue the orders. LRDG never suspects who the puppet master is that planned the missions and pulls the strings to make them happen. They believe the assignments originate from Grey Pillars."

Maj. Randal said, "Dudley's a genius."

"Bagnold got his fingers rather badly burned," Lady Jane said. "Probably never understand why—pigeonholed now in some inconsequential position as a result of his overreaching."

"Unfortunately, Ralph is of no value to us. Dudley shall not want Raiding Forces having any direct contact with him now."

"Not good," Maj. Randal said. "I wanted to learn how the man planned his patrols."

"We shall find someone," Lady Jane said. "LRDG view the desert as their Number One enemy. You are going to see it differently: a safe haven to escape into after striking a blow."

"Roger that," Maj. Randal said. "Only, I need to learn how to do it."

"While Bagnold was a wonderful innovator, a skilled organizer and the perfect man to form the LRDG—dreamed up the concept and sold the idea to Wavell after Jumbo Wilson turned him down flat—as the unit commander, he was essentially a desert explorer in uniform," Lady Jane said.

"We need a *tactician* to advise you, John."

***

"I KNOW YOU PLANNED TO GO TO ACHNACARRY, KING," Major John Randal said to the mercenary from RAF Habbaniya who had elected to join Raiding Forces. "But I need you back here as soon as you finish parachute training."

"Been looking forward to the challenge, sir," King said. "Hard training—they say the Commando Castle provides the best in the world. Wanted to earn my own Fairbairn Fighting Knife."

"Yeah, well, keep the one I gave you," Maj. Randal said. "We're forming a desert raiding unit. I need you in it."

"Soldiering in the sun," King said. "Count me in, Major. The desert is my oyster. 'Right man, right job' – like it says in your rules."

"Good," Maj. Randal said, "you're flying out tonight. A cable has been sent to No. 1 British Parachute School. Skip the first week—it's mostly physical fitness. Do weeks two and three: second week is Apparatus Training, and the third is Jump Week.

"Get back here as soon as you graduate. Seaborn House will have an officer escort you on board an aircraft the same day."

"Yes, sir," the merc said.

***

LIEUTENANT DICK COURTNEY AND HIS TWO STRIKERS, X-ray and Vanish from the Gold Coast Border Police, arrived back in Cairo. Major John Randal had Lt. Courtney brief Lieutenant Roy Kidd on what to expect from the training at No. 1 British Parachute School and at Achnacarry. Also, to make sure he had all the kit he needed for the courses.

Maj. Randal hated to lose Lt. Kidd for over two months, but he wanted him to have the benefit of the training—it would pay off later.

Sergeant Major Mike "March or Die" Mikkalis, DSM, MM, came in next. He had the three ex-Foreign Legion corporals who had served with him as guerrilla company commanders in his 1st Mule Raiding Battalion. The men had taken the creative *noms de guerre* Smith, Jones and Brown.

With him was the 10th Lancer Lieutenant Westcott Huxley, whom no one had wanted in their Mule Raiding Battalions when 1 Guerrilla Corps (Parachute), Force N was formed in Abyssinia. He was wearing a Military Cross ribbon for his actions with the 1st Mercs. Lt. Huxley was incapable of pronouncing the letter *R,* but he was fluent in French, German and Italian.

Sgt. Maj. Mikkalis swore by him.

The young officer had been offered a permanent position in Raiding Forces.

Maj. Randal turned Sgt. Maj. Mikkalis and the three corporals over to Captain the Lady Jane Seaborn. She gave them the task of preparing the villa designated Raiding Forces Headquarters (RFHQ) for the arrival of troops. The men would be returning from their leave over the next two weeks.

Lt. Huxley was assigned to Lieutenant Penelope Honeycutt-Parker, whose father had once commanded the 10th Lancer Regiment. His job was to assist with the establishment of a desert navigation course for Raiding Forces personnel that she and Brandy were organizing. There was a lot to be done to obtain all the specialized celestial almanacs, sun compasses, logarithmic tables, map boards, protractors, dividers, etc. necessary to teach celestial navigation.

Maj. Randal, Brandy and Lt. Honeycutt-Parker drove out to the villa for a meeting with Sgt. Maj. Mikkalis and his three corporals.

"Raiding Forces has been alerted for deep desert raiding operations," Maj. Randal said. "The details are classified—not at liberty to discuss them at this point."

Sgt. Maj. Mikkalis and the corporals perked up. All four men were veterans of the French Foreign Legion. They had cut their military teeth in the sand.

"Raiding Forces will initially have two Squadrons—one designated as the Desert Squadron and the other as Sea Squadron. What we need to do today is start thinking about what specialist personnel the Desert Squadron will require.

"Lt. Honeycutt-Parker and Mrs. Seaborn are here because before the war they spent six months searching for the Lost Oasis of Zerzura and know desert exploration firsthand."

Four pair of hard-case eyes shifted to the women. In their minds, Lt. Honeycutt-Parker and Brandy earned instant respect by having journeyed into the Great Sand Sea, where no European had set foot before. Equipped with only the supplies they could carry, they had ventured into a region where hostile nomadic natives who hated infidels were likely to appear at any time.

More than a few experienced explorers with established reputations who had gone into the desert in search of the Lost Oasis were still there—bones bleaching in the sun.

"My plan, which I'm making up as we go," Maj. Randal said, "is to bring in Jack Merritt's Sudanese Defense Force Company to establish a Forward Operating Base (FOB) in the Western Desert somewhere and garrison it. Jack's training with the LRDG right now.

"The Lounge Lizards have been promised to me, but after all their attachments were pulled out, they're back to being the smallest regiment in the British Army, only about fifty officers and men total. Currently they are marching on Iraq, so we cannot factor them into our immediate plans.

"N Squadron, Phantom, have joined Raiding Forces. You can expect Major Adair's men to arrive here tomorrow, so be ready. Eight patrols of one officer and six men plus a HQ troop—approximately sixty-five men total.

"Fifteen Chevrolet trucks we can convert for desert patrolling will be available in the next couple of weeks.

"That's what we have to work with, initially," Maj. Randal said. "Now, tell me what we're going to need in the way of specialists."

"I take it we are going to be operating like the Long Range Desert Group," Sgt. Maj. Mikkalis said, "30-cwt trucks patrolling?"

"That's the idea," Maj. Randal said. "Only, we'll do things our way. 'The First Rule is There Ain't No Rules' is in full force and effect. I want your best thoughts."

"Any chance I can visit the LRDG and observe their operation?" Sgt. Maj. Mikkalis said.

"I'll see what we can work out," Maj. Randal said.

"Navigators," Brandy said. "Minimum of one per patrol. To be on the safe side, every officer and NCO should at least understand the basics of celestial navigation."

"Drivers," Sgt. Maj. Mikkalis said. "Every man has to be able to drive. Have to set up a desert driving course—it's an acquired skill."

"Mechanics," Lt. Honeycutt-Parker said. "At least one fitter per patrol; breakdowns in the desert are commonplace. We shall need a complete stand-alone, fully-staffed workshop at our FOB capable of handling any repair.

"Winches on every vehicle and heavy-recovery vehicles at the FOB to tow broken-down patrol trucks or any damaged enemy transport you capture."

"Armorers," Sgt. Maj. Mikkalis said. "One per patrol and a section at the FOB. Each vehicle will carry at least one machine gun, possibly more, and that adds up to a lot of guns to maintain. Desert patrolling is hard on weapons.

"Do you happen to know what type of MGs we are going to have, sir?"

"The RAF is replacing its Vickers K models; those for sure," Maj. Randal said. "Have to use captured Italian guns for the rest."

"Machine gunners, sir," Corporal Smith said, "capable of disassembling and assembling their weapons blindfolded—train them ourselves, Major. You cannot possibly have enough men in Raiding Forces qualified to the skill level we will demand."

"While we're on armaments," Maj. Randal said, "our scope-mounted Boys Anti-tank Rifles are a classified weapon.

"We need canvas covers made—to keep 'em concealed from prying eyes going to and from our patrol areas. Never discuss the No. 32 scopes being mounted on the Boys with anyone. Spread the word—is that clear?"

"Clear!"

"One with each patrol," Maj. Randal said, "preferably two."

"That means snipers," Sgt. Maj. Mikkalis said.

"Our best shooters," Maj. Randal said. "Key part of my plan."

"Wireless operators," Corporal Brown said. "One long-range radio truck per patrol."

"Phantom," Maj. Randal said, "should have what we need."

"Medical personnel," Brandy said. "Every man trained in first aid. One medic per patrol—a surgeon at the Forward Operating Base with a fully-equipped field hospital."

"Explosives, sir," Corporal Jones said. "Every man on patrol explosives trained—qualified to put down a hasty minefield to attack an enemy convoy or to discourage pursuit.

"One demolitions man per patrol with the ability to locate and clear enemy mines."

"Parachute rigger detachment," Maj. Randal said. "May not do much jumping in the desert, but we will resupply by air—extend the range of the patrols."

"Linguists," Brandy said. "Arabic, German and Italian speakers with each patrol."

"Administrative staff," Sgt. Maj. Mikkalis said.

"Phantom has an HQ troop," Maj. Randal said. "Use them."

"John, I strongly advise that you turn all of Raiding Force's administrative and personnel matters over to the Royal Marines," Lt. Honeycutt-Parker said. "One would not want Lady Jane to feel snubbed."

Maj. Randal said, "What could I have been thinking?"

6

LOOSE LIPS SINK SHIPS

CAPTAIN A. W. "SAMMY" SANSOM WAS WAITING for Major John Randal in the lobby of Shepard's Hotel. The two retired to a quiet corner.

"Your trucks are ready, Major."

"That was quick," Maj. Randal said. "Where can I pick 'em up?"

"Ready," Capt. Sansom said, "means they have been secured. I arranged for the Royal Army Ordinance Corps (RAOC) to modify them to the same standard as the LRDGs. In fact, that's who the fitters have been led to believe the Chevrolets belong to. My men altered all the numbers and painted LRDG's symbols on the bumpers.

"Do not do anything to cause the mechanics to think differently."

"When can I have 'em?" Maj. Randal said.

"Desertizing is a major rebuild," Capt. Sansom said. "Three weeks, maybe longer—much has to be done to bring street Chevrolets up to the standard you people will require for patrolling where you are going."

"Let me run up to my room," Maj. Randal said. "I'll be right back."

"Don't bother," Capt. Samson said. "Keep your shiny trinket."

"I promised the man a watch for the trucks," Maj. Randal said.

"That was then; this is now," Capt. Sansom said. "No need to honor your agreement."

"Really," Maj. Randal said, "and why might that be?"

"The party of the second part turned up dead."

"Who killed him?"

"You did," Capt. Sansom said.

"*What?*"

"Four little letters: LRDG. The moment you said them out loud, Cairo's most active car thief was a dead man. We could not afford a professional criminal knowing the connection."

Capt. Sansom pulled a photo out of the inside pocket of his jacket. Maj. Randal saw a grainy picture of the crook with no name, lying on his back with a bullet hole in his forehead, slightly off-center between his eyes.

"Never thought I would have to be lecturing you about operational security. Not taking this seriously, Major?"

"I was just..."

"They say 'loose lips sink ships,'" Capt. Sansom said. "You sank his."

***

MAJOR JOHN RANDAL HAD NEVER BEEN A GOOD STUDENT. He had always been more interested in guns, girls and horses in school, not necessarily in that order. For the past five days Lieutenant Penelope Honeycutt-Parker and Brandy had been tag-team tutoring him in celestial navigation.

The women had their work cut out for them.

Maj. Randal had to take readings at noon and midnight. The sun was straight overhead at noon in Egypt so he had to wait until the sun compass would cast a shadow in order to get an azimuth.

At night, clouds sometimes obscured the stars when he tried to shoot them.

Then he had to work through the table of logarithms. To be safe, the problem had to be done twice. In the Great Sand Sea, a small deviation could send a patrol swanning out into oblivion.

The math was not simple.

When doing land navigation with a map and compass, a 3-degree error is built in. A lensatic compass is only so accurate. In the desert, a 3-degree error could mean agonizing death.

To find a well, locate an oasis or rendezvous with another patrol, you had to hit it dead-on.

Maj. Randal was five miles outside Cairo, bent over the hood of one of the Phantom trucks, struggling to make it happen. Mastering celestial navigation was a lot harder for him than the training he had done at No. 1 Parachute School or Achnacarry.

It did not help that Brandy was reclining on a folding lounge chair in a halter top and short shorts, taking in the sun, while he tried to work.

Day and night for nearly a week, Maj. Randal had been at it. He was determined to master the skill. There was no way he was going to take out a long-range deep desert raiding patrol without being able to do his own navigation—not that he had any intention as serving as a patrol navigator.

Still, a commander of Special Forces needs to lead. In the Great Western Desert, for the most part, leading meant finding your way. It is not easy.

Maj. Randal was finishing his calculations. Brandy was reading a letter from her son, Lieutenant Randy "Hornblower" Seaborn, DSC, RN. She started laughing, which was not particularly noteworthy. Brandy laughed nearly all the time.

"You shall love this story, John," Brandy said, when he brought her his findings to review.

"The Navy relieved Father from convoy duty. So he took command of the MGB-345 while Randy was in Abyssinia with the Emperor's column."

"The Razor got beached?"

"On his last voyage to Malta, he had three ships sunk out from under him. The Admiralty felt he had done his bit at his age," Brandy said. "Typically, he went straight to the Navy Yard where the MGB-345 was undergoing a refit, speeded up the work, conducted sea trials, and now Raiding Forces has an admiral in command of a gunboat."

Maj. Randal said, "That's pretty funny."

Brandy giggled, "Now Father is refusing to give the 345 back to Randy."

"Admiral Ransom commandeered his grandson's boat," Maj. Randal said. "How's Hornblower taking that?"

"Less than happy," Brandy said, "A Seaborn family feud is in the making. He wants you to order Father to give him his boat back."

"Me?"

"The Razor works for you now, John," Brandy laughed. "The 345 is assigned to Raiding Forces—not the Navy."

"Hell no, negative on that," Maj. Randal said. "Leave me out of it. I'll cable Randy to come out here to be my navigator."

"He wants a sea command," Brandy said. "Randy had quite enough of being a dry-land sailor riding a mule in Abyssinia."

"I've got a boat for him," Maj. Randal said. "We'll send a message as soon as we get back. He can come out here to operate with the Sea Squadron."

"*You* have a boat for Randy?"

"Affirmative," Maj. Randal said. "He'll have to provide the crew."

"This I want to see," Brandy said.

"Hide and watch."

"You are serious?"

"Absolutely," Maj. Randal said. "Hornblower may still have to go out as navigator on my patrols. These logarithms are bigger than me."

"Practice makes perfect, handsome."

"Did I ever mention," Maj. Randal said, "that you remind me of my old high school student teacher?"

"Thank you, John."

Apparently Brandy knew about Miss UCLA.

***

MAJOR JOHN RANDAL WAS SITTING ALONE IN A CORNER of the Long Bar in Shepard's Hotel. He was waiting for Captain the Lady Jane Seaborn. The bar was packed, as usual.

There was a civilian in a tailor-made bush suit who seemed vaguely familiar sitting at the bar. The man was sleek as a seal—tanned, clean shaven with gray hair neatly parted. He handled himself with the ease of a wealthy sportsman. Maj. Randal could not get a good look at his face.

GG, the Italian prisoner of war captured by Force N in Abyssinia, came out the swinging doors behind the bar carrying a plate of beefsteak and eggs and delivered it to the man in the bush suit. Lady Jane had secured GG a temporary job at Shepard's until his exact status could be worked out. Now it had been decided he would be the chef for Raiding Forces Headquarters.

Maj. Randal noted that the two acted like old friends. He was reasonably sure he knew the man from somewhere, too. There was an almost imperceptible bulge under the jacket; maybe that was why he seemed so confident.

Then, when the man raised his fork, Maj. Randal could see his watch. A Panerai: Maj. Randal was wearing a wrist compass made by the same firm that he had captured off an Italian submarine.

The wristwatch he did recognize. Maj. Randal had shot the general who owned it.

The man at the bar glanced in the mirror, spotted him in the corner and turned around on his bar stool—Waldo Treywick.

In Abyssinia, with a snow-white beard and a bad haircut, the old poacher had looked twenty, maybe thirty, years older. Waldo immediately came over.

"Thought I was going to have to come pull you out of some Ras's private jail," Maj. Randal said. "You all right, Mr. Treywick?"

"Couldn't be better, Major," Waldo said. "Sorry to hear they busted you down from Brigadier."

"Easy come, easy go," Maj. Randal said.

"Yeah, well, you was a damn good Brigadier," Mr. Treywick said. "Best I ever seen—saw a few back in the day when me and P. J. Pretorius was scoutin' squareheads in the last 'en.

"Ain't wearin' your fancy ivory handles anymore either, I notice."

"Retired from active service," Maj. Randal said. "Lady Jane put a pair on her side arm."

"Heard 'bout that," Waldo said. "Better watch yourself, Major. That woman is catnip to you—got Rita and Lana; now your ivories.

"Find what you and Capt. McKoy were looking for, Mr. Treywick?" Maj. Randal asked, hoping to change the subject.

"Thought you were getting yourself in trouble when we pulled out of Abyssinia and you two stayed back."

"Mission accomplished," Waldo said. "We was out in less than a week. Except for Frank; took him a little longer because he brought out a pack train. Finally hitched a ride with a convoy outta Addis Ababa on the way back to Kenya runnin' empty.

"Never asked what he was packin'."

"What *was* he packing?" Maj. Randal said, lighting a Player's with his hard-service Zippo. "If you don't mind me asking."

"Gold," Waldo said. "I never exactly explained it to you, Major, but I was guiding a museum archeologist from Chicago when we was captured…meaning I was. He got away. We found Solomon's lost treasure—at least we found the Ras who claimed *he* found it."

"Really?"

"You blew the man off his mule," Waldo said, "the day you emancipated me and the girls."

"So you and Capt. McKoy have King Solomon's treasure?" Maj. Randal asked.

"I don't think we do," Waldo said. "The archeologist, *he* thought so because that's what he was searching for and sorta had already convinced himself of it when we hit pay dirt. They wrote it up that way in the Chicago newspaper.

"Only the Ras discovered us a-sneakin' around, and we had to make a run for our lives and couldn't bring any of it back as proof.

"You don't have to take my word for it. I read the story a couple of years later in the newspaper. We could probably find a copy. It was real good—the professor told a great tale: 'war drums beatin',' slave's sweat glistenin' in the moonlight while they was laborin' in the gold mine. Real good writin'—only it wasn't King Solomon's lost treasure, and there wasn't any gold mine."

"What exactly did you find, Mr. Treywick?" Maj. Randal asked.

"The Ras had been raidin' and lootin' temples for years, and he had a pile of stolen treasure—diamonds, rubies and other precious stones—buckets of 'em. Had a lot of gold too, but most of it was coins—not mined ore or bars.

"Pretty sure it was a military payroll out of the Sudan that got knocked over back in the day—a camel caravan that went missin'; people been searchin' for it ever since.

"The Emperor would kill the Ras quick—or maybe not so quick if he ever found out he had been a-robbin' those religious shrines and you hadn't already done smoked the man."

"So, what happened?" Maj. Randal asked.

"Me and Joe went back and got the booty," Waldo said. "Frank, he was day labor, not in on the cut."

"You knew where the Ras had his treasure cached all along?"

"Yeah," Waldo said. "But it didn't do me no good even after you dropped him with your '03. Not with a quarter million Italians patrollin' the countryside. No way to get the loot out over the border."

"Gold and precious stones would have been useful raising our guerrilla army, Mr. Treywick," Maj. Randal said.

"That's what I thought too," Waldo said. "Probably why I didn't mention it at the time."

"Where's the treasure now?" Maj. Randal said.

"The gold coin is crated up and stored in the basement of the U.S. Envoy's office in Nairobi," Waldo said. "Joe, being a U.S. Marshal and all, no one will ever inspect the crates, them being sealed and marked 'Property of the U.S. Marshal's Service.' We ain't exactly sure what to do with it. . . . Did you know they made it illegal for an individual citizen to own gold in America?"

"Heard that," Maj. Randal said.

"The jewels is sittin' in a bank in Beverly Hills," Waldo said. "Joe had hisself escorted on a plane out of Kenya by the local FBI representative as a professional courtesy, and then his plane was met by a couple of federal marshals in L. A. when it landed.

"He never went through customs," Waldo said.

"What've you been up to, Major?"

"Found a stash of gold bars," Maj. Randal said, "but the British Secret Intelligence Service got 'em."

"Shoulda planned ahead," Waldo said. "Let me and Joe handle the details."

"Well, I didn't know you men were in the international money smuggling business," Maj. Randal said.

"Besides, I was busy at the time."

7

DESERT SQUADRON

BRIGADIER RAYMOND J. MAUNSELL, COLONEL DUDLEY Clarke and James "Baldie" Taylor met in A-Force Headquarters located at No. 6 Sharia Kasr-el-Nill. The top floors of the building housed a bordello. It was the perfect cover. No one paid the slightest attention to which British officers were coming and going.

There were too many to count…they came and went at all hours.

Col. Clarke had recently returned from Turkey. On the way back to Cairo he had slipped into Syria, where he had conducted a forward reconnaissance of several key Vichy French military installations in the event that British intervention was necessary due to the recent escalation of French collaboration with Nazi Germany.

Jim Taylor had flown in that morning from RAF Habbaniya for the meeting. The ground fighting was over at the station but sporadic air attacks continued. German planes bombed the base the afternoon before he departed…the Luftwaffe aircraft landed in Syria to refuel before flying on to Iraq.

The military/political situation with Vichy French Syria was spiraling out of control. Events were rapidly coming to a head. For all practical purposes, the Vichy government had become a co-belligerent with the Nazis.

However, there was no time to deal with that problem at present.

"You met with Major Randal?" Col. Clarke said to Brig. Maunsell.

"I did," R.J. said. "Briefed him, as per your request. The Major recognized the tactical possibilities. Not only is he willing to organize a desert force along the lines of the LRDG dedicated to raiding…he offered to provide a Commando-type squadron to strike the Via Balbia from the sea."

"Excellent," Col. Clarke said. "You advised him we wanted to have a desert patrol up and running in the next six weeks?"

"Yes," R.J. said. "On the way back to meet up with his ah…girlfriend after our meeting, the Major made arrangements for a notorious local car thief to steal 15 Chevrolet trucks of the model the Long Range Desert Group uses."

"Surely you jest?" Col. Clarke said.

"Have to be careful with the Major," Baldie said. "Give him an order…"

"We are learning that," R.J. said. "Maj. Randal has been studying celestial navigation. In fact, he is establishing a course to train his Raiding Forces personnel in the skill when they return from their leave.

"Turned a young 10th Lancer lieutenant loose on the military establishment in Cairo to secure the necessary equipment Raiding Forces needs for desert patrolling. He has turned out to be an uncanny scrounger. Police reports are pouring in daily. This morning it was 200 pair of sunglasses, disappeared from an RAF depot. All the logarithm tables have gone missing from one of the local schools. The list goes on…"

"Most likely an orphanage," Col. Clarke said, "knowing the 'Shiny Tenth'."

"Did you inform the Major we would do our best to honor his request for supplies and equipment?" Jim asked.

"I expressed to Major Randal," R.J. said, "that it would be prudent to start planning how to structure Raiding Forces, Middle East. Gave him a thumbnail sketch of the situation now that Rommel has changed the military equation, showed him the map, and explained it was our wish for him to have his first desert patrol in the field in six weeks' time.

"The Major went off like a shot…never made any requests.

"Squadron N, Phantom, had completed a signals course prior to being assigned," R.J. said. "Major Randal purloined them for Raiding Forces…no going through channels, no official authorization, simply told the squadron commander to report to RFHQ."

"Phantom complied?" Col. Clarke asked. "No written orders…?"

"With alacrity."

"Where is Raiding Forces Headquarters located?" Col. Clarke asked. "I was not aware there was one."

"Twenty-five miles west of Cairo, where the river has its confluence with the coast," R.J. said. "Belonged to a member of King Farouk's Royal Family. Lady Jane acquired it somehow."

"Jim," Col. Clarke said, "in addition to your other tasks, plan on supervising Raiding Forces in the future. In fact, when practicable, wrap up your work up north. We shall find a replacement for you.

"Concentrate on Raiding Forces Afrika Korps interdiction project exclusively."

"Nothing I would rather do," Jim said.

"The LRDG is performing strategic reconnaissance, monitoring enemy road traffic, running a desert taxi service to insert intelligence agents behind the lines and performing rescue missions for downed RAF pilots," Col. Clarke said. "The unit is over-tasked.

"The quicker we can get Randal's people in the field, taking the pressure off the LRDG, the better for everyone. Make it your top priority."

"We still have our Ambassador trapped in the embassy in Baghdad," Jim said. "As soon as Habforce reaches RAF Habbaniya in the next day or so, it will launch a counterattack against the Golden Square. Once the rescue is effected, I can devote my full attention to the Rommel issue."

"Commando raids along the Mediterranean coast are something we need to capitalize on," Col. Clarke said. "Find out what the Major requires and ensure it is made available to him…why GHQ has not pursued the concept before now is hard to fathom."

"If Raiding Forces can envelop the Via Balbia's sea flank," Jim said, "it opens up limitless opportunities to strike Rommel's line of communications."

"Major Randal can be allowed to know he will be asked to perform certain tasks for A-Force from time to time," Col. Clarke said. "However, in the grand scheme he needs to be led to believe he is working for you, Baldie, not me. In fact, the less direct contact I have with him, the better.

"Point Randal in the right direction, give him general guidance and let him press on. Naturally, we shall call on Raiding Forces to perform missions from time to time... through you."

"I understand," Jim said.

"Disrupting Rommel's logistical lifeline is the most critical assignment in Middle East Command...period," Col. Clarke said. "Top priority. Be relentless in its execution...allow no obstacle to stand in your way."

"Raiding Forces has a rule, 'Right Man, Right Job'," Jim said. "Major Randal and I are a good team..."

"I am well aware of that, Baldie," Col. Clarke said. "Undoubtedly, you two shall make the Desert Fox regret this day for the rest of his life."

"You can bet we will."

***

MAJOR JOHN RANDAL WAS IN HIS PRIVATE SUITE at RFHQ, which was as big as a small house. It was located on the third floor of the main building, with a view of the Nile out one bank of windows and the Mediterranean out the other. One corner had been turned into a miniature war room with maps pinned to the walls and an easel and chalkboard.

He was diagramming a table of organization and equipment (TO&E) for Raiding Forces, Middle East, on the board. Abyssinia had been bush league...taking on the Afrika Korps in its own backyard was going to be the Big Show. Maj. Randal knew detailed preparation was crucial to success.

Captain the Lady Jane Seaborn came out of the bathroom from her shower in a short robe, drying her thick mahogany hair.

"Running late," she said. "Lt. Huxley and I are meeting with an Air Marshal to organize a supply of oversized balloon tires. Perfect for the Chevrolet trucks. We need to arrange for a constant source of supply from the RAF once Desert Squadron takes the field…Brandy says we cannot have enough tires."

"Try to keep 'Don't Dance' out of trouble," Maj. Randal said. "As much stuff as he's stolen, we'll be lucky if we don't all get thrown in prison."

"Coming from you, John," Lady Jane said, flashing her heart attack smile, "that's a major compliment."

Maj. Randal felt the familiar ice-pick-through-the-chest sensation. Being around Lady Jane never got old. In fact, the more he was, the more he wanted to be.

That had never happened before…not with any woman.

"Tell Huxley," Maj. Randal said, "thanks for the Ray-Bans."

When she was leaving, Maj. Randal said, "Would you ask Sergeant Major Mikkalis to come up on your way out?"

"Dinner this evening," Lady Jane said, "the two of us…no army business."

"I guess," Maj. Randal said, "the Kit-Kat Club is out…"

This time the smile was almost lethal.

Sergeant Major Mike "March or Die" Mikkalis knocked on the door.

"Come in," Maj. Randal said. "Take a look at this."

The chalkboard had a rough diagram drawn on it that was pyramidal in shape, with two main columns running down with a lot of lines sticking out from them. About a third of the lines had names chalked in. Clearly, the TO&E was a work in progress.

At the top was RFHQ. Major Clive Adair's name was next to it. Slightly below that was a line running out that was labeled RFFOB, with Captain Lionel Honeycutt-Parker's name. But nothing was cast in stone. Honeycutt-Parker might be better at RFHQ…the big Royal Dragoon was a topnotch organizer.

Or, he might choose to stay in England at Seaborn House. Raiding Forces was running several operations into enemy-occupied France. Capt. Honeycutt-Parker might elect to command Raiding Forces, Europe.

A lot depended on what Major Sir Terry "Zorro" Stone chose to do. He might want to be Deputy Commander or he might want command of a squadron…then everything would change.

The leg down to the left was labeled 'Desert Squadron'. Captain Taylor Corrigan was chalked in as the commander. Three lines ran out from it: one labeled 'Lieutenant Jeffery Tall-Castle'; one labeled 'Lounge Lizard officer'; the last one was blank. All three of those lines had one other line running out from them, for a second in command…those were all blank.

The three commands, patrols of 15 trucks, two officers and 30 men, were based on what Maj. Randal knew to be the original Long Range Desert Group organization.

The leg down to the right was labeled 'Sea Squadron'. Captain Jeb Pelham-Davies was chalked in as commander. Of the three arms sticking out from it, only one was labeled…'Lieutenant Pip Pilkington'.

"What do you think?" Maj. Randal said.

"Quite a few blank spaces on your chart, Major."

"You'd have made it a lot easier if you'd kept your temporary commission and taken command of one of the patrols," Maj. Randal said.

"Negative, sir," Sgt. Maj. Mikkalis said. "I intend to enjoy myself…what I am doing now is my idea of the best assignment the Army has to offer."

"How're we going to fill the officer billets?" Maj. Randal said. "My guess is they're always going to be a problem."

"There are several officers we have never met at Seaborn House, sir," Sgt. Maj. Mikkalis said. "You can ask Capt. Corrigan for recommendations. Every officer had to recruit his replacement before being allowed to deploy to Force N…you gave the order.

"The Captain signed off on each one."

"There's nine Phantom officers," Maj. Randal said, "of unknown quality."

"Not entirely, sir," Sgt. Maj. Mikkalis said. "We know they are not reluctant to serve behind enemy lines. Most of them commanded detachments with Force N."

"We'll evaluate each one on a case-by-case basis," Maj. Randal said. "Phantom hand-picked 'em, but that doesn't mean they'll meet Raiding Forces standards.

"I only want Achnacarry-trained people, officers and men for the Sea Squadron.

"Desert Squadron, that's another story. Not everyone will want to be out on a patrol in the unexplored Great Sand Sea for weeks on end. That's special work... nothing like we've trained for."

"Capt. Corrigan and Capt. Pelham-Davies will have ideas about which of the Force N company commanders who served in their Mule Raiding Battalions (MRB) they want in their new commands.

"Bring back some of the junior officers you did not initially invite to join Raiding Forces, sir.

Maj. Randal said, "We can commission any of the Bimbashis they recommend."

Sgt. Maj. Mikkalis said, "Major, you concentrate on the officers... leave the NCOs and other ranks to me."

"Can do," Maj. Randal said. "What about raising a French patrol using your three corporals and King as the basic building block?"

"The corporals are ex-French Foreign Legion," Sgt. Maj. Mikkalis said. "Not 'Free French', sir... none of them are from France."

"Really?" Maj. Randal said. "I didn't know that."

"Very few Frenchmen serve in the Legion," Sgt. Maj. Mikkalis said.

"We can organize a patrol of Legionnaires... desert men. No great trick to recruit volunteers, sir."

"Who do we get to be their commander?" Maj. Randal said.

"'Lt. Huxley," Sgt. Maj. Mikkalis said. "Speaks French like a native and the men will follow him."

"Do it," Maj. Randal said. "We'll see how Huxley works out."

"I talked to King before he left," Sgt. Maj. Mikkalis said. "He's planning on being your bodyguard when he gets back."

"Let him have any job he wants," Maj. Randal said.

"Give me a week or so to locate the Legionnaires, sir," Sgt. Maj. Mikkalis said.

"No Germans," Maj. Randal said, "not in Raiding Forces."

"My thoughts exactly," Sgt. Maj. Mikkalis said. "Nazis were known to have infiltrated the Legion...when I was a member before the war started, sir.

Maj. Randal said, "Try not to recruit any."

"God help the man in Raiding Forces," Sgt. Maj. Mikkalis said, "that I suspect of being a spy."

8

BETTER LATE THAN NEVER

MAJOR JOHN RANDAL AND CAPTAIN THE LADY JANE Seaborn were out by the pool at RAF Habbaniya. The last time he had been at the base almost two weeks ago, the pool area had served as his Command Post for the provisional Strike Force.

Then, the Royal Air Force base had been under siege. A division of Golden Square rebel troops had occupied the heights outside the wire. Things were relatively peaceful now, except for the odd air attack by Iraqi and German aircraft. The Iraqi Army had packed up and gone home.

No one really knew why.

A dusty 1914 model Rolls Royce armored car pulled up to the club. Major Sir Terry "Zorro" Stone KBE, DSO, MC, stepped out, accompanied by Captain James "Jimmy" Roosevelt, USMCR.

2nd Life Guards troops, serving in the lorried infantry role attached to the Lancelot Lancers Regiment, *aka* Lounge Lizards, dismounted from their trucks and surrounded the area as if to secure it.

Kingcol had arrived.

"Hi Terry," Lady Jane said. "Jimmy, how did you manage to find yourself associated with the Lancers?"

"Flew down and linked up with Habforce," Capt. Roosevelt said. "Traveled with Kingcol, the advance column, under Brig. Joe Kingstone."

"Joe is said to be our best cavalry brigadier," Lady Jane said.

"Have to feel for Joe," Capt. Roosevelt said. "More blue-blooded nobility riding in his column than Henry V had at Agincourt…four baronets, three barons, two viscounts, a pair of earls, one duke and a highly-decorated knight of the realm with a striking resemblance to Errol Flynn.

"Seemed like I was on a back lot in Hollywood…Kingcol marched out into the unknown, sublimely confident that they would be able to fight their way through and relieve the beleaguered cantonment in the nick of time, the day *after* we had already relieved ourselves…I never said anything, not wanting to discourage anyone.

"The cavalry has arrived."

"Better late than never," Maj. Randal said.

"Good to see you too, old stick," Maj. Stone said. "Spent the entire siege poolside, I take it, while my regiment force marched across a thousand miles of burning sand, risking all to save the likes of you from the clutches of an army of blood-thirsty Iraqi devils bent on Holy Jihad."

"Fighting hard the whole way?" Maj. Randal said.

"Glubb Pasha's 'Girls'…the Arab Legion out of Jordan, engaged in a couple of minor skirmishes en route," Maj. Stone said. "My Lancers never fired a shot.

"The only unpleasantness we encountered came from my old regiment, the 2nd Life Guards," Maj. Stone said. "They have been thoroughly browned off the entire trip."

"Why might that be?" Maj. Randal said.

"The troopers were dismounted. Re-flagged as lorried infantry. Had to shoot their horses before we departed, which did nothing for morale," Major Stone said.

"How dreadful," Lady Jane said. "What could possibly cause them to shoot their horses?"

"Not likely to let the Arabs have their cherished blacks," Maj. Stone said. "Even for a price. Better to put them down."

"Instead of the armored cars the regiment has long been promised, the men were packed in trucks like sardines, lorried infantry. Bitter about that...an affront to their dignity."

"The swankiest cavalry regiment in the army," Lady Jane said. "Who would blame them?"

"My former commanding officer loathed finding his squadron placed under my command. The ignominy of being called a 'Lounge Lizard' was the final straw."

Lady Jane giggled. She was solely responsible for the regiment being nicknamed the 'Lounge Lizards'...even commissioning the unit identification marking, the silhouette of a turquoise gecko that looked like it had been run over by a gravel crusher.

Rumor was that Maj. Stone had been disinherited over the symbol. The Lancelot Lancers *was* the family regiment, and his father, the Duke, had not been amused.

"Outranked your old CO," Maj. Randal said. "Hate it when that happens."

"Exigencies of war," Maj. Stone said. "Ours is not to reason why..."

"Personally, I'm proud of my association with the Lounge Lizards," Capt. Roosevelt said. "Damn fine outfit.

"Shoving off across trackless desert with nothing but a compass azimuth to go by, who knows where the water holes might be, was one of the most daring undertakings in military history... even with the siege broken."

"Now that you're here," Maj. Randal said. "Time to go to work."

***

THE AIR HEADQUARTERS CONFERENCE ROOM was packed. Colonel Ouvrey Roberts issued his Operations Order for an attack on Fallujah beginning at dawn the next day. Recently arrived in the room were Major General George Clark, commander of Habforce, and Vice Air Marshall John D'Albiac, the new Air Officer Commanding (AOC), RAF Habbaniya.

Brigadier Joe Kingstone was surprised to discover that his boss, whom he thought had been traveling in the follow-up Habforce column, had arrived by air at the base ahead of his Kingcol...the advance party.

Neither senior commander was happy with the plan that Col. Roberts put forward.

Maj. Gen. Clark wanted to command the attack personally but was talked out of it. No one thought it a good idea since he had only arrived that day. He agreed to allow Col. Roberts to continue in command...reluctantly.

VAM D'Albiac was livid. Col. Roberts' plan called for integrated air-ground operations; a dangerous precedent, in his opinion. The RAF's mission was to defeat the Luftwaffe – not be on call to support ground formations on the whim of some *army* officer. VAM D'Albiac clearly did not grasp that the only reason the Iraqi rebel forces besieging RAF Habbaniya had been defeated was because of the close coordination and cooperation between the RAF and army.

He intended to file a complaint with his higher headquarters over the egregious misuse of RAF assets.

Major John Randal was sitting in the back of the room between Major Sir Terry "Zorro" Stone and Squadron Leader Tony Dudgeon. When he tried to introduce the two officers, Maj. Randal discovered that they already knew each other from Eton.

Sqn. Ldr. Dudgeon drawled, "Our new commander appears to be a bigger fool than our last one."

Sitting with them was the poet, author, politician and Kingcol intelligence officer Lieutenant Somerset de Clair. He was piqued that the inhabitants of RAF Habbaniya were not overjoyed to be rescued...actually believed they had relieved themselves.

Ingrates.

Col. Roberts had a tough nut to crack in his objective...Fallujah. The town sat astride the Euphrates River, on the road to Baghdad 30 miles away. The key strategic feature was the 177-foot-long bridge that linked Fallujah to

Baghdad. The problem was that the Iraqis had flooded the low-lying areas by breaching the Euphrates' 'bunds' to allow the river to flow in. Most of the western approaches to the long, iron bridge were under water.

That ruled out a *coup de main*. The element of surprise was critical to prevent the Iraqis from blowing the bridge. The bridge was of strategic importance to the follow-up operation of driving onto Baghdad to engage the Golden Square rebel forces.

It needed to be taken intact.

Paramount to Col. Roberts' strategy was avoiding the inevitable bloodbath that would result from street fighting in Fallujah.

Maj. Randal thought that the concept of the operation he put forward was excellent...simple, easy to understand and daring. The plan maximized the capabilities of the different combat arms available.

There were two phases.

Phase One consisted of a Psychological Warfare campaign aimed at Fallujah and scheduled to begin shortly after the briefing. The RAF would drop leaflets advising the Iraqi defenders to surrender. A massive British Army was advancing on the town. The same one that had routed the rebel forces on the escarpment outside of RAF Habbaniya... wholly fictional, of course.

Why die in the bombing attacks that were to come?

Simultaneously, Fallujah was to be cut off from all communications with Baghdad. Low flying Audaxes under the command of Sqn. Ldr. Dudgeon would buzz through the telephone lines and cut them with their propellers. In the cases where there was more than one line, the pilot would land. The bombardier would jump out and chop down the nearest telephone pole with an ax.

Sqn. Ldr. Dudgeon whispered, "Thanks, Major...your crazy stunts were a bad influence on Col. Roberts – he believes we are all supermen."

"Flying into telephone cables," Maj. Randal said, "does sound chancy."

Phase Two was a three-pronged assault on Fallujah. Troops would advance across Hammond's Bund, then cross the gap the Iraqis had blown in it to flood the area using an improvised ferry…then storm the bridge.

Simultaneously, Kingcol—led by the Lancelot Lancers—would cross the Euphrates by another improvised ferry…a modified pleasure boat brought up from Lake Habbaniya at Sin-el-Dhibban, and threaten Fallujah from the northwest.

Before dawn, a company of the King's Own Royal Regiment (KORR) would be flown in to air-land on the Fallujah-Baghdad road, set up a roadblock and cut the town off from reinforcements. The KORR, having accomplished the world's first strategic airlift when it deployed to Iraq from India, was now itching to make bold tactical use of its newfound air mobility.

"Major Randal," Col. Roberts said, "will drop by parachute in advance, with a small party of Commandos to mark the landing ground for the KORR."

From start to finish, the purpose of the exercise was to cause the Iraqis to feel isolated, then panic, abandoning Fallujah and fleeing without putting up a fight.

"I would not be standing in the road, old stick," Maj. Stone said under his breath, "when the Iraqi Army realizes it has pressing business in Baghdad."

"Roger that."

***

MAJOR JOHN RANDAL WAS ON THE GROUND OUTSIDE of Fallujah, not far off the road to Baghdad behind enemy lines. He was frantically chopping at a creosote-soaked telephone pole with an ax. Sun, sand and the winds of time had turned it into a petrified log.

It was not going down.

Squadron Leader Tony Dudgeon was sitting in his idling Audax, laughing his head off while watching Maj. Randal's exertions.

Finally in desperation, Maj. Randal took an M-36 Mills Bomb out of his pocket, wired it to the pole, pulled the pin and made a run for the airplane. He had never felt more foolish in his entire life.

KAAAABOOOOM!

"Go back and cut the wires," Sqn. Ldr. Dudgeon shouted over the motor.

Maj. Randal ran back and cleaved the telephone lines lying on the ground. He was not having his best day. This was the craziest mission he had ever been on.

Sqn. Ldr. Dudgeon had dragooned him into coming along.

He was never going to make that mistake again…flying with a daredevil pilot medically classified as combat-fatigued. Bad move. Maj. Randal planned to find a way to get some payback on the Squadron Leader first chance…provided he lived through the rest of the mission.

The plan was to cut the phone line in two more places.

Maj. Randal did not have to get out of the Audax with the ax again. Sqn. Ldr. Dudgeon clipped the cables by flying through them…an even more hair-raising experience. Purposely flying at low level, barely skimming the desert floor while aiming dead center between two telephone poles—straight at the wire in an attempt to cut it with the propeller—is not rational behavior.

Most aviators spend their entire careers trying to *avoid* flying into telephone lines.

An hour later, Maj. Randal, Captain the Lady Jane Seaborn, Sqn. Ldr. Dudgeon, Major Sir Terry "Zorro" Stone, Captain Jimmy Roosevelt, Jim Taylor and Squadron Leader Paddy Wilcox were in the RAF Habbaniya Officer's Club laughing uproariously at Sqn. Ldr. Dudgeon's recounting of the afternoon's adventure.

The action was more entertaining in the telling than in the doing.

Veronica Paige joined the group. Soon she and Lady Jane were engaged in an intense private conversation.

Maj. Randal wondered what that was about.

***

MAJOR JOHN RANDAL ARRIVED AT THE AIRFIELD at 0400 hours. Lieutenant Westcott Huxley was there with Corporals Smith, Jones and Brown. Squadron Leader Paddy Wilcox and Jim Taylor were in the Hudson running through their pre-flight checklist.

There were four ancient bi-winged Vickers Valentias queued up in line with a platoon of troops in full combat gear gathered around each one.

Captain Valentine Fabian walked up and saluted, even though it was pitch-dark.

"Nice to serve with you again, Major."

"Your troops ready to go, Captain?"

"Yes, sir,"

"The quicker you exit," Maj. Randal said, "the better."

"We spent most of yesterday running de-planing drills, sir."

"Good," Maj. Randal said. "See you on the ground."

Colonel Ouvrey Roberts and Major Ted Everett arrived. After speaking briefly with Maj. Randal, the two went around and visited each planeload of the King's Own Royal Regiment. The mission was high-risk, high-reward. Inserting the KORR rifle company behind the Iraqi forces as a blocking force was the first tactical airlift the British Army had ever attempted and tension was high.

A lot could go wrong.

Lt. Huxley and the ex-Foreign Legion corporals were chuted up. Maj. Randal gave each man a thorough jumpmaster's inspection. He went on board the Hudson and checked the steel cable to which the jumpers would attach their static lines. Next, he taped the edges of the door from which they would be exiting.

Then he strapped on his own parachute.

Everyone would be jumping with a duffel bag of 5-gallon cans containing a kerosene and motor oil concoction sealed inside. Maj. Randal's contained a smoke pot. Once on the ground, the men would set up the cans at intervals and light the fuel they contained to mark the landing ground for the Valentias.

Maj. Randal would light off the smoke.

It was hoped that the troop transport pilots would be able to see Maj. Randal's white smoke in the pre-dawn light to help judge wind drift on the ground. The touchdowns, made in bad light on an uncertain landing surface behind enemy lines, would be tricky. Even a slight miscalculation could result in tragedy.

No one had ever done this before.

"Ready, Lieutenant?"

"Wojew, suw," Lt. Huxley said. "Weady as we'll evew be."

Maj. Randal said, "Right."

9

TACTICAL AIR ASSAULT

"STAND UP," MAJOR JOHN RANDAL ORDERED.

Lieutenant Westcott Huxley and the three ex-Foreign Legion corporals struggled to their feet. The Hudson had reached cruising altitude after taking off. The flight to the Drop Zone was only a matter of minutes.

"HOOK UP!"

The four Raiding Forces men clicked their snap hooks on the steel cable. Then, balancing themselves, they slipped the safety wire through the tiny hole. It was like trying to thread a needle on a bucking horse.

"CHECK STATIC LINES!"

The jumpers rattled their static lines back and forth and pulled down on them to make sure they were locked.

"CHECK YOUR EQUIPMENT!"

Everyone ran their hands over their weapons and other personal gear. The idea was *not* to find anything wrong. There was little time to fix any deficiency and they were going to jump no matter what.

"SOUND OFF FOR EQUIPMENT CHECK!"

"OKAY, OKAY, OKAY," Lt. Huxley, jumping number two behind Maj. Randal, stuck out one arm in the proscribed manner and shouted, "ALL OKAY!"

Captain James "Jimmy" Roosevelt, along to observe his first parachute operation, gave Maj. Randal a thumbs up. Watching men preparing to jump from a plane in flight was proving to be considerably more stressful than he would have thought. It was dark out, who knew what was waiting for them on the ground, and it was a long way down.

The jumpers were not wearing reserve parachutes. U.S. Army paratroopers wore reserves. Capt. Roosevelt knew there is no sure thing. The lowest bidder gets the contract. At least that was conventional military wisdom.

James "Baldie" Taylor came out of the pilot's compartment and made his way to the rear of the plane. He was going to retrieve the static lines once the jumpers had exited the airplane.

"Everything copacetic?" Jim asked, using a term Maj. Randal never heard anywhere except on airborne operations. It did not mean 'is everything is fine and dandy?'…it meant 'are you in good enough shape to jump?'

"Roger that, General."

Jim was no longer using the rank of Major General like he had in Abyssinia but, as a mark of respect, Maj. Randal no longer called him "Baldie."

"Illuminate the landing ground, load your men on the first Valentia out and I will see you back at RAF Habbaniya for breakfast, Major," Jim said.

"Sounds like a plan."

"We will ride out after and watch Zorro make his river crossing," Jim said. "On to Baghdad."

The red light next to the door blinked three times.

"ONE MINUTE!" Maj. Randal shouted. "CLOSE ON THE DOOR!"

Maj. Randal reached out and grabbed the rim that ran around the exit door with his fingertips, then arched his body outside the aircraft. The wind distorted his facial features and ripped at his faded green jungle jacket.

He could see the road coming up through the dark. Squadron Leader Paddy Wilcox made a slight adjustment and the airplane lined up directly over it. From here on, one spot was as good as the next.

The light on the wing turned green.

Maj. Randal swung back inside.

The expression on Lt. Huxley's face was no longer what you might expect to see on a dilettante from the most wealthy cavalry regiment in the army who got his 'Rs' confused. Eyes narrowed to slits, the skin on his cheekbones stretched tight, he looked ready to bite a steel spike in half.

Behind him the tough-as-nails corporals were closed up tight, wanting out of the airplane.

"FOLLOW ME," Maj. Randal barked, "LET'S GO!"

On this exit, Maj. Randal was more than a little careful with his duffel bag containing the smoke pots. His ribs were still sore from the last time he had jumped a bundle. He was not taking anything for granted. However, parachuting from a Hudson was a more gentlemanly affair than jumping out of a cramped little Walrus amphibian.

They were exiting from 1,000 feet – twice the normal height of a combat jump. The idea was to give everyone time to shake out their bundles if there were any entanglements. There were not supposed to be any Iraqi troops in the area. No one was expected to be shooting at them.

While there were no guarantees on that, the Drop Zone had been selected to be away from any known Iraqi positions.

"One thousand, two thousand, three…," Maj. Randal felt the gentle tug of the X-chute pop open and deploy, always a good feeling. He looked up. No blown panels, no twisted lines.

Out of Maj. Randal's peripheral vision he could glimpse the other four parachutes staggered above and behind him. Down below he could faintly see the desert floor. There was not much of a breeze. The early morning air was heavy, so he was drifting down slow and easy for a change.

Also, he was coming in forward, which in his personal experience was rare. It made things a lot easier.

Maj. Randal did not pull a slip, he simply reached above his head, gripped the risers in each hand, brought his elbows together with his forearms protecting his face, bent his knees and rocked his boots to make sure his knees were *not* locked, and with his chin tucked down hard on his chest waited for his toes to touch down.

There was the familiar blurring sensation, a whisper of silk, and then he landed in a soft patch of sand. He made a split, almost unconscious, decision to make a right-side parachute landing fall – swiveled right, fell and hit all five points of contact – toes, calf, thigh, buttocks, and side of back – in the correct sequence.

Springing up, Maj. Randal pulled the safety clip of the quick-release device on his chest and hammered it with his fist. The parachute harness immediately came apart and dropped to the ground. He untied the leg rope attached to the bundle of 5-gallon cans, un-slung his 9mm Beretta MAB-38 submachine gun and glanced around to see how his troops were doing.

The men were floating down silently. Maj. Randal walked to his parachute with his arms outstretched and rolled the canopy up in the approved figure-eight method. Then he stuffed it in its parachute bag, lined up the snaps and clipped them shut.

By the time he had removed the smoke pot from the duffel bag, Lt. Huxley was there, lugging a .45 Thompson submachine gun. One by one, the corporals arrived. Everyone was down and ready to go with equipment in good working order.

Now, all that was necessary was to set up the cans. The team had synchronized their watches prior to the jump. The flares were to be lit at 0445 hours.

"Let's do it," Maj. Randal ordered. "Rally on the smoke as soon as you light 'em off."

The men disappeared into the dark, moving out on their appointed missions, guiding on the railroad. Their job was to set up the flares beside the tracks to mark the landing ground. The marked portion of the improvised landing air strip was 500 yards in length.

At the prearranged time, the landing lights came on. Up in the pre-dawn sky, the Valentia troop transports swooped in and landed. The pilots demonstrated nerves of steel—and no small amount of skill—setting down right between the improvised flares, trusting to Maj. Randal's team to have selected a suitable place to land.

It was asking a lot for them to accept – with no questions asked – that the ground was capable of handling their large transports. A stretch of road with potholes could have spelled instant disaster.

Captain Valentine Fabian led his company of the King's Own Royal Regiment (KORR) off the first plane at a dead run. Maj. Randal had his team standing by, ready to board. The KORR officer saluted crisply as the two groups passed each other.

"Good luck," Maj. Randal called, as his men trotted by heading for the Valentia – mission accomplished.

"Nice job, Major," Capt. Fabian shouted. "Lighted up like a regular airport."

The Raiding Forces team was loaded seconds after the last KORR trooper deplaned. The pilot wasted no time. He began his take off run as soon as they were on board.

The big, obsolete bomber, the same model Maj. Randal and Lieutenant Butch "Headhunter" Hoolihan, DSO, MC, MM, RM, had jumped from into Abyssinia, was one of the slowest aircraft still in service. So slow that when you looked down at something on the ground it did not seem to move. Nevertheless, they were landing back at RAF Habbaniya in 10 minutes.

Jim and Capt. Roosevelt were standing by with Flanigan when the Valentia landed. Maj. Randal and Lt. Huxley climbed into the policeman's waiting car with them. They set off to observe the final stages of the Euphrates river crossing by the Lancelot Lancers, the 2/4 Gurkhas, two companies of the Levies and an improvised half battery of the howitzers that Strike Force had captured from the Iraqis during the raid on Wolf's Teeth.

The ferryboat was being hauled back and forth on a wire hawser the Madras Sappers and Miners had thrown across the 750-foot stretch of the river. The operation was well underway by the time they arrived. Major Sir

Terry "Zorro" Stone's Rolls Royce armored cars could be seen on the far bank providing security for the troops as they crossed over.

As the sun came up, Colonel Ouvry Roberts ordered the attacking forces to advance on the town in small bounds, taking their time according to plan. The concept of the operation was to give the Iraqis the opportunity to either surrender or pull out without a fight in the built-up area. Major General George Clark was on the scene, observing.

He lost his nerve.

Despite his promise to keep out of the tactical handling of the battle, Maj. Gen. Clark demanded that Col. Roberts immediately push his troops into Fallujah. The General was an excellent organizer and administrator. He was no battle commander – and today it showed.

Col. Roberts coolly ignored him.

After a planned pause to consolidate at 1445 hours, a massive air attack went in, with the RAF dropping 10 tons of bombs. The Levies troops, who had crossed the Bund, rushed the steel bridge. Then the Lancelot Lancers, *aka* Lounge Lizards, in their Rolls Royce armored cars, accompanied by their attached squadron of 2nd Life Guards in the lorried infantry role, looped around and entered Fallujah from the flank, capturing 300 prisoners.

Even the dispirited Life Guardsmen perked up at the easy success of the perfectly-executed maneuver.

Not a single battle casualty was taken by any of the attacking units. The Iraqis, fearing that they were surrounded upon discovering the KORR astride the Baghdad Road to their rear, high-tailed it for parts unknown without putting up a fight.

Col. Roberts had orchestrated a magnificent victory.

By 1600 hours the Hudson was winging its way back to Cairo. Besides Captain the Lady Jane Seaborn, Lt. Huxley and the three ex-Foreign Legion corporals, on board were: Mr. Zargo, Ace, Queen, Jack, Joker, Flanigan, Veronica Paige and "The Great Teddy."

Lady Jane explained the manifest to Maj. Randal.

"Jim is bringing Mr. Zargo and his people down to work with Raiding Forces Desert Squadron. Veronica is going to be helping A-Force on a new project Dudley is organizing…she has to enlist or be drafted. All women under 40 are being called up.

"I shall take Teddy to England when I attend Mandy's commissioning ceremony. Off to Eton to finish his education."

"Eton?"

"John," Lady Jane said, "it is a simple fact that English schools have a pecking order. Eton is at the top. We *do* want Teddy to have a good start."

"I want to recommend the kid for a medal," Maj. Randal said. "Just wondered how you fixed it."

Spotting Flanigan walking down the isle, Maj. Randal said, "What's your plan?"

"Lady Jane recruited me to be her driver, Major," Flanigan said. "When Mandy returns, we will have the old Habbaniya firm back together again."

Maj. Randal pushed his cut-down bush hat over his eyes to get some long overdue sleep.

"That'll be swell."

Veronica, Mandy, Lady Jane…life as he knew it had ceased to exist.

***

MAJOR JOHN RANDAL AND CAPTAIN THE LADY JANE Seaborn walked up the stairs to their private suite located on the top floor at RFHQ. Captain "Geronimo" Joe McKoy and Waldo Treywick were inside, sitting on a couch in the corner of the living room where the maps on the wall were positioned. They were having a grand time studying the chalkboard marked up with the proposed 'Raiding Forces, Middle East Table of Organization.'

"John," Capt. McKoy said, "you're going at this all wrong."

10

MISSION BRIEF

JAMES "BALDIE" TAYLOR WAS STANDING in front of a small group
in Major John Randal's (and Captain the Lady Jane Seaborn's) private suite
at Raiding Forces Headquarters (RFHQ). People were seated on the small
couches and extra chairs that had been provided for the briefing. The soldier
of fortune, King, back from No.1 Parachute School, was standing guard
outside the door.

Present were: Major John Randal; Major Jack Merritt DSO, MC; Major
Clive Adair; Captain Jeb Pelham-Davies DSO, MC; Captain Taylor Corrigan
DSO, MC; Captain "Pyro" Percy Stirling DSO, MC; Lady Jane; Lieutenant
Randy "Hornblower" Seaborn; Captain James "Jimmy" Roosevelt (in golf
togs, having played a round of golf with Field Marshall Sir Archibald Wavell
that morning in his capacity of unofficial ambassador for his father, President
Franklin D. Roosevelt); Captain "Geronimo" Joe McKoy; Lieutenant
Penelope Honeycutt-Parker; Lieutenant Pamala Plum-Martin; Brandy
Seaborn; and Waldo Treywick.

Jim was a high-ranking member of MI-6, the British Secret Intelligence
Service, though that was classified "Need to Know."

The only two people in the room who knew were Lady Jane and Lt.
Pamala Plum-Martin – both of whom were also members of the SIS.

They all worked under the cover story of being Special Operations
Executive, an organization so secret even its initials were classified.

It was not clear who MI-6 was trying to confuse, the Germans or other British intelligence organizations. SOE was certainly fooled. It had all three on the payroll. Maj. Randal had an idea they were MI-6 but he did not have a "Need to Know," so officially he did not.

"This may be the oddest group I have ever briefed," Jim said. "I have no inkling why some of you are here, and others are present over my objection.

"Major Randal prepared the attendance list.

"He has not explained his reasoning to me. Understand this: everything said in this room is classified Most Secret. No one outside of those sitting here right now have any need to know what is briefed today.

"Parker, you and Mrs. Seaborn consider yourselves employed by me as of right now. If you have not signed the Official Secrets Act already, you will before this day is over.

"Captain McKoy, you and Waldo are carried on my roster of contract agents—volunteer—non-paid. Welcome to SOE, boys.

"Captain Roosevelt, you are cleared to go home and tell your father every word I say."

"I work for Bill Donovan," Capt. Roosevelt said.

"Apprise Wild Bill too," Jim said. "He has been coordinating with us privately for the last six months. No one else, Jimmy."

"Thanks, Baldie."

"What does the U.S. Marine Corps doctrine have to say about logistics?"

Capt. Roosevelt, there as an observer, was caught off guard being singled out for a question. "The Marines are an amphibious force. We take the fight to the enemy on foreign shores in distant and remote places. Logistics establishes limits on what is operationally possible."

"Remember that last sentence," Jim said. "Think about it every day, all day. Think about it at night. 'Logistics establishes limits on what is operationally possible.'

"Strategic Raiding Forces has been assigned a starring role in the most important campaign being fought in the Middle East today—a war against the Axis *logistics system.* The objective is to make it difficult—if not impossible—for the Afrika Korps to sustain itself in the field.

"From December 1940 through February 1941, Field Marshal Wavell conducted OPERATION COMPASS against the Italians. It was successful beyond anyone's expectations. Unfortunately, Wavell had to stop short of finishing them off because Middle East Command was ordered to divert troops to Greece and then to Crete.

"Nevertheless, Hitler was shocked by the scope of the Italian losses as a result of COMPASS. He believed that if Italy lost Tripoli it would be knocked out of the war. A decision was made in Berlin to send a *Sperrverband*—a blocking force of two German divisions, the 5th Light Division and 15th Panzer Division under General Erwin Rommel—to prevent that from taking place.

"The German High Command's aim is to keep Italy in the war, thus shielding the Romanian oil fields in Southeast Europe.

"General Rommel sees it differently. Instead of Afrika Korps being a bulwark for the Italians, the Desert Fox has concluded that if he can control the Mediterranean coastline, Germany will be able to ship supplies from Italy to Africa unmolested. With that kind of a support pipeline, he would be able to seize the oil fields in Libya, Iraq and Iran.

"The Nazis win the war..."

Jim said, "Rommel landed in theatre on 14 February '41. Two days later, the leading elements of Afrika Korps landed at Tripoli. Two weeks later, disregarding direct orders to take his time and build up a supply base before initiating combat operations, Rommel launched his first offensive to recapture Cyrenaica.

"Many of his tanks were phony: Volkswagens with cardboard strapped on the sides to look like panzers. Even so, Afrika Korps drove all the way to

Tobruk, where a part of our Eighth Army—consisting largely of Australian troops—is currently under siege.

"That is the bad news," he said.

"The good news is that now the Desert Fox has a 1,200- to 1,500-mile-long supply lifeline—one of the longest in modern history. He has to haul every item Afrika Korps needs—water, ammunition, food stocks, fuel, parts, etc.—with him.

"Actually, Rommel's logistical infrastructure is considerably longer than that— originating in Italy. His supplies have to be freighted across the Mediterranean, the vast majority of war materiel by ship, under constant attack every inch of the way by Royal Navy surface craft, submarines and the Royal Air Force.

"When the Axis merchantmen reach Africa, they dock in one of the three major ports the Axis controls.

"Then the provisions have to be transported by truck and/or rail to the front— subject to air attack by the RAF and the chance ambush by the LRDG.

"Now, you—Strategic Raiding Forces—are joining the battle to focus exclusively on Rommel's overland supply route.

"Exactly how you go about it I leave to Major Randal, our resident guerrilla warfare expert." Jim said.

"Questions?" When no one said anything, he told them, "I will be followed by Colonel Cromwell, chief logistics officer, Middle East Command. The Colonel will provide more detailed insight on Afrika Korps' supply challenges."

Colonel Terrance Cromwell was ushered into the room by King at the door.

"Gentlemen," Col. Cromwell said, "the claim has been made that professionals talk logistics and amateurs talk tactics. I shall not say that, of course, considering that in this room sit some of the best small-unit tacticians Britain has to offer. But mark it down—the desert war is a war of logistics.

"Think of Afrika Korps as a giant, fire-breathing dragon with a voracious appetite, dragging a 1,200 mile-long tail. Most subscribe to the age-old theory, 'if you cut off the head, the body dies.' I submit, which would you rather tangle with? Big teeth breathing flames or a long, defenseless appendage?

"The Axis is almost entirely dependent on sea transport for sustenance. Every stick of Rommel's provisions has to be shipped from the Continent. Once in country, it has to be hauled to the front by road and rail across vast distances in all weather. And the coastal roads are notoriously prone to flash flooding.

"Afrika Korps has what we logisticians tend to describe as an 'out of whack, tooth-to-tail ratio'," Col. Cromwell said.

"When you glance at a map, what appears to be an enormous theatre of operations in actuality turns out to be a narrow—approximately fifty-mile wide—strip that runs along the Mediterranean coast. It's the only terrain where high-speed armored formations can maneuver—where the battle will be won or lost.

"More importantly for your purposes, it's the only ground that can support Afrika Korps' supply columns.

"Apart from a few remote desert tracks, which, if used, will greatly increase wear and tear on Rommel's precious vehicles, there is only one hard surface road network: the Via Balbia. It stretches endlessly along the coast.

"There are only two rail lines in the entire theatre: one in Tripolitania and the other in Cyrenaica."

Maj. Randal made eye contact with Capt. Stirling. "Pyro" Percy was likely the most experienced railroad buster in the war on either side, a member of the famed 17/21 Lancers, the "Death or Glory Boys". A great believer in the "P for Plenty" formula, when Capt. Stirling blew something up, it stayed blown up.

Capt. Stirling grinned.

The Desert Fox was going to have to learn to cope without his railroads.

"The operations, and quite possibly, the intelligence types," Col. Cromwell was saying, "will advise you that Rommel's 10-ton fuel carriers are the most strategically important target on the African continent. Not true. *Any* truck is invaluable.

"A motorized force of one division requires 350 tons of supplies a day. To transport that quantity 300 miles, my staff estimates thirty-nine convoys of thirty 2-ton trucks each is required. Bear in mind, it's 700 miles from Tripoli to Benghazi and another 350 miles from Tobruk to Alamein. My staff expects a third of his vehicles will be out of action performing maintenance at any given time. It takes a minimum of 5,000 trucks on the road to sustain the Afrika Korps.

"The math is enormous, irrefutable—and Rommel's supply problem is a never-ending, all-consuming nightmare." Col. Cromwell said.

"While a German aircraft that is destroyed can be replaced by flying in another from Italy, every truck you knock out has to be replaced by a long, high-risk sea voyage. Which means those ships carrying replacement trucks will *not* be carrying tanks, artillery, troops and ammunition.

"And, the truck could be lost at sea, which means the Germans would have to send out *another* to replace the replacement.

"The ground transport problem feeds on itself. Best estimates are the Desert Fox will consume 50 percent of his total fuel allocation for Afrika Korps simply topping off the vehicles in his supply convoys.

"Now, subtract the losses to his fuel supply convoys caused by the RAF, the LRDG and your raids on the Via Balbia once they get going. The actual percentage of fuel available to the Afrika Korps for combat maneuvers is going to be quite small.

"In conclusion, if British Forces can carry out a war of attrition on the German logistics system, and our army is able to hold the Afrika Korps off long enough now that Lend Lease is in effect, there is only one outcome: we win by materiel superiority."

Cromwell ended his briefing quietly. "The numbers do not lie; nor do they boast or exaggerate," he said.

Maj. Merritt went next. As a Life Guards corporal, he had been Maj. Randal's No. 2 during Commando training at Achnacarry and on the first early raids. Given a commission in the field as a part of Force N in Abyssinia, he had been seconded to the Sudan Defense Force (SDF) as an acting captain.

The SDF was an elite mechanized unit. British officers assigned are temporarily accorded the privilege of serving at one grade higher rank. That made him a lieutenant, acting captain, temporary major.

At the end of the Abyssinian Campaign, Maj. Merritt's company had been attached to the Long Range Desert Group in anticipation of being assigned to Raiding Forces, Middle East once it was up and running.

"The LRDG is the best deep-desert penetration unit operating in the Middle East command," Maj. Merritt said. "It was originally conceived for reconnaissance and raiding against the Italians behind their lines across the Great Sand Sea. Today the Group is performing map survey work, road watch, strategic reconnaissance, and providing a desert taxi service to deliver agents to their operational areas for various intelligence agencies.

"Patrols carry out the occasional raid which they call 'beatups'.

"The original three founders, Bagnold, Clayton and Pendergrass, were all experienced prewar desert explorers. The first troops were New Zealanders, drawn mostly from their division cavalry squadron. After six months, the men were to return to their unit, their government not wanting their citizen soldiers to serve under British command permanently after the bloodletting during the last war," Maj. Merritt said.

"Starting out," he said, "the LRDG had three patrols later increased to five consisting of fifteen 30-cwt Chevrolet trucks heavily modified for desert operations. After protracted negotiations, the New Zealand HQ eventually agreed to allow one patrol to remain. To fill the vacancies by the departing personnel, volunteers were accepted on a temporary basis from the Guards, Yeomanry and other units.

"Today the LRDG has five patrols each made up of two officers and thirty men. They serve on six-month rotating tours that can be extended on an individual case-by-case basis by invitation. The Group does not mix the patrols. The result is that there is a Guards Patrol, a Yeomanry Patrol, New Zealand Patrol etc.—each with its own unique personality. Bagnold founded the unit, organized it and commanded it brilliantly for a year but has since moved on to become a staff officer at GHQ. Clayton assumed command but was captured leading a patrol. Pendergrass is currently in command." Maj. Merritt said.

"The LRDG operates out of the Oasis at Kufra.

"The Group has been misused lately," Maj. Merritt said, "having to guard the oasis, administer it and run long supply convoys from Cairo to their Forward Operating Base. In addition, GHQ unleashed a wave of publicity about their success as desert raiders and then started to believe their own press. As a result, the patrols have been assigned fighting missions best carried out by armored car squadrons, which have not ended well.

"My impression is that the LRDG made its reputation against Italians; it remains to be seen how they fare against the Afrika Korps. And they need to get back to their original mission: long range, deep desert patrolling."

The Vargas-girl-looking Royal Marine, Lt. Plum-Martin, was up next. "I am filling in for Squadron Leader Wilcox today—he is away flying. Earlier this week the two of us flew up to Kufra to observe the LRDG air operations.

"Lt. Col. Pendergrass is a private pilot. He flies his own plane, a small Waco. The Group has two of them. The RAF has not been cooperative— LRDG had to buy their airplanes privately then encountered difficulty getting authorization to paint Allied identification roundels on them.

"Because of the fantastic distances covered over hostile terrain, the two Wacos always fly formation together. If one is forced down, the other can

land and pick the pilot up or mark the location for a patrol to come to the
rescue if there is no place suitable to put down.

"The LRDG uses their aircraft exclusively for liaison, Lt. Plum-Martin
said. "Paddy is not likely to be satisfied being an aerial chauffer when our
Walruses have bomb racks, guns mounted, and we have a squadron's worth
of Canadian bush pilots back from leave who love flying and fighting."

Maj. Clive Adair followed Lt. Plum-Martin. He gave a brief description
of the long-range communications capabilities of Phantom.

When he concluded, Captain A. W. "Sammy" Sansom, Chief of Cairo
Counterintelligence, was escorted in.

"The LRDG has a highly-classified, Most Secret counterintelligence
operation in play. That information is not to leave this room," Sansom said.
"The Germans have a master spy named Count Lazzlo Almasy. Prior to the
war, the Count was a desert explorer and a member of the Royal Geographic
Society. In fact, he frequently went on expeditions with Bagnold, Clayton
and Pendergrass.

"Nowadays, Almasy is a Nazi intelligence officer. He operates a desert
taxi service similar to the LRDG—infiltrating spies into Egypt for the
Special-Purposes Training and Construction Company No. 800,
Brandenburger Regiment and the Luftwaffe's special missions
Kampfgeschwader 200 (KG200), under the command and control of SS
Colonel Otto Skorzeny and Brigadier Walter Schellenberg of the Abwehr,
respectively.

"The count is as dangerous as a viper, Sansom said. "The LRDG is
tasked with tracking down, capturing and/or killing him.

"Unfortunately, the Group is not suited for clandestine work. Their
problem is compounded by the lack of any known photos of Lazzlo. Only
Bagnold, Clayton and Pendergrass know what he looks like.

"Pendergrass is busy commanding the Group, Bagnold is sitting at a
desk in Cairo pushing paper, and Clayton is behind the wire in the bag."

Brandy said, "Parker and I know Lazzlo."

Capt. Sansom froze. "How is that possible, Mrs. Seaborn?"

"We were on expedition together before the war."

"Lazzlo is quite depraved," Lt. Honeycutt-Parker drawled. "A strong preference for young Arab boys—not illegal in this part of the world or even frowned on in certain quarters."

"Would you recognize Almasy if you saw him again?" Capt. Sansom asked.

"Absolutely."

"I need to get with you two ladies immediately upon conclusion of this briefing," Capt. Sansom said.

Next, King escorted in Major Vladimir Peniakoff, *aka* "Popski." The Major was a rotund, fortyish Russian raised in Poland. From an affluent family, he spoke a half-dozen languages.

Living in Egypt when the war started and looking for adventure, Popski divorced his wife, packed his two daughters off to private school in South Africa, and somehow managed to wrangle a "hostilities only" commission from the British army.

"I command the Libyan Arab Commando," Maj. Peniakoff said. "The Senussi inhabit the region you will be operating in. They have been occupied by and at war with Italy for many years.

"The Italian 'Butcher' Graziani slaughtered their sheiks by throwing them out of airplanes over their villages and hanging others in public from piano wire—a slow, painful death. The Senussi hate the Italians, are ambivalent to the Germans—though they respect their ability as warriors—and see the British as their savior.

"Originally, the plan was to arm the Senussi and wage a Lawrence-of-Arabia-style guerrilla war. That has been shelved as a bad idea, though you must continue to hold out the promise to do so later in order to entice the tribesmen to provide intelligence, watch over your secret supply dumps and serve as guides.

"Trust the nomadic desert tribes, but not the town Arabs—many of whom wish to ingratiate themselves with the Italians."

"Beware of informers," Maj. Peniakoff said.

Maj. Randal spoke last. He kept it short and simple. "Raiding Forces, Middle East is going to reorganize. Initial plans are to have two squadrons. A Desert Squadron for land-based raiding and a Sea Squadron to carry out pinprick raids along the coast targeting the Via Balbia.

"You people are the key players."

***

JAMES 'BALDIE' TAYLOR ARRIVED IN COLONEL DUDLEY Clarke's Cairo office thirty minutes after the meeting at RFHQ concluded. He did not have an appointment.

"You are not going to believe what Raiding Forces has," Jim said.

"What?"

"Phantom has a long-range radio at RFHQ Cairo capable of communicating direct to its regimental Headquarters outside London," Jim said. "When Wavell's staff found out about it, the idea of messages not vetted by GHQ being transmitted out of theatre back to the UK nearly gave them apoplexy."

"I can imagine it would," Col. Clarke said.

"GHQ ordered Maj. Adair not to send any communiqués containing operational details, unit or commander assessments—which is precisely what the Phantom Regiment was organized to do. However, he was allowed to set up the radio equipment because staff did not want to appear to be censoring Phantom."

"A wise and prudent plan," Col. Clarke said.

"The equipment has to be *tested,*" Jim said.

"Tested?"

"To carry out regular radio tests, Phantom placed a Marconi set at Raiding Forces HQ at Seaborn House. Major David Niven, who I understand used to work for you, stationed a detachment there to operate it," Jim said.

"Now, Maj. Randal has his own personal, highly secure means of private communications between RFHQ Middle East and RFHQ Seaborn House. Phantom plans to send personal messages back and forth to their wives and girlfriends as radio checks."

"Incredible," Col. Clarke said. "Are you making this story up?"

"Come see for yourself."

"I shall take your word for it," Col. Clarke said almost beside himself. "Do not let anything—and I mean *anything*—disturb that working arrangement."

"My thoughts exactly," Jim said.

"I shall contact Colonel Menzies immediately," Col. Clarke said. "We can use Phantom to provide MI-6 and A-Force a secure back channel to talk to each other covertly as frequently as we like with no one—meaning GHQ—the wiser.

"Guard that radio with your life!"

11

WHAT THE HELL IS A JEEP?

"AIN'T NOTHING IN THE WORLD BETTER," Captain "Geronimo" Joe McKoy said, "than forming a new military organization. Can't think of anything I like being a part of more."

"It would help," Major John Randal said, "if we knew what we were doing."

"That's the beauty of it," the silver-haired cowboy said. "You got yourself a clean sheet of paper—know where you're going, John; you just ain't real sure how to get there."

"Don't forget that correspondence course in business administration Joe took, Major," Waldo said.

"'The problem is the solution' might come in handy. Solved our mule situation."

Maj. Randal said, "I'll try to keep that in mind.

"Tell me again, Captain, why you think my organization chart's all wrong."

"The Sea Squadron is a no-brainer," Capt. McKoy said, taking out a cigar. "Raiding Forces has the best-qualified officers and men in the world available to fill it.

"Desert Squadron—that's another story. You ain't a desert man, John. So you're a-operatin' in the dark.

"Now me, I grew up in Arizona, served in the Rangers, and I was Chief-of-Scouts for Blackjack Pershing on the Punitive Expedition—commanded the Apache Scouts as you may recall.

"All that was desert work," Capt. McKoy said.

"Just about the time we got back from down Mexico way, the U.S. declared war on the Kaiser, and the army decided to send a cavalry division to the Middle East to serve alongside Allenby's boys, who was mostly Australian Light Horsemen at that time.

"We was organizing a division out of a bunch of the cavalry regiments stationed down at Fort Sam Houston in Texas. Supposed to be called the 1st Cav but ended up being the 15th for some reason. Then the big brass decided to break it up and convert the whole shebang into artillery regiments.

"I was in charge of the advance party to Egypt. We got shipped out before the breakup. Thirty U.S. Cavalry scouts. We got there, but the rest of the division never made it—being broken up like I said.

"My troop was equipped with six Model T Fords, so they turned us into a Light Car Patrol. No. 7 on the British books. We called ourselves No. 1 United States Light Car Patrol.

"We operated all over this country, then up into Palestine and Syria for the entire war," Capt. McKoy said. "Know it like the back a' my hand."

"So," Maj. Randal said, "what's wrong with my plan?"

"You're a-fixin' to ape the Long Range Desert Group," Capt. McKoy said. "Those boys run fifteen truck patrols: 30-cwt. You don't want to do that."

"Why not?"

"Two reasons," Capt. McKoy said. "Takes a lot of fuel to sustain that many vehicles on patrol, and you can't hide fifteen Chevrolet trucks from the air in the desert.

"Enemy air is going to be your big problem, John.

"Find you some Ford pickups, jack 'em up, put those air force balloon tires on 'em, do all the other desert modifications to the radiator and pack on the machine guns. What you want is a small, nimble, hard-hitting patrol with heavy-duty firepower.

"Five...six gun trucks per patrol, max, up to six machine guns per— plenty good medicine."

"Finding qualified officers is my major headache," Maj. Randal said. "You're doubling my pain, Captain."

"Not really," Capt. McKoy said. "I'll want a patrol. You're going to take one, so that only leaves us one more extra officer patrol leader than the ones you're already looking for, John."

"The problem is, fifteen trucks is too many," Waldo said, scratching his head. "But we need us fifteen trucks worth a' firepower. So, the solution is cut a regular patrol in half, double up on the machine guns.

"Pretty good, Joe. 'Problem is the solution.' Just like they said it would be in your correspondence course."

"What qualities am I looking for in a patrol leader, Captain?" Maj. Randal asked.

"A motorized desert patrol is a different animal than, say, your infantry deal or pinprick Commando raid team commander," Capt. McKoy said. "Your patrol leader has to be thinking three moves ahead all the time. What you want is a deliberate man—a tactician who can be bold when an opportunity comes up but possessed of a cool brain.

"Patrols don't move all that fast through desert terrain, so a patrol leader has plenty of time to think things out in advance on the roll, make a plan, and work it out in his head before he has to put it into action.

"Sometimes a patrol might need to pre-stage dumps of fuel and water in advance to set up their next mission," Capt. McKoy said. "Other times a patrol will abandon some vehicles temporarily to conserve gasoline—load everybody into just a couple a' trucks and make a push to reach a distant objective.

"From time to time, a patrol might cache a truck full of goods, fuel, water and parts in a secret location they can use later as a field-expedient supply depot. Been known to do that with a broke-down vehicle so they have it in place to cannibalize for parts at a later date, in an emergency.

"Desert patrolling is sort of like a chess match, you're always working out your next move. Like I said, thinking three moves ahead."

"How hard is it to master?" Maj. Randal said.

"Not that difficult," Capt. McKoy said. "Lots of men from a lot a' different backgrounds has been real successful at it. Navigation can be tricky, but most of it's dead reckoning. Once you understand the basics of desert operations, the rest comes pretty easy.

"The tactics is the main part.

"Your Patrol Leader has to be the big chief —see the whole picture, make the plans, lead from the front, do any advance reconnaissance, while always keeping an eye on water and fuel consumption.

"'It's good to have a Plan B,'" Capt. McKoy said, quoting from the Rules for Raiding that Maj. Randal had composed. "'Plan missions backward. Know how to get home.'

"The patrol members have to be picked men. Every man has to be able to drive. Have to be shade tree mechanics, radio operators and armorers. Somebody needs to know a little medicine.

"Patrolmen need to not get discouraged when things don't go according to plan 'cause they seldom do. And they have to enjoy working out in the blue—living wild, counting on each other for survival.

"You want to cross-train your people in the field every chance you get, so every man knows every other man's job—training never stops."

Maj. Randal said, "Sounds like a lot can go wrong."

"Lighten up, John," Capt. McKoy said. "You're overthinking this. You'll make a top-notch desert operator. I'm almost beginning to feel sorry for ol' Rommel."

"Yeah," said Waldo, "the Desert Fox don't have no idea what's in store for him once you get Raiding Forces goin,' Major.

"His problem *ain't* gonna be the solution."

***

"WHERE AM I GOING TO FIND FORD PICKUP TRUCKS?" Major John Randal asked, thinking about a certain car thief with a bullet hole in his brain—no help there.

"There *is* a Ford Dealership in Cairo, John," Captain the Lady Jane Seaborn said. She was putting on her earrings on the way out of their suite at RFHQ. "I shall drop by and see what is available while I am in town."

"Really," Maj. Randal said, "why didn't I think of that? Go shopping. How hard can that be?"

"Remember, lunch at Groppi's."

"Roger that," Maj. Randal said, going back to studying his TO&E diagram on the blackboard.

"Lieutenant Hoolihan," King announced.

"You learn which knife and fork to use, Butch?" Maj. Randal asked. He was glad to see the young Royal Marine.

"Yes, sir," Lieutenant Butch "Headhunter" Hoolihan said. "Top down, outside in, and if you are not 100 percent sure, watch the Colonel's wife and use whatever piece of silverware she picks up next."

"Works every time," Maj. Randal said. "You look like a movie star with all that fruit salad on your chest, stud."

"You made the recommendations, sir," Lt. Hoolihan said. "I thought Lady Jane was joking when she informed me about the investiture ceremony. Then when the King pinned the DSO ribbon on my tunic, I was sure he had picked up the wrong one."

Lieutenants are rarely awarded the Distinguished Service Order—a decoration reserved for field grade officers and above in the rigid British honors system.

"No mistake," Maj. Randal said. "You earned it, Butch. Come over here and take a look at this organizational chart I'm working on.

"We're setting up a Desert Squadron and a Sea Squadron.

"The Desert Squadron will operate similar to the LRDG. The Sea Squadron will be carrying out small-scale raids against the Via Balbia road system that runs along the Mediterranean coastline. Bad guys have roadhouses every fifteen miles or so for about 1,200 miles.

"In addition to troop leaders, I'm going to need an operations officer, an intelligence officer, most likely a motor officer and probably some other officers I haven't thought of yet.

"Where do you see yourself fitting in, Butch?"

"'Right Man, Right Job,'" Lt. Hoolihan quoted. "Sea Squadron for me, if that meets with your approval, sir."

"Thought you'd say that," Maj. Randal said. "What I'd really like is for you to be my assistant patrol leader in Desert Squadron..."

"Sir, I shall..."

"Negative," Maj. Randal said. "We need you leading raids, Butch. I'll give you a troop."

"A Royal Marine's dream assignment, sir," Lt. Hoolihan said.

"Well, we have a problem," Maj. Randal said. "Hornblower is out here, but he doesn't have a ship. Do you remember that partially wrecked dry dock on the Jubbah River we passed on the way in to Kismayo?"

"You mean the one with the three Italian MAS motor torpedo boats up on blocks inside?"

"That's it," Maj. Randal said. "Get with Randy. Pam will fly you two up there this afternoon. Commandeer the boats and bring 'em back here. Take Mr. Treywick with you."

"Yes, sir."

"Don't let anyone or anything stand in your way," Maj. Randal said. "We need at least one boat in operation immediately.

"Carry out your first raid as quick as you can organize your troop, and Randy can get a boat seaworthy. Pick yourself two lieutenants and twenty men, all Commando School graduates. I'll give you two weeks."

"My pleasure, sir," Lt. Hoolihan said. "Good to be back."

***

MAJOR JOHN RANDAL AND CAPTAIN "GERONIMO" JOE McKoy met Captain the Lady Jane Seaborn for lunch. Groppi's was packed. The war was good for the restaurant business in Cairo.

"I went by the Ford dealership," Lady Jane reported. "Only have half a dozen pickup trucks, all but one used. The owner is going to check with the dealership in Alexandria to inquire what they might have in inventory. Pickups are not very popular in this part of the world. We may find it difficult to acquire them in the numbers needed for Desert Squadron."

"Not popular?" Capt. McKoy said. "That's down right un-American."

"Egyptians prefer larger trucks," Lady Jane said.

"The army considers vehicles designed for the civilian market to be too flimsy for military applications…which means there are not many pickup trucks to be had for us to choose from."

"We're going to need a lot more than six," Maj. Randal said.

"I was in the Lend-Lease Office earlier," Lady Jane said, "to inspect the latest manifest of shipments arriving from the U.S.

"Do either of you happen to know what a Bantam might be?"

"Bantam?" Maj. Randal said.

"There's a half-broke car company in the States," Capt. McKoy said, "goes by that name."

"A consignment of Bantam Military Cars was off-loaded this morning," Lady Jane said. "Tiny little toys—one-quarter ton. No one can imagine any military use for them.

"We can have the lot."

"Bantam Military Car," Maj. Randal said. "How many?"

"Fifty," Lady Jane said. "Convertible, two to four passengers, three speed, 4x4 all-wheel drive, fold-down windscreen.

"Little rag-top runabouts, cute as can be—boxes on wheels."

"Cute is good," Maj. Randal said. "We'll take 'em."

Lady Jane rewarded him with a blinding smile.

"Bantams," Capt. McKoy said, rolling a cigar between his fingers, "might be what they call 'jeeps.'"

Maj. Randal asked, "What the hell is a 'jeep'?"

12

BUTTERFLY BOY

MAJOR JOHN RANDAL WAS STUDYING HIS TO&E DIAGRAM of Desert Squadron in his suite at RFHQ. Maybe he was overthinking the problem like Captain "Geronimo" Joe McKoy said. Desert Squadron had finally come together like a puzzle—all at once the pieces fit.

Captain Taylor Corrigan would command the Squadron. He was an extraordinarily talented cavalry officer from the Blues, had commanded a Mule Raiding Battalion with Force N and was the best fit for Desert Squadron.

Captain "Pyro" Percy Stirling, $17^{th}/21^{st}$ Lancers "The Death or Glory Boys," would be a patrol leader on detached duty, an independent patrol tasked with going after the two Axis rail lines: Railroad Wrecking Crew II. Maj. Randal was not sure whether or not to count his patrol as one of the six he intended to raise. Probably not.

Captain Lionel Chatterhorn, MC, Vulnerable Points Wing, had arrived from leave to assume personal command of the security detail at RFHQ.

When Maj. Randal briefed him on Raiding Forces' new mission profile, Capt. Chatterhorn said, "I have always felt a yearning to someday get involved in desert exploration."

Capt. Chatterhorn was a mature officer. Not only was he a security professional, he had also been pressed into service in Force N as a guerrilla troop commander, where he had demonstrated exceptional leadership abilities.

Maj. Randal assigned him one of the patrol leader slots on the spot.

Lieutenant Jeffery Tall-Castle, MC, Yorkshire Dragoons Yeomanry, also a Force N guerrilla troop commander who had distinguished himself in Abyssinia, was assigned to be a patrol leader.

Lieutenant Westcott Huxley was penciled in to be the patrol leader of the Foreign Legion/Free French patrol. Maj. Randal had reservations about this assignment. Huxley was very young. When they had formed Force N in Abyssinia, none of the Mule Raiding Battalion commanders had wanted him in their unit.

And, last but not least, Capt. "Geronimo" Joe McKoy was granted his wish to lead a patrol.

Maj. Randal planned to have a small patrol of his own but did not have the details worked out yet.

Bimbashis Airey McKnight, Cord Granger and Jack Masters were all being commissioned as lieutenants and recalled to Raiding Forces. The three had served as platoon leaders in the Railroad Wrecking Crew under Capt. Stirling in Force N. They would be assigned as assistant patrol leaders.

Their demolitions experience was going to be invaluable.

Frank Polanski had shown up at RFHQ. The ex-U.S. Marine, soldier-of-fortune and local advisor to Capt. McKoy in Abyssinia was looking for work. In the Marines, Frank had been a heavy weapons specialist. Maj. Randal assigned him to be the Desert Squadron armorer.

On paper, he was now a contract employee of Special Operations Executive.

Desert Squadron was going to need three additional assistant patrol leaders. Lieutenant Dirk Van Rood, a Force N guerrilla troop commander, was being brought back to Raiding Forces to fill one of them. Maj. Randal was counting on Lieutenant Roy Kidd filling another when he returned from training in a few weeks.

Recruiting was underway to find the specialist personnel needed for the patrol's drivers, navigators, snipers, mechanics, radio operators, machine gunners, etc. Maj. Randal conducted the initial screening. He wanted combat-experienced men—not fake- brave, the crazy-tough or anyone who tried to ingratiate himself during the interview.

Maj. Randal was looking for men who could think for themselves.

Raiding Forces had the authority to recruit any man from any regiment. Only one out of ten people who volunteered were picked. Those men were then assigned to Sergeant Major Mike "March or Die" Mikkalis for further evaluation.

Sgt. Maj. Mikkalis and the three Foreign Legion corporals, Smith, Jones and Brown (ably assisted by King from time to time when his duties allowed), conducted a brutal seven-day selection course, which ran round the clock and allowed only about four hours' sleep for the candidates the entire week. Those who survived then had to pass a final interview with Captain Jeb Pelham-Davies, who placed the men he accepted into a replacement pool.

From that group, the patrol leaders chose the personnel they wanted for their patrols. The men finally assigned to Desert Squadron had to agree to successfully complete a parachute course at a later date in order to remain on status with Raiding Forces.

A message arrived from Seaborn House. Captain Lionel Honeycutt-Parker, OBE, requested permission to stay in England and take command there.

Maj. Randal had been expecting him to come back to help organize and then run RFHQ. However, he had given the Royal Dragoon the option to select his next assignment. Now he had to find a replacement, and that was not going to be easy.

Major Clive Adair, who was working round the clock to amalgamate Squadron N, Phantom into Raiding Forces, was going to have to take on added responsibilities.

Lieutenant Pip Pilkington, MC, reported in. He was an explosives expert. In Abyssinia he had blown down the sides of two mountains, trapping an Italian convoy of reinforcements out of Addis Ababa bound for the battle at Kern. Maj. Randal assigned him to be his Chief-of-Demolitions, with a roving assignment to serve where needed in either Desert or Sea Squadron.

Lovat Scouts Munro Ferguson and Lionel Fenwick arrived from their home leave. They were immediately assigned to recruit and train the snipers needed to operate the scoped Boys .55 Anti-Tank Rifle that would be carried aboard one jeep in every patrol in Desert Squadron.

Capt. Pelham-Davies was tapped to command Sea Squadron. He was a former instructor at Achnacarry—the famed Commando School. The troops had respected him so much that they petitioned Maj. Randal to recruit him for Raiding Forces, making him the only officer invited in by the men. Capt. Pelham-Davies had served as a Mule Raiding Battalion commander in Force N.

As a Special Forces officer, he had no peer.

Unlike for Desert Squadron, Maj. Randal and Capt. Pelham-Davies had a good idea of what was needed for Sea Squadron, which would have two troops of twenty men and three officers, plus an HQ section, Life Boat Service section and a scratch Royal Navy flotilla. However, Capt. Pelham-Davies had his work cut out for him to get it organized.

Lieutenant Randy Seaborn and Lieutenant Butch "Headhunter" Hoolihan were away securing captured Italian MAS torpedo boats.

Lt. Hoolihan was Capt. Pelham-Davies' only Raiding Forces officer assigned to date, though he had twenty Achnacarry-qualified men from Force N ready to go, plus a detachment of Life Boat Servicemen who had served in Abyssinia.

The rest would have to be brought in from Raiding Forces, Seaborn House. Maj. Randal had specified only Achnacarry-trained personnel for Sea Squadron. Amphibious, pinprick raiding was specialist work and required highly qualified operators to be successful.

What that meant was officers and men, many of whom had not served in Force N, coming out to Egypt. New, hand-picked, highly qualified personnel being infused into Raiding Forces, Middle East, was a good thing.

Training was taking place nonstop at RFHQ.

Lieutenant Penelope Honeycutt-Parker and Brandy Seaborn were conducting desert navigation classes. Maj. Randal was going out with them daily, practicing his newly acquired skills. Navigation was something every man needed to be familiar with, even if they never served as patrol navigators.

Frank Polanski had assembled a complete armory of the weapons the patrols were likely to encounter—from pistols to heavy machine guns. He was holding weapons classes (friendly and enemy) to familiarize every member of Raiding Forces Desert and Sea Squadron with disassembly, assembly and live firing of all small arms in the Middle East. Raiders were allowed to carry personal weapons of their own choosing on operations, provided they could demonstrate proficiency with them.

Capt. McKoy was running a desert driving school. He had found a large patch of soft sand, complete with high dunes that looked like mounds of sugar, which was perfect for his designs. Every man aspiring to serve in Desert Squadron had to pass the driving course or be RTU'd—Returned to Unit.

Driving was a requirement that was not optional. Capt. McKoy did not grade on the curve. His course was pass/fail.

The ex-Arizona Ranger came by Maj. Randal's suite.

Maj. Randal went over the revised TO&E with him.

"Looks like she's shaping up," Capt. McKoy said. "You got a wide range of patrol leaders there, from me to a teenager who talks like Donald Duck. We'll see who outperforms who."

"Yes, we will," Maj. Randal said.

"It'll be real interesting," Capt. McKoy said. "This ain't my first rodeo, so I've sorta got the edge—but you got yourself some good men lined up."

"How's the driving going, Captain?" Maj. Randal asked.

"I tell you, John," Capt. McKoy said, pulling out a cigar, "We need ourselves some 'Mericans.

"Australians from the Outback would be real good, but their government won't allow 'em to serve under British command. They don't get it—you ain't British.

"New Zealand farmers have a lot of experience driving rough country, but they already have a patrol with the LRDG, and that's all the men Gen'l Freyberg's gonna let go, so we won't be getting any of them.

"The handful of South Africans and Rhodesians we got is good, real good—but there ain't enough of 'em.

"English boys just don't have the depth of driving experience we need. Some ain't never drove before, never owned a car, and they ain't much hand at being mechanics. You can't teach that kind of stuff overnight, John."

Maj. Randal said, "You're right about that."

"Patrolmen need to be able to completely tear down their vehicle and rebuild it with bailing wire and scrap iron if need be," Capt. McKoy said. "You can't call AAA when you have a breakdown out in the blue.

"We need us some shade tree mechanics from the USA—farm boys and ranch hands who was driving by the time they could see over the top of a steering wheel, used to working on beat-up pickup trucks during the week.

"Like to drag race on weekends."

"Where are we going to get U.S. citizens," Maj. Randal asked, "willing to volunteer for British Special Forces?"

"I got an idea, maybe," Capt. McKoy said. "I'll get back to you."

"How are the Bantams working out?" Maj. Randal asked.

"We hit us a home run, John," Capt. McKoy said. "Lucked out.

"Once people discover those little jeeps can go anywhere, anytime, we won't be able to lay our hands on another one for love or money."

"That good?" Maj. Randal said.

"Superior to the Model Ts we had in No. 1 U.S. Light Car Company back in the day—by a long shot.

"When one gets stuck in soft sand it ain't all that much trouble to get 'er unstuck."

"Think they're big enough?" Maj. Randal said.

"I absolutely do," Capt. McKoy said. "If Lady Jane has a chance to round us up any more of 'em, tell her to take all she can get. We're going to make our living with these gun jeeps."

"Gun jeeps?"

"Weld machine gun mounts all over 'em. Put a pedestal in the back with an Italian 20 mm Breda Model 35 on some of 'em. Two mounts in front—each sporting a pair a' twin Vickers Ks .303s, for the driver and passenger. Frank's working on it."

"That's more guns than some fighter planes carry," Maj. Randal said.

"Smoke anything that rolls—up to a medium tank," Capt. McKoy said. "We're talking serious firepower."

"OK," Maj. Randal said. "I'll inform Jane of your desire for more jeeps."

"You do that, John—we ain't never going to look back."

"One question," Maj. Randal said. "What does *jeep* stand for?"

"I don't think anybody knows—not for sure," Capt. McKoy said.

"It's a military mystery."

***

"DINNER TONIGHT WITH THE FIELD MARSHAL, JOHN," Captain the Lady Jane Seaborn said. "Wear your best walking-out uniform.

"Captain McKoy and Mr. Treywick are also on the invitation list."

"I can't think of anything," Major John Randal said, "I'd rather not do."

"Decorations, please," Lady Jane said, touching up her lipstick. "No excuses."

Maj. Randal seldom wore his medals, preferring only a simple pair of parachute wings.

"Ahhh…"

"Humor me," Lady Jane said, flashing a beautiful smile. "After all, you *are* my hero."

Maj. Randal said, "Since you put it that way."

He never stood a fighting chance with her.

The dinner was a private affair at the Wavell residence. Conversation was limited. Field Marshal Sir Archibald Wavell was known to be taciturn. Tonight, he barely spoke at all.

The Field Marshal had a lot on his mind.

Following the final course, after brandy and cigars were produced, Maj. Randal brought out his old 26th Cavalry Regiment Zippo. FM Wavell said, "Interesting lighter; would you mind if I look at it?"

The Field Marshal inspected the Zippo carefully. He observed the crossed sabers, noted the inscription—"Our Strength is in Loyalty"—and found what he expected: a small butterfly engraved on the lid.

Hmmmm. Those two tended to checkmate each other.

FM Wavell remembered the dinner all those many months ago when his American guest, Colonel William "Wild Bill" Donovan, had inquired about Maj. Randal, and the subject of his Philippine service in the U.S. Army had come up.

"Butterfly Boys" is what women of a certain profession in the Islands and other places in the East call men who "flit from flower to flower."

The Field Marshal handed the lighter back without comment. He glanced at his aide, who immediately departed the room and returned with a silver tray on which rested three small blue boxes.

"Maj. Randal," the young Captain said, "if you, Captain McKoy and Mr. Treywick will please rise."

FM Wavell pinned the Order of the British Empire on an unsuspecting Capt. McKoy and Waldo Treywick. "We shall dispense with the reading of the full text tonight—for extraordinary service to King and Country in the wilds of Abyssinia."

"Now," FM Wavell said, "Lady Jane, if you will perform the honors."

Lady Jane removed Maj. John Randal's insignia of rank and replaced them with badges denoting a lieutenant colonel: a crown over a four-pointed star.

"A brigadier of guerrilla irregulars in a remote place is one thing," FM Wavell said. "A lieutenant colonel charged with a theatre-level strategic mission at the very epicenter of a major campaign in the only command in the world where British ground troops are in direct contact with German Forces is quite another. Serious responsibility demands a serious rank.

"Congratulations, Colonel."

13

GREAT SAND SEA

LIEUTENANT COLONEL JOHN RANDAL WAS STANDING in the cockpit OF the Hudson winging its way far out into the desert. It was approaching 0500 hours. The sun would be coming up shortly. Squadron Leader Paddy Wilcox was in the left seat. James "Baldie" Taylor was in the co-pilot's chair.

"LRDG," Jim said, "needs to evacuate the patrol leader of Y Patrol...came down with malaria. Since the patrol was sent out to support Raiding Forces Desert Squadron's (RFDS) clandestine intelligence mission, Col. Pendergrass suggested having you replace him.

"Valuable experience...only thing better than observing a patrol is commanding it. Gives you an opportunity to see how the Raiding Forces field intelligence mission, which I have not had time to brief you on prior to now, works."

"I didn't know we had an intelligence mission," Lt. Col. Randal said. "When did that happen?"

"Mr. Zargo and the four mercs we brought down from RAF Habbaniya," Jim said. "They infiltrated into the tribal region where RFDS will be working, spread out across the desert, penetrated the villages and oases and have been establishing an intelligence network among the Senussi.

"The tribesmen want weapons to fight the Italians…bad idea. If we arm them, the Senussi will start raiding. When that happens, it's a given that the Italians will overreact and annihilate the tribe.

"I wondered where Mr. Zargo disappeared to?" Lt. Col. Randal said.

"Zargo went straight to the field," Jim said. "He plans to weave an invisible web around the enemy camps, place agents in their headquarters, and have watchers at their airfields, supply dumps and along the main roads."

"Exactly the kind of hard intelligence Raiding Forces needs," Lt. Col. Randal said. "I don't want to have to wander around the desert looking for targets of opportunity."

"The Senussi revel in intrigue…a natural talent for espionage," Jim said. "They come and go; no one pays them any attention. The tribesmen see everything, and know everything, in this part of the world.

"Our problem is that we need to improve on Zargo's ability to transmit the information his Senussi spies collect.

"LRDG operates out of their Forward Operating Base (FOB) at Kufra Oasis, 650 miles from Cairo. We have been authorized to set up a permanent Raiding Forces detachment there…fitters for repairs, supply dump, fuel storage facility, etc.

"Zargo has located a small, semi-lost oasis where Desert Squadron can establish its own Patrol Base…a place named Xara, approximately 80 miles from Kufra. We call it 'Oasis X.'

"RFDS can stage there to operate against the Axis coastal road network or into the interior of Libya if necessary."

"Sounds good, General," Lt. Col. Randal said.

"Major Merritt has elements of his Heavy Squadron at X now, getting it organized.

"Jack is running convoys 900 miles out," Lt. Col. Randal said. "Is there any kind of road?"

"No road," Jim said. "Have to drive 10-ton fuel tankers across barren desert to Kufra and then on to Oasis X cross-country, utilizing unpaved tracks and camel caravan routes. That's the only way we have to transport the fuel to stockpile for the RFDS patrols. Some convoys may take up to four weeks to make the trip, depending on weather."

"Can Jack do that?" Lt. Col. Randal said.

"No choice," Jim said. "Not going to be easy. Especially if the Luftwaffe catches one of his convoys on the march."

"Guess I've been so focused on reorganization," Lt. Col. Randal said, "that the scale of the operation hasn't completely registered with me yet."

"That's OK, Colonel," Jim said. "You take care of the teeth...let me worry about the tail until we can find the right man to come in and take over the job.

"Then we can both concentrate on the business of killing Nazis."

"Works for me," Lt. Col. Randal said. "As much trouble as it's going to be to supply Oasis X, we need to make every patrol count."

"Look at it this way," Jim said, "if it's this difficult for us to supply one squadron, imagine what the Desert Fox has to be going through with all of Afrika Korps to maintain."

"Roger that," Lt. Col Randal said. "Raiding Forces may only be capable of small-scale raids, General...but we can give Rommel something to think about."

***

LIEUTENANT COLONEL JOHN RANDAL, CAPTAIN "Geronimo" Joe McKoy, Lieutenant Pip Pilkington, Lieutenant Westcott Huxley and King shouldered their gear and swung out of the back of the Hudson. A cluster of bearded desert warriors passed them on the way to board the aircraft. The two groups did not stop to exchange pleasantries.

There were 15 Chevrolet trucks scattered about the desert, bristling machine guns and stacked with supplies. A tall, bearded Yeomanry lieutenant escorted Lt. Col. Randal's party to his command gun truck. The Hudson taxied for takeoff before they had their gear on the truck.

"Lieutenant Fraser Llewellyn, Royal Wiltshire Yeomanry, sir," the LRDG officer introduced himself. "Welcome to Y-Patrol."

They spread a map out over the hood of the gun truck.

"We are here, sir," Lt. Llewellyn said as he pointed to a spot on a mostly blank map. "Our mission is to rendezvous with an intelligence agent at this location day after tomorrow. Y-Patrol is ready to move when you are.

"Any questions, sir?"

"Negative," Lt. Col. Randal said...not exactly telling the truth. He had a lot of questions but he was not going to ask them. Not now. "Let's roll."

"Ride with me, Llewellyn, and let Lt. Pilkington travel in your truck...he can get some practice desert driving."

"Sir!"

Lt. Col. Randal climbed in behind the wheel, Capt. McKoy rode shotgun, King on the .303 Lewis pedestal-mounted machine gun, and the two lieutenants in the back.

Lt. Llewellyn gave Capt. McKoy the azimuth so that he could adjust the sun compass on the dashboard. The order-of-march was the patrol commander's truck selecting the route and leading the way, navigator's truck, then radio truck, with the fitter's truck bringing up the rear of the column in the event of a breakdown. With spacing between the gun trucks, the patrol strung out over a quarter of a mile on the move.

Lt. Col. Randal clicked on...it felt good to be back in the field with a combat command on the move. That said, he felt like he had landed on the moon. He could see as far as the eye could see in every direction and there was only emptiness.

Never in his life had he felt so isolated and alone.

"Ain't nothing like the Great Sand Sea," Capt. McKoy said, taking out a cigar. "Most of the desert is limestone, not sand...but this part is different. You take you a piece a' land the size of Indiana and you pour sand on it 'till it's about three, four hundred feet deep, then you take a great big rake and wiggle it through that sand pile, making ridges and valleys, stand back, take a look and that's what you're dealing with.

"Some people say the terrain features are always changing, moving around because the sand is always getting blown away, but I don't think so. Personally, I believe the ridges are pretty much permanent. For every grain of sand that blows away, two more arrive…what do think, John?"

"I have no idea."

"Rainfall is generally scanty," Capt. McKoy said. "Along the coastal band where we'll be doing most of our best work, you can get a good six to eight inches a year but you get 'em in about three or four months and they come in big cloud bursts which can cause flash flooding. When it rains the desert becomes a bog…ain't good for animal travel or vehicles."

"Saw that," Lt. Col. Randal said, "when the Iraqis flooded the road to RAF Habbaniya."

"Out here in the middle of the Great Sand Sea, well, you might get a half inch of rain or so per year and that's it," Capt. McKoy said.

"The population is entirely dependent on water. The people living along the coastal belt are semi-nomadic. Move from place to place as the vegetation dictates, to support their flocks.

"Your oasis-dwellers who live in the interior, well, they're permanent inhabitants of their isolated wells and springs. Some are so cut off they have their own language.

"Game is mighty scarce," Capt. McKoy said. "There's some gazelle in places, rabbits and wild jackals.

"But the interesting part is the bones. I've seen mammoth and crocodile and they shouldn't ought to a' been there. One time, we came across the bleached skeleton of a giant whale. Explain that."

"A whale in the middle of the desert?" Lt. Col. Randal said, keeping an eye on the sun compass to make sure he was on azimuth. "Has to be a story there."

"I don't know what it is," Capt. McKoy said.

"Now, the Libyan plateau is about 500 feet...virtually uninhabited because it's waterless, except for old Roman cisterns built in ancient times to gather rain water.

"They're monsters...must a' took a lot of work to build and there's a whole bunch of 'em. You'd a' thought people out here would a' kept those cisterns up, water being such a hot ticket item...but naw, they just let most of 'em run down."

"The farther south you travel into the desert, away from the coastline, the desert gives way from stones to fine gravel. The monotony is unbroken by any conspicuous terrain features and in a lot of places you can drive in a line, straight as an arrow for 100 miles."

"Sounds like you know the desert well, Capt. McKoy," Lt. Llewellyn said.

"I served with No.1 U.S. Light Car Company out here in the last one," Capt. McKoy said. "Probably hasn't changed much.

"Take that sun compass...Captain Claude Williams invented it for the Fords."

"I thought Colonel Bagnold was responsible for the mobile sun compass," Lt. Llewellyn said.

"He may have refined it some," Capt. McKoy said, "but Captain Williams improvised the first sun compass in about 1917. I used one back then and I didn't see Bagnold anywhere.

"The Cap'n, now he was a New Zealand sheepherder...those New Zealand boys make good desert hands."

"In LRDG, we rate the New Zealand Patrol as our best," Lt. Llewellyn said. "Rhodesians are second and the Yeomanry...Y-Patrol, well, we are third. The Guards are last."

"Problem is, you can't take a lensatic compass reading on the roll in a steel automobile," Capt. McKoy said, continuing his explanation of the improvised sun compass.

"Got to stop every so often and move off 20 yards or so to take your reading because the motor and the metal affect the compass. Captain Williams, he got tired a' stopping and dismounting, so he came up with the idea of bolting a steel sundial on the dashboard of a Model T Ford on top of a metal plate. The plate had degrees filed in it to set the azimuth you want to follow.

"Shoot your azimuth, dial 'er in and all the driver has to do is keep the shadow straight on his line-of-march. Every once in a while whoever's riding shotgun has to adjust the dial to keep it aligned with the sun, but you can do that on the move and keep on going.

"Don't get much simpler than that."

***

AFTER A LONG DAY OF DRIVING, Y-PATROL LAAGERED as the sun went down. The patrolmen were issued their daily ration of rum and lime juice. The troops immediately brewed up.

Nights were the best time on patrol. Men gathered around their vehicles, prepared the evening meal…LRDG rations were famous for being the tastiest in the service. The troops visited from group to group, swapping stories about the day's adventures. Then everyone went to work readying their trucks, weapons and personal equipment for the next day's march.

"Patrol's sort a' like a wagon train in the cowboy movies," Captain "Geronimo" Joe McKoy said, "circled up at night."

When the sun went down, the sand cooled rapidly and it got cold fast. Lieutenant Colonel John Randal had been spending time during the desert nights practicing celestial navigation, so he knew what to expect. He brought along his fur-collared Italian bomber jacket captured in Abyssinia.

The perfect piece of gear.

Capt. McKoy was holding court around the fire at the command truck, "So, I was on a patrol somewhere out in the blue one time back in the day, a' helping this Royal Geographic Society surveyor named Dr. Ball with his observations, hoping to fill in a few spots on what was pretty much a nothing-there map. He was deaf as a stone, but a mighty cool customer when it came to celestial alignments.

"The enemy could a' been closing in or his plate a' beans might a' been gettin' cold, but as long as the star he was a' workin' on didn't go shooting off somewhere and drop out of the field of his telescope, he didn't care about a thing in the world.

"Precision being a mania with the Doc, and the idea that the known position of the port of Matruh might be off by a few hundred yards, was pretty much a major calamity to his way a' thinkin'.

"Part a' my job was the difficult and delicate task of taking the Berlin – or maybe the Paris – time signals off the wireless receiver to ascertain the chronometer error. Extreme accuracy was important in this endeavor because it was deemed desirable to estimate the error to within $1/10^{th}$ or at least $1/5^{th}$ of a second.

"The Doc and me had been doing this nightly for a couple a' weeks. I was gettin' mighty good at it, so I didn't think much of the deal when he asked me to help him with a final night's observations to pinpoint Matruh to settle the little matter of its exact longitude and latitude.

"Now, the way it works, wireless time signals are sent out from Berlin at midnight...0200 hours Egyptian time. Paris follows from the Eiffel Tower. But German signals are considered to be the most accurate on planet Earth, so naturally they're the ones we used.

"Personally, I was glad to help the Doc from a purely humanitarian standpoint. It was awful to think the poor devils at Matruh might be a half-mile or so out to sea without even knowing it.

"Now, the plan called for some pretty tricky work. The Doc had prepared an elaborate program, 'a dozen or so pairs of stars to shoot, which would keep us going at intervals till 0200 hours. At that point in time, like I said, the German radio signals would occupy us for approximately a half-hour and then the evenin's entertainment would conclude with one last but all-important observation.

"When 0800 hours rolled around, we had everything ready to go, theodolite adjusted dead level perfect, books, lights, pencils, etc. all ready and in their place. Minutes before the first stars were due to appear, a few small clouds began to drift across the sky like they was racing each other and they blotted out the big moment.

"Our first observation was a bust.

"'We can spare some sets'," the Doc said, laid-back and easy like. "'Next up will be a beauty'.

"Well, we lost that one too, and the three after that. Gamma this, Delta the other thing, and Aquarius on the half shell were each in turn obliterated by drifting scud. 1000 hours rolled around and the Doc, though optimistic, was getting a trifle ground down from the strain…him being a perfectionist.

"So, we took a short break for a shot of medicinal brandy.

"Fortified, we went back for the next observation, lost it…adjourned for another swig, then back to the theodolite. Failed again, back to the bottle and so on and so forth. We continued to give mouth-to-mouth resuscitation to that bottle a' Hennessey, but we finally lost her about midnight and I was forced to crack the seal on another one.

"Now the Doc, he was more optimistic the longer this went on. But me, I was going down the tube—figuratively speaking—not being a college man except for a couple a' correspondence courses. I'd had about enough stargazin'.

"At 0200 hours we took the German time signals. By now we had been tryin' to take observations, strikin' out and fortifyin' ourselves with brandy for hours. The Doc staggered over from the wireless set to the theodolite for the last and final pair of stars on his target list.

"Our star was visible to the southeast, so was its twin blinkin' to the southwest… absolutely perfect.

"The thing to understand is that those two stars had to be observed at equal altitudes and within a few minutes of one another…one risin', the other descendin'.

"We caught the first 'un, man, what a shot…booked the results to a $1/10^{th}$ of a second. The Doc – glued to the eyepiece – zeroed in on the second star, eager to finish our observations. But a tiny cloud began to chase that little sparkler way up there in the stratosphere.

"'It's in the field,' the Doc shouted, 'two minutes will do it. Uh-oh, no, it's not. I can see it. No, I can't.'

"And boys, that was all she wrote."

Lieutenant Westcott Huxley said, "What happened, Captain?"

"Nothin'," Capt. McKoy said. "We got skunked."

"Try learning," Lt. Col. Randal said, "to take those readings from Brandy Seaborn while she's sunbathing."

14

THE CAMEL'S NOSE

LIEUTENANT COLONEL JOHN RANDAL HAD BEEN BRIEFED on the Western Desert. Early travel was along the camel caravan routes called "masrabs." The LRDG also used them as much as possible. Some were known and some—secret routes used by smugglers and slave dealers—were not.

Most of the desert made for reasonably good travel—unless there was the rare rainstorm. Then the gullies and ravines became swift-running rivers or lakes, and the sand turned into what was known as the "Arab mud bath."

The swaths of soft sand were the most difficult to negotiate and posed the greatest obstacle.

Most travelers avoided the soft areas, especially the high dunes. The blown sand could only be traversed with great effort, which was what made the region so attractive to raiders. A determined band could attack out of the Great Sand Sea, knowing that they could escape back into it, safe from pursuit.

The Italians had only one unit, the Auto-Saharan Company, capable of operating in the interior of the Western Desert, and it only patrolled in Axis-held territory as an anti-LRDG unit. The Germans did not have any deep-desert units.

The Great Sand Sea was such a vast, remote place that even the enemy air forces seldom overflew it—mechanical failure resulting in a forced landing was an automatic death sentence. Both the Germans and Italians viewed the desert as an obstacle. LRDG—and now Riding Forces—saw it as a safe haven.

Lt. Col. Randal drove the lead truck in the Y-Patrol column. Ahead, he could see the sand was soft. He shifted into low gear and plowed into it. The 30-cwt Chevrolet truck—transformed into a sort of big convertible pickup by removing the top of the cab and windscreen—struggled on.

The truck luffed like a sailboat on a choppy lake.

Lt. Col. Randal's years of driving in the sand dunes on the beach when growing up in California—reinforced by Captain "Geronimo" Joe McKoy's desert driving lessons at RFHQ—paid off. The Chevrolet kept churning, though it was a highly anxious feeling, expecting to sink out of sight at any second. The command truck squiggled forward until it eventually came to a hard patch of sand.

The trick was to *never* apply the brakes.

The navigator's truck followed in the tracks and pulled up beside the command truck. However, the third truck, containing the radio, started to sink. The passengers baled off and ran around to the back of the truck and started to push frantically.

"Sand channels," Lieutenant Fraser Llewellyn shouted, standing up in the command truck and looking back. "Keep it moving. You lads do not want to have to unload the bloody truck."

Two of the LRDG troopers ran to the side of the Chevrolet and unbuckled the yellow perforated sand mats strapped to the sides of every truck. Then they dashed to the back of the truck and slid them under the rear tires.

The wheels spun, kicking up sand, gripped and gained traction. The Chevrolet moved forward a few inches. Men were shoving and shouting. No one wanted to have to unload the water cans, cases of machine gun ammunition, landmines, rolls of 808 plastic explosives, boxes of rations, etc., and carry all of it by hand to firm ground, where they would have to reload everything when the truck finally made it there.

Temperature was over 100 degrees, and there was no shade.

The truck lurched forward and ran off the sand channels. The men quickly snatched them out and rushed around to put them under the wheels again before they sank in. It looked like a Chinese fire drill, but in fact, the LRDG men knew exactly what they were doing and had the process down to a science.

Moving inch by agonizing inch, using a combination of sand channels, mats and muscle, the Chevrolet finally reached hard surface. The LRDG patrolmen threw themselves down on the ground, exhausted.

Standard Operating Procedure (SOP) stipulated that when a truck became stuck, everyone else would keep going. The crew of the stalled vehicle was responsible for getting unstuck. The idea was to keep the column moving until it reached the safety of hard ground. Then—and only then—could the other men go back and help their mates if they still needed it.

It was a point of pride in the LRDG for the crew of a truck that became mired in soft sand to get out of it by themselves.

Desert travel is not for the lazy or easily discouraged. Victory is measured in fractions of inches at times. Teamwork was essential for success. The life of a desert raider was man and machine against the elements as much as against an armed enemy.

"Two weeks a' this," Capt. McKoy said, "and it's like you been doin' it all your life. That's the one good thing about desert work—you can pick it up pretty fast if you stick to it.

"Six months operating in the sand, and you're a nomad."

"The run from RFHQ to Oasis X," Lt. Col. Randal said, "should be a good shake-down cruise for our patrols. Your driving classes helped, Captain. Keep it going for all new recruits."

"Didn't hurt that you been drivin' all your life, John," Capt. McKoy said. "Can't teach experience."

Lt. Col. Randal said, "You're probably right about that."

"Why I said we need us some 'Mericans."

***

DESERT NAVIGATION REQUIRES THE NAVIGATOR to constantly be checking three things: watch, compass and the fuel gauge. By juggling the calculations of time-of-march, direction and fuel consumption, it is possible to have a rough idea of your location. It's called "dead reckoning," and with practice, the experienced desert hand is seldom lost.

Provided, that is, he knows where he started. If a desert traveler ever gets disoriented, a map and compass are virtually worthless. There are no terrain features to locate that will help orient the map.

The only way to find yourself if you are truly lost in the desert is by celestial navigation, and that is a difficult skill to master. Plus, it requires the right equipment and complicated calculations.

Desert Arabs are never lost. No one knows how they do it. Nomads simply know their way. However, they make miserable guides for a motorized patrol because they have little or no experience in navigating at the speed a truck travels, which throws off their innate sense of direction and distance.

Navigation was a never-ending problem, with no easy solution.

At sundown, just before the sun began to be swallowed up, a pair of riders leading a spare horse swam into view in the distance, flickering like a mirage. Lieutenant Colonel John Randal was driving, picking the best ground for the convoy and monitoring his watch, compass and fuel gauge. He knew that the trucks were getting close to the point where Y-Patrol was supposed to rendezvous with the intelligence agent Lieutenant Fraser Llewellyn had briefed him about when he flew in.

Nevertheless, King, manning the .303 Lewis machine gun, went on a heightened state of alert when the two riders appeared.

Captain "Geronimo" Joe McKoy pulled his 9mm Beretta MAB-38 out of the leather boot mounted outside the open cabin on the frame of the truck. He affixed the submachine gun's magazine and racked a round into the chamber, never taking his eyes off the riders in the distance.

His movements, while unhurried and casual, were very, very professional.

Lt. Col. Randal said, "There a password?"

"Our people are supposed to wave a red handkerchief," Lt. Llewellyn said. "It's up now, sir."

"I see it."

The mercenary who went by the name Joker was sitting on his horse, with a wizened Arab on another animal beside him. The tribesman was wearing a black eye patch over one eye. The old man's other eye looked mostly white.

Was he blind?

"Laager here," Joker said. "Colonel, you are coming with me to meet Mr. Zargo. We will be back tomorrow night."

"Can that man see?" Lt. Col. Randal said.

"Not much, Colonel," Joker said.

"He's our guide?"

"Yes, sir."

As Lt. Col. Randal swung up on the spare horse, Capt. McKoy said, "Things can get a little weird in the desert sometimes."

"This would be one of 'em," Lt. Col. Randal said. "See you when I see you."

Joker was wearing a black cloak, as was the semi-blind guide. He tossed one to Lt. Col. Randal.

"We ride at night," Joker said, "to avoid the odd traveler. Mr. Zargo does not want the word out that you are here at this point in the game. Later, he says, when the time is right, we will make a big production of your arrival."

Lt. Col. Randal put the dark robe on over his uniform and off they rode. They cantered through the pitch-dark for four hours over broken ground. The guide never hesitated. He seemed to know exactly where they were going.

Eventually the horses ended up in a defile. Everyone dismounted. The blind man and Joker had an animated conversation.

"What's he saying?" Lt. Col. Randal asked.

"The guide wants me to crawl up on the ridge and see if I can spot a rock cairn with the profile of a camel's nose," Joker said. "The tent village where we will find Mr. Zargo will be just over the ridge to the left of the rock."

"Are you nuts?" Lt. Col. Randal asked. "It's midnight, the wind is howling and a blind man wants you to skyline a rock in the pitch dark?"

"You asked what the man said, Colonel."

"I'll do it," Lt. Col. Randal said.

He scrambled up the incline on his hands and knees. Peering over the top, using the night vision technique of offset viewing—not looking directly at what you want to see—Lt. Col. Randal was able to make out the rough outline of a rock that looked like a camel's nose faintly visible in the dark and distance.

Unbelievable.

The guide disappeared with the horses. Joker and Lt. Col. Randal slipped into the camp. In this part of the world, there were no permanent structures—only tents. A shadow appeared out of the darkness.

"Welcome, Colonel," Mr. Zargo said, leading them up the wadi through an unseen crack in the cliff. He lifted a heavy curtain and led them out of the night into a fantastic cavern, brightly lit with pressure lanterns. Oriental carpets covered the floor, carpets hung from the walls, and two sofas piled with cushions were in the middle of the room.

A scene out of *One Thousand and One Nights*.

Mr. Zargo clapped his hands, and a retainer appeared with a teapot and glasses.

Time was short.

"My main source of information," Mr. Zargo said, "consists of Italian-speaking Senussi working as servants in the headquarters, messes and homes of the Blackshirts. The Italian officers talk freely in front of them and leave documents lying around. They never suspect their domestic help can speak or read Italian.

"Later at night, the servants meet friends in the street or their tents, words are exchanged and a rider is dispatched with a well-memorized message. Eventually those messages are delivered to me through the good services of one sheik or another.

"Each of my people, all men you know, has his own network. We have intertwined the entire region in a spider web of invisible agents."

"Outstanding," Lt. Col. Randal said.

"Have to put up with a lot of local political intrigue," Mr. Zargo said. "Some sheiks use cut-outs so no one will ever know who is actually responsible for providing my organization the information.

"The Senussi hate the Italians—that is why they perform this service. However, it is necessary to be very careful. There are turncoats and traitors among them. It is not unheard of for a sheik to use the Blackshirts to eliminate political rivals."

"Tell me about the military situation," Lt. Col. Randal said.

"Rommel has taken firm command of all operations, even though the Italian Armed Forces have many times the number of German troops in the country. The Nazi divisions are the tip of the spear, and the Italians have been relegated to supporting them—a role they are more than happy to perform."

"What does that mean," Lt. Col. Randal asked, "exactly?"

"Italian troops are detailed to guard all the fixed bases and provide security for the supply convoys traveling the Via Balbia. Their combat formations take their orders directly from General Rommel's Headquarters, even though many of the senior Italian officers outrank him.

"From now on, British troops will be fighting German-led Italians."

"So," Lt. Col. Randal said, "Raiding Forces tries its best to avoid Germans and attack the Italians—that how you see it, Mr. Zargo?"

"That is how I would do it," Mr. Zargo said, "if I were you, Colonel."

"Since I'm here," Lt. Col. Randal said, "can you give me a target that Y-Patrol can raid before we return to base?"

"Hoping you might ask," Mr. Zargo said. "We are about seventy-five miles from the Via Balbia. There are roadhouses all along it—generally spaced every fifteen miles as rest stops for the enemy convoys. Make good targets, particularly if you can catch a convoy at one late at night.

"The Italians have a fuel dump approximately twelve miles east of the nearest roadhouse," Mr. Zargo said. "Unguarded, except for a barbed wire fence to keep out thieves. Covers an area of about fifteen acres—fairly substantial in size.

"Then there is a Regia Aeronautica landing ground located thirty miles west of the roadhouse. Not a very large base. A half squadron of Savoia-Marchetti S.73 transports are stationed there. Security is lax. The Italians have no reason to fear a ground attack.

"You can take your pick, Colonel."

"Why not hit 'em all?" Lt. Col. Randal asked.

It was not really a question.

15

POWDER RIVER

COLONEL DUDLEY CLARKE AND JAMES "BALDIE" TAYLOR were meeting at A-Force HQ. The situation in Vichy France-controlled Syria had reached the boiling point. The use of Syrian airfields by Luftwaffe aircraft to fly in direct support of the Golden Square rebels in Iraq was confirmed.

French collaboration with Nazi Germany was out in the open…there was no sugar-coating it, no matter how much anyone wanted to ignore it or how much another problem in the Middle East Command was unwanted.

The Greek intervention had been a fiasco, Crete turning out even worse and the Golden Square had very nearly succeeded in overthrowing the British condominium in Iraq. The rebels would have, if Hitler had honored his commitment to support them with airborne troops.

The word had come down from GHQ that Vichy French Syria was going to be invaded to preempt any farther escalation of Nazi meddling. Britain was going to war with Vichy France. The problem was, as usual, that Field Marshal Sir Archibald Wavell did not have any troops to spare for the campaign…he was already fighting on five fronts.

The Germans had started running military materials into Syria by the Taurus railroad, an extension of the Oriental Express that permitted travel from Berlin to Basra. Neutral Turkey was turning a blind eye to the cargo on the trains crossing their territory.

The concern at GHQ was that sooner or later the Germans would try slipping in a load of tanks. The problem was complicated by not having the diplomatic luxury of letting it happen before reacting. The first shipment could tip the balance of power in the Western Desert.

A daring scheme had been concocted to air-land a platoon of Royal Engineers in Vichy France territory to take out the last bridge before Tel Kotchek…on the Syrian side of the border. The only problem was that there was no one experienced enough to evaluate the prospects of the proposed operation.

Col. Clarke and Jim Taylor were trying to figure out how to avert another embarrassing failure…British Forces had suffered a long string of them lately.

"Can we arrange to have Randal flown back here to consult on this?" Col. Clarke asked.

"Y-Patrol is carrying out a series of raids tonight as we speak," Jim said. "We can have Col. Randal picked up and flown back to RFHQ tomorrow."

"Know what I like most about Randal?" Col. Clarke said. "He always plans his operations meticulously in advance before he carries them out. Veronica Paige tells me that what he did at RAF Habbaniya deserves to be written up and studied at the army staff college."

At that very moment, Lieutenant Colonel John Randal was driving down a pitch-dark stretch of single-lane, hard-top Via Balbia, leading two other gun trucks looking for the enemy roadhouse. They knew it to be somewhere along there, but were not exactly sure where.

He was winging it…an armed joy ride.

Over a slight rise in the road, the three LRDG trucks ran headlong into a column of German trucks coming from the opposite direction. No one had thought enemy convoys traveled at night…it was believed they laagered at the roadhouses.

Lt. Col. Randal's trucks had their lights off. The Germans had their distinctive cat's eye running lights on. He had not seen or even thought about them since Calais...bad memories.

The situation was instantly glass-house crazy...totally insane.

"Fire 'em up," Lt. Col. Randal ordered, drawing his Colt .38 Super out of his chest holster and pressing the accelerator to the floorboard. Before he could get off a round, Captain "Geronimo" Joe McKoy was firing short, efficient bursts from his .303 Lewis gun into the cabs of the trucks at a 45-degree angle down the road as they raced past.

King was tracking right behind Capt. McKoy's tracers with his own, cracking out crisp bursts of six from his .303 Lewis gun. Lieutenant Westcott Huxley and Mr. Zargo were shooting their Thompson .45 submachine guns point-blank into the sides of the enemy trucks as they raced by.

"Powder River," Capt. McKoy shouted, "Let 'er buck!"

Lt. Col. Randal was fighting the wheel with one hand and firing his pistol with the other.

All guns in the three LRDG trucks that could be brought to bear—six .303 Lewis machine guns and a number of personal weapons—were putting out a concentrated cone of firepower. Muzzle blasts from the combined guns were deafening. Tracers lit up the night. Hot brass being ejected from the guns was bouncing around the interior of the Chevrolet gun trucks.

Men were screaming.

The trucks of the German drivers killed or wounded swerved wildly. Other drivers instinctively took evasive action, running off the road, with several trucks rolling over when they left the hard surface and hit the soft sand at speed.

Some drivers panicked and slammed on their brakes, only to have the vehicle following them rear-end their truck at speed.

Chaos reigned on a small stretch of highway.

Surprise was so complete that some of the Germans believed an airplane had strafed the column. Confused Nazi gunners fired their machine guns into the air.

Others mistakenly thought the LRDG trucks were British armored cars.

The action was over in seconds. It seemed like an hour. The LRDG trucks sped past the tail end of the enemy column, guns blazing, and were swallowed up in the night.

Lt. Col. Randal had no idea how much actual damage had been inflicted...the encounter gave new meaning to the term "meeting engagement". The idea of going back to make an assessment never occurred to him.

Squadron Leader Tony Dudgeon had once told him that the way to strafe an airfield was make one showy pass and never *ever* make a second gun run.

Y-Patrol got the hell out of Dodge.

***

LIEUTENANT PIP PILKINGTON—WITH TWO GUN TRUCKS and Joker acting as his guide with the aid of one of the local Senussi—was making his way through the desert to the 15-acre Axis fuel dump. The plan was to penetrate the dump, set up delayed charges and exfiltrate to the rendezvous with Lieutenant Colonel John Randal and Lieutenant Fraser Llewellyn, who was off on his own carrying out a raid on a Regia Aeronautica landing ground.

Lt. Pilkington had replaced Lieutenant "Pyro" Percy Stirling as the Raiding Forces Demolitions Officer. He had a roving commission to serve with either Desert Squadron or Sea Squadron as needed – depending on the mission.

Tonight he was going to take out an Italian fuel dump.

Joker halted the patrol.

"Let's go take a look, Lieutenant," the merc said. "We're a half mile from the objective."

The two walked through the night until they came to a rusted, three-strand wire fence surrounding the 15-acre fuel storage dump. What the fence was supposed to do was subject to speculation...there were no guards on duty. Anywhere.

The ground enclosed by the fence was dotted with scrubby trees and overgrown with thorny thistle bushes. Lt. Pilkington thought it seemed more than a little spooky, an enemy installation with no one home. He and Joker toured the fuel dump for about an hour.

The store of gasoline was laid out in lots of 25 to 30 drums lying next to each other on the ground. There were 103 lots, averaging 25 barrels per lot, which came to well over 100,000 gallons of gasoline.

"Go bring up the trucks," Lt. Pilkington ordered. "We have our work cut out for us."

The trucks arrived shortly. It was necessary to prepare the dump so that it all went up at one time. To do that required 'daisy chains' made from gun-cotton primers threaded on a 5-foot length of primer cord...an instantaneous fuse that looks like a common electrical cord.

The gun-cotton primers were in the shape of a truncated cone the size of a large pipe bowl and had a longitudinal hole through their centers. Five primers per daisy chain were spaced out and held in place by knots in the cord. On one end of the cord a detonator was fixed with adhesive tape...into the detonator was crimped a time igniter (a device that was intended to set off the detonator at a certain time after the safety pin had been pulled).

The daisy chains had been prepared in advance. They had to be put in place and the detonators—which were carried separately for safety—inserted. There was a lot of work to do.

All the daisy chains were placed in one Chevrolet and it was driven—through a hole snipped in the wire—to the center of the fuel dump. Each of the LRDG men was assigned a pie-shaped sector spreading out from the truck in a wagon wheel formation. Each man had a dozen daisy chains they were responsible for. The plan was for them to lay one under each cluster of drums they could locate in their area of responsibility.

Placing demolitions properly is painstaking work.

The Y-Patrol men went at the task methodically and they did not get in any hurry. The LRDG operators were all trained in the rudiments of explosives. However, none of them had ever taken on a project this large and the troops were excited.

The dump was going to make a big boom when it went up. And the Germans were going to be very unhappy with their Italian allies for their failure to secure the site... it was not going to be easy to replace that much fuel.

As the LRDG patrolmen returned to the trucks from time to time to get additional daisy chains, they were chuckling when they passed each other in the dark. This was too easy.

However, it was a lot of fun.

Sure beat the monotony of hiding beside a road, counting enemy trucks and armored fighting vehicles passing by in the heat of the day.

Two hours after departing the gasoline dump and heading for the rendezvous, Lt. Pilkington ordered the two trucks to stop. He looked at his watch. The demolitions should have gone off by now.

Nothing.

Sometimes with explosives, the best laid plans turn to naught...he felt sick. Timers had been known to be defective. Something had to have gone badly wrong. What?

At 0210 hours in the far distance the skyline turned yellow. Flames leaped skyward, danced, and lit up the landscape for miles and miles and miles. Drums of gasoline blasted into the air like rocket ships and then exploded, creating blazing orbs of fiery rain that sparkled slowly down to earth.

The sight was fantastic—otherworldly—a light show beyond description.

The scrub brush was tinder. Fire turned from gold to red, and then a wall of smoke billowed up, rolling like a giant tidal wave. Wind fanned the conflagration. The entire desert was burning, and still, explosions were erupting while waves of flames rippled on the ground.

Nothing had prepared Y-Patrol for such a result from their labors. The devastation defied all expectations.

Several LRDG men began to think about the possibility of volunteering for service in Desert Squadron. Raiding Forces was going to be where the action was…Lt. Col. Randal was clearly not into strategic reconnaissance or having his troops serve as a taxi service.

***

LIEUTENANT COLONEL JOHN RANDAL PULLED OVER to the side of the road. The three gun trucks of the LRDG's Y-Patrol under his direct command were a mile past their chance encounter with the German convoy. Before he could exit the driver's seat, Lieutenant Westcott Huxley baled out of the back of the Chevrolet and trotted down the road in the dark to check on the other two trucks.

That is what officers are supposed to do – see to the welfare of their troops.

Captain "Geronimo" Joe McKoy pulled out a pair of thin cigars and offered one to Lt. Col. Randal as he was changing the magazine on his Colt .38 Super.

"Powder River?" Lt. Col. Randal said, sticking the cigar between his front teeth. "Let 'er buck?"

"Living the moment, John," Capt. McKoy said. "Things was getting downright Western."

"Convoys are not supposed to travel at night," Mr. Zargo said.

"Yeah, well," Lt. Col. Randal said, "there's always that 10 percent who don't get the word."

"How far up ahead," Capt. McKoy said, "you reckon that roadhouse is located?"

"We should be there," Mr. Zargo said.

Navigation in the desert without any terrain features to use as reference points to guide on is different than in other types of topography. Being 'there' is a relative term. It meant within a mile or two.

Once you were 'there', you had to search to find your objective.

That was what Lt. Col. Randal had been doing driving down the hardball… searching for the roadhouse they intended to raid.

The wise navigator intentionally misses his target left or right. That way, once he has traveled the correct distance, he knows which direction to hunt for the point he wants to find.

"No casualties, suw," Lt. Huxley reported, climbing back in the truck with his Thompson submachine gun cradled in his arms. "Some of the lads seem 'wather shook up'."

"Welcome to Raiding Forces, gentlemen," Mr. Zargo said, "where being shook up seems to be a way of life."

"'Weady to 'woll, suw."

"Anyone get a count on the trucks?" Lt. Col. Randal said, shifting into low gear and letting out the clutch.

"Twenty-three," King said. "Between the two of us, Captain McKoy and I managed to put rounds into every one of them, Colonel."

"Seemed like a hundred," Lt. Col. Randal said.

The roadhouse was a quarter mile farther up the Via Balbia. The building was blacked out but light could be seen inside around the edges of the blackout screens. A dozen trucks were parked haphazardly beside it. Men were standing outside smoking. The red tips of their cigarettes glowed in the dark.

No one was on guard.

Lt. Col. Randal pulled up next to the roadhouse and stopped when he was sure all three LRDG gun trucks had an unobstructed field of fire. No one paid the new arrivals any attention. The nearest British troops were over 600 miles away.

And Afrika Korps used a lot of captured British Army trucks…nothing unusual here.

The signal to engage was Lt. Col. Randal firing a magazine loaded all tracers from his 9mm Beretta MAB-38 submachine gun.

He pointed his weapon at the group of glowing cigarettes and squeezed the trigger. The night was pitch-dark one second and a blazing inferno the next. Six Vickers Lewis .303 machine guns firing in unison raked the parked trucks, turning them into cheese shredders.

Then the gunners shifted their fire to the blockhouse. Y-Patrol shot it to pieces. Every patrolman not manning a Lewis gun was firing a submachine gun… the LRDG preferred .45 caliber Thompsons.

The cone of fire from the combined automatic weapons at point-blank range was devastating. There was shattering glass, the screams of men in the building, tracers streaking and disappearing as if swallowed up. The blockhouse was riddled.

Lt. Col. Randal let the engagement run for what seemed like a long time, but in fact, was only about a minute. Then he fired a green flare from his Very pistol. That was the signal to shift the fire away from the blockhouse and back to the trucks.

Lt. Huxley jumped out, ran up to the roadhouse and slammed himself against the wall next to one of the shot-out windows. He primed an M-36 Mills grenade, and then pitched it inside. The first one was quickly followed up by two more.

Three bright flashes and muffled *WHUUUMPH, WHUUUMPH, WHUUMPH*s occurred fours seconds later.

The young 10th Lancer swung around, kicked in the bullet-splintered door and emptied his .45 Thompson submachine gun inside. Lt. Huxley swung back outside the door, changed magazines, and then went back again, shouting something unintelligible and emptying a second stick magazine inside the building. Then he tossed in another grenade before trotting back to the command gun truck.

That was more action on his part than the original plan had called for.

"I couldn't make out what the Lieutenant was yelling," Capt. McKoy said, recharging his Lewis gun.

"Whatever it was," Lt. Col. Randal said, "Huxley seemed genuinely sincere."

Capt. McKoy said, "Reckon he was having trouble with his R's?"

"I doubt anybody noticed."

***

LIEUTENANT FRASER LLEWELLYN DROVE ACROSS the desert and arrived at the Regia Aeronautica landing ground. That, in desert navigation terms, is a hole-in-one. He was pleasantly surprised to have accomplished the feat.

Unfortunately, most of the aircraft expected to be found there were absent. Only two Breda Ba.88 Lince twin engine bombers were visible. Lt. Llewellyn attacked straightaway.

The plan called for the 10-truck patrol to arrive in the dark, move up as close as possible to the field without actually driving on to the Italian base, and from long range, strafe the planes with all 20 of Y-Patrol's .303 Lewis machine guns.

Twenty machine guns is *massive* firepower.

When the patrol opened fire, the two Italian bombers were turned into junk in the blink of an eye. Not that they were any great loss...the Lince bomber was so poorly designed the rumor was that it had to take off in the direction it intended to fly because it did not have enough power to complete a turn at low altitude.

A machine gun that tried to engage from one of the flak towers was instantly snuffed out by a withering hailstorm of .303 caliber steel jacketed rounds.

Discretion clearly being the appropriate choice in the face of such concentrated firepower tonight, the remainder of the Blackshirts chose not to shoot at the LRDG patrol.

One Italian defender did manage to drop a single round down a mortar tube before the gun trucks turned their attention to his position and obliterated it with their combined guns. The shell arched up and came down with unerring accuracy, exploding in front of the command gun truck.

A piece of shrapnel pierced the radiator, sending up a plume of white steam.

No problem. The bearded warriors of the LRDG really were the best in the business. A steel cable was produced and a tow affected while Lt. Llewellyn shifted to another truck to continue the fight with no interruption or slackening of performance.

Lt. Llewellyn had his 10 Y-Patrol trucks en route to the rendezvous point within five minutes of initiating his attack. Hit and run...he was thinking the LRDG should consider pulling more ops like this.

Desert raiding held a lot of promise.

16

AIN'T REAL GOOD

LIEUTENANT FRASER LLEWELLYN WAS THE FIRST to reach the rendezvous. The LRDG men set up a dispersed perimeter in a wadi, camouflaged their gun trucks, and went about the task of repairing the damaged radiator on the command truck. The patrolmen were seasoned professionals. They spent every spare minute working on their vehicles or their gear.

There was always plenty to do.

Lieutenant Pip Pilkington was the second to arrive an hour before sunrise. The LRDG men were quick to share the story of their night's adventures with each other. Both parties had successfully completed their mission.

It was a happy camp.

Shortly after sunrise, several Arab horsemen appeared on the ridgeline in the distance. They observed the Y-Patrol perimeter from a careful distance and then disappeared into the desert.

The sun came up red hot.

Messerschmitt 109s – a pair of them – arrived three hours later. They flew straight to the wadi where the gun trucks were parked. The German pilots knew the exact location of each truck, even though the Chevrolets were camouflaged. The desert-tan fighters with light blue underwings and black crosses painted on their fuselages went to work.

Standard Operating Procedure (SOP) in the LRDG was for patrolmen to *never,* under any circumstance, return fire at enemy aircraft. The logic was that trucks and equipment could be replaced, experienced desert operators could not.

Firing at attacking enemy aircraft would not only result in the loss of trucks and equipment, but there would be wounded or dead patrolmen.

Not firing meant the patrol would only lose trucks and equipment…at least that was the theory.

When the attack began, the LRDG patrolmen scattered and sought shelter away from their vehicles. The attack went on for a long time. The German pilots knew in advance exactly where the trucks were concealed, had orders to punish the raiders, and were methodical in carrying out their mission.

Lt. Pilkington was hiding in a small gulley running off the wadi, crouching under the exposed roots of a scrubby acacia tree. He looked over and saw Lt. Llewellyn leaning against the withered trunk of another tree. The LRDG officer gave him a wave and went back to reading a book as the air attack continued.

Truck after truck was destroyed. The strafing went on and on and on. The Me 109s departed but reappeared shortly – rearmed and refueled – to continue the attack. They did not quit until every LRDG truck was smoking.

Lieutenant Colonel Randal's three gun trucks were the last to arrive at the rally point. He could see the tall columns of smoke from the burning Chevrolet trucks miles out. Even before driving up, it was clear that the scope of the disaster was catastrophic.

There was good news and bad news.

Only two of the LRDG patrolmen had been wounded, both minor…the good news. All of the trucks were a write-off. Most of the equipment was unsalvageable. Worst of all, the water cans were shredded and there was virtually no water left.

Lt. Llewellyn pointed to the map, "Kufra is located 500 miles east. The nearest LRDG emergency supply dump is located at LG 173 – an abandoned RAF Landing Ground approximately 200 miles straight line from here.

"We have 60 men and three trucks but there is not enough fuel remaining to drive 200 miles, particularly if we load down the trucks with passengers.

"We have water for two days if we ration it."

"You have situations like this," Lt. Col. Randal said to Captain "Geronimo" Joe McKoy, who was leaning over the map, "back when you were in No. 1 U.S. Light Car Company?"

"Naturally, the radio is shot to pieces," Capt. McKoy said. "Ain't real good, John."

Lt. Col. Randal said. "OK…we'll form two columns. You take the three trucks, the two wounded men and make for the abandoned landing ground.

"Llewellyn and I will bring the rest of the men on foot."

"Naw, John," Capt. McKoy said. "I don't want to do that. Let Lt. Llewellyn ramrod the trucks. I'd rather march with you."

"Captain…"

"Take a look at the men," Capt. McKoy said. "Most of 'em wearing sandals or soft, slip-on desert boots. Seems kinda foolish facing a 200-mile forced march, don't it…those sandals ain't gonna last five miles."

"Yeah," Lt. Col. Randal said. "That salty, Desert Rat-look so popular in Cairo does seem pretty stupid right about now.

Lt. Llewellyn was wearing shorts and sandals. He did not say anything. He was feeling foolish.

"This march is gonna get ugly," Capt. McKoy said. "Now if these boys see an 'ole cowboy like me a' leadin' the way maybe they'll be a little bit more motivated to keep up with the column."

"Good point," Lt. Col. Randal said. "You set the pace, Captain."

"Bear in mind, John," Capt. McKoy said, "the minute those trucks drive off, we have to go on the plan we ain't ever gonna see 'em again. Those Nazi flyboys might get 'em or who knows what…anything can happen out here in the blue.

"We have to make it on our own hook."

"Lady Jane told me I needed a 'desert tactician' to advise me," Lt. Col. Randal said. "Never thought it'd turn out to be you, Captain."

"Ain't that a daisy?"

***

Y-SERVICE INTERCEPTS WERE DELIVERED TO COLONEL Dudley Clarke at A-Force HQ. Afrika Korps was throwing a temper tantrum over the loss of its gasoline supplies. The Luftwaffe was screaming about the attack on its landing ground…they had thought its location a secret. The worst outcry, however, was over the assault on the roadhouse and the audacious shooting-up of a convoy 600 miles behind the lines.

The German intelligence people had sorted out that it had not been a Desert Air Force night fighter strafing the convoy, but they still believed the encounter had been a brush with a patrol of British armored cars. The idea that an enemy armored car regiment could operate that far behind their lines was disconcerting.

The only defense against armored cars was armored cars or tanks, but Afrika Korps did not have any of those to spare for the purpose of escorting convoys. There were simply too many convoys, too many miles, the demand at the front…meaning Tobruk was all-consuming.

The Italians did have a number of armored car regiments, consisting mostly of laughably obsolete Lanica IZM cars of ancient vintage, armed with a pair of 8mm machine guns. They were ordered to begin patrolling the Via Balbia immediately. The task was impossible…secure 1,200 miles of nothingness around the clock.

Col. Clarke was ecstatic. The idea had been for Lieutenant Colonel John Randal to gain a little field experience. No one had expected him to do much more than ride around in the desert with Y-Patrol and become acclimatized.

Certainly it had never occurred to anyone that Lt. Col. Randal would orchestrate the most successful series of raids in the last eight months.

What most pleased Col. Clarke was the news that the Germans were confused as to what had actually taken place. A-Force was in the business of confusing the enemy. He began to see unimagined possibilities for Desert Squadron.

GHQ was euphoric. The destruction of the fuel dump electrified a despondent group of staff types at Grey Pillars who daily grappled with the realization that Afrika Korps was unstoppable...tank on tank.

However, cut off his fuel supplies and the Desert Fox would not be able to execute his brilliant tactics. It did not matter what kind of military genius Rommel was or how superior German tanks were if they ran out of gas.

Victory was as simple as that.

Field Marshal Sir Archibald Wavell sent a courier to A-Force with a hand-carried message that he wanted to see the commander of Raiding Forces. Have him returned to Cairo by the most immediate means.

"The Field Marshal intends to decorate Colonel Randal," Col. Clarke said, reading the communiqué.

"And, we need to talk to him about the Syrian bridge project. How quickly can we bring Randal back?"

Jim Taylor said, "LRDG informed me that Y-Patrol failed to report in during its last two scheduled radio checks."

"What does that mean?"

"Patrols have to stop and set up a 16-foot antenna for their long-range radio to reach Kufra," Jim explained. "Takes time and effort. The LRDG has commo checks preplanned twice a day at specific times for each patrol in the field. Y-Patrol has failed to come up on the net during the last two reporting periods."

"What does that mean, Jim?"

"Could be their radio has malfunctioned," Jim said. "Not what we want to hear, Dudley, but not necessarily bad news."

"No," Col. Clarke said, "definitely not what I want to hear."

"The LRDG is not overly alarmed," Jim said. "They have this sort of thing occur all the time…not out of the ordinary in their line of work."

"Find Y-Patrol, Baldie," Col. Clarke ordered. "Do it now. I have no intention of sitting around wringing my hands, with the Field Marshal breathing down my neck, waiting for LRDG to develop a sense of urgency."

"Squadron Leader Wilcox is at Kufra," Jim said. "I will message him to initiate an aerial search immediately.

"Probably nothing to worry about."

"Try telling that to Lady Jane," Col. Clarke said.

"I am going to leave that task to you, Jim."

***

"TAKE THREE TRUCK CREWS, AND TWELVE MEN, counting yourself," Lieutenant Colonel John Randal ordered. "The two wounded and your nine weakest men…you know who they are. Make for LG 173."

"I will fill up the trucks with water and fuel and then double straight back on my tracks," Lieutenant Fraser Llewellyn said.

"You do that," Lt. Col. Randal said.

"Keep marching, Colonel," Lt. Llewellyn said. "We can pull this off."

The three trucks drove out of sight. A lonely feeling settled in immediately after they had gone. Two hundred miles is a lot of empty desert to cross on foot with water in short supply.

"Mr. Zargo," Lt. Col. Randal said, "you, King and Joker fall in behind me. Now would be the time to break out your best Murder Inc. act."

The three mercenaries glanced at each other. They fell in behind Lt. Col. Randal, standing shoulder to shoulder, fingering their weapons…looking hard as nails.

Lieutenant Westcott Huxley slid in next to the trio of mercs with his Thompson submachine gun held across his chest by its pistol grip. King gave the "Don't Dance" 10th Lancer lieutenant a flint-eyed nod.

On command, the remaining 44 men of Y-Patrol assembled.

"I came out here," Lt. Col. Randal said, "to find out how the LRDG operates. So far all I've learned is what *not* to do. Short pants and sandals...some of you men don't even have personal weapons. Left 'em in the trucks when you took cover.

"Captain McKoy is going to lead this march, 200 miles as the crow flies. Keep up...stragglers put the column at risk.

"I'll shoot any man who falls out...personally."

There was not much in the way of a response from Y-Patrol. They were experienced desert hands. The men knew what they were facing.

"Is that clear?" Lt. Col Randal said. "Am I going too fast for anyone?"

***

THE FIRST SANDAL STRAP BROKE IN LESS THAN THREE miles. The sun was on fire. The desert was a sauna. There was no breeze. Y-Patrol was in a lot of trouble.

Some men tried repairing their sandals. That failed miserably. Others tried cutting off the ends of their shirttails and wrapping their bleeding feet. No joy.

The fashionable butter-yellow, slip-on desert boots did not fare much better. Basically high-topped loafers, they were loose and not intended for serious walking. Blisters were a problem.

After a while, most of the men were marching barefoot. That might have been all right if the desert was soft sand. Unfortunately, it was in great part limestone with scrubby brush and stunted prickly plants.

You could track the column by the blood on the ground. To survive, Y-Patrol needed to cover 50 miles a day. In the condition the troops were in, they would be lucky to do 15.

For the LRDG personnel the journey was turning into a death march.

For Lieutenant Colonel John Randal, the Raiding Forces personnel and the mercs attached to the patrol, it was a stroll in the sun.

Mr. Zargo took the opportunity to continue briefing the Raiding Forces commander on the state of affairs in the jebel as they marched.

"The Arabs reported Y-Patrol to the Germans for a cash reward. That is how the pilots knew the exact location of each parked truck."

"So," Lt. Col. Randal said, "we can trust the desert nomads except for the ones we can't?"

"Politics in the jebel can be complicated," Mr. Zargo said, "at times."

"I see," Lt. Col. Randal said.

"As for targets, Colonel," Mr. Zargo said, "the Germans and the Italians have established clandestine landing grounds scattered across the desert, with water and fuel cached at them. They use the LGs as emergency landing strips, intermediate places their planes can land to refuel on long flights or, from time to time, they will fly in a bombing squadron to stage from one of them."

"Can you pinpoint these secret air strips?" Lt. Col. Randal said.

"Many of them."

"Make good secondary targets," Lt. Col. Randal said. "When we have a patrol in the area they can raid it."

"I would have expected," Mr. Zargo said, "that airfields would be a principal target for Raiding Forces."

"Negative," Lt. Col. Randal said. "Our primary is the Via Balbia, which includes fuel dumps as well as enemy traffic…10-ton fuel carriers at the top of the list, but any enemy transport is a prime target. I don't want my patrols wasting time crossing long stretches of unexplored desert to attack an airstrip that may or may not be abandoned when they get there."

"I understand, Colonel," Mr. Zargo said.

"My plan is to take down targets you identify for us along the coastal corridor," Lt. Col. Randal said. "Raid something, somewhere, a long way from each other, every night.

"Hit and run."

"Operate Apache style," Captain "Geronimo" Joe McKoy said. "Ghost in and out of the desert, do a little damage and then disappear like a puff a' smoke into thin air. Come back, do it all over again.

"This is gonna get real good, John."

"You were right, Captain," Lt. Col. Randal said. "Y-Patrol was too large with 15 trucks. Let's cut our patrols down to six, like you suggested. More agile, easier to conceal."

"Desert raiding is no job for 30-cwt trucks," Capt. McKoy said. "Work fine for what the LRDG specializes in: long-range strategic reconnaissance, running supplies to distant locations and hauling secret agents to the field.

"Not for us, though. You're gonna love what our modified Bantam gun jeeps can do when we get 'em all out of the shop. I guarantee."

Lieutenant Westcott Huxley strode in their direction. He had been moving up and down the column, shouting encouragement to the men. For every mile they marched, he marched two or maybe three. Somehow the young lieutenant had managed to learn most of the troop's names.

The LRDG has relaxed military standards. People are called by their first names – even the officers.

"Wight, left, wight, left," Lt. Huxley called. "Keep going, Collin – step it out – one foot in fwont of the othew."

"Put a sock in it, Westcott," Collin said, "…sir."

17

TROUBLE COMES AT YOU FAST

THE HUDSON FLEW OVER THE LIMPING Y-PATROL COLUMN at 1525 hours of the second day. Squadron Leader Paddy Wilcox buzzed them at haircut altitude, kicking up dust devils as he went screaming past. The patrolmen were shouting and waving.

Lieutenant Colonel John Randal had kept the patrol marching most of the night. Nevertheless, the men had only traveled approximately twenty-five miles. While no one was going to die now and none of the damage was permanent, the men were nearly all crippled.

That is, the ones who had been wearing sandals and soft, slip-on desert boots. Lt. Col. Randal, the mercs, and the Raiding Forces personnel were not even tired. It was a lesson not lost on the future Raiding Forces Desert Squadron operators.

"Out here in the deep blue," Captain "Geronimo" Joe McKoy said, "trouble comes at you fast—ain't no warning. Need to be prepared."

"I don't get it," Lt. Col. Randal said. "The LRDG has been in business a year; they've had people make survival-forced marches that dwarf this hike. And still, their troops take to the field like they are going on a picnic."

"Ain't no good answer to that one, John."

The LRDG was a highly specialized special force. They were able to travel to distant places across unmapped, trackless desert and stay in the field for long periods of time. While it was easy to find things about the unit to criticize, it was not going to be so simple to duplicate their skills or their successes.

Lt. Col. Randal knew Raiding Forces was not going to be able to simply plop volunteers into gun jeeps, send them on their way and have instant desert raiders. RFDS needed to acquire the specialized knowledge necessary to give it the confidence required to operate in the dangerous environment into which it was surely headed. His problem was that the squadron did not have the luxury of time to develop it.

Lt. Col. Randal was toying with an idea that might stack the deck in their favor—just a little.

The Hudson came back around. A canvas packet trailing a three-foot-long white cloth streamer flew out the bay door. Lieutenant Westcott Huxley ran to retrieve it.

As the plane thundered over, Lt. Col. Randal blinked out "WATER" with a flashlight. Sqn. Ldr. Wilcox rocked his wings to acknowledge he understood the message. Then the Hudson made a lazy circle and headed back in the direction from which it had come.

Lt. Huxley handed Lt. Col. Randal the message from Sqn. Ldr. Wilcox: "STAND FAST. R-PATROL WILL ARRIVE YOUR POSITION FIRST LIGHT TOMORROW."

When the patrol heard the news, most of the men simply fell down right where they were standing. No shade—no problem. They went to sleep on the ground in the sun.

The casual observer would have thought the men were dead.

At 1745 hours, the Hudson returned. Sqn. Ldr. Wilcox lined up at 1,000 feet. Parachutes began to appear in trail behind the airplane, looking like swimming octopuses. Then they blossomed into full canopy.

Y-patrol roused itself. The troops made a rush to secure the containers when they came down. The chutes supported water cans.

"Take charge of the DZ," Lt. Col. Randal ordered Lt. Huxley. "Don't let anyone at the water. King, you and Joker are on the Lieutenant."

"Parachutes make good tents to get outta the sun," Capt. McKoy said. "Exceptin', we don't have any tent poles and there ain't a halfway decent tree within a hundred miles."

Lesson learned: In the desert you have to bring everything with you or do without. There is little to be able to improvise with and no living off the land.

***

R-PATROL ARRIVED AT 0630 HOURS. The New Zealanders happened to have been passing by fifty miles north, returning to Kufra after completing a mission, when they were ordered to go to the aid of Y-Patrol.

It picked up the troops and continued on to the oasis.

Mr. Zargo and Joker hitched a ride with R-Patrol. When they reached their operational area in the Jebel el-Akhdar, they would drop off and continue their intelligence mission.

Lieutenant Colonel John Randal, Captain "Geronimo" Joe McKoy, Lieutenant Pip Pilkington, Lieutenant Westcott Huxley and King rode with the patrol until it came to a hard patch of desert suitable for Squadron Leader Paddy Wilcox to land on. At 1030 hours, the Hudson arrived to pick them up.

"We are going to put down at Kufra to refuel, and then I have orders to fly you straight on to Cairo, Colonel," Sqn. Ldr. Wilcox said. "Lady Jane will be standing by to pick us up when we arrive."

"Radio ahead," Lt. Col. Randal said. "Have Major Adair meet the plane when it lands to refuel."

"Lt. Huxley," Lt. Col. Randal said, "When we ran into that convoy, what was the first thing you recognized?"

"Wecognized, suw?"

"What alerted you the trucks were Nazis?"

"Cat's eyes headlights, suw," Lt. Huxley said. "Vewy distinctive."

"Think it might be a good idea to mount 'em on RFDS gun jeeps?"

"Bwilliant, Colonel," Lt. Huxley said. "Make us look like Nazis."

"Give us an edge," Capt. McKoy said. "Pretty good, John."

"Pwobably none of the Gewman lights available—we can impwovise though," Lt. Huxley said.

"Leave the details to me, suw."

Major Clive Adair, the commander of N Squadron, Phantom, was on the dirt landing strip when the Hudson touched down at the LRDG desert patrol base. He came onboard while the refueling was taking place.

"Clive," Lt. Col. Randal said, "some time ago Captain McKoy recommended Desert Squadron field small six-gun jeep patrols instead of the large fifteen truck patrols like the LRDG deploys. We intend to do that.

"Can you outfit six radio jeeps for RFDS and still be able to rig six of our Chevrolet trucks with radios so we can loan them to the LRDG for their patrols?"

"Why would we want to provide radio trucks to the LRDG, sir?" Maj. Clive Adair asked.

"I want you to go to Colonel Pendergrass," Lt. Col. Randal said. "Offer to supply him six Chevrolet 30-cwt trucks equipped with Phantom radio crews in exchange for him supplying RFDS with a dozen skilled desert operators."

"Have to obtain the additional radios from regiment in the UK," Maj. Adair said. "You *do* realize the implication of what you are doing, sir."

"What might that be?" Lt. Col. Randal said, accepting a thin cigar from Capt. McKoy.

"Infiltrating the LRDG," Maj. Adair said. "Phantom—meaning Raiding Forces—will be handling all their patrol communications *and* running the commo center here at Kufra. You will have penetrated the most hush-hush operational unit in the Middle East Command, Colonel."

"Really?" Lt. Col. Randal said, holding the cigar out for the lighter the ex-Rough Rider offered, locking eyes with Capt. McKoy over the flame.

"I want good men—navigators, NCOs, the best the LRDG have. Drive a hard bargain, Clive."

"Regiment will definitely love your plan, sir—a feather in our cap. Most likely ship us the radios on a top-priority flight with an officer escort," Maj. Adair said. "Insinuating Phantom into military organizations by making ourselves useful is what we do."

"As far as negotiating favorable terms—like taking candy from a baby, sir. LRDG is badly in need of enhanced long-range communications."

"Make it happen," Lt. Col. Randal said. "We need those men."

***

DROP-DEAD GORGEOUS CAPTAIN THE LADY JANE SEABORN was waiting when the Hudson landed at the RAF field outside Cairo. Flanigan had parked her white Rolls Royce on the tarmac. She was standing at the bottom of the ladder when Lieutenant Colonel John Randal came down the steps and she gave him a huge kiss.

He was startled by the passion. "I was only gone a few days."

"You are supposed to spread alarm and despondency among the enemy," Lady Jane said, holding his arm, "not *me.*"

"All we did was shoot up some trucks," Lt. Col. Randal said. "Pip took out a fuel dump—but it was unguarded—raided a small landing ground, but it was a non-event too. Then the bad guys strafed the LRDG laager so we had to walk..."

"Grey Pillars sees it differently," Lady Jane said. "You four are due in the Field Marshal's office as soon as we can drive you there."

"Can't we shower first—change into fresh uniforms?"

"Straight from the field," Lady Jane said. "Those are my orders."

The group was ushered into Field Marshal Sir Archibald Wavell's spacious office the moment they arrived at GHQ. It was empty. Before they could sit down, the Field Marshal came in, accompanied by his aide.

The aide called, "ATTENTION!"

"Lady Jane," FM Wavell said, "will you assist?"

"My pleasure, Sir Archibald."

The aide passed her a blue box.Lady Jane opened it and handed the decoration inside to FM Wavell.

"Bar to your Distinguished Service Order," FM Wavell said. "Your third—very impressive, Colonel."

"What?" Lt. Col. Randal said, "I didn't..."

"The lift in morale your exploits gave to my staff," FM Wavell said, "is deserving of far more than a mere colored ribbon."

Unbeknown to Lt. Col. Randal—because he did not have a need to know—was the fact that the GHQ staff was in the final stages of planning OPERATION BATTLEAX, a counterattack designed to relieve Tobruk. The planners badly needed a shot in the arm of self-confidence, considering that almost to a man the general staff believed the German Afrika Korps to be unbeatable.

"Lieutenant Pip Pilkington," the aide said, reading off his list of honorees.

"Reports are that the conflagration when the Nazi fuel supply dump went up turned night into day," FM Wavell said, taking the Military Cross from Lady Jane. "Try to make that event a regular occurrence, Lieutenant. Congratulations on a well-deserved bar to your MC."

"Lieutenant Westcott Huxley," the aide said.

"I know your grandfather," FM Wavell said. "What in the blue blazes is a 10th Lancer doing serving with a band of cutthroats like Colonel Randal's?"

"Natuwal fit, suw," Lt. Huxley said. "Waiding Forces don't dance eithew."

"A bar to your Military Cross—family will be proud."

"Captain Joe McKoy," the aide said, "U.S. volunteer."

"We British have the time-honored tradition of awarding military decorations to the citizens of other nations who perform military service deserving of the honor in time of war. Getting to be a habit—second time in two weeks I have decorated you," FM Wavell said, eyeing Capt. McKoy's pair of ivory-gripped Colt Single Action six-shooters.

"Not your first experience of war in the desert, I understand, Captain."

"I commanded No. 1 U.S. Light Car Company," Capt. McKoy said, "back in the last one."

"Light Cars," FM Wavell said. "Remember the companies well. Never received the recognition they deserved."

Then they were back outside in the Rolls Royce. The entire ceremony had lasted less than five minutes. Brevity was FM Wavell's stock in trade.

"That your doing, Jane?" Lt. Col. Randal said as Flanigan drove.

"Simply the 'arranging for you to be at the ceremony' part," Lady Jane said. "Today was Archie's idea."

"All I did was drive a truck," Lt. Col. Randal said.

"Medals ain't for us, John," Capt. McKoy said. "They're to impress the Short Range Shepard's Patrol boys who sit in an office for a living and hang out in their shorts and desert boots at the Long Bar in Shepard's at the end of the duty day."

Lt. Col. Randal said, "Roger that but..."

"When your basic armchair commando sees a decorated combat man, makes 'em think the mundane job they're a-doin' every day—pushing pencils—amounts to something. And it does."

"Somebody's got to send us the beans and the bullets," Capt. McKoy said, "so we can go kill bad guys."

Lesson learned: Actions taken hundreds of miles behind enemy lines are magnified far out of proportion to actual damage inflicted when viewed through the prism of distance by higher command.

That cut both ways.

General Erwin Rommel was equally as impressed as FM Wavell. The only difference being that the Desert Fox did not want to pin a medal on Lt. Col. Randal.

Or any other member of Raiding Forces. He wanted them dead.

***

THE ROLLS ROYCE THREADED ITS WAY THROUGH CAIRO traffic. It arrived at a home in the suburbs. "The Great Teddy" was standing outside with a suitcase. Captain the Lady Jane Seaborn went to the door of the house to speak to the 15-year-old boy's aunt.

Teddy climbed in the back seat of the limousine with Lieutenant Colonel John Randal and Captain "Geronimo" Joe McKoy.

"I understand you and Lady Jane are not flying out to England for a couple of weeks," Lt. Col. Randal said.

"Yes, sir," Teddy said. "Mandy will be getting her commission in two weeks, and I shall be starting classes at Eton."

"Perfect," Lt. Col. Randal said. "Are you prepared to accept a mission in the interim?"

"Yes, sir," Teddy said, peering out from behind his Coke-bottle glasses.

"What I am getting ready to tell you is classified," Lt. Col. Randal said. "You will not discuss it with anyone not in Raiding Forces. Is that clear?"

"Clear, sir," Teddy said.

"This is Captain McKoy," Lt. Col. Randal said. "I want you to work with him to develop a way to camouflage our jeeps in the open desert—primarily from air attack.

"What are your questions?"

"What is a jeep, Colonel?"

"A small car," Lt. Col. Randal said. "Your mission is to teach us how to make 'em invisible—think you can?"

"Magicians make things appear, and they make them disappear, sir," Teddy said. "We need to develop a way to puzzle the enemy pilots so that they are not able to find your jeeps, or to trick them into seeing what they hope to see so they mistakenly attack the wrong target."

"You do that, Ted," Lt. Col. Randal said, "I'm going to owe you. Be thinking of some way to pay you back."

Teddy said, "Already know what I want, sir."

"What might that be?"

"A night out at the Kit-Kat Club."

18

MR. FROGSPAWN

MAJOR SIR TERRY "ZORRO" STONE ARRIVED AT RAIDING Forces Headquarters. He had turned over command of the Lancelot Lancers Yeomanry Regiment, *aka* Lounge Lizards, to his older brother at the conclusion of the fighting to quell the Golden Square rebellion in Iraq. Now he was reporting for duty with Raiding Forces.

Lieutenant Colonel John Randal had finally been able to take a shower, shave and put on a fresh uniform when Flanigan informed him, "Maj. Stone to see you, Colonel."

"Hello, Terry," Captain the Lady Jane Seaborn said, fixing one of her earrings as she was leaving with Lieutenant Westcott Huxley for an appointment in town. "John has simply been beside himself waiting for you to arrive.

"Dinner with us tonight?"

"Absolutely, love to."

After Lady Jane breezed out, Maj. Stone said, "Lady Jane just gets better- looking...her husband Mallory is a bloody fool.

"You ever call his ex-girlfriend, Rocky?"

"Negative."

"Have her phone number?" Maj. Stone asked.

"I do."

"Maybe you should turn it over to me, old stick," Maj. Stone said, "for safe-keeping."

"Don't give it back," Lt. Col. Randal said, "no matter what I say."

"You would do the same for me," Maj. Stone said, putting the slip of paper with the phone number on it in the breast pocket of his blouse. "That's what friends are for."

Changing subjects, Lt. Col Randal said, "We've been reorganizing Raiding Forces for operations in Middle East Command, Terry."

He showed Maj. Stone the work-in-progress TO&E chart sketched on the chalkboard.

"Our mission is to raid the Via Balbia around the clock. Hit and run...high tempo. Enemy transport is our primary target. There's going to be a Desert Squadron and a Sea Squadron. You can have any job you want...we'll reshuffle assignments if you decide you'd like to command a squadron."

"You have N Squadron, Phantom too, I see," Maj. Stone said, studying the chart. "Excellent!

"No. 9 Motor Machine Gun Company, SDF...Jack Merritt, very good. You have it marked 'Heavy Squadron'?"

"LRDG is letting us stage out of their base at Kufra," Lt. Col. Randal said, flipping the cloth covering off a map of Raiding Forces' area of proposed operations... the entire Western Desert and everything that adjoined it. "And we're organizing a Patrol Base at a place called Oasis X.

"Jack is running long-distance convoys with 10-ton fuel trucks across trackless desert between the Sudan and there. He'll also be establishing clandestine fuel dumps across the desert to serve as emergency re-supply stations for our fighting patrols.

"In addition, Heavy Squadron will be responsible for all other support, maintenance and vehicle recovery towing missions."

"Sounds like an impossible job," Maj. Stone said.

"If anyone can do it," Lt. Col. Randal said, "Jack's the man."

"Raiding Forces has quite a lot of area to cover, old stick," Maj. Stone said, as he lit a Player's while studying the map. "Rather enormous assignment, actually…true combined operation – air, sea and land."

"Enough to keep us busy," Lt. Col. Randal said.

"Raiding Forces has become a small, private army," Maj. Stone said.

"You need to bring in Jack Black. Make him your Deputy Commander (Logistics). Jack's the best in the business…he'll take all support planning off your shoulders.

Lt. Col. Randal said, "What about you?"

Maj. Stone picked up a piece of chalk and immediately below 'Lt. Col. Randal' at the top drew a long line to one side. He labeled it "MI-9."

"Escape?"

"I have been tapped to become the Middle East MI-9 Officer," Maj. Stone said. "It's an A-Force task but the plan is to place it under the Raiding Forces umbrella. Dudley Clarke and Norman Crockett have had this project in the works for some time."

"I see," said Lt. Col. Randal.

"Wear two hats," Maj. Stone said. "Deputy Commander Raiding Forces (Operations) and MI-9 Chief-of-Station. Think of Escape as a fifth squadron."

"A fifth squadron?"

"On paper," Maj. Stone said. "Veronica Paige will be running the MI-9 shop out of A-Force HQ for the time being. All Raiding Forces is expected to do is supply personnel to carry out certain jobs from time to time."

"Veronica," Lt. Col. Randal said. "She's *very* capable."

"Exactly what she said about you, John," Maj. Stone said.

"MI-9," Lt. Col. Randal said, "like the mission. Could be good, Terry."

"Operate theatre-wide," Maj. Stone said. "Opens up a lot of possibilities for Raiding Forces…conduct joint operations. There is a little more to it than merely recovering escapers or evaders.

"MI-9 is an intelligence function.

"By the way, you shall be getting the Lancelot Lancers soon enough. I see you have the regiment penciled in as a patrol in Desert Squadron."

"Yeah, but there's only going to be 18 men max in one of our RFDS patrols," Lt. Col. Randal said. "What do you suggest we do with the rest of the Lounge Lizards?"

"Let me think on it," Maj. Stone said. "When I was with the LRDG before you came out here, we were operating against a string of isolated Italian forts at vast distances, so the larger patrols were a necessity.

"I see the advantage of reducing patrol size for high-speed pin-prick raiding."

"We need to be able to strike hard, disappear fast," Lt. Col. Randal said, "and be small enough to conceal ourselves from the aerial pursuit that's bound to follow.

"What's going to make RFDS work is accurate intelligence – which gives us the ability to concentrate at the point of attack and mobility…small patrols with a lot of firepower."

"Need to be careful about breaking up the Lancers," Maj. Stone said. "It's already the tiniest regiment in the army.

"Might it be possible to form two patrols?"

"Form a Lounge Lizard Squadron, keep the regiment intact if that works better for you," Lt. Col. Randal said. "It's your call. I don't think we're going to have a job for your brother, though."

King, who had replaced Flanigan on duty, stuck his head in the door, "Mr. Frogspawn to see you, Colonel."

"Really?"

"What the man said, sir," King said. "American…"

Maj. Stone said, "This should prove interesting."

"Well," Lt. Col. Randal said, "show him in."

A stocky man in shirt and slacks with a military haircut walked through the door. He said, "Jimmy sent me, Colonel."

"Jimmy?"

"You know….*J.R.*"

"No," Lt. Col. Randal said, "why don't you tell me?"

"Yes, sir. My name is Rawlston…Hank W., ex-Technical Sergeant, U.S. Army. Jimmy, meaning Capt. James J. Roosevelt, United States Marines, told me to explain we – meaning the five men I have with me – are the advance party."

"Advance party of what?"

"The American Volunteer Group," ex-Tech. Sgt. Rawlston said. "Most of the AVG are pilots and ground crew and they're headed out to China to fight the Japs. Our guys are primarily infantry, with a few cavalry and armored people, and we're coming out here to help kill Nazis."

"J.R.…ah, Jimmy, think this up," Lt. Col. Randal said, "all by himself?"

"Some guy named McKoy wired, suggesting the idea to recruit prior service civilian volunteers for Africa," ex-Tech. Sgt. Rawlston said. "Claimed you needed shade-tree mechanics."

"Affirmative," Lt. Col. Randal said, "men who can improvise."

"That would be us, Colonel. All recently discharged, given early-outs from army forts in West Texas, New Mexico, Nevada, Arizona and Southern California, and used to working in a desert-type environment. What I've brought you for starters is a light-wheeled vehicle maintenance section, including tools.

"There's another 24 U.S. volunteers en route – straight-up soldier types, be here any day. As I understand the plan, Colonel, we'll serve under you until the U.S. gets in the war.

"Not really sure what happens after that."

"You men are volunteering for Raiding Forces as private individuals?" Lt. Col. Randal said.

"Yes, sir."

"You understand that you'll be expected to jump out of airplanes, go behind enemy lines and be subject to military discipline?"

"Just don't make us eat any cucumber sandwiches," ex-Tech. Sgt. Rawlston said. "We ain't real fond of high tea."

Maj. Stone said, "How do you feel about crumpets?"

***

LIEUTENANT COLONEL JOHN RANDAL AND SQUADRON Leader Paddy Wilcox took a cab to A-Force HQ. Since there was an operating bordello in the building, no one was going to notice a couple of officers arriving or departing – particularly if they took public transportation…the perfect deception.

They might as well have been invisible.

Colonel Dudley Clarke and James "Baldie" Taylor were waiting.

"Everything we discuss today is classified," Jim said. "We are not having this conversation. You were never here."

Lt. Col. Randal clicked on.

"A Berlin to Baghdad railroad has been the dream of the German Empire for ages," Jim began, going straight to it. "The last stretch of the line, the Taurus Railway, was finally completed late last year.

"Now it poses a strategic threat to Great Britain.

"The last thing we need is for the Nazis to use the railroad to transport men, material and armored fighting vehicles across Syria by rail to Afrika Korps.

"Our problem is that the Vichy French are openly collaborating with the Germans. They have recently allowed the Luftwaffe to land at their Syrian airfields, refuel and take off to fly combat missions in support of the Golden Square's rebellion in Iraq.

"The Vichy government in France is afraid the Germans will occupy their overseas colonies should they refuse the Nazis the right to cross their territory. At this point, in our eyes, Vichy France has stepped over the line from passive, occupied, neutral country to that of an active, full-blown ally of an enemy combatant.

"The Taurus Railway cannot be allowed to become a German supply route. Give Rommel even a modest increase in men and equipment and he will drive all the way to the Suez Canal. If the Afrika Korps manages to capture the Canal, we lose the war.

"Are you following me so far, Colonel?"

"Seems clear enough," Lt. Col. Randal said, lighting a cigarette with his battered Zippo.

"East of Aleppo, Syria," Jim said, as he lifted a canvas cloth and revealed the map that was resting on the tripod stand, "are a series of tunnels and railway bridges. The closest span to Tel Kotchek has been selected as a target to be taken down.

"A former Canadian bush pilot, Flight Lieutenant Christopher Bartlett, flying out of RAF Habbaniya, has proposed landing a Valentia aircraft—with a dozen Royal Engineers on board—next to the bridge and blowing it up. Seems he heard about your raid on the Iraqi gun position during the siege and believes he can duplicate Plum-Martin's feat of landing on the Bund.

"Col. Clarke and I have asked you here today to give us your professional opinion. Do you believe this operation has a reasonable chance of success?"

The target bridge was located in the far north of Syria near its border with Turkey. As far away from RAF Habbaniya or any other British air base as it could possibly be.

Sqn. Ldr. Wilcox flipped up his trademark black eyepiece so that he could use both of his better-than-perfectly-good eyes to study the map.

"Photo reconnaissance?"

Col. Clarke handed the pilot a manila folder. "I made an unauthorized detour along that particular stretch of the rail line when I was in Turkey recently…not supposed to cross the border into Syria but I managed to slip in. You shall find my photos of the bridge in there as well."

"Dudley does not understand," Jim said. "He is not supposed to be going undercover playing at being a secret agent."

"You cannot have all the fun, Baldie," Col. Clarke said. "Even I like to get out of the office from time to time."

"What's your initial reaction, Colonel?" Jim asked.

"Don't do it," Lt. Col. Randal said.

"Why not?" Col. Clarke said. He was clearly the originator of the plan.

Lt. Col. Randal did not believe for one minute that some obscure flight lieutenant had dreamed the mission up—agreed to fly it, maybe—but he never originated the concept-of-the-operation.

"Raiding Forces Rules," Lt. Col. Randal said, "'Plan missions backward. Know how to get home'. The objective is 200 miles inside Syria. If this raid goes bad, there is no way home."

"I *have* read your rules," Col. Clarke said. "The engineers land next to the tracks on that long stretch of open ground in the photos. They deplane, set their charges, load back up and fly out…'short and simple'.

"What say you, Squadron Leader?"

"French Moran fighters are quite good…pose a serious threat during entrance and egress," Sqn. Ldr. Wilcox said. "Have to land in broad daylight. Any mishap on wheels down and the mission is a total write-off.

"Colonel Randal is right…don't do it. A million things can go wrong, sir."

"All operations have risks," Col. Clarke said. "The greater danger is for the Nazis to reinforce Afrika Korps by rail."

"Achievable results have to justify risk," Lt. Col. Randal said. "A squad of Royal Engineers will only be able to damage the structure. What do you think the French are going to be doing while they're placing the charges?"

"Would it change things," Col. Clarke said, "if I told you that putting the bridge out of action temporarily is all we need to accomplish in order for the mission to be considered a success?"

He was not at liberty to reveal that OPERATION EXPORTER, the ground invasion of Syria, had been given a green light.

Britain was going to war with Vichy France.

"Provided the ground troops are expendable," Lt. Col. Randal said, "it's doable… with a little luck."

"You agree, Squadron Leader?" Colonel Clarke said.

"The flying phase is problematic," Sqn. Ldr. Wilcox said. "It's a long-shot, Colonel. The landing is high-risk."

"Any way to improve our chances, gentlemen?" Col. Clarke asked.

Lt. Col. Randal said, "Thought you were never going to ask."

***

SERGEANT MAJOR MIKE "MARCH OR DIE" MIKKALIS was sitting in THE small, white-washed building that served as the Raiding Forces Command Post at Kufra. No one much liked the oasis. There were flies during the day, mosquitoes at night, scorpions and poisonous snakes at all hours. Also, the LRDG troopers in from patrol were required to shave, stand reveille, pull guard duty and hold regular formations.

There was a lot of what was known in the army as 'bull' – not what you might expect in a special force.

For the last few weeks, Sgt. Maj. Mikkalis had been spending as much time as possible observing LRDG operations. Time that was sandwiched in between recruiting, conducting brief but intense selection courses back at RFHQ, and training the new volunteers accepted for Desert Squadron.

Most volunteers never made it past the interviews. Those who did faced a harsh selection course. Approximately 10 percent of the men who applied made it through selection and the training phase which followed.

Men who did not measure up in training were RTU'd. Those men who completed the training had to then be asked to join a patrol by one of the patrol leaders. Men who did not 'fit' were RTU'd.

Once operations commenced, men who did not perform up to Raiding Forces standards in the field were going to be RTU'd. There were a lot of ways for a volunteer to end up packing his bags. It was not easy to pass all the barriers to entry into RFDS.

The idea was to keep out anyone who did not have what it took to become a member of the Raiding Forces organization, and, in large part, that decision was made by the men of Raiding Forces themselves.

Sgt. Maj. Mikkalis had served in the French Foreign Legion, the King's Royal Rifle Corps and Raiding Forces since its inception. He had a pretty clear idea what he was looking for in the way of a new recruit. It did not matter what unit a man had come from or what his previous military background had been, as long as he possessed the requisite desire and could perform to standard under extreme stress.

That said, desert experience was priceless.

"Private Nelson, LRDG to see you, Sarn't Major."

"What can I do for you, Nelson?"

"Here to volunteer for Raiding Forces, Sarn't Major," Private Nelson said. "Word is you will be accepting men from the LRDG…want to get at the head of the queue."

"You were in Y-Patrol…had all your trucks shot up," Sgt. Maj. Mikkalis said. "Marched back with Colonel Randal. He nearly killed you, you're still limping.

"Now why would you want another taste of what the Colonel has to offer, Nelson?"

"The whole bloody patrol was bloody well crippled, Sarn't Major…bloody sandals and desert boots. Sad bunch of bearded brigands and desert highwaymen, we was," Pvt. Nelson said.

"Colonel Randal and the other Raiding Forces people acted as if they were on a bloody stroll in the park. You could bloody hear 'em chatting up their next operations – working out the details as if they didn't have a bloody care in the whole bloody world… the lot enjoying themselves, like.

"Type of officers I bloody well want to serve under…sign me up.

"Liked the sound of those missions too…had enough skulking around behind a bush, peeking out watching the bloody Afrika Korps drive by, counting bloody trucks and tanks so some rear-area staff bloke can stick bloody pins in a map."

"How long have you been assigned to the LRDG?" Sgt. Maj. Mikkalis asked.

"Came in with the first draft of Yeomanry almost a bloody year ago, Sarn't Major. I *am* a desert rat…certified."

"Welcome to Raiding Forces, Nelson."

"Lt. Llewellyn to see you, Sarn't Major…"

Intelligence Note Number 9

MOST SECRET INNER ALLIED BUREAU ENEMY ORDER OF BATTLE ASSESSMENT

Large parties of German tourists have been sighted flooding into Vichy French Syria. The visitors are for the most part military age, physically fit, single males. A number have been observed crossing the border to Iraq.

19

NO PLAN B

LIEUTENANT COLONEL JOHN RANDAL SHOUTED, "SIX MINUTES!"

The Hudson was streaking through the pitch-black enemy sky. Well, maybe not enemy. No war had been declared yet—but it was going to be when he and his men were finished doing their work to the railway bridge on the northern border between Vichy French Syria and Turkey.

"STAND UP!"

Three heavily-armed paratroopers struggled to their feet. The plane had been flying for a long time, and their legs were cramped. The paratroopers—and Lt. Col. Randal—were dressed in 6th Foreign Infantry Regiment, French Foreign Legion uniforms.

"HOOK UP!"

Lieutenant Westcott Huxley, Corporal Jones and King connected their snap links to the steel cable that ran down the length of the aircraft slightly above shoulder height. Each man threaded the steel safety pin into the tiny hole that appeared once the snap link was seated. Then they bent the wire down on the far side to lock it in place.

It takes concentration, a steady hand and cool demeanor to accomplish that simple task while getting ready to jump out of a bucking airplane flying at low altitude in the dark of night behind the lines a long way from home.

"CHECK STATIC LINE!"

King, jumping last, turned around and let Cpl. Jones trace his yellow static line into the parachute container on his back. Then he turned around and inspected Cpl. Jones' line, while he in turn checked Lt. Huxley's. Everyone rattled their static lines to make sure they were firmly hooked up.

"CHECK YOUR EQUIPMENT!"

The jumpers ran their hands over their equipment. This was not a good time to find something that was not where it was supposed to be. They were going to jump no matter what they found—not that they were going to find anything out of place. Each man had been checking his equipment consciously or subconsciously on the entire flight to the drop zone.

"SOUND OFF FOR EQUIPMENT CHECK!"

King shouted, "OK!"

He slapped the leg of Cpl. Jones, who shouted, "OK!"

Then he slapped Lt. Huxley's leg and shouted, "OK!"

Making eye contact with Lt. Col. Randal, the young 10th Lancer shouted, "ALL OK!"

Lt. Col. Randal turned to the open door of the Hudson, wedged one of his rubber-soled, canvas-topped raiding boots on the right side of the door, then the other on the left side of the door. He reached up and felt for the ledge of the door with the fingertips of his right hand and then his left, clamping his fingers in the weld. Standing spread-eagled, he arched his body outside the aircraft and looked in the direction of flight.

The Hudson was thundering toward the DZ. Up ahead in the distance, he could see the railroad bridge swimming into view. The plan was for the aircraft to fly past the bridge for a half mile or so until it would be out of sight of any French troops that might be guarding it. Then the team would jump beside the first straight stretch of the tracks.

Not the best of plans but the only one Lt. Col. Randal could come up with on short notice and no ability to recon the drop zone prior to the mission.

He swung back inside the aircraft, and glanced at the lime green digits on his black-faced Rolex watch——strapped next to the Panerai wrist compass on his left wrist, made by Rolex on contract for Italian frogmen.

"ONE MINUTE!"

The red light was glowing. The Hudson was flying at 500 feet. The bridge flashed below.

The light flashed green.

"LET'S GO!"

The prop blast rolled Lt. Col. Randal sideways when he exited the aircraft in a tight tuck position. Lt. Huxley came into sight over his left shoulder, and the other two jumpers were spilling out behind him. The Hudson flew on.

For a moment, things were taking place in slow motion. Then the X-type parachute deployed gently, as they always did, and he was pulled up short when the canopy cracked open. It was a pleasant sensation.

Jumping at 500 feet is not for the faint-hearted. There was not much time for Lt. Col. Randal to enjoy the ride or to get prepared for the single most important aspect of the experience remaining, second only to the parachute opening—the landing. Every action had to be automatic; there was no time to think.

Lt. Col. Randal was coming in backward. One second, things were happening in slow motion, and the next he was screaming in, unable to see where he was going. Beneath his boots the ground blazed. Then he was down, feet and knees together, but NOT locked landing—limp and rolling onto the five points of contact of a parachute landing fall. He made a very respectable PLF—actually felt good about it.

Then in one practiced movement, Lt. Col. Randal leapt to his feet, hammered the quick release on his chest and dropped his parachute harness. Instinctively, he brought the 9mm Beretta MAB-38 submachine gun up and was scanning to verify they were alone on the drop zone. He heard the swish of silk over his head, then Lt. Huxley touched down with a muffled clatter of equipment, followed immediately by Cpl. Jones and King.

When it was clear they had landed undetected—at least for the moment—the men coolly went through the stretched arm, figure-eight drill of winding up their parachutes, stuffing the canopy into the lightweight parachute bag they jumped in with, tucking in their chest straps, lining up the long row of snaps, buttoning the bags and throwing them over their head onto their shoulders like packs. Within minutes the team was prepared to move out.

King was on point, with Lt. Huxley next, followed by Cpl. Jones. All three were fluent French speakers. Lt. Col. Randal did not speak French. He pulled rear security.

The team patrolled down the track in the direction of the bridge, toward the area Flight Lieutenant Christopher Bartlett had selected as a landing ground for the Vickers-Valentia. The ancient airplane with the Royal Engineers onboard was airborne forty-five minutes behind the Hudson – scheduled to touch down shortly after sunrise, provided the landing zone was suitable for it to land.

Lt. Col. Randal's first task was to walk the ground and determine if it would, in fact, suffice.

The sky was beginning to lighten when the team patrolled around a curve in the tracks and came to the meadow-like area chosen to land the Vickers-Valentia. The field was solid. There were no obstructions.

The landing ground was a GO.

Lt. Col. Randal and Cpl. Jones stayed there to mark it. They were using a new technique. When the Vickers-Valentia approached, the two men would ignite red railroad flares at both ends of the strip.

No one had ever thought before of using common railroad flares to mark a DZ or LZ. The flares were lightweight, easy to carry, simple to ignite and were designed to be highly visible night or day. If there were any French guards on the bridge, they would think the flares were some sort of railroad signal—nothing to be alarmed about.

At least that was the plan.

Lt. Huxley and King advanced down the tracks to the bridge. Both men were armed with .22-caliber High Standard Military Model D semiautomatic pistols with silencers to eliminate any sentries they might encounter. King was hoping to get a chance to use his Fairbairn Commando knife if the opportunity presented itself.

It was not known if the French posted guards on the bridge at night.

There was no reason to. Vichy France was not at war. And the bridge was as far away from British (the only conceivable enemy) territory as physically possible. Turkey, only a few miles up the tracks, was neutral, and there was zero chance that it would attack the French colony.

Lt. Huxley and King strolled across the long span of the bridge. There had not been any guard posted on the near side that the team had parachuted in on. That was a positive sign, they thought.

Before reaching the far side, both Raiding Forces men saw the flash of a cigarette being lit. Not so good. They went on high alert but continued walking casually toward the end of the bridge.

The two were dressed in 6th Foreign Infantry Regiment, Foreign Legion uniforms. Both men spoke fluent French. There was no reason for their appearance to raise undue alarm.

Their story, if challenged, was that they were patrolling the railroad track. Which was true.

When Lt. Huxley and King reached the far side of the bridge, they encountered two Syrian battalion du Levant troopers standing guard. The men were sporting the traditional purple facing on their uniforms and white kaffiyeh head-dresses. As hoped, the sentries were not alarmed.

Lt. Huxley shot them. Four rounds, two each, *Whicccch, Whicccch, Whicccch, Whicccch.*

Both guards were dead on the ground while King, who prided himself on being a professional—and quick—was still bringing up his pistol. He glanced sideways at Lt. Huxley, who was holstering his .22 High Standard Military Model D, unruffled.

"Fowtunes of waw—unfowtunately," Lt. Huxley said.

"Nice work, Lieutenant," King said, as he grabbed one of the dead Syrians by the legs and started dragging him out on the bridge. Lt. Huxley caught up and grabbed the man's arms. They swung him back, then forth, then let go when the body was over the edge—heave ho.

It was a long way down.

Lt. Huxley and King tossed the other body off also.

The Vickers-Valentia flew low over the bridge and along the tracks. Lt. Col. Randal ignited his flare at one end of the LZ, and Cpl. Jones ignited one at the other. The airplane passed over, circled and came back for a landing.

The Royal Engineers were disembarking before it rolled to a complete stop. Lieutenant Pip Pilkington stepped off and gave Lt. Col. Randal a casual salute.

"Demolitions team reporting for duty, Colonel," he said.

"There's your objective, Lieutenant," Lt. Col. Randal said. "Light it up, Pip."

"My pleasure, sir."

The Royal Engineers trotted toward the bridge, carrying huge packs of guncotton explosives. The bridge was a massive structure. Normally a demolitions project of this magnitude would take hours to properly prepare—maybe a full day.

Lt. Col. Randal had given Lt. Pilkington thirty minutes to do the job.

The Royal Engineers knew exactly what was expected of them. However, they were combat engineers, not Commandos. The men had been having second thoughts on the plane flying in. None of them had ever expected to air-land 200 miles behind enemy lines to carry out a demolitions job.

The troops went to work with a will. They wanted to get this mission over with in a hurry—and go home.

Lt. Col. Randal decided to cross the bridge to check on Lt. Huxley and King. Everything was going like clockwork. This was one for the books—operations never went this smooth, even in training.

"Any problems?" he asked when he walked up.

"Negative," Lt. Huxley said. "Mission accomplished, suw."

"There were two guards," King said.

"Really."

"Lieutenant iced 'em. We tossed the bodies in the gorge, Colonel."

"Both?" Lt. Col. Randal said.

"Both," King said.

"Good job, Huxley."

On the other bank, the Royal Engineers could be seen withdrawing off the bridge. Lt. Col. Randal glanced at his watch. Right on schedule, according to plan.

Time to pull out.

KAAAAAAABOOOOOOOOOM!

"What the . . ."

The bridge wobbled, broke in half and the top part toppled over into the valley, taking almost the entire length of the span with it. It was a catastrophic demolition. Lt. Pilkington and the Royal Engineers had performed beyond expectation.

That bridge was out of action.

Unfortunately, the explosives detonated prematurely or someone got happy fingers and set them off early. Either way, Lt. Col. Randal, Lt. Huxley and King were stranded on the far side with no way to reach the airplane.

On the far bank, Lt. Pilkington held his arms out as if to say, "I have no idea how that happened."

"Not good," Lt. Huxley wailed uncharacteristically, almost beside himself. "Weally, weally, wotten . . ."

"What are you going on about?" Lt. Col. Randal said, staring at the destruction.

So much for a textbook-perfect operation. Across the way, the Royal Engineers were all back aboard the Vickers-Valentia.

"My date with Pam, suw," Lt. Huxley said, "tomowow night."

The airplane started to taxi, and then lifted off. It came back around and roared overhead, rocking its wings: "good-bye."

"*You*," Lt. Col. Randal said, "have a date with Pamala Plum-Martin?"

"Woger, suw," Lt. Huxley said. "Not going to appweciate being stood up—pwobably nevew happened to hew befowe."

"Plum-Martin's older than you," Lt. Col. Randal said. "Besides, she only goes out with fighter pilots."

"Pam invited me, Colonel," Lt. Huxley said. "Damn engineews."

"You're right, Lieutenant," Lt. Col. Randal said. "You do have a problem."

There was no Plan B.

20

WHY NOT TAKE A CAB?

"WE CAN STRIKE NORTH AND EXFILTRATE across the border into Turkey, it's not far," King said. "Zargo farmed me out on contract to some well-connected individuals up there a while back.

"If we get to a telephone, they will make arrangements to have us picked up. We should be on a commercial flight to Cairo by sundown."

"Pewfect," Lieutenant Westcott Huxley said.

"I've been to Turkey," Lieutenant Colonel John Randal said. "The Secret Police asked me not to come back."

"Istanbul about a year ago...ten months?" King said. "Captain McKoy was performing at the Palace Hotel?"

"That's about right," Lt. Col. Randal said.

"Big flap," King said. "A female SS officer – Gretchen von something or other – was murdered, along with her bodyguard, a Brandenburger Commando, in a room at the Palace. Rumor had it an American shot them both.

"Ring any bells, Colonel?"

"You shot a *woman,* suw?" Lieutenant Huxley said.

"Degenerate Nazi," King said. "Good looking ...Lady Jane's evil twin."

"I won't be going to Turkey," Lt. Col. Randal said, "any time soon."

"In that case," King said, "our only option is to escape and evade to the Palestine border a good 200 miles...and how to pull that off? The Vichy French are not going to be happy about us blowing up their bridge."

"Why not," Lt. Huxley said, "take a cab?"

***

CAPTAIN "GERONIMO" JOE MCKOY and "The Great Teddy" were onboard a Seagull piloted by the Vargas girl-looking Royal Marine, Lieutenant Pamala Plum-Martin. They were flying over a patch of desert not far from Raiding Forces Headquarters outside of Cairo. Capt. McKoy was in the co-pilot's seat and Teddy was standing behind them, leaning over the front seats looking out the windscreen.

"Jeeps, eleven o'clock," Lt. Plum-Martin said.

Down below could be seen six little box-shaped vehicles attempting to park in defilade. They were clearly visible from the air. However, Lt. Plum-Martin knew their exact position...in fact, it might have been difficult to locate the patrol if she had not known where to search.

"Tell them to put up the camouflage netting," Capt. McKoy said. "Let's see how she works."

The Walrus winged out into the desert for a half hour to give the patrol time to erect the special netting Teddy had designed to make the jeeps blend in with the terrain. The primary color was pink.

No one knew what to make of that.

When the patrol leader radioed Lt. Plum-Martin that the patrol was ready, she flew back over the location. The jeeps were virtually invisible. Had they not known where the six vehicles were positioned, it would have been almost impossible to spot them from the air.

"That pink sure did the job," Capt. McKoy said. "Reckon I owe you one...had me doubting, ol' son."

"Me too," Lt. Plum-Martin said. "I thought you might be color blind, Teddy, when I saw your nets."

"Colonel Randal told me the Luftwaffe went straight to where Y-Patrol was laagered because nomadic Arabs saw them and turned informer for a reward," Teddy said.

"He said the LRDG trucks attempted to conceal themselves but the enemy pilots knew the exact location of each one."

"Exactly the way it went down," Capt. McKoy said. "Patrol was under netting… didn't help one little bit because those Nazi flyboys had accurate intel.

"Shot the trucks to pieces…took their time about it too."

"The purpose of camouflage is to confuse," Teddy said, "not conceal."

"Didn't know that," Capt. McKoy said. "I always thought the idea of camouflage was to hide something."

"OK, Pam," Teddy said, "radio the patrol to execute Plan B."

The Walrus circled out into the desert again to give the troops on the ground time to carry out the order. This time, when Lt. Plum-Martin received the call to return, they spotted the six jeeps immediately from a long way out. Now the vehicles were under a different pattern of netting – easy to distinguish.

"Teddy," Capt. McKoy said, "you're a genius, partner!"

"I would roll in on that target in a heartbeat," Lt. Plum-Martin said, "definitely."

Down below the patrol had inflated blow-up dummy jeeps of a pattern "The Great Teddy" had devised, and Lady Jane had ordered prototypes constructed for today's test.

The patrol placed the inflatable decoys where the gun jeeps had been parked, moved the jeeps to a new location and put the pink netting back up. The dummies were covered in standard issue pattern camouflage netting but the patrolmen did an intentionally sloppy job…parts of the fake jeeps could be seen poking out of the mesh.

With the dummy jeeps serving as a distraction, the real ones were invisible to the eye.

"Each patrol needs to be issued with a supply of pyrotechnics and smoke pots," Teddy said. "That way, when attacked, the men can simulate the distractor jeeps being destroyed and burning. That will contribute to the illusion."

"Good idea," Capt. McKoy said. "We'll have to come up with an SOP for when to put out the decoys and deploy the smoke bombs, but you done cracked this case, Ted.

"And that ain't no little deal."

***

LIEUTENANT RANDY "HORNBLOWER" SEABORN turned the Italian MAS motor Torpedo Boat up the river, toward the floating dock outside of Raiding Forces HQ. Lieutenant Butch "Headhunter" Hoolihan and Waldo Treywick were on board. The mission to secure the boat had taken longer than expected.

It had been an odyssey.

The three had flown to the port town of Kismayo. There they secured ground transport and traveled up the Jubba River to the improvised dry dock Force N guerrillas had discovered when they moved into the city ahead of Major Sir Terry "Zorro" Stone's armored car regiment, the Lancelot Lancers.

When Lt. Hoolihan and Waldo last saw the dry dock it had housed three pristine MAS boats.

When they arrived on this trip, the roof of the boathouse covering it was half in. There were only two boats inside. One was badly damaged. The other was going to need quite a bit of work to make it seaworthy. Lt. Seaborn made a quick survey and decided to cannibalize the worst boat for parts and restore the second.

The question was, "Where was the third boat?"

While making arrangements with the Royal Navy to float both MAS boats and have them towed down river to the shipyard at Kismayo to begin repairs, inquiries were made. The third boat, it turned out, had been requisitioned by the RAF and was in service as a recreational watercraft at the local officer's beach club.

The RAF did not want to give it up.

What to do? Lt. Seaborn called his mother.

Brandy Seaborn and Lieutenant Penelope Honeycutt-Parker flew in on Lieutenant Pamala Plum-Martin's Seagull. The two went straight to the Officer's Club. When they left, they had reserved the liberated Italian motor torpedo boat for a 'fishing expedition' the next day for Lieutenant General Alan Cunningham, they claimed.

A discreet private party…no need to log it in. The General was, after all, married.

And there was no necessity for a boat captain. Brandy, who identified herself as Miss Wilson – even though she was wearing a wedding ring with a diamond the size of a bird's egg – explained that she was qualified to handle the yacht.

"No problem, Miss Wilson."

The group of South African Air Force pilots who had reserved the craft was bumped unceremoniously. No excuse given.

Brandy and Lt. Honeycutt-Parker picked up the yacht the following morning. The women cruised to the Port of Kismayo shipyard where Lt. Seaborn, Lt. Hoolihan and Waldo were waiting. The three boarded the boat and set a course for RFHQ, which was a long voyage and required passage through the Suez Canal.

As soon as they cleared sight of land, Lt. Plum-Martin landed on the Red Sea next to the boat. Brandy and Lt. Honeycutt-Parker transferred to the Seagull. They flew back to RFHQ to continue with their other commitments, working with MI-5 on a classified project and training navigators for RFDS.

Lt. Seaborn, Lt. Hoolihan and Waldo settled in for a long cruise.

The 55-foot MAS boat was a beauty. Normally it carried a pair of torpedoes and a single anti-aircraft machine gun. However, all organic weapons had been removed when it was converted to sporting purposes.

Fully loaded with a crew of 10, it was capable of 45 knots... at least that was what the Italian Navy claimed.

Lt. Seaborn planned to use the boat to carry Sea Squadron Commandos on high-speed coastal pin-prick raids against the Via Balbia. He was not going to need torpedoes, but anti-aircraft machine guns were a must. The boat would be operating close in shore and some heavier caliber guns might also be an asset to shoot up trucks running down the coastal road at night, provide fire support for the Sea Squadron raiders, or possibly to carry out gunnery missions against point-type targets of opportunity along the coast.

Lt. Seaborn, the youngest officer of his grade in the Royal Navy, favored heavy firepower on his boats. He was a fighting sailor from a long line of fighting sailors and, though young, a highly experienced special operations naval officer.

Maj. Stone and Captain Jeb Pelham-Davies, Sea Squadron's commanding officer, were waiting on the dock.

***

JAMES "BALDIE" TAYLOR SAID, "I do not believe I can break the news to Lady Jane...not again."

"Someone has to," Colonel Dudley Clarke said, "...not going to be me."

"Not much information to go on," Jim said. "The message Phantom received from RAF Habbaniya sent by Lieutenant Pilkington was bare bones. 'MISSION ACCOMPLISHED STOP RANDAL, HUXLEY and KING MISSING IN ACTION STOP'."

"What does Squadron Leader Wilcox have to say?" Col. Clarke asked.

"He flew directly back to RAF Habbaniya after making the drop," Jim said. "He was going to wait there to fly Randal, Huxley, Pilkington and King back here after they extracted with the Royal Engineers. Paddy did not learn the three had gone MIA until the Vickers-Valentia landed."

"Where is he now?"

"On the way back here with Lieutenant Pilkington," Jim said. "The Vickers-Valentia bringing out the Royal Engineers only flies about 75 mph…it took nearly five hours flying home to RAF Habbaniya. With that much time elapsed, there was no way to attempt to mount a rescue."

"Most likely Randal and the other two will be picked up and detained…we need to have people traveling with the leading elements of *EXPORTER* to liberate Randal and his men immediately when we launch into Syria. I want senior operatives capable of dealing with the politics of the situation," Col. Clarke said.

"Notify Y-Service to keep their ears open for any signals intelligence they can pick up, confirming Randal's apprehension and place of detention."

Jim said, "I can have a team standing by ready to go in. We need Colonel Randal back here ASAP. Lead it myself…we have a situation."

"What?"

"Raiding Forces was alerted this morning to take part in *BATTLEAX*. GHQ Middle East wants a series of raids on Rommel's lines of communication during the attack to relieve Tobruk."

"Has GHQ Middle East settled on a date?" Col. Clark asked

"Raiding Forces has orders to commence their raids in support of *BATTLEAX* ten days from now…no exact date for the operation was provided."

"Can Desert Squadron have patrols in place ready to go," Colonel Clark asked, "in that period of time?"

"Probably not," Jim said. "We really need Colonel Randal if we are to have any hope of meeting GHQ's deadline. He has been working full-time to organize RFDS, choosing his patrol leaders, running a recruiting and selection program, getting equipment organized and training key personnel.

"The Lancelot Lancers have not been released from Kingcol, which means that RFDS is understrength."

"The Prime Minister may be over-extending British Forces, ordering Wavell to strike out on two fronts at virtually the same time," Col. Clarke said. "Some say the Field Marshall is exhausted and not making the best decisions...whisper is his days in command are numbered.

"No one could have done a better job out here than Wavell," Jim said. "But, he was badly off the mark about RAF Habbaniya...wanted to concede Iraq to the Golden Square from day one. Did not want to fight on another front. Now he is being ordered to attack in two different directions.

"Hate to admit it but the man may be fatigued." Col. Clarke said. "He has been my patron. I shall hate to see him go.

"De Gaulle promised the Prime Minister that once the Syrian attack goes in, the Vichy French will throw down their arms and rally to his Fighting French Forces. Churchill is flogging Wavell to invade immediately. On top of which, the GHQ staff has convinced themselves that *EXPORTER* is going to be a walkover."

"There is no intelligence to confirm that," Jim said. "In fact, my information is the exact opposite.

"The Vichy French Armed Forces consider De Gaulle a traitor. If Free French Forces—or as he calls them, the 'Fighting French'—lead the charge tomorrow, what is going to result is a civil war in Syria and Lebanon."

"Honor is a central component of the French officer corps psyche," Col. Clark said. "Appearance is paramount. The local French military may see our invasion as an opportunity to demonstrate to the world that they can fight after all."

"Bad blood runs deep between the UK and France," Jim said. "The Frogs claim we ran out on them at Dunkirk, and we are carrying out round-the-clock bombing raids against the Nazis in French territory on the continent, causing civilian casualties. And, they are furious with the Royal Navy for sinking the Vichy fleet to prevent it from falling into Hitler's hands.

"Fair to say more than a few French officers hate us worse than they do the Nazis."

"GHQ may not be giving all those issues enough weight," Col. Clark said. "My guess is *EXPORTER* is not going to be so easy."

"Which brings up another problem," Jim said. "Colonel Randal was in a pistol fight onboard the French submarine *Surcouf*...shot several Vichy naval officers.

"That's right," Col. Clarke said, "I had forgotten."

"Could turn nasty," Jim said, "if he is taken prisoner."

"You might choose to leave out the detail about the *Surcouf* gunfight when breaking the news to Lady Jane that her boyfriend is MIA in Vichy French Syria after blowing up one of their prize railway bridges," Col. Clark said.

"I would...if I were you, Baldie."

***

THE GYPSY CAB HAD BEEN DRIVING down the scenic coast road at breakneck speed for six hours. King was in the front seat, talking to Amed, the driver, while Lieutenant Colonel John Randal and Lieutenant Westcott Huxley dozed in the back. They were headed for the Palestine border, which was only a short distance ahead.

Amed had been promised a handsome bonus if he could make it before dark. The story he had been given was that Lt. Col. Randal, an American recruit serving in the 6th Foreign Infantry Regiment, French Foreign Legion, had never learned to speak French to Legion standard and was being summarily kicked out of the regiment...escorted to the border by Lt. Westcott and King (both of whom spoke French fluently) and given his walking papers.

The Legion no longer required his services.

Amed did not believe one word of the story. He had been a taxi driver for many years. And he had rented his cab out to members of the Legion before. These three were not fooling him.

They were deserting.

Military matters meant nothing to him. Amed had no interest in what the three Legionnaires were up to. All the Syrian was concerned with was collecting his bonus…a fare was a fare.

He was driving like a maniac. Unfortunately, for the sake of his gratuity, he was not going to make it in time. The sun was going down. When it did, dark set in fast.

The moon came up.

The cab was getting close to the border. There were two towns to go, Iskanderuna and Naqoura, then across into Palestine. With no curfew, no probation from traveling at night, or any restriction against driving with the headlamps on, they were making good time.

King said, "Take us across into Palestine, Amed, and we will pay your gratuity anyway…provided you keep driving south until we tell you to stop."

In the back of the cab, Lt. Col. Randal was thinking that if this had been a war movie, the enemy would have heavily-armed checkpoints every few miles or so to inspect papers and subject anyone who passed by to a field interrogation to verify people were who they claimed to be. However, it was Vichy French Syria and the taxi had not encountered a military or police barrier the entire trip.

Not a single guard had been posted on any of the series of bridges they drove over, along the sheer cliff face next to the sea. That was hard to explain, considering the alarm must have spread that a bridge had been attacked earlier that morning.

Clearly the Vichy French were unaware that three British Commandos had been left behind following the raid and were escaping & evading.

Amed ran into his first military roadblock at the bridge in a valley on the south side of Iskanderuna…ten Australians in slouch hats, five Palmach (the full time professional arm of the Jewish Haganah), a lieutenant from the King's Dragoon Guards (Armored Cars) and Rashid Taher, their Arab guide. The taxi screeched to a halt. A forest of .303 Enfield Mark III rifles was leveled at the vehicle.

Moshe Dayan, the leader of the Palmach team, recently released from a British prison, stepped up to the driver's window, holding a .455 Webly revolver.

"Everyone step out of the car," Dayan ordered.

EXPORTER was set to launch at 0230 hours. Lt. Col. Randal and his party had run headlong into the tip of the spear sent out in advance of the main body to secure the Iskanderuna Bridge. The occupants of the taxi exited, being very careful not to do anything that might be interpreted as hostile.

"My Gawd," the KDG lieutenant said, "When did you badge over to the bloody Frog Legion, Westcott?"

"Don't shoot, boys," Lt. Huxley said. "I have a hot date I'm twying to make in Caiwo."

21

PREPARE TO MOVE OUT

"THIS IS A WARNING ORDER," LIEUTENANT COLONEL JOHN Randal said. "Are you prepared to copy?"

He was not asking a question…it was a formal declaration that this was a mission alert. The men in the Operations Room at Raiding Forces Headquarters (RFHQ) knew immediately that they were going into action. The jovial atmosphere in the room instantly changed to intensely professional.

Present were James "Baldie" Taylor, Major Sir Terry "Zorro" Stone, Squadron Leader Paddy Wilcox, Major Jack Black, Major Jack Merritt, Major Clive Adair, Captain "Geronimo" Joe McKoy, Captain Taylor Corrigan, Captain "Pyro" Percy Stirling, Captain Lionel Chatterhorn, Captain the Lady Jane Seaborn, Lieutenant Jeffery Tall-Castle, Lieutenant Westcott Huxley, Lieutenant Fraser Llewellyn, Lieutenant Airey McKnight, Lieutenant Cord Granger, Lieutenant Jack Masters, Lieutenant Penelope Honeycutt-Parker, Brandy Seaborn and Sergeant Major Mike "March or Die" Mikkalis.

Absent was Lieutenant Dick Courtney, who was in the Gold Coast, recruiting men for his gun jeep patrol.

"SITUATION," Lt. Col. Randal said. "Raiding Forces has been alerted to put Desert Squadron in the field immediately."

Tension in the room shot sky high. Everyone present knew Raiding Forces Desert Squadron (RFDS) had not been formed yet. This directive was a surprise.

"MISSION: RFDS will place three patrols of six gun jeeps each in the field to support *OPERATION BATTLEAX*...Middle East Command's counterattack to retake Tobruk. Patrols will operate out of Oasis X on a line between Tobruk and Tripoli. Patrols will harass, harry and interdict isolated enemy installations and lines of communication.

"EXECUTION: RFDS will commence raiding operations within the next eight days."

There was a gasp from the people in the briefing. It might take longer than a week to reach Oasis X from RFHQ. No one present had ever made the journey before...not driving there directly across the desert.

"CONCEPT OF THE OPERATION: RFDS will form three provisional patrols of six gun jeeps. The patrol leaders will be Capt. McKoy, Capt. Chatterhorn and myself. Capt. Corrigan, RFDS commander, will move by air to Oasis X immediately this day to establish the Squadron Headquarters.

"The three patrols designated Red, White and Blue will depart RFHQ at first light tomorrow. Patrols are to move independently by a route of their choosing to Oasis X. Patrols must be prepared to conduct independent raids and ambushes against isolated enemy installations in their AO and Motor Transport along the Via Balbia upon command.

"COMMAND AND SIGNAL: One jeep in each patrol will be manned by a Phantom radio team, which will be responsible for all communications.

"ADMINISTRATION AND LOGISTICS: Get in your jeeps and drive like hell to Oasis X. Major Black, operating from here at RFHQ, and Capt. Corrigan from X, will have figured out the rest of it by the time you get there...maybe."

The group laughed. RFDS was going to be flying by the seat of their pants. No sense trying to deny it.

"Now, listen up," Lt. Col. Randal said. "We can do this, but it's going to take a lot of effort and a can-do attitude by everyone involved. We're short of almost everything, not all the jeeps are ready to go, and you'll have to improvise on the fly.

"I'm stacking these patrols officer-heavy so that everyone who's slated to be in a leadership position later can gain desert experience. The most effective leaders will eventually command...keep that in mind, gentlemen.

"You can expect to be in the field for at least a month. As we get the other jeeps ready and as the rest of our personnel arrive and complete their training, RFDS will create additional patrols...eventually we should have a minimum of six.

"A list of patrol members will be posted as soon as the three patrol leaders decide on who's assigned to which patrol.

"Patrol leaders meeting in my quarters immediately following this briefing... Capt. Corrigan will chair.

"Lady Jane, Lt. Honeycutt-Parker, Brandy and Lt. Huxley, stand fast.

"Let's do it."

***

"HUXLEY," LIEUTENANT COLONEL JOHN RANDAL said, "You're my assistant patrol leader. I'm going to stay here at RFHQ for a few days, which means you're going to lead the patrol to Oasis X."

"Suw!"

"Take the patrol leaders meeting for me...pick us a good team. Let me see your patrol roster before you notify the troops."

"Woger that, suw."

Captain the Lady Jane Seaborn, Lieutenant Penelope-Honeycutt Parker and Brandy Seaborn huddled in a corner of the Operations Room.

"Ladies," Lt. Col. Randal said, "here's the situation...Lt. Llewellyn, who has volunteered over from the LRDG, is our only experienced navigator.

Everyone else is one of your students. I can't send out patrols with student navigators, no matter how good they are."

Brandy and Lt. Honeycutt-Parker looked at each other.

"A crime, John," Brandy said, "...epic."

"Yes, it would be," Lt. Honeycutt-Parker drawled, "actually."

"Jane," Lt. Col. Randal said, "where have Rita and Lana disappeared to?"

"Charm school," Lady Jane said, "in Alexandria."

"*Charm school*...get the girls back here," Lt. Col. Randal said. "Have Pam fly in to pick 'em up this afternoon if necessary."

"I shall make the arrangements," Lady Jane said.

"I'll assign Rita to Parker, and Brandy, you take Lana," Lt. Col. Randal said. "Flip a coin. One of you travel with Capt. McKoy, and the other with Huxley and me. Llewellyn is going with Chatterhorn.

"OK with you two?"

"Perfect," Brandy said. "I am traveling with you, John."

"Where would you like me, John?" Lady Jane asked.

"What's your thought?" Lt. Col. Randal said.

"Oasis X," Lady Jane said. "I was scheduled to fly out to attend Mandy's graduation, but that's out of the question now...we have a long laundry list of things at the Oasis that have to be done."

"Negative," Lt. Col. Randal said.

"No?"

"Go to Mandy's commissioning...make those jumps with her like you promised," Lt. Col. Randal said. "Leave tomorrow...get her an early-out if you can."

"Love to...are you certain?"

"You girls take a day, go shopping...have fun," Lt. Col. Randal said. "Then come back here on the double and get X organized.

"I'll give you a check. Buy Mandy a present for me...something nice."

"John," Lady Jane said, "are you all right?"

"Mandy was a real trooper at Habbaniya," Lt. Col. Randal said.

"I had to shoot her horse, Blackie."

***

CAPTAIN JEB PELHAM-DAVIES and Lieutenant Randy "Hornblower" Seaborn were standing by, having been summoned to see Lieutenant Colonel John Randal.

"Can you have Sea Squadron ready to carry out raids by next week?" Lt. Col. Randal said, lighting a cigarette.

Capt. Pelham-Davies said, "Difficult, sir."

"Why might that be?"

"We only have one MAS boat," Lt. Seaborn said, "unarmed, sir."

"Don't fight anybody, Randy," Lt. Col. Randal said, "Slip in, insert a raiding party, mine the coastal road, come home and do it again the next night until I tell you to stop."

"That is a problem, sir," Capt. Pelham-Davies said. "It's 400 nautical miles from RFHQ to Tobruk…our AO runs from there to Tripoli."

"What's your plan?" Lt. Col. Randal said.

The two officers hesitated. Lt. Seaborn said, "We want to establish a forward operating base at Tobruk, sir."

"Tobruk is surrounded by the Afrika Korps," Lt. Col. Randal said. "Under attack around the clock, could be overrun any day. You want to relocate there and set up shop?"

"Our only option, sir," Lt. Seaborn said. "We have to stage closer to our target area."

"Lt. Hoolihan has his sea raiding troop ready to go," Capt. Pelham-Davies said. "Sea Squadron's second troop is onboard a convoy en route from Seaborn House as we speak, sir. Could take a month to get here."

Lt. Seaborn said, "Butch's troop is going to see hard service before his Commandos can get a respite, sir. We do not want to degrade them unnecessarily with long periods at sea traveling to their targets."

"Yeah," Lt. Col. Randal said, "I can see how that's a problem."

"Sea Squadron has no choice but to displace closer to our target area, sir." Lt. Seaborn said. "Tobruk is the *best* place we can."

"Worst plan I've ever heard," Lt. Col. Randal said.

"Get it done."

***

SQUADRON LEADER PADDY WILCOX, Major Jack Merritt and Sergeant Major Mike "March or Die" Mikkalis were standing by to see Lieutenant Colonel John Randal.

Maj. Merritt said, "Utilizing the LRDG's base at Kufra to stage for operations at Oasis X is a mistake, sir. We do not gain anything by using it as an intermediate stop. Be better to blaze a new route direct to X."

"Can you do that?" Lt. Col. Randal said.

"Not sure, sir," Maj. Merritt said, "but worth a try. If you look at the map, Kufra is a good place to launch deep desert exploration or reconnaissance missions.

"However, Raiding Forces is primarily tasked with operating in the other direction against the coastal road network. What we need is a safe haven located in the desert behind the Great Sand Sea, from which RFDS patrols can strike out at the coast then retreat back into. X gives us that capability – but there is no need to add the extra miles it takes to reach it by routing through Kufra… a long, unnecessary dog leg."

"The road is already established," Lt. Col. Randal said.

"Nobody likes it at Kufra," Sgt. Maj. Mikkalis said. "Snakes, fleas, flies and the LRDG runs the place like it's a peacetime establishment. Reveille, retreat, duty parades, guard mount, stand-to and they expect RFDS to participate. Our lads are better off out of there, Colonel."

"We're going to have to do most of those things at X," Lt. Col. Randal said.

"At least Raiding Forces will be in charge," Sgt. Maj. Mikkalis said, "meaning me."

"Your call, Jack," Lt. Col. Randal said. "Can you cut a road to Oasis X...that's the question."

"I can shave off approximately 200 miles by going direct," Maj. Merritt said. "The trick will be setting up supply dumps to stage as we go. We will have to run a shuttle setting up the fuel caches...inching our way forward, leapfrogging our dumps."

"How long will that take?"

"Four to six weeks, sir."

"We don't have that much time, Jack."

"That's how long it took me to reach X going through Kufra, sir," Maj. Merritt said. "You have sufficient fuel stored there now to operate gun jeep patrols for three weeks.

"The problem is, Colonel, you do not have a reserve to evacuate the administrative and supply personnel if the oasis comes under ground attack."

"I see," Lt. Col. Randal said.

Looking across the room, he made eye contact with Major Jack Black, who immediately came over to join the conversation.

"Desert war is a war of logistics," Maj. Merritt said. "Requires considerable drop-ahead planning. Then we have to work like a colony of ants, going back and forth shuttling our supplies to X, establishing dumps of fuel in order to have enough to be able to reach it.

"We have to operate with outdated trucks that weren't designed to be driven in the desert...with no spare parts when they break down...and do all that under constant threat of enemy air attack."

"As you increase the number of RFDS patrols operating out of X, Colonel," Maj. Black said, "the supply problem multiplies exponentially."

"You two Jacks work it out," Lt. Col. Randal ordered. "I don't care how we get there."

"We have a similar problem with our Walruses," Sqn. Ldr. Wilcox said. "Whichever route, the flight to X is long and dangerous. To be safe, I recommend our SOP be to fly in pairs so that if one plane goes down, the other can land and pick the pilot up or stay on station until a rescue party can arrive."

"Makes sense," Lt. Col. Randal said.

"Additionally," Sqn Ldr. Wilcox said, "what we need to do is establish an emergency lifeline of water and food dumps every 15 miles from RFHQ to X along the air route. That way, if a plane goes down, the passengers can walk to the oasis if they have to, by going from cache to cache."

"Can we do that?" Lt. Col. Randal asked.

"Easy enough to cache water and food stockpiles as we convoy out," Maj. Black said, "but when we do, it means that much less fuel we are able to transport to X...less operating time for the gun jeep patrols until we have the emergency dumps in place."

"How long is *that* going to take?"

"No way to tell, sir," Maj. Merritt said. "Could be up to three months before we have everything completely in place. Then Heavy Squadron will face a constant struggle to keep the dumps and emergency caches re-supplied."

"The Walrus is not the ideal aircraft for long-range desert operations," Sqn. Ldr. Wilcox said. "Sand and dust do not do airplane engines any good. They only have the one. What we need are twin engine models like the Hudson."

"What are the chances of us getting any twin engine airplanes?" Lt. Col. Randal said.

"We might be able to obtain a couple of Avro Ansons," Sqn. Ldr. Wilcox said. "Obsolete, only used as multi-engine trainers nowadays...a limited number perform coastal patrols. The Navy probably has a couple in their inventory that they won't miss.

"Small...only carry four passengers, but not a bad aircraft for what we want them for."

"See what you can do, Paddy," Lt. Col. Randal said.

"The trouble is, Colonel, the RAF will not cooperate with us," Sqn. Ldr. Wilcox said. "The LRDG had to resort to buying two Wacos using private funds – and then the Air Force would not provide any maintenance support. We're going to run into the same problem."

"Get with Jim Taylor," Lt. Col. Randal said, "maybe he'll have a thought.

"I don't."

***

LIEUTENANT COLONEL JOHN RANDAL went in search of Captain the Lady Jane Seaborn. She was sitting on a desk, with her booted legs crossed, talking on the phone.

Lady Jane said, "I shall send the car around." Then hung up.

"Tell me about that long laundry list," Lt. Col. Randal said, "we need to do at X."

22

BOLD TALK

FRANK POLANSKI AND EX-TECHNICAL Sergeant Hank Rawlston escorted Lieutenant Colonel John Randal on an inspection tour of the gun jeeps being readied for assignment to the Red, White and Blue patrols.

"Bantams don't take as much work to get ready to go as them Chevrolet trucks you was originally planning to use do, Colonel," ex-Tech. Sgt. Rawlston said.

"We need to install the sun compass on the hood – which ain't real difficult, remove some of the grills on the front of the engine cowling to get better airflow and install the LRDG water condenser on the radiator…which is the hardest part."

"Water condenser?" Lt. Col. Randal said. "That's a new one…what's the story?"

"Geronimo Joe and Lt. Llewellyn was out here arguing about the condensers yesterday," ex-Tech. Sgt. Rawlston said. The Lieutenant claimed it was some Col. Bagnold who invented 'em but Capt. McKoy, he said naw, they had 'em back in the last one when he was out here in the Light Car Companies, whatever those were…invented by some desert exploring scientist, Dr. John Ball, according to Joe."

"What's a condenser do, exactly?" Lt. Col. Randal asked.

"When the engine overheats," ex-Tech. Sgt. Rawlston said, "first thing, the water-cooled radiator boils over. Water is too precious to be allowed to spill out on the ground. So, this guy Dr. Ball rigged up a special hose device so that when the water in the radiator boils over, it's collected and recycled…the guy was a genius.

"We've put 'em on every jeep, Colonel. Had to modify 'em a little to fit but they work fine."

Lt. Col. Randal said, "I don't know much about jeeps."

"Simple mechanical design," ex-Tech. Sgt. Rawlston said. "Easy to maintain and a breeze to repair in the field…carry spares, have a breakdown, replace the part, continue to march.

"Bantam built the original. Didn't win the big government bid though…Willys did. Our first bunch, they're Bantams, but the second lot Lady Jane got for us is Willys."

"Any difference?" Lt. Col. Randal said.

"Not much, Colonel," ex-Tech. Sgt. Rawlston said, chewing on the stub of a cigar. "The Willys come packed in a wood crate so we have to assemble them.

"Ain't that hard but takes a little time."

"How many do you have ready to go?" Lt. Col. Randal said.

"Thirteen could pull out right now," ex-Tech. Sgt. Rawlston said. "Count on your other five by tomorrow. I got you a command jeep set up, Colonel…ready to roll."

"Frank?" Lt. Col. Randal said.

"We're finishing up installing the gun mounts," the ex-U.S. Marine said. "We'll have all the guns up by the time Hank gets done."

"Run the weapons down for me," Lt. Col. Randal said.

"Every jeep is equipped with a pair of twin Vickers K Model .303s, one pair mounted on the driver's side and one pair on the passenger's. Hank takes off the windscreen…fire out the front. Another pair of Vickers Ks is mounted on a pedestal in the back, good for a full 360-degree field of fire," Frank said.

"One jeep in each patrol will carry an Italian Breda 20mm on its pedestal for extra heavy punch.

"What you really want, Col. Randal – and I've asked Lady Jane to keep her eye open for any that show up on the Lend Lease manifest – is *Ma Deuces*...M2 Browning .50 cals. Put 'em on the pedestal mounts instead of the Vickers Ks...that's some serious knock-down power working for you."

"What about the Boys .55s?" Lt. Col. Randal said.

"One jeep in each patrol will be equipped with a sniper modified AT Rifle... carry it in a steel case bolted in the back to protect the scope," Frank said. "When you need to snipe something, simply whip the Vickers Ks off the pedestal and slap on the Boys...only takes a couple of seconds to install."

"Nice, Frank," Lt. Col. Randal said.

"Ain't all, Colonel," the ex-U.S. Marine said. "One jeep in each patrol will carry a mortar on board. Could be decisive when you attack one of those roadhouses on the Via Balbia.

"Good work, men," Lt. Col. Randal said. "Keep at it, all three RFDS patrols need to pull out of here at daybreak."

"No problem, Colonel," ex-Tech. Sgt. Rawlston said. "We'll have 'em ready for you."

"May look like toy cars," Frank said, "but Raiding Force's jeeps got an attitude...each one has as many guns as your average RAF fighter. Our patrols carry more machine guns than LRDG patrols twice their size."

Lt. Col. Randal said, "You really packed on the firepower."

***

LIEUTENANT COLONEL JOHN RANDAL encountered James "Baldie" Taylor as he was walking back into RFHQ's Operations Room to find Lieutenant Westcott Huxley.

"Jack tells me you plan to stop using Kufra as your intermediate staging base," Jim said.

"Which Jack?"

"Merritt."

"That's what he recommended," Lt. Col. Randal said.

"We are not having this conversation," Jim said. "*Whatever* you decide…do not close out your entire Raiding Forces detachment at Kufra. At a minimum, keep the long range Phantom set up in place.

"Continue to provide signals support for the LRDG."

"Yes, sir," Lt. Col. Randal said.

"One of the things I like about you, Colonel," Jim said, "is you never ask questions I am not going to answer…truthfully."

"General," Lt. Col. Randal said, "what I've learned…you never ask me to do something without a reason."

"True," Jim said. "Not that it has always worked out so wonderful for you."

Captain "Geronimo" Joe McKoy marched past with a crowd of eager lieutenants…all seasoned veterans of Force N. He was holding a long, unlit cigar in one hand, barking out a series of orders rapid-fire. RFDS had one patrol getting organized in a hurry.

"John," Capt. McKoy called, "you mind if our patrol takes the White designator?"

"No problem, Captain," Lt. Col. Randal said. "It's yours."

"Outstanding," Capt. McKoy said. "The good guys always wear white hats."

Captain Lionel Chatterhorn was across the room, assembling his team of officers. He appeared to be taking a more measured approach. The security specialist was a mature officer originally handpicked by Captain the Lady Jane Seaborn to protect Raiding Forces at Seaborn House. In Abyssinia he had transitioned into a troop commander by necessity and proved to be a superb combat leader.

When Lt. Col. Randal and Jim walked over, Capt. Chatterhorn said, "We like Red, sir."

"You got it."

Lt. Huxley came into the operations center.

"Let's see the patrol roster," Lt. Col. Randal said.

He scanned the list of names, "Too many...18 men – that's a full strength patrol."

"Wojer suw, undewstood," Lt. Huxley said. "Fow the initial pawt of the twip, we go out fouw to a jeep in some vehicles. When we weach X, the extwa men will dwop off befowe we deploy on our opewational patwols. Majow Adaiw, Capt. Stiwling and Lt. Pilkington awe stwap hanging to get expewience.

"Mistew Tweywick, well, I am not suwe why he wants to come with us, suw."

"I'm not exactly sure either, Lieutenant," Lt. Col. Randal said lighting a cigarette.

"Lt. Gwanger will be ouw patwol demolitions specialist when we go into action."

"What's GG doing on here?" Lt. Col. Randal said.

"Lady Jane," Lt. Huxley said, "she made me pwomise to have you all in one piece and well-fed when she wetuwned, suw."

The list included the former Legionnaires, Corporals Smith, Jones and Brown, plus 16 names of men Lt. Col. Randal did not recognize.

"Who are these people?"

"Eight are Foweign Legion volunteews wecruited fow the 'Fwee Fwench' patwol I'm to lead when the jeeps awe available, suw.

"One is a Yeomanwy man volunteewed ovew fwom the LRDG, Nelson...with us on the Y-Patwol mission.

"Six are Amewicans."

"You can't have the light vehicle repair team, Westcott," Lt. Col. Randal said. "Rawlston has to get the rest of the jeeps serviced...then he'll set up shop at X to refit the patrol vehicles when they come in from the field...they're not going out on patrol."

"The *new* Amewicans, suw," Lt. Huxley said. "Captain McKoy said they make the best dwivers. Awwived while you wew issuing the Wawning Owdew, suw...I wecwuited six."

Lt. Col. Randal looked across the room and made eye contact with Lady Jane. She immediately cut short her conversation with Major Jack Black and came over.

"Jane," Lt. Col. Randal said, "what's the story on the new people Lt. Huxley's telling me about?"

"Came in earlier," Lady Jane said. "A contingent of 24 U.S. volunteers. One of my Marines is getting them settled in their quarters.

"Westcott solicited a half-dozen volunteers from the group to drive his jeeps. Another of my Marines is kitting out those men with field gear and weapons."

"Who did the picking?" Lt. Col. Randal said.

"The group leader...Travis McCloud," Lady Jane said. "Former captain, Infantry, United States Army."

"Good choices, Lieutenant," Lt. Col. Randal said, taking another look at the roster. "Most of the men in Blue Patrol—*my* patrol—are going to end up in your patrol when you get one."

"Wojew, suw," Lt. Huxley said, "It's Good to Have a Plan B."

"Huxley," Lt. Col. Randal said, winking at drop-dead gorgeous Lady Jane, who was trying not to laugh, "let's make a deal."

"Suw?"

"You strike 'Roger' from your vocabulary and I may actually let you have a patrol."

"Wilco...suw."

***

BRIGADIER GEORGE DAVY AND COLONEL DUDLEY Clarke arrived in Captain the Lady Jane Seaborn's Rolls Royce. She escorted them out to the quad where Red, White and Blue Patrols of Raiding Forces Desert Squadron were going through a round robin of training stations preparatory to deployment.

That the Director of Military Operations for Middle East Command would take the time out of his workday to visit RFHQ—when he had both the invasion of Syria in progress and the counter-attack to relieve Tobruk in the final stages ready to commence– was an indication of how much importance he placed on the future success of RFDS.

James "Baldie" Taylor joined them on their inspection.

Brig. Davy and Col. Clarke worked hand and glove. It was A-Force commander's firm policy that his organization and its satellite units, like Raiding Forces, fall under the Operations Division of GHQ…not Intelligence.

Strange, considering that one of the best-kept secrets in the war— second only to ULTRA—was that Col. Clarke reported to, and worked directly for, 'C', Colonel Stewart Menzies, DSO, Chief of MI-6, *aka* the British Secret Intelligence Service.

Currently Brig. Davy and Col. Clarke were in the early stage of a Most Secret deception campaign against the Desert Fox, General Erwin Rommel, called PLAN A-R…'Anti-Rommel'.

The "story" being fed the Axis in bits and pieces was that British and Free French Forces planned a multi-pronged attack on the Afrika Korps supply lines from Tobruk to Tripoli.

Layforce, consisting of A Troop drawn from 3 Commando, 7 Commando, 8 Commando (Guards) and No. 11 Commando (Scottish), was slated to make an amphibious landing to sever the Via Balbia. The idea was to cut the Afrika Korps surrounding Tobruk off from its base of supplies in Tripoli.

1SAS Brigade (Notional)…meaning it did not actually exist…was moving from the Transjordan to Egypt, equipped with gliders to stage for an airborne attack in support of the Commandos of Layforce.

Free French troops working in conjunction with Raiding Forces would make long-range strikes against the Axis lines of communications from the desert flank.

American armored specialists had arrived to train the British in the use of their new 'air-conditioned' tanks. The Germans, new to the Western Desert, believed that tanks could not be operated for long periods during the intense heat of the summer. But air-conditioned tanks could.

PLAN A-R was an elaborate ruse. There was no 1SAS Brigade...it being one of Col. Clarke's favorite notional units. There was not going to be a full-scale Commando landing, though the Commandos of Layforce were real enough. There was not a single glider in Africa; however, dummy gliders had been built (nicknamed MECCANOS) and moved to a disused airfield near Cairo where the Luftwaffe promptly subjected them to several bombing attacks.

And there were no air-conditioned tanks.

There *was* going to be a series of small-scale raids on the Afrika Korps supply lines from the desert and sea flank. RFDS and Sea Squadron constituted the only real part of the plan.

The fact that Raiding Forces actually did have a contingent of American volunteers and some French Foreign Legion men in its ranks was icing on the cake for the sake of the deception. Col. Clarke, the world's master of military deception, was overjoyed with that development, which he intended to exploit to its fullest extent.

At the first station, ex-Technical Sergeant Hank Rawlston had the hood up on a jeep and was pointing out to Red Patrol the mechanical features to be found on the Bantam Light Reconnaissance Car.

"One jeep in the patrol will be designated as the fitter vehicle – have mechanics on board...travel last in the column. Each vehicle in the patrol will carry at least one vital spare part...enough so that you guys can just about rebuild yourselves a complete jeep if need be.

"Questions?"

"Why's the bloody thing called a jeep?"

"Classified," said ex-Tech. Sgt. Rawlings, who had no idea what the answer was. "Next question..."

"The Great Teddy" was lecturing on camouflage techniques at his station. He demonstrated the blow-up dummies. The boy had spent time working with Lieutenant Fraser Llewellyn, who had volunteered over from LRDG to develop an SOP for when/where to deploy them.

"Any time your patrol is spotted by an enemy surveillance aircraft," Teddy said, "the moment it departs, immediately laager and put up the pink netting to cover your patrol cars.

"Then back-track on your line-of-march and deploy the dummies in a likely location. Cover them with your conventional army-issue netting..."

At his station Squadron Leader Paddy Wilcox briefed on patrol tactics *vis-à-vis* enemy air.

"One thing everyone in the Long Range Desert Group agrees on is that enemy air is the biggest threat. Do not stop if attacked on the move. The LRDG never fires on an enemy aircraft under any circumstance. RFDS is currently evaluating that policy...use your discretion until advised differently."

"When attacked by enemy aircraft," Sqn. Ldr. Wilcox said, "stay on course. If you are traveling in column formation, immediately break out of it and come on line... each driver choosing his own path. Then, when the enemy begins its attack run, the jeep it has targeted needs to make a hard, 90-degree turn right or left and hammer down on the accelerator.

"Play your cards right, and you might cause the enemy pilot to fly into the ground, trying to keep you in his sights. Moving targets making hard turns are difficult for a diving airplane to stay with.

"Now this is important. *Never* travel in a single-file column formation unless the terrain absolutely dictates. We conducted aerial tests, working with a party on the ground. The trail left by a patrol where one jeep travels in the tracks of the vehicle in front of him is highly visible from the air.

"However, we discovered that when the jeeps broke out of line it was difficult to spot the tracks from the air.

"Lesson learned: Travel in an open formation, spread out as wide as possible whenever the terrain allows."

Frank Polanski demonstrated the weapons systems mounted on the jeeps. Right away a couple of problems became apparent. The U.S. volunteers and the ex-Foreign Legion men had never worked with the Vickers K machine guns. The Italian Breda 20mm was a new weapon to virtually everyone, including the Force N veterans who had served in Abyssinia…they had encountered the weapon but most had never operated it.

Frank made a note to discuss the situation with Lieutenant Colonel John Randal. He intended to recommend one man in every patrol be a heavy weapons expert. Nights could be spent on weapons familiarization classes.

Lt. Col. Randal briefed Raiding Forces Area of Operations (AO) and tactics.

"The purpose of the exercise," Lt. Col. Randal said, "is to arrive unexpected and unannounced from out of nowhere in the dark of night, inflict damage on enemy motor transport, installations, and personnel, then disappear back into the desert. Hit and run… over and over again.

"Enemy wheeled vehicles are our primary target…10-tonners at the top of the list. However, all motor transport is worth its weight in gold to Afrika Korps.

"Never leave any enemy truck behind without firing it up.

"Striking hard and fast and then disappearing into the desert to do it all over again somewhere else will force the bad guys to rethink. Rommel will have no choice but to increase road security on the Via Balbia to protect his line-of-communications and to beef up security at his fixed installations all across the Western Desert.

"Men, armored fighting vehicles, and motor transport will be siphoned off from the fighting front and tied down guarding some remote area against an attack that will never come.

"Because we never hit the same place twice…unless we do.

"Pick the time and place, concentrate your force at the point of attack and *never* fight the bad guys when the bad guys want to fight you.

"The plan," Lt. Col. Randal said, "is to take the tactics we perfected in the mountains of Abyssinia to the Western Desert…ghost in and out of the vast sand sea, riding gun jeeps instead of mules and shoot up everything in sight.

"Guerrilla war and plenty of it."

***

BRIGADIER GEORGE DAVY SAID TO Colonel Dudley Clarke as they were departing RFHQ, "Anyone read Colonel Randal in on PLAN A-R?"

"Not I," Col. Clarke said. "Colonel Randal has been led to believe he works for SOE, not A-Force…what he does not know cannot be revealed under interrogation in the event of capture."

James "Baldie" Taylor said, "Colonel Randal does not possess a 'Need to Know' the details of PLAN A-R."

Brig. Davy said, "Certainly seems to have figured it out."

Captain the Lady Jane Seaborn said, "John took one look at the map the moment he was informed of Raiding Forces' new mission and knew straightaway what tactics were wanted and the effect they would have on Afrika Korps if properly executed."

"You believe that 'hit and run' lecture was anything more than bold talk, Lady Jane," Brig. Davy said, "to motivate the troops?"

"Colonel Randal is going to carry out the mission you heard him brief, Brigadier," Lady Jane said.

"Your deception has become *very* real…minus the Layforce Commandos and the 1SAS glider landings."

***

LIEUTENANT COLONEL JOHN RANDAL ACCOMPANIED Captain the Lady Jane Seaborn and "The Great Teddy" to the seaport where the Flying Clipper was docked, ready for boarding.

Lt. Col. Randal wondered which Duke or Admiral's party Lady Jane bumped to get seats.

Red came into the VIP lounge. She said, "Teddy, how would you like me to show you around the Clipper? The pilot invited you up to the cockpit to see how they fly the airplane."

"Ted," Lt. Col. Randal said, "you get out of school, get a commission some day… I'll always have a place for you in Raiding Forces."

"Yes, sir!"

When they were alone, Lady Jane put her arms around Lt. Col. Randal's neck. A tear trickled down her cheek. "John, I have cherished every moment of the time we have spent together these last few weeks."

"Ah…"

"Do try to be more careful," Lady Jane said. "Mandy's right…you are too reckless."

"Wasn't my fault that bridge blew when it did," Lt. Col. Randal said. "Or that the Luftwaffe shot up all those Y-Patrol trucks. I wasn't even there when it…"

Lady Jane said, "Mallory is pressing for a reconciliation."

Lt. Col. Randal said. "I figured he would."

23

BLUE

LIEUTENANT COLONEL JOHN RANDAL DECIDED TO JOIN Blue Patrol early on the third day. There was only so much he could do at RFHQ. Major Sir Terry "Zorro" Stone did not need him looking over his shoulder.

Major Jack Black did not require supervision doing his job…logistics for such a widespread unit as Raiding Forces was complicated enough without having his commander asking unnecessary questions.

Sea Squadron was in the process of relocating to Tobruk, preparatory to launching their first amphibious pin-prick raids.

Sergeant Major Mike "March or Die" Mikkalis' recruiting/training program was running like a Swiss watch, even though he was losing several of his instructors who were headed to Oasis X with the patrols.

Sgt. Maj. Mikkalis helped the Raiding Forces commander make his decision when he told Lt. Col. Randal, "This is the best job I've ever had – anytime, anywhere. Now, go kill someone and let me get on with it, sir."

The night before he departed, Capt. A. W. "Sammy" Sansom arrived unannounced at RFHQ.

"You need an aggressive counterintelligence program at Oasis X, Colonel," Capt. Sansom said. "Bad form to have Axis agents living in your forward operating base, observing and reporting on RFDS."

"Could be a problem," Lt. Col. Randal said.

"Never trust the natives," Capt. Sansom said. "Intrigue is inbred in their culture. Play both sides against the middle if they get a chance. You want to make sure not to give them one."

Lt. Col. Randal said, "Recruiting a counterintelligence officer for X was on Lady Jane's 'to do' list when she got back from the UK...may not be coming back, now."

"I have some leave time accumulated," Capt. Sansom said. "Why not let me fly in to survey the situation. Make an assessment, develop a catalog of recommendations... suggest someone for the job as your onsite counterintelligence chief.

I can conduct the preliminary vetting of the locals...spy the spies."

"You'd do that?" Lt. Col. Randal said.

"Absolutely," Capt. Sansom said. "I may ask a favor in return someday, but count me in."

"Fair enough," Lt. Col. Randal said. "We need the help."

***

LIEUTENANT PAMALA PLUM-MARTIN flew in low over blue patrol. The jeeps were halted on their line of march. A yellow smoke grenade blossomed.

Mindful of the last time he had jumped from a Walrus, Lieutenant Colonel John Randal exited the door with extreme caution. Today he was not carrying much extra gear in addition to his personal weapons...only his modified Brixia 45mm shoulder-fired mortar and five rounds. Another 40 rounds were stowed aboard his command jeep down below, along with the rest of his equipment.

Captain "Geronimo" Joe McKoy had originally built the Brixia in the field behind the lines in Abyssinia by stripping the base plate and most of the other parts, except the action and barrel, off an Italian 45mm mortar and bolting on a cut-down rifle stock so the weapon could be fired from the shoulder instead of the sitting position the way it had originally been designed.

The result was crude but effective…a stubby, sawed-off shotgun type weapon capable of launching a high-explosive round that traveled so slow you could watch it in flight. When the 45mm grenade detonated, it was a gratifying experience. Trees fell down, things blew up…always an attention-getting explosion.

The gunsmiths at Westley Richards had recently spent several weeks refining Capt McKoy's field expedient prototype.

Lt. Col. Randal had an idea that the shoulder-fired 45mm mortar was going to be a great truck buster. The weapon had worked to good effect against convoys in the mountains of Abyssinia. Five more were on order. Eventually, there would be one per patrol.

Lieutenant Westcott Huxley, Brandy Seaborn and Waldo Treywick were waiting when he touched down. Lana Turner rolled up his X-type parachute and stuffed it in his parachute bag. The canvas bag went into the back of the jeep that King was leaning against, cleaning his nails with a Fairbairn Commando knife.

The American volunteer, ex-Captain Travis McCloud, was sitting at the wheel.

Brandy spread a map out over the hood.

"We are here," Brandy said, "skirting along the southern border of the Qattara Depression. The plan is to cut south of the mysterious oasis at Siwi to avoid being seen by the inhabitants. Our fun starts when we encounter the Great Sand Sea.

"Fair sailing so far, John."

"Jeeps working out?" Lt. Col. Randal asked.

"Best little truck ever made, Colonel," Waldo said. "Never seen anythin' to beat 'em. Better 'n mules. Climb or run over whatever gets in their path…bust through brush, ain't temperamental, don't kick, bite or hold a grudge."

"The lads have become attached to the Bantams, suw," Lt. Huxley said. "The way cavalwymen awe to chawgews.

"Almost like being back in the wegiment...except, Colonel, jeeps *can* dance."

Lt. Col. Randal took command. Nothing was said, but prior to his arrival, the journey had resembled a desert exploration expedition. Now it was a war patrol.

Every man (and woman) present was a free spirit with the heart of an adventurer. That was fine as far as Lt. Col. Randal was concerned, except that freelance enterprises operating on their own in the vastness of the Western Desert and beyond had to exhibit perfect discipline, pay rigorous attention to detail, and be totally focused at all times. Danger was always present...from the elements or enemy.

Tragedy could strike at any time and it came fast.

Lt. Col. Randal wanted everyone dialed in to everything taking place. Monotonous, mind-numbing attentiveness to perpetually tedious duties and minor tasks was a greater virtue than boldness when on patrol. Getting things done right was more important than getting things done fast.

Deliberation was paramount.

There were three questions Lt. Col. Randal required every patrol member to know the answer to at all times: 'Where am I?', 'Where is the enemy?' and "Where are the friendly forces?'

On every halt, he gathered the patrol around and critiqued their performance. Lt. Huxley translated for the Foreign Legion men who had not yet mastered English.

Lt. Col. Randal demanded the patrolmen perform the same task, the same way – no matter how simple – over and over until it was second nature.

"Sailors," Brandy said, "understand the value of repetition, repetition, repetition."

"So do soldiers," Lt. Col. Randal said. "Don't like it much...except in the best units."

"Blue Patrol is going to be the best of the best," Brandy said. "I know you, John."

"Yeah, but then Huxley gets to fight it," Lt. Col. Randal said. "Most of these men are slated for his Free French patrol."

"What a completely unselfish act of leadership," Brandy said. "You could be working up your own team…you continue to impress, John."

"Negative," Lt. Col. Randal said. "Huxley selected Blue's personnel. I was busy at the time. Have to keep your eye on 'Don't Dance'…pretty slick operator."

Immediate action drills began.

The idea was: Know what to do and do the same thing the same way, every time…react instinctively without having to stop and think.

Lt. Col. Randal ordered air guards posted on each jeep at all times during the hours of daylight. Weapons had to be kept immaculately clean— not easy in a desert environment—vehicles meticulously maintained, and every man had to be able to reach in the back of his jeep and come out with the item needed – grenades, belt of ammunition, hand-held torch, etc. without having to hunt for it.

Blue Patrol ran drill after drill after drill – some while halted and others while on the move.

Routine can be boring or it can be reassuring. The troops came to realize that Blue Patrol was going to be able to execute like a well-oiled machine when the chips were down. That knowledge bred confidence, which morphed into unity and *esprit de corps*.

Later, Lt. Col. Randal intended to implement cross-training so that every patrolman could perform every other man's job.

Before Red, White and Blue patrols had departed RFHQ, Lt. Col. Randal decreed that shorts were forbidden. No slip-on desert boots or sandals could be worn except at night around camp and then only when the trooper's canvas-topped raiding boots were dangling around his neck by their laces.

Getting caught without your boots was grounds to be RTU'd.

Headgear ran the gamut from cowboy hats, berets, slouch hats and kepis, to baseball caps sporting the logo of the U.S. volunteer's favorite sports teams.

Military uniformity had no value…preparedness did. No one was *ever* to be separated from his individual weapon (at minimum a pistol), compass, wristwatch, map case or canteen of water.

Any member of the patrol who did not conform to Lt. Col. Randal's standards would be RTU'd.

When Blue Patrol halted for the evening, the drivers immediately began their vehicle maintenance. Gunners cleaned their machine guns. Then everyone cleaned their personal weapons.

The mechanics from the fitter's jeep went around and checked on every other vehicle to consult or offer a hand with repairs. Everyone worked. Anyone who did not immediately pitch in voluntarily would be RTU'd.

Corporal Brown, the senior corporal acting in the capacity as patrol sergeant, measured the water and fuel and then brought the numbers to Lt. Col. Randal. Patrolling was all about the numbers. It was a balancing act.

Before daylight was lost, a class on disassembly and assembly of the Vickers K machine gun and the Breda 20mm was held for the U.S. volunteers and Foreign Legion men new to the weapon.

Only when all work details were over did GG serve the evening meal. The patrol messed together and every patrolman had an equal share of the rations.

After supper, the Phantom radio team set up their long-distance antenna. They made their scheduled radio checks and then tuned in to BBC London…sometimes Radio Occupied Paris or Berlin. The sounds of the music wafted out across the moonlit desert.

Radio operators were good-naturedly threatened that if they failed to play 'good stuff', they would be RTU'd.

When the stars came out, Brandy set up the theodolite to establish their position. Lt. Col. Randal, all the officers, Corporals Smith, Jones and Brown and anyone else interested in learning the mysteries of celestial navigation assembled to observe.

Brandy explained each step as she worked.

In between taking the observations, which was a timely process, Lt. Col. Randal held court from a canvas folding chair. He critiqued everything that the patrol had done during the day. Then the meeting was open...anyone could comment, criticize, praise or make suggestions, regardless of rank or position.

Ideas were floated and debated, and those deemed worthy were ordered implemented the next day. Suggestions that had seemed like good ideas previously—if tried and found lacking—were eliminated. Patrol tactics were a constantly evolving process.

Afterwards, patrolmen gathered around their jeeps and brewed up tea or coffee. Later, the men visited with friends at the other jeeps. Night was a pleasant time.

Blue Patrol lived in its own world...a private army conducting a private war, free from meddling by higher authority or inane service regulation. The men were made to feel as if they were privileged members of a unique military organization that was harder to *stay* in than to get in. Oddballs were welcome. Misfits were not. Anyone who did not mesh would be RTU'd.

A patrol is a mobile fighting clan...only as strong as its weakest link. And that man was always in peril of being replaced by a better operator. Each patrolman had to constantly demonstrate that he was a top professional and continue to operate at peak performance or his services would no longer be required.

Lt. Col. Randal realized that constant pressure to perform would cause the patrolmen to develop a certain amount of paranoia. And, in his mind, that was not a bad thing. He wanted the men constantly looking over their shoulder.

A perfectionist—some thought a martinet—when it came to patrol tactics, Lt. Col. Randal demanded that every patrolman think and act tactically at all times. Failure to do so would result in being RTU'd.

The Western Desert was not a safe place. It did not forgive mistakes.

Blue Patrol maintained a 25 percent alert at night…one man in four was always awake on guard. There was almost no way that conventional enemy forces, German or Italian, would attack after dark, but nomadic marauders lurked in the desert…sometimes in fairly large bands. RFDS had to remain vigilant.

Anyone who fell asleep on guard duty would be RTU'd.

Blue Patrol was up well before daybreak. Lt. Col. Randal liked to be moving at the crack of dawn. He was a firm believer that distance traveled early was better than time made up by traveling late at the end of the day.

First thing, Lt. Col. Randal set the sundial on the compass bearing Brandy provided…worked out the night before. Next, he read the speedometer. Then he set two watches. His Rolex regulated to standard military Double Daylight Savings Time.

A second watch, the plainest from the gaudy collection liberated from the Iraqi Air Marshal's quarters in the BOQ at RAF Habbaniya, was set to Greenwich Mean Time and then attached to a ring on the jeep's dashboard.

When the sun lightened the sky enough to see, the gun jeeps moved out. Order-of-march was: the command jeep (which in Blue Patrol was also the navigation jeep… normally it would be the second vehicle), Lt. Huxley's jeep containing the Phantom operators, three jeeps under the command of Corporals Smith, Jones and Brown, with the fitter's repair jeep always last.

When traveling in trail formation, the pedestal machine gun men were instructed to check to their rear every few minutes to make sure the jeep behind them had not lost contact with the column. To double-check every half hour, Lt. Huxley dropped back to make sure all patrol vehicles were accounted for. It was easy to get separated in the rough country – some of which was heavy with thick bushes.

Patrolmen quickly learned that things strapped to the outside of their jeeps could be knocked off and lost. At stops, the jeep crews would bring the dropped gear they had found along the way forward to see who it belonged to. After a time, packing the jeeps became an art form and that problem went away.

As the patrol rolled along, Lt. Col. Randal said, "McCloud, how did you end up out of the army in charge of a group of American Volunteers?"

"I was the officer-in-charge of the Airborne Committee at the Infantry School at Ft. Benning, sir," ex-Capt. McCloud said. "Teaching airborne tactics...not that we actually knew anything about 'em.

"We had formed the Test Platoon to conduct experiments with parachute operations. Later, the 501st Parachute Infantry Battalion was authorized. I had recently been penciled in to the next parachute battalion being raised by Major Bill Lee when Jimmy came down and recruited me, sir."

"So, you're a paratrooper?"

"Yes, sir," ex-Capt. McCloud said. "Airborne all the way."

"When I form my patrol," Lt. Col. Randal said, "you'll be part of it...later I'll see about letting you organize one of your own. Not sure what to do about the fact that you and your men are civilians...technically mercenaries."

"Not anymore, sir," ex-Capt. McCloud said. "Major Stone badged us into the Lancelot Lancers."

"Really?"

"The men were not so sure about joining a high-toned private family cavalry regiment," ex-Capt. McCloud said, "until Lady Jane pointed out Zorro's boys were also known as 'Lounge Lizards'...then it was all good with the troops."

Lt. Col. Randal said, "No kidding."

"Colonel, if Lady Jane had suggested they enlist in the FANY's," ex-Capt. McCloud said, "my boys would have said, 'sign me up'."

Lt. Col. Randal said, "I know the feeling."

***

BEFORE BLUE PATROL REACHED THE SOFT SAND of the Great Sand Sea, Lieutenant Colonel John Randal decided to begin running tactical maneuvers. The idea was to let the gun jeep crews practice fighting mock battles. He briefed the tactics on the next halt.

With the patrol gathered around in a semi-circle, Lt. Col. Randal said, "Whenever a jeep moves, it needs to be supported by another gun jeep. Always concentrate on covering each other at all times...constantly checking your fields of fire to ensure they're clear.

"The pedestal gunner passes directions to the driver, so the jeep is always in position to instantly provide covering fire to the vehicle to its immediate front.

"There are two ways for a mounted patrol to travel...by leaps and by bounds."

One of the ex-Foreign Legion men raised his hand. Lieutenant Wescott Huxley translated. "He would like to know what's the diffewence between a leap and a bound, suw."

Lt. Col. Randal tossed five stones out on a smooth patch of sand and knelt down next to them where everyone could see. Taking two of the rocks, he demonstrated. "Working in pairs, a 'leap' is like the game of leapfrogs...one jeep swings around the other, which provides cover with its guns...advances for a short distance and then halts.

"Then, when the lead jeep has taken up a firing position, the second jeep leapfrogs past it. That's what is called 'moving by leaps.'

"It can also work with three or more jeeps," Lt. Col. Randal said, adding a third stone and demonstrating the move again with the rocks.

"Moving by 'bounds' is when one jeep advances while it is being covered by one or more other jeeps...then takes up a firing position," Lt. Col. Randal adjusted the rocks.

"Now at this point, the follow-up jeep or jeeps move forward to join the first jeep while it covers them. Then the first jeep advances again and the movement is repeated. That's called moving by 'bounds'.

"The idea is that there is always at least one stationary machine gun covering any jeep moving forward.

"Is that clear?"

"CLEAR, SIR!"

"Now," Lt. Col. Randal said, "when we have the enemy in sight and are in the full attack mode, we will sometimes be driving hard and fast, shooting up everything in our path. When that happens, you *still* have to constantly be aware of supporting the vehicle to your immediate front, keeping a clear field of fire at all times – as if the patrol was moving by leaps or bounds.

"Is that clear?"

"CLEAR, SIR!"

Drills began immediately.

***

BLUE PATROL HIT THE GREAT SAND SEA. They had to cross it to reach Oasis X…100 miles, more or less. And as Brandy had predicted, the fun began. The crossing sounded like a long way to a group of men who had never attempted anything like it before.

In fact, the idea seemed impossible.

Southwest of the Qattara Depression, standing on a flat, gravelly desert floor, the dunes took on a strange and unusual formation. A single sand dune could run from one to 50 miles in length and be as tall as 200 feet. The sand that made up the dunes was perfectly fine, the consistency of sugar, with straight ridgelines that appeared to be serrated at the top like the edge of a saw. The dunes were only a few hundred feet in depth and very narrow at the top.

The dunes ran on and on like waves, as far as the eye could see. Sometimes they were miles apart, sometimes a few hundred yards apart, and sometimes they actually merged. The soft sand was impenetrable except by specially-outfitted vehicles.

The men of Blue Patrol, new to the desert, looking at the Great Sand Sea for the first time, were overwhelmed by the majesty of the natural obstacle and the absurdity of thinking about attempting to drive across it. Standing at its bottom, a 200-foot tall sand dune, with the fine sand blowing at the top, looked like Mt. Everest. And there were a lot of them – one right after the other.

"Only 100 miles," one of the French Foreign Legionnaires said.

"Hell's bells," said one of the U.S. volunteers in a Texas twang, "might as well be a hundred *million*."

Blue Patrol attacked straightaway. At times when a jeep bogged down— the flat valleys in between the dunes were particularly treacherous, with the sand, being soft and seemingly without bottom—the crew could extricate their jeep by pushing while the driver worked to make it to harder ground.

Standard Operating Procedure was that if a jeep got stuck, the others kept going until they reached firm ground. Then when the patrol was safe, everyone could go back, pitch in and help the crew of the bogged vehicle.

Other places where there were no hard spots for some distance, the 6-foot yellow sand channels strapped to the sides of each jeep were broken out and placed under the wheels, stretching out like a small, perforated steel rail line.

Private Nelson, a transfer from the LRDG, demonstrated their use.

The patrol went one at a time, and as a jeep passed over one of the 6-foot sections of channels, men would grab it up, run to the front of the line and pitch it back down…"channel throwing." The skill was an art as much as a science and the enterprise a team sport. A relay race.

The battle against the Great Sand Sea was on. Men labored, jeeps struggled and the sun beat down. Victory was measured in inches. Time seemed to stand still.

The soft sand in the valleys was the big problem. Hard places were non-existent. The jeeps became bogged unless they stayed on the sand channels.

Drivers inched their way up the slope of the dunes, wheels churning – the ground being firmer the steeper the incline. Four-wheel drive and the light weight of the jeeps gave them the capability to traverse terrain previously impassable…even to the vaunted LRDG.

The trick was to gain speed toward the top of the saw-toothed ridgeline…but it was also the danger. The far side could be a sheer drop-off for 40 to 50 feet. A jeep gaining momentum might zoom over the top, become airborne and crash into the valley.

Pvt. Nelson advised that when the floor of the sand valleys had been negotiated and the assault on the crest was ready to commence, a party of men on foot make their way to the top first. When the jeep driver drove up the slope, gaining speed toward the summit as the ground firmed, it needed to stop before sailing over.

The men were there to help slow the jeep at the peak. Then, man-handling it, roll the vehicle over the top *very* carefully. Sometimes they used ropes or the winch mounted on each vehicle to lower the jeep down.

Blue Patrol took four days to traverse the Great Sand Sea. A snail's pace…Lt. Col. Randal's fault. He conducted a patrol debriefing after every soft patch and ridgeline was conquered.

However, during those four days drivers learned to feel their way in the sand. Channel throwers developed the skill of building a moving hard top on the run. Teamwork was perfected.

And the fear of being in the desert evaporated.

A sense of confidence developed that Blue Patrol could conquer anything… together. Drive out into the vastness and keep going forever. No problem.

Nothing could stop them.

24

X

LIEUTENANT COLONEL JOHN RANDAL was driving the command jeep. Brandy Seaborn was studying her map. King was on the pedestal-mounted twin .303 Vickers K machine guns, and Lana was riding in the jump seat in back.

"We should be coming to the escarpment above X any moment now, John," Brandy said. "I intentionally missed left. When you see the valley, break right. Follow the line of cliffs, and they will lead you straight to the oasis."

"Roger," Lt. Col. Randal said.

Brandy was playing it smart—cheating. It is almost impossible to strike a point-type target by dead reckoning without any terrain features to go by, from a hundred miles out.

The experienced navigator misses on purpose left or right so when they reach the distance they are supposed to travel—a relatively easy calculation—and do not see their target, they know which direction to turn to locate it.

In this case, a slight miss to the right, north of Oasis Xara, would put Blue Patrol out of the narrow sand channel connecting the Great Sand Sea to the Calanscio Sand Sea. They would be lost, driving into another giant, unexplored ocean of sand.

Not to worry—Brandy hit X dead on the money.

"What a magical place," Brandy said, when Blue Patrol drove out of the sand on to the hard limestone above the oasis.

Xara was tucked in tight on the southern side and protected by the saddle connecting the Great Sand Sea to the Calanscio Sand Sea. On the map, the two sand seas drooped down—looking something like the ears of a hound dog—enveloping the oasis on three sides and isolating it from the outside world. It was not an easy place to get to, and there was no real reason to go there, so visitors were rare.

The LRDG base at Kufra Oasis was 200 miles farther on, due south. Siwi Oasis was 125 miles due east, back across the Great Sand Sea. Jaghbub, a small city which contains the tomb of the founder of the Senussi faith and is their Mecca, was eighty miles due north on the far side of the saddle.

The Port of Tobruk, under siege by the Afrika Korps, was a little over 140 miles farther on, due north past Jaghbub. RFDS's area of operations (AO) ran from the port all the way to Tripoli, approximately 750 miles along the Mediterranean coast.

Oasis X was the perfect clandestine base to stage raiding patrols that would operate against the coastal highway—the Via Balbia. Gun jeeps could slip across the sand saddle at its narrowest point, to where the soft sand sea turned back to limestone desert, and in a single day be within striking distance of the coast.

In the movies, an oasis is a small grove of palm trees surrounding an inviting pool. That was what Lt. Col. Randal was expecting as Blue Patrol wound its way down the escarpment out of the Great Sand Sea.

What he found was Xara, a village carved into the side of the limestone cliffs with houses hacked out of solid rock running down the slope to the valley, where an underground river bubbled up from springs in the porous limestone below. Palm trees and other cultivated orchards (primarily dates) grew thick along the course of the river for about a mile before it dived back deep underground. Sparkling pools of water were dotted here and there.

In ancient days, a company of Roman Legionnaires had been posted there. The soldiers had constructed aqueducts to carry water to their barracks and to the private quarters of the officers. They continued to work, though were badly in need of repair.

There was the ruin of a Roman bath. All that remained was the tile-lined pool, still being spring-fed and a pile of rubble.

A Temple of Venus had once been the most prominent structure at the oasis. Now, it was also a ruin. Only a few stones remained.

Xarans were clearly not very good at preventive maintenance.

Brandy said, "Legend has it that Alexander the Great visited to consult the oracle."

Lt. Col. Randal said, "Must have really been desperate for advice."

The company of Legionnaires stationed at X was not recalled home to Rome before it fell. Over time, the abandoned soldiers assimilated into the population. In appearance, the Xarans were olive-skinned, thin individuals with fine, aquiline features.

The children were beautiful but as timid as hares.

The agriculture of the oasis would support 600 people. The population must never exceed that number. When there was a birth, there had to be a death.

How that worked was a mystery.

Most of the higher class of Xarans spoke Arabic, but among themselves they used their own language, which had a curious singsong intonation suggestive of Chinese.

The local religion was Senussi, a fanatical form of Mohammedanism. However, the people were lax in the matters of faith. It was said they had the morals of alley cats.

The Xarans' only allegiance was local. The boundary of the oasis was the outer limit of their world. They did not care who won the war.

The arrival of RFDS was viewed as a business opportunity. And it was a chance to improve the gene pool, the way the Roman Legion had all those many years ago.

Nothing more.

***

THE OASIS WAS BUSTLING when Blue Patrol drove in. Major Jack Merritt had stationed a detachment of his No. 9 Motor Machine Gun Company Raiding Forces Heavy Squadron at X to guard the petroleum, oil and lubrication (POL) he had delivered in the first convoy.

Red and White Patrols were already there. Sergeant Major Mike "March or Die" Mikkalis and Frank Polanski had arrived earlier that morning with an additional four Bantam gun jeeps. They had left after Blue Patrol and reached the oasis before it. Captain A. W. "Sammy" Sansom was onsite, organizing a counterintelligence operation. Mr. Zargo had relocated to X to run his network of intelligence agents. James "Baldie" Taylor had flown in with Squadron Leader Paddy Wilcox.

Captain Taylor Corrigan, RFDS commander, escorted Lieutenant Colonel John Randal to his quarters.

Captain the Lady Jane Seaborn had visited Xara several weeks earlier, bringing a planeload of tea—the favored currency. She had met with the local sheik who ruled the oasis, in order to make arrangements for RFDS. As was typical, she had secured the bluest of the blue chip real estate for Raiding Forces.

RFDS Tactical Operations Center and Lt. Col. Randal's quarters were located at the top of the cliff.

To reach them, it was necessary to wind your way up a narrow street to the top. There, Lt. Col. Randal found a spacious condominium carved out of the face of the rock cliff. Lady Jane had furnished it with piles of oriental carpets and white, gauzy mosquito netting. The bathroom had a tile bath the size of a small swimming pool. The view was spectacular.

Like everything else Lady Jane touched, the accommodations were first-rate, especially considering they were located in the middle of nowhere. Lt. Col. Randal did not plan on spending much time there, but the quarters would be something to look forward to returning home to after an extended combat patrol in the desert.

Lt. Col. Randal walked out of the bath wrapped in a towel, after soaking for a half hour. Lieutenant Mandy Paige breezed in. She was carrying an armload of boxes—presents.

"Where did you come from?"

"Pam and I flew up just now. Roy Kidd is back. He came with us. Lady Jane has been detained in England—personal business."

"How'd you like jumping out of airplanes…Lieutenant Mandy?" Lt. Col. Randal asked, lighting a cigarette with his old U.S. 26th Cavalry Regiment Zippo.

"Lieutenant Mandy?"

"You don't really expect me to call you Lieutenant Paige?"

"No, John," Lt. Mandy laughed. "That *would* be over the top. Loved parachuting. Better than sex!"

"That's more information," Lt. Col. Randal said, "than I needed, Lieutenant."

"Mr. Chatterley sent you brand-new khaki battledress uniforms," Lt. Mandy said. "Time to retire your old jungle fatigues."

Waldo strolled in.

"You need to introduce me to your tailor someday, Colonel," Waldo said, as he admired one of the uniforms Lt. Mandy had draped over the couch. "Lieutenant Huxley tells me no one does a buttonhole like Chatterley's Military Tailors."

"You should know—you've been wearing the uniforms he made me for the last six months," Lt. Col. Randal said. "Take a couple, Mr. Treywick."

King arrived, "I'm on the door, Colonel."

"Try this on," Lt. Col. Randal said, pitching the merc one of the boxes. "We're about the same size."

"Thanks, chief."

"Lady Jane said that is exactly what you would do," Lt. Mandy said, as Lt. Col. Randal retreated into the bathroom to get dressed. She had more of the tailor-made uniforms tucked away in her room.

"In no particular order," Lt. Col. Randal called to Lt. Mandy, "I want a patrol leader's conference—no, make that happen first, next fifteen minutes. Have Captain Corrigan and Lieutenant Huxley sit in.

"We'll meet on the deck.

"I want to see Mr. Zargo, Captain Sansom and Major Adair after that."

"Exactly like Strike Force at RAF Habbaniya," Lt. Mandy said. "Back behind enemy lines, and you are in charge."

"We're not about to be overrun," Lt. Col. Randal said, "and the only thing surrounding us is sand."

"I hear you have been reckless again while I was gone, John," Lt. Mandy said.

"What are you talking about?"

"Lost on a patrol in the desert and MIA in a country we were not at war with, until *you* parachuted in and blew up one of their bridges."

"Wasn't like it sounds," Lt. Col. Randal said.

"That's your story," Lt. Mandy said. "Lady Jane says she discovered a white hair."

Sgt. Maj. Mikkalis walked in as Lt. Mandy was dashing off to organize the meetings.

Lt. Col. Randal came out of the bath in a lightweight khaki uniform cut in the traditional safari jacket military style with large bellows pockets, dark leather buttons and epaulets.

"Thanks for bringing the jeeps, Sar'nt Major. You flying back to RFHQ?"

"Not a chance, sir," Sgt. Maj. Mikkalis said. "You didn't actually believe I was going to stay home and let *you* have all the fun? Mad Dog finally arrived—left him in charge of training."

"I'll take the four jeeps you brought out, plus my command jeep—form a patrol," Lt. Col. Randal said.

"You can be my patrol sergeant."

"Negative," Sgt. Maj. Mikkalis said. "I'm going out with Lt. Huxley, sir—Blue Patrol."

"Really?"

"Give Cpl. Brown a check ride," Sgt. Maj. Mikkalis said. "Performs up to expectations, he can put up sergeant's stripes."

"Brown's fine," Lt. Col. Randal said, "knows his stuff."

Jim Taylor showed up.

"RFDS has been ordered to take the field immediately, Colonel. BATTLEAX is set to commence in forty-eight hours. How long before you can have your patrols ready to move out?"

"We have to rearm and refit," Lt. Col. Randal said. "I need a little time to organize a new patrol. White and Red patrols can pull out later today.

"Blue and the new patrol will be ready to go sunrise tomorrow."

"Outstanding," Jim said. "The Prime Minister has ordered Wavell make a major push—vital to have RFDS out harassing Afrika Korps' lines of communication.

"BATTLEAX is the most significant operation attempted in the Middle East to date. If it fails, Rommel's next stop is Alexandria and then Cairo—nothing in between to slow him down."

"I'm having a patrol leader's meeting in a few minutes," Lt. Col. Randal said. "After it's over, Mr. Zargo will be here to go over the target list he's prepared.

"You might want to sit in, General," Lt. Col. Randal said, "prioritize it for us."

"Nothing I would rather do."

***

LIEUTENANT COLONEL JOHN RANDAL WAS OUT ON THE DECK
UNDER A canvas pavilion with Captain "Geronimo" Joe McKoy, Captain
Lionel Chatterhorn, Captain Taylor Corrigan and Lieutenant Westcott
Huxley.

The patrol leaders were discussing their experiences of the last week. Lt.
Col. Randal was listening to their reports, while at the same time running
through a mental checklist of things that needed to be accomplished in order
to have RFDS ready to take the field.

Time was short and a lot had to be done.

"How'd you like the experience of being a patrol leader?" Lt. Col.
Randal asked Capt. Chatterhorn.

He was considering pulling the security specialist off Red Patrol and
using him to run the counterintelligence operation at X—Lieutenant Fraser
Llewellyn could take his place as patrol leader.

"Enjoyed every minute of it, sir," Capt. Chatterhorn said. "We had a
fairly steep learning curve when the patrol encountered the soft sand, but the
lads picked up on things after a while. The Americans taught us all a lot
about driving.

"Lieutenant Llewellyn and the two volunteers from the LRDG were a
treasure trove of desert lore. Looking forward to going out again."

So much, Lt. Col. Randal decided, for the idea of pulling Capt.
Chatterhorn off patrol duty.

Lieutenant Mandy Paige brought out a tray of drinks. She glanced at Lt.
Huxley. The 10th Lancer had never met Lt. Mandy—he perked up.

"Reach out for Lieutenant Kidd," Lt. Col. Randal said to Lt. Mandy.
"Tell Roy to get here ASAP. Find Travis McCord; have him report at the
same time."

"Right away, John. Anything else?"

"Have Sgt. Maj. Mikkalis draw up a roster of the troops he brought out
with him," Lt. Col. Randal said. "Give it to Roy."

"Yes, sir."

"Captain McKoy, you and Lionel provide Taylor the names of your people to be RTU'd," Lt. Col. Randal said.

"Who are we getting rid of, Huxley?"

"Suw?"

"What men are Blue Patrol going to RTU—if any?"

"Jamison and Wentworth, suw."

"Put 'em on the list."

Of the fifty-four handpicked men who had departed RFHQ en route to X, eight men assigned as patrolmen on Red, White and Blue patrols were being returned to unit for not making the grade.

Major Clive Adair would not be continuing on patrol, as he had other pressing duties at X. Of the straphangers that came out with Blue Patrol, only Captain "Pyro" Percy Stirling and Waldo would be available for the upcoming operation.

Lt. Col. Randal needed to make adjustments to the existing patrol personnel—shuffle men to fill his new patrol. He knew it was not good shaking up patrols at this early stage.

Under the circumstances, he had no other choice.

Raiding Forces Rules for Raiding called for "Right Man, Right Job." Achieving that with men new to desert operations on patrols that had yet to develop cohesion was going to require thought.

"I have been informed," Lt. Col. Randal said, "RFDS has to have all patrols in the field as soon as possible. How quickly can you be prepared to move out?"

Capt. McKoy took his cigar from between his front teeth, "White Patrol can move out in two hours, John."

"You sure, Captain? You can take a little more time if you need it."

"Ammo, water and gas, and we're gone," Capt. McKoy said. "Anybody ain't ready to go gets left."

"Lionel?"

"We can follow Captain McKoy out, sir."

"Westcott," Lt. Col. Randal said, "showtime, stud—you've got Blue Patrol. Be ready to pull out at first light tomorrow."

"Wilco, suw," Lt. Huxley said without the slightest hesitation.

"All of you may be required to give up some of your people," Lt. Col. Randal said, "to round out the new patrol I'll be forming.

"Sorry to have to do that."

"No problem, John," Capt. McKoy said. "You take any of my boys you want."

Capt. Chatterhorn and Lt. Huxley both nodded.

"There won't be time to conduct a formal squadron Operations Order," Lt. Col. Randal said. "Each patrol will issue its own. You'll be provided an assigned AO and a target list and are authorized to carry on as you see fit.

"Operate at night," Lt. Col. Randal said. "Hit and run. Ambush, snipe, mine the roads and shoot up the roadhouses. Surprise, speed, violence of action—then be gone. No pitched firefights.

"Is that clear?"

"CLEAR, SIR!"

"Let's go do it."

***

LIEUTENANT ROY KIDD APPEARED as the meeting of patrol leaders was breaking up. He was armed with his pair of P-08 Lugar pistols, a High-Standard Military Model D .22 with a pouch for a silencer given him by Lieutenant Colonel John Randal, and a nickeled Fairbairn Commando Knife he had been awarded upon graduation from the Commando School at Achnacarry, Scotland.

Lt. Kidd was also wearing parachute wings. He had crammed a lot of tough training into a short amount of time.

"Mr. Treywick," Lt. Col. Randal said, "Meet Lieutenant Kidd—with me at Habbaniya. Served in India, hunted tiger and leopard in his spare time.

When they had a problem with a bad cat, the local officials asked Roy in to deal with it."

"Leopard man, huh," Waldo said. "I always try to avoid 'em myself— once they get a taste for eatin' people.

"Prudent policy," Lt. Kidd said.

Ex-Captain Travis McCloud arrived a few minutes later.

He was showing his U.S. Army Parachutist Wings to Lieutenant Mandy Paige when Lt. Col. John Randal waved for him to join them out on the deck.

"We're going to form another patrol—Violet. Four gun jeeps and my command jeep," Lt. Col. Randal said.

"Roy, you're my assistant patrol leader. Travis, you take one of the jeeps—vehicle commander.

"We need to pick our team, three men per jeep. Travis, you select drivers from your volunteers. I'll drive the command vehicle."

"Roger."

"Here's the Violet Patrol personnel roster that Sgt. Maj. Mikkalis drew up, sir," Lt. Kidd said. "He said one of the jeeps is a Phantom radio jeep, one is a fitter's jeep crewed by three U.S. volunteers, and one carries a Breda 20mm—the gunner's name is Polanski."

"Good man," Lt. Col. Randal said, scanning the list. "Ex-U.S. Marine, a mercenary in Abyssinia before joining Force N, then Raiding Forces. He's been working as RFDS armorer."

The only other names he recognized were Lovat Scouts Lionel Fenwick and Munro Ferguson and Rifleman Ned Pompedous. He handed the list back

"You know the drivers assigned to the other patrols," Lt. Col. Randal said to ex-Capt. McCloud. "If you need to shuffle any of your people around by pulling them off Red, White or Blue Patrols to get the men who work together best, do it now."

"Colonel," ex-Capt. McCloud said, "I don't know the men all that well. We were recruited from different forts and thrown together in a hurry to get out here."

"In that case," Lt. Col. Randal said, "leave the men who drove the jeeps out here in place and pick three U.S. volunteers from the list."

"Yes, sir."

"We've got Frank on the 20mm, Fenwick and Ferguson will take the pedestal-mounted Vickers Ks, King's on the gun on my jeep. Pompedous can take one.

"Waldo, you fill a vehicle commander slot—pick your team. Percy will handle demolitions. GG's coming over from Blue Patrol to do the cooking, and serve as Italian interpreter."

Lt. Kidd said, "Everyone we need, sir, except a navigator and a patrol sergeant."

"Any LRDG transfer," Lt. Col. Randal said, "listed as a navigator?"

"One man," Lt. Kidd said. "Sgt. Maj. Mikkalis has him penciled in for Blue Patrol."

"How are you two men at celestial navigation?" Lt. Col. Randal said, lighting a cigarette.

"I don't even know what that is, sir," Lt. Kidd said.

"Brandy's so good-looking," ex-Capt. McCloud said, "I could never concentrate when she was trying to teach us how—enjoyed watching her shoot the stars, though."

"Had the same trouble," Lt. Col. Randal said. "Navigation's going to be a problem."

25

NEVER KICK A CAMEL CHIP

LIEUTENANT COLONEL JOHN RANDAL WAS STUDYING the TO&E diagram he had drawn of Violet Patrol on a blackboard that was set up on a tripod in the living room of his quarters at Oasis Xara. He was working on filling in the blank slots. Rita and Lana were out on the deck, admiring the view. Lieutenant Mandy Paige was on the field phone that ran to a switchboard in the Operations Center.

Violet Patrol consisted of five gun jeeps. Lt. Col. Randal was going to drive the command jeep. The other jeeps would be driven by the new U.S. volunteers who were, at this stage of the game, an unknown factor—they would have to prove themselves on operations. Waldo, ex-Captain Travis McCloud, and Lieutenant Roy Kidd would command jeeps.

Those assignments had already been decided.

Captain "Pyro" Percy Stirling would also command a jeep, even though he was not slated to be a permanent member of the patrol. He was going to reconstitute the Railroad Wrecking Crew as soon as the jeeps were available.

The rest of Violet Patrol consisted of two American mechanics in the fitter's jeep; Rifleman Ned Pompedous, who had been with Lt. Col. Randal since Swamp Fox Force at Calais; Lovat Scouts Lionel Fenwick and Munro Ferguson, who had been with him since they had been recruited for OPERATION BUZZARD PLUCKER to snipe German pilots in France; the two Phantom operators who had been with 1 Guerrilla Corps (Parachute),

Force N, Headquarters; Private Nelson, who had been badged over from the LRDG; former U.S. Marine Frank Polanski on the 20mm; King; and GG.

Lt. Col. Randal liked the way his patrol was shaping up on paper. With the exception of the seven new Americans, he was going to be surrounded by men he had served with before. Violet did not have a patrol sergeant. Special Forces NCOs were in high demand and short supply.

"Have Rifleman Pompedous report to me," Lt. Col. Randal said.

"Yes, sir," Lt. Mandy said.

"Major Adair," King called.

"Clive," Lt. Col. Randal said, as the Phantom Squadron N commander walked in.

"Your Phantom operators are gradually being integrated into Raiding Forces—pretty soon they'll be indistinguishable from the rest of my people. You OK with that?"

"Absolutely, sir," Major Clive Adair said. "The squadron feels like it was our lucky day when I ran into you in the Long Bar at Shepard's, Colonel."

"In that case," Lt. Col. Randal said, "I'm appointing you Mayor of X."

"Sir!"

"Do what it takes to get this place shipshape. Lady Jane got us to where we are now, but she's away in England and may not be coming back.

"Before she left, Lady Jane advised me that we needed a Political Officer. I'm not sure exactly what they do, but until we find one, you're going to have to be ours."

"No problem, sir," Maj. Adair said. "Phantom officers are trained in the art of fawning high-ranking senior officials—military and civilian.

"That's one of the insidious ways we gain information. Brown-nose the brass and local politicians."

"We don't want the natives restless, Clive," Lt. Col Randal said. "No drums beating in the night."

"Understood, sir."

"Capt. Sansom is here now, setting up a counterintelligence program," Lt. Col. Randal said. "We'll be bringing in a counterintelligence type to handle the operation after he goes back to Cairo, but I want you to be on top of it. Know everything going on here at X—you own the place."

"You can count on it, Colonel."

Lt. Mandy returned to the suite.

"My former aide at RAF Habbaniya," Lt. Col. Randal said. "Mandy's available to work for you when I'm away on operations—very capable."

"Must be," Maj. Adair said, "to be one of Lady Jane's Marine officers."

"She is," Lt. Col. Randal said. "You may have trouble keeping the boys at bay, though."

"What boys?" Lt. Mandy said. "All we have around here are cutthroat killers."

"I'll be having a series of meetings later," Lt. Col. Randal said. "Be a good idea to sit in, Clive."

"Yes, sir."

"Pompedous," King announced as Maj. Adair was leaving, "reporting as ordered, Colonel."

"Rifleman," Lt. Col. Randal said, as the former Swamp Fox Force man marched through the door, "I'm short an NCO in Violet Patrol. Go see Lt. Kidd."

"Sir?"

"Move out—Corporal."

Lieutenant Pamala Plum-Martin arrived, wearing a tailored flight suit, looking as if she had stepped out of the pages of a glossy magazine, as usual.

"Nice place, John—love the view."

"Lady Jane's doings," Lt. Col. Randal said.

"Paddy and Baldie talked the Navy into providing Raiding Forces two Ansons," Lt. Plum-Martin said. "I shall be flying to RAF Habbaniya for twin-engine certification/transition."

Pinned above the parachute wings on Lt. Plum-Martin's flight suit was a type of pilot's wings that Lt. Col. Randal had never seen before. The glamorous Royal Marine was one of the few people in the service authorized to wear both.

"What kind of wings are those, Pam?"

"Auxiliary Transport Service," Lt. Plum-Martin said.

"What...?"

"The RAF refuses to issue wings to women," Lt. Mandy said. "Chauvinists."

"Why not?" Lt. Col. Randal said. "You fly combat missions."

"No provision for female RAF pilots in the King's Regulations," Lt. Plum-Martin said. "Only ATS wings for us girls."

"That's ridiculous," Lt. Col. Randal said.

"No one needs to know what operations I fly," Lt. Plum-Martin said. "Classified."

"I'm not supposed to tell you this, Pam," Lt. Col Randal said.

"Wanted it to be a surprise—you've been awarded the Distinguished Flying Cross with bar."

"*Surprise,*" Lt. Plum-Martin said breathlessly. "I'm thunderstruck, John!"

"Go, Pam," Lt. Mandy said.

"Give your fighter pilot boyfriends something to think about," Lt. Col. Randal said.

"Love you, John," the Vargas Girl-looking Royal Marine said as she hugged him. "You take better care of your troops than anyone."

"Since you brought up the subject of my troops, stay away from Huxley," Lt. Col. Randal ordered. "I need his mind on his business—too young for you anyway."

Lt. Mandy said, "Oooooh!"

"*Ciao,*" Lt. Plum-Martin laughed, planting a red lipstick kiss on Lt. Col. Randal's cheek. "I'm off.

"Keep your eye on John while I'm away flying, Mandy. He needs adult supervision."

King stuck his head in the door as Lt. Mandy was attempting to wipe the lipstick off John's cheek. "Capt. Sansom and Zargo to see you, chief. Maj. Adair is with them."

"Send 'em in."

Jim Taylor arrived at the same time. The men went out on the terrace to the chairs under the canopy.

Lt. Col. Randal signaled Lt. Mandy to join them. Rita and Lana, not wanting to be left out of anything interesting, drifted over to stand behind his chair.

Capt. Sansom went first. "You have a static native population here at X, constant at 600 people. The locals have no loyalty to the Axis or to us, which means you can never trust them.

"On the other hand, treat the people fairly and you have no reason to fear them either.

"That stipulated, Colonel, maintain an aggressive counterintelligence program at all times. Sooner or later, one of the denizens will recognize an opportunity to turn a nice, fat profit selling information to the opposition.

"Human nature—guaranteed."

"Who do we get to run it?" Lt. Col. Randal asked.

"Me, Colonel," Mr. Zargo said, tapping his pipe. "Counterintelligence is my forte. I can continue to direct my network of field agents at the same time—kill two birds with one stone."

"Perfect," Lt. Col. Randal said. "We're in good hands, then."

Squadron Leader Paddy Wilcox arrived, wearing his trademark black eye patch.

Mr. Zargo unrolled a map and laid it out on the table. Everyone moved in to get a better look.

"Based on my original instructions," Mr. Zargo said, "the Area of Operations for RFDS's first mission was broken down into three intelligence gathering sectors. Jim had advised me that he thought three patrols would be all that RFDS would have ready to take the field in time for BATTLEAX.

"Left to right they are as follows: Benghazi east to Derna, approximately 200 miles. Derna east to Tobruk, approximately 100 miles. Tobruk east to Sollum—the farthest point east that Axis forces have penetrated—approximately 100 miles.

"However, because the extreme western sector is twice as large as the other two, I assigned two of my agents, Joker and Queen, to cover it— roughly splitting the sector in half. Jack covers Derna to Tobruk. Ace is responsible for the area from Tobruk to Sollum.

"Now, with four patrols going out, I recommend that you adopt the same boundary between Benghazi and Derna that Joker and Queen use. Assign one patrol to operate east of the line and one to operate west."

Lt. Col. Randal studied the map, "Roger."

"Grid coordinates will be supplied to each of the patrol leaders before they depart X, giving the location where to rendezvous with my agents.

"My men will serve as guides for the duration of the operation. Each of my people will have a target list he has developed over the last few weeks— everything on the list has had eyes-on reconnaissance.

"Colonel Randal instructed me to identify soft targets. He specified that patrols fighting their way to an objective was not an option. With that in mind, we have identified truck parks, fuel dumps, ammunition caches, blockhouse rest stops and other enemy installations, such as small landing grounds and radio relay stations, that depend primarily on their remoteness for security.

"Some targets are completely unguarded.

"Murder, Inc.—as my men have unfairly been characterized on occasion," Mr. Zargo said, "will escort the patrols to the objective."

"True," Lt. Mandy mouthed silently.

"As a consequence of their previous association with Colonel Randal during the siege of RAF Habbaniya," Mr. Zargo said, "my operators are highly anticipating the prospect of working with RFDS."

Jim said, "Enemy motor transport is RFDS's designated primary target—but that's not the case on this patrol, gentlemen.

"This time out, the purpose of the exercise is to strike as many targets as possible in the shortest time possible, with the goal of forcing Rommel to siphon off combat troops from the fighting front to guard static rear-area installations.

"Your mission is to assist BATTLEAX by degrading the enemy units at the point of Desert Forces' attack."

"In that case," Lt. Col. Randal said, "our best bet is to raid isolated Italian installations in hopes that the Germans will be forced to go to their aid."

"I agree," Jim said, "concentrate on the Italians—make them scream."

"We can do that," Lt. Col. Randal said. "We've had practice."

***

LIEUTENANT COLONEL JOHN RANDAL, Lieutenant Mandy Paige, Rita Hayworth and Lana Turner strolled down the narrow winding street to inspect Violet Patrol. Lieutenant Roy Kidd, ex-Captain Travis McCloud and newly-promoted Corporal Ned Pompedous had been organizing the patrol while he was occupied with RFDS's administrative and operational details.

Violet Patrol was stacked heavy with Americans: eleven patrol members were U.S. citizens.

No one had intentionally planned it that way.

Seven of the men had never heard a shot fired in anger. And they did not know their patrol leader, Lt. Col. Randal. Which meant they did not respect him.

King was there ahead of them waiting, wearing an evil smirk. He had a 12x18-inch square of tin nailed to the trunk of a palm tree. Waldo was wearing an expression that looked akin to the cat that ate the canary.

Lt. Kidd called the patrol to fall in.

Lt. Col. Randal had not been expecting this. Without a word, he produced one of his 1911 Colt .38 Supers. Shooting fast, he cracked off ten rounds, ejected the empty magazine, replaced it with a fully charged one, and fired ten more rounds. Waldo walked over to the tree and removed the tin rectangle.

He wandered back and showed it to the troops.

There was a "V" of bullet holes shot square in the middle: V for Violet. A hush fell over the U.S. personnel (everyone else had seen this stunt before). King took the tin and wired it to the front bumper of the command jeep.

The new men watched silently as he worked.

"Patrol briefing at 1600 hours," Lt. Col. Randal said. He did not feel as good as he had earlier. Violet Patrol looked better on paper than it did in person.

On the way back up the cliff, Lt. Mandy said, "Nice pep talk, John."

"I didn't say anything."

"You let your guns do the talking."

***

LIEUTENANT COLONEL JOHN RANDAL, Captain "Geronimo" Joe McKoy and Captain Taylor Corrigan were looking at a map spread out on the hood of White Patrol's command jeep. The patrol was drawn up and prepared to move out as promised—right on time. The men were standing by in their jeeps, ready to go.

White Patrol was easily the best fighting organization in RFDS. Capt. McKoy had carefully selected his officers and men. Each of the gun jeeps was commanded by a former Bimbashi, now promoted to lieutenant, or

Yeomanry (Reserve Cavalry) lieutenant, from his 5 Mule Raiding Battalion, 1 Guerrilla Corps (Parachute), Force N. All the other ranks had come from his battalion, including the two Phantom radio operators. The only men who had not served in Abyssinia with him were the three U.S. volunteers manning the fitter's jeep.

The old Arizona Ranger's troops would follow him over a cliff.

Jim Taylor walked up and stood looking over Lt. Col. Randal's shoulder as he gave Capt. McKoy a last minute frag order.

"Our AO has been broken down into four sectors," Lt. Col. Randal said, tapping the map with the tip of his Fairbairn Commando knife.

"Running left to right, west to east: Ack, Beer, Charlie, Don. Since you're pulling out first, Captain, White Patrol has drawn Ack—the farthest west. Rendezvous with Joker at this location," Lt. Col. Randal pointed with the flat of his double-edged blade.

"We're going to play this the way we did in Abyssinia—raid the Italians to make Rommel send German troops to save 'em. You can hit remote fixed installations during the day, then move down to the Via Balbia and shoot up convoys or blockhouses at night.

"Radio silence for the next three days, then come up on the net and give Capt. Corrigan a situation report. Regularly scheduled sit reps after that. Keep operating as instructed until ordered differently.

"Questions?"

"Commence the fight," Capt. McKoy said, "the minute we reach our AO?"

"Affirmative."

Capt. McKoy stuck his hand up in the air and made a circle. Six Bantam jeeps cranked up in unison. He climbed in his command vehicle, adjusting the binoculars that were dangling on his chest.

"Good hunting, Captain," Lt. Col. Randal said.

"Never kick a camel chip on a hot day, John," Capt. McKoy said, sticking a cigar between his front teeth. "Hasta luego, amigo."

White Patrol snaked its way up the escarpment, crested the top and moved out of sight.

"What do you suppose," Jim said, "the old cowboy's comment about camel dung was supposed to mean?"

"Captain McKoy is of the opinion that RFDS is being rushed into action, General," Lt. Col. Randal said, "before we're trained and ready."

"'Geronimo' Joe is not entirely alone in that line of thinking," Jim said.

"Field Marshal Wavell voiced the same concern to the Prime Minister when he was ordered to conduct BATTLEAX. Wavell worries that his Desert Force is being hurried into an attack that the ground troops are neither organized for nor prepared to conduct, and under new, recently appointed commanders they do not know—like your Desert Squadron."

"Mention camel chips?"

"Metaphorically."

***

CAPTAIN LIONEL CHATTERHORN'S RED PATROL was briefed next. His patrol was stacked almost entirely with personnel picked from his elite Vulnerable Points Wing security personnel, who had parachuted in to Abyssinia to guard 1 Guerrilla Corps (Parachute), Force N Headquarters. They were older men—professionals at securing high-value installations—who lately had been engaged most often in small-scale raiding.

Like Lt. Huxley, he had chosen U.S. volunteers as his jeep drivers because of their driving skills.

Capt. Chatterhorn was a deliberate officer. He planned his missions with care, made sure each of his men knew what was expected of him, rehearsed them to do it and kept his troops under tight control.

"Red Patrol will be operating in Beer Sector," Lt. Col. Randal said as he pointed to the map.

"Captain McKoy will be in Ack sector to your immediate west. Lt. Huxley will be working Charlie sector to your east. Rendezvous with Queen at this location," Lt. Col. Randal tapped the map with the tip of his Fairbairn. He'll provide you target intelligence and serve as your guide.

"Priority goes to out-of-the-way, lightly guarded Italian facilities during the day. Raid the coastal road system area under cover of darkness. You don't have to do big things—damage is as good as destruction on this patrol. Hit and run."

"Understood, sir."

"The idea, Lionel, is to spread alarm and despondency—no prolonged firefights."

Capt. Chatterhorn said, "Cry havoc."

"Roger that," Lt. Col. Randal said, "and plenty of it."

Red Patrol rolled out immediately.

***

LIEUTENANT COLONEL JOHN RANDAL AND LIEUTENANT Westcott Huxley were sitting out on the terrace of his suite. A map of RFDS's AO was spread out on the table. They were going over every detail of Blue Patrol's sector, Charlie, step by step.

Lt. Col. Randal was trying to anticipate every possible contingency.

He enjoyed working with young hard-charging officers. What Lt. Col. Randal did *not* like was sending them on deep penetration operations where no one could come to their aid if they ran into trouble.

This time out, Blue Patrol was going to be entirely on its own. The desert was a dangerous place at the best of times. Throw in the Afrika Korps, the Italian Army, the Luftwaffe, the Regia Aeronautica and the odd marauding band of hostile Arabs, and it was incredibly dangerous.

RFDS patrols departing X would be in survival mode from the moment they crossed the LD. A patrol could roll out and vanish without a trace. Everyone knew that.

"I won't be coming down to inspect your patrol," Lt. Col. Randal said.

There was a reason. Blue Patrol needed to feel Lt. Huxley was in command and that he had Lt. Col. Randal's full confidence. The last thing the new patrol leader needed was for his commander to appear to be looking over his shoulder—worried prior to the mission.

Which he was.

"Tomorrow before Violet pulls out, I'll drop by and wish your troops well."

"Wilco."

"Cavalry officers," Lt. Col. Randal said to the young 10th Lancer, lighting a cigarette with his old battered U.S. 26th Cavalry Regiment Zippo, "are trained to react instantly—instinctively.

"I'm going to give you a piece of advice, Westcott: don't."

"Suw?"

"No matter how bad the situation, no matter how fast events are developing, even if it's all going south, there's always a few seconds to think things through.

"Make a plan, *then* execute the hell out of it."

"Yes, suw," Lt. Huxley said, "I shall wemembew, Colonel."

"You do that."

***

AT 1600 HOURS LIEUTENANT COLONEL JOHN RANDAL issued his Patrol Order to the officers and men of Violet Patrol in their assembly area. The men were drawn up in a semicircle, sitting cross-legged on the ground. Lieutenant Roy Kidd and Captain "Pyro" Percy Stirling held up a map of the AO so that they could see it.

The briefing was a full five-paragraph Patrol Order: Situation, Mission, Execution, Administration & Logistics, and Command & Signal. Lt. Col. Randal took his time. He talked the patrol through everything it would do from the time he finished the order until the time they arrived in the AO and linked up with Ace to begin their operations. The briefing was detailed—however, no one was allowed to take notes.

Violet Patrol could not risk having anyone captured and the mission compromised.

Immediately upon conclusion of the briefing, Violet Patrol climbed in their gun jeeps and drove up on the escarpment. There Lt. Col. Randal put the troops through a series of rehearsals for two hours. Then the patrol returned to X.

Upon arrival back at the oasis, he conducted a detailed inspection of men, equipment and vehicles. Lt. Col. Randal quizzed each man on his job, the job of the other men in his jeep, and specific items of importance that had been covered in the briefing. He was accompanied by ex-Captain Travis McCloud and Waldo Treywick.

When Lt. Col. Randal was finished, he ordered Violet Patrol to fall in around him. "LD time is 0500 hours. Expect to fight when we reach our AO. Be ready."

Then he departed the area.

After he was gone, ex-Capt. McCloud said, "Never saw a Patrol Order, Rehearsal and Final Inspection carried out any better—even at the Infantry School at Ft. Benning where the instructor cadre put on canned demonstrations they rehearse for weeks."

"You new boys ain't seen nothin' yet," Waldo said. "The Colonel operates on a whole 'nother level when he's in immediate proximity of the bad guys."

"Roger that," Lt. Kidd said. "Things are about to get interesting."

***

LIEUTENANT COLONEL RANDAL WAS SITTING OUT ON THE TERRACE, cleaning his pistols by the light of a kerosene lamp. Lieutenant Mandy Paige was at the table with him, sipping a glass of wine. Rita and Lana were leaning over the rail, taking in the view. X was spectacular at night, with candles flickering in the houses down the cliff and torches lining the single winding street.

From time to time, the girls would drift over to the table, then away again.

"Your slave girls rub up against you like cats," Lt. Mandy said.

"They're not my slaves, Mandy," Lt. Col. Randal said. "Besides, the girls work for Lady Jane now—Royal Marines."

"Not what Rita and Lana say," Lt. Mandy said. "Made it quite clear to me they *belong* to you. I am pretty sure there are laws against having slaves."

"Really," Lt. Col. Randal said. "I thought Lady Jane had commandeered 'em."

"Rita and Lana gave her the same story," Mandy said.

"Well, I'm loaning 'em to you, Mandy," Lt. Col. Randal said. "Girls have instructions to never let you out of their sight while I'm gone."

"Excellent, my own private security detail."

"Don't you go anywhere without 'em—that's an order."

"Lady Jane said you make her feel safe," Lt. Mandy said. "You make me feel safe too, John."

"That's nice," Lt. Col. Randal said, racking the slide on his 9mm Browning P-35.

"I met Mallory."

"How'd that go?"

"Movie star looks," Lt. Mandy said. "Easy to see why Lady Jane married him."

"Yeah—that's what I thought too."

26

FOX HUNTING

AT 0400 HOURS, LIEUTENANT COLONEL JOHN RANDAL came out of his bedroom, carrying a small, canvas parachute bag containing his personal items. His 9mm Beretta MAB-38 submachine gun was slung over his shoulder. King had packed the rest of his gear in the command jeep. He found Brandy Seaborn and Lieutenant Penelope Honeycutt-Parker sitting on the couch—kitted up.

"I was hoping to sneak out without having to run into you two," Lt. Col. Randal said.

"No luck, handsome," Brandy said. "Parker and I are reporting for duty."

"Negative," Lt. Col. Randal said. "This is a fighting patrol—not a desert exploration or training mission."

"How would it look," Brandy asked, "to have the patrol named in honor of Lady Jane's favorite color, wandering around lost in the desert?"

"Violet needs a navigator, John," Lt. Honeycutt-Parker said. "Now you have two."

Lt. Col. Randal said, "Not going to happen."

"Are you absolutely firm?" Brandy said.

"Roger that," Lt. Col. Randal said.

The two women gave him looks. He walked out the door. This was no time for debate.

Violet Patrol was drawn up and ready to move out when he arrived.

Jim Taylor was there waiting. "I plan to ride a short distance with you, Colonel. Have a chance to go over some things. One of the Chevrolet trucks will tag along and bring me back.

"Then, I am flying to Cairo."

"Good," Lt. Col. Randal said, stowing his gear in the back of the command jeep. He was clicked on, tuned in to the upcoming patrol, thinking several moves ahead.

On the run across the narrow 100-mile saddle of the Great Sand Sea, he was planning to have each of the vehicle commanders ride with him from time to time. Also, the new men would each get a chance in the passenger seat of the command jeep so that he could spend time with them too. Lt. Col. Randal was not going to waste a moment on the drive to the AO—Violet Patrol was a work in progress.

Training would continue right up until the fighting commenced.

The morning was pitch-dark and cold before sunrise. Lt. Col. Randal walked over to Blue Patrol's assembly area. Captain Taylor Corrigan had been there ahead of him, made his inspection, and already departed the area.

Capt. Corrigan had been diplomatically staying in the background while his boss was at X. He was probably going to be glad to see him long gone, Lt. Col. Randal thought, so that he could get on with the business of organizing RFDS. Hard to blame the Captain—he would have felt the same way.

"Mowning, suw," Lieutenant Westcott Huxley said with a salute.

"Morning," Lt. Col. Randal said. "Let's do a quick walk-around of your patrol, Lieutenant."

Sergeant Major Mike "March or Die" Mikkalis joined the two officers. The three went to each gun jeep. Lt. Col. Randal spoke briefly with the vehicle commanders.

Blue Patrol was stacked with old desert hands. Not only were many of the men veterans of the French Foreign Legion, they had also served in Force

N in Abyssinia in Sgt. Maj. (then acting Captain) Mikkalis' 1st Mule Raiding Battalion, which had operated in the Danakil Depression—an evil place.

The patrol had jelled on the trip out from Cairo. The U.S. volunteers clearly liked the idea of being associated with a group of "crazy mercs." Lt. Col. Randal was confident that the shared experience of combat would forge Blue Patrol into an outstanding operational unit.

When the inspection was complete, Lt. Col. Randal ordered, "Lt. Huxley, take command of your patrol. Follow Violet out.

"Good luck and good hunting."

Immediately upon arriving back at his command jeep, Lt. Col. Randal gave the command, "Saddle up."

Capt. Corrigan was there to see them off.

"I know you want to concentrate on tactical operations, Taylor," Lt. Col. Randal said. "First, you have to get all six patrols out here to X.

"Once that's out of the way, you can get down to business—assessing Mr. Zargo's intelligence reports, selecting targets, planning missions, Command and Control of your patrols—get your operational rhythm going.

"Probably want to take out a patrol or two yourself."

"Yes, sir," Capt. Corrigan said. "I do plan to, Colonel."

No leading from behind in Raiding Forces.

"Capt. Corrigan," Lt. Col. Randal ordered, "take charge of Desert Squadron; don't let anything stand in the way of getting it organized and getting your squadron's patrols ready to take the field."

"Sir!"

Lt. Col. Randal climbed in behind the steering wheel of his command jeep. King was on the twin .303 Vickers K pedestal-mounted machine gun, sitting on the spare tire bolted to the back. Jim Taylor was sitting in the passenger seat.

The sun came up flaming. The sky turned from crimson to gold, then blinding white, as the five jeeps gunned their engines and rolled out up the cliff. The morning went from cold to hot with no in-between.

Jim briefed Lt. Col. Randal on the current state of the military situation theatre-wide as they drove. "Crete surrendered two days ago. The bulk of our forces on the island are now prisoners of war—lost nearly all the Commandos from Layforce."

"I thought we outnumbered the Germans," Lt. Col. Randal said. "How'd that happen?"

"We did outnumber them. General Freyberg is a highly decorated, experienced combat veteran—but this time he got it wrong. Decided to station his troops along the coast to guard against an amphibious invasion, which never came, because the Royal Navy had sunk most of the German troop transports at sea.

"Freyberg did not recognize the strategic significance of the island's airfields—failed to secure them adequately. The Nazis dropped parachutists to seize the strips. Once the landing grounds had been captured, the Germans air-landed a tough mountain division.

"Things quickly spiraled out of control from there. Should never have happened—but it did."

"We're going to have to win one, General," Lt. Col. Randal said, "sometime."

"Not in Greece, not in Crete," Jim said, "and so far, not in Syria."

Lt. Col. Randal said, "EXPORTER was supposed to be a walkover."

"Yes, it was. General de Gaulle promised Prime Minister Churchill that the Vichy French would lay down their arms and rally to his Free 'Fighting' French if we invaded," Jim said.

"Since our side tends to view the Vichy French as Nazi collaborators, we believed him. Our thought was that the French military would see the light, welcome us with open arms and, given the opportunity, join the fight against the Third Reich."

"No?" Lt. Col. Randal said.

"Unfortunately, the French officer corps sees it differently. They believe their duty is to serve France—de Gaulle is a traitor.

"The French hate the Nazis, but England is an ancient enemy. The military have convinced themselves that we ran out on them at Dunkirk. Then we sank their fleet to prevent it from falling into German hands. And now, with the RAF bombing their cities on the Continent, causing civilian casualties, more than a few Frenchmen hate us worse than they do the Nazis."

"See how they might," Lt. Col. Randal said.

"Our troops have found themselves embroiled in a bloody civil war in Syria," Jim said. "If the French had fought as hard against the Germans as they are fighting us now, we would still be in France holding off the evil Nazi hordes at the Maginot Line."

"What impact," Lt. Col. Randal said, "will the Syrian situation have on us?"

"None directly," Jim said. "EXPORTER is a lot like what the Abyssinian Campaign has turned into, with the Duke of Aosta still holding out in a remote mountain redoubt—an insignificant backwater.

"We will prevail, but it will take time—low priority at this point.

"The misfortune is, GHQ has found itself with the bulk of its troops and war materiel frittered away fighting meaningless battles—in Greece, Crete, Abyssinia, Libya and now Syria—that could be put to better use in the Western Desert against the Germans—the real threat."

"Sounds like," Lt. Col. Randal said, "we're attriting ourselves."

"The good news is that the Nazis are too," Jim said. "While you were patrolling out to X, Hitler invaded Russia. That's what I wanted to talk to you about, Colonel."

"Russia?"

"Now we understand why Hitler failed to send in the German Air-Landing troops he had promised the Golden Square to support their revolution in Iraq. The Nazis needed every man they could scrape up for the Russian invasion."

"All I know about Russia," Lt. Col. Randal said, "is: it's big; Napoleon tried to take it; winter set in . . ."

"What else do you need to know?" Jim said. "Hitler has to be insane to launch a two-front war. Only a madman would take such a risk."

"What's it mean, General?"

"Two schools of thought: the naysayers are convinced the Russians will fold up without much of a fight; Hitler will capture all their military hardware and draft the defeated Russian soldiers into his army—making it the most powerful military machine the world has ever seen.

"The optimists say, *now* there's no way the Germans can win this war."

"What camp are you in?" Lt. Col. Randal asked.

"Purely academic, in my opinion," Jim said. "England could go down in flames long before the Russian campaign is ever decided."

"Yeah," Lt. Col. Randal said, "but that operation has to have some impact on us."

"Agreed. My guess is that sooner rather than later, Hitler will come to view Africa as a German backwater," Jim said. "A theatre he can no longer afford to lavish reinforcements on. That's where Raiding Forces fits in the picture.

"With Lend Lease gearing up, the way we win is by attrition. We can replace our losses. Not so the Nazis. Every truck, every armored car, every field piece Desert Squadron can destroy becomes virtually irreplaceable.

"Hit the Desert Fox often and hard, Colonel," Jim said. "Your mission for the foreseeable future is to conduct a steady drumbeat of small-scale pinprick raids against Afrika Korps—drive Rommel crazy.

"Mess with his mind."

"Can do," Lt. Col. Randal said. "Raiding Forces is good at that."

***

LIEUTENANT COLONEL JOHN RANDAL WATCHED the Chevrolet 30-CWT drive back in the direction of Oasis X. When it was out of sight, he strolled back to the tail end of the small Violet Patrol column. When he reached the last jeep, he leaned against the side and lit a cigarette with his hard-used Zippo.

"OK, ladies," Lt. Col. Randal said, "you can come out now."

The three Americans aboard the fitter's jeep were grinning from ear to ear. Brandy and Lieutenant Penelope Honeycutt-Parker threw back the tarp they were hiding under in the back of the jeep.

"Hot under there?"

"How did you know we were here?" Brandy demanded.

"Gave up too easy," Lt. Col. Randal said. "Not your style."

"You noticed," Brandy said. She laughed.

"Now, no one can blame me when you get killed," Lt. Col. Randal said. "I've got witnesses, right, guys?"

"We're shocked, sir," the driver said. "Stowaways."

"Right under the barrels of my Vickers Ks," the machine gunner said.

"Where's your gear?" Lt. Col. Randal said.

"In your command jeep," Lt. Honeycutt-Parker said.

Lt. Col. Randal said, "Noticed that extra rumble seat bolted in the back."

"I drive," Brandy said, "you practice navigation."

***

LIEUTENANT PENELOPE HONEYCUTT-PARKER, whom the Americans had nicknamed "Legs," traded places with ex-Captain Travis McCloud in his jeep. Now he was riding in the jump seat bolted sideways behind the driver's seat in the command jeep. Lieutenant Colonel John Randal, riding shotgun, was carrying on a conversation with him while Brandy drove.

"How do you think your men are settling in?" Lt. Col. Randal asked.

"I'd say we're off to a fast start," ex-Capt. McCloud said. "You made a great first impression, Colonel."

"Really?" Lt. Col. Randal said. "I didn't think it went so well."

"Showed up with Mandy—definite eye candy in everyone's book—and two hot slave girls, didn't say a word, shot the lights out, turned around and left.

"The boys were impressed."

"Rita and Lana aren't my slaves," Lt. Col. Randal said. "Graduated charm school—overdoing the eye shadow."

"Not the story Waldo tells," said ex-Capt. McCloud. "Mr. Treywick has been filling us in on Force N—at least the unclassified parts."

"Really."

"Did you know he was with P. J. Pretorius, sir? Scouted the cruiser *Köenig* up the Rufiji River in the Great War—read about their exploits in junior high school."

"He's mentioned P. J.," Lt. Col. Randal said.

"According to Waldo, you've killed more man-eating lions than any white hunter in Africa," ex-Capt. McCloud said. "Says you're not very good at it, though."

"Mr. Treywick said that?"

"Claims you're not much of a reconnaissance man either—a trail of dead bodies everywhere you go."

Brandy twittered, stifling a laugh.

"McCloud," Lt. Col. Randal said, "tell your men not to believe everything they hear."

***

VIOLET PATROL HIT THE SOFT, WINDBLOWN SAND at the saddle between the two sand seas. The patrol swung out online as dictated by SOP, to make their tracks more difficult to spot from the air. Lieutenant Colonel John Randal called for a halt so the men could dismount to get a last-minute briefing.

Brandy said to the assembled troops, "There are certain driving tricks to remember—always keep to high ground so you can turn downhill when a soft patch comes along. Pick up momentum to get through it.

"Ribbed sand—butter yellow in color—is generally hard and safe. Shining purple patches are usually liquid bogs.

"Never brake hard. If you do, the wheels will dig in.

"When you come to a tall sand dune, go to second gear *early* before the slope begins—then charge it."

"Brandy," Lt. Col. Randal said, after Violet Patrol continued to march, "you never mentioned any of that on the way out. When we get back to X, write it all down—give it to the men."

In the distance appeared a huge dune barrier a mile wide and 300 feet high. Brandy brought the command jeep to a stop.

"Time to let some air out of the tires," Brandy said.

"Why might that be?" Lt. Col. Randal asked, as King hopped out of the jeep to carry out her orders.

"Letting down the pressure gives the tire an inch or two more bearing on the surface of the tread," Brandy said. "We are going to need all we can get."

"I see," Lt. Col. Randal said. "Pass the word to the other jeeps, Travis."

When Violet Patrol had made the adjustment to their tires, Brandy attacked the tallest sand dune.

She floored the jeep in second gear, pointing it straight uphill. A yellow plume of sand shot up, and the front tires lifted off the ground. Rear wheels churning, the jeep was running up to the slope but there was no sensation of movement. Only by looking at the speedometer was it possible to confirm they were moving.

It was one of the wildest rides Lt. Col. Randal had ever experienced—unbelievable. He was afraid the jeep was going to flip over backwards.

When Brandy reached the top, she came off the accelerator and the front end came back down. As soon as the wheels touched the sand, she skidded sideways to a halt right at the side of the precipice, before plunging over.

"For the record, Brandy," Lt. Col. Randal said, peering over the edge of the sheer drop-off, "you're a stud."

"That's a rodge'," Ex-Captain Travis McCloud said.

"Affirmative," King said. "I will ride with you anytime, anywhere, Mrs. Seaborn."

"Why didn't you volunteer how to do this to Blue Patrol on the way out?" Lt. Col. Randal said.

"You had LRDG people," Brandy said. "They were teaching the basics of desert driving," Brandy said. "This is a slightly more advanced technique."

"Slightly..."

The other jeep drivers down at the bottom—drag racers and hotrod men—were watching in amazement, mixed with a healthy dose of apprehension. No one had ever seen anything to match that run.

Lieutenant Penelope "Legs" Honeycutt-Parker explained the procedure to the drivers. It sounded simple enough.

Then, to no small surprise, one after the other they mirrored Brandy's tactics and duplicated the stunt—the men had not been convinced it would actually work when they attempted the climb.

Once over the top, the jeeps labored their way down the far slope secured by ropes. Then the Americans demonstrated that the trip out from Cairo had been well-spent learning how to handle driving in sand. They romped through the desert.

Soft patches were spotted from a distance (an acquired skill) and avoided whenever possible. Only on a rare occasion did a gun jeep become stuck.

When that happened, the crew simply dismounted, lifted up the front of the jeep and set it back down on the yellow, steel-plate sand channels. Then the men did the same with the back wheels.

Four-wheel drive did the rest. Within minutes, the vehicle would be on its way.

Once, when a jeep had all four wheels buried, another crew drove over—being careful to stay on sold ground—walked a steel cable down, hooked up and winched it out. The men seemed to view getting their jeeps out of a problem as an interesting challenge—nothing to be discouraged about.

Lt. Col. Randal was well-pleased. He had not expected this level of driving skill so early in the operation.

Violet Patrol raced across the 100 miles of treacherous soft sand. The whole world was sand—millions and millions of tons of it. Nothing lived there except for the occasional Painted Lady butterfly that flittered by.

The patrol made the crossing in a little over eight hours.

The jeeps pulled out onto the hard, stony limestone surface of the Western Desert. They wound through a landscape that looked like something out of a fairy tale set in hell.

Ten thousand years of nonstop wind, in a region where it never rained, had carved weird features on the faces of the hills and outcroppings of the sandstone rocks.

Everything was bone-dry. Hot. Glaring. Desolate.

The *khamsin* was unrelenting—a hot, dry, sandy wind.

Violet Patrol came back in trail formation on the hard surface and snaked its way through wadis dotted with patches of scrub acacia bushes between the parched hills, twisting and turning, running at speed.

By 1600 hours, the patrol had arrived at a terrain feature called Parrot's Head. It was an extraordinary hill featuring a tiny neck with a big rock balanced on top that looked exactly like—a parrot's head.

Ace was sitting in the shadow of the hill.

He and Lt. Col. Randal immediately held a council of war over a map spread out on the hood of the command jeep. Ex-Capt. McCloud, Captain "Pyro" Percy Stirling, Lieutenant Roy Kidd and Waldo Treywick gathered around. Brandy stayed behind the wheel with her driving gloves off, filing her nails.

There were no terrain features on the map: it was mostly blank except for one contour line around the border. The only markings were Ace's notations indicating enemy positions he had reconnoitered.

"How would you like to take down an Italian munitions dump, Colonel," Ace asked, "to get the ball rolling?"

"Love to," Lt. Col. Randal said.

"There's a cave an hour's march from here, at a small oasis called Zazerbo, where the Eyties have cached a stockpile of land mines," Ace said. "Lot of mines—no guards.

"Make a terrific bang."

"Have you been inside, Ace?" Lt. Col. Randal asked.

"I have, Colonel," Ace said. "It's a massive complex. The main cavern has a series of chambers running off it, a long way back inside. The mines are stacked floor-to- the ceiling, about fifteen to twenty feet high—thousands of them."

"What kind of mines?" Capt. Stirling asked.

"Italians have four basic types in their inventory," Ace said. "B-4 anti-personnel mines, B-2 anti-tank mines, four-igniter mines and Ratchet RR Model railroad mines. All there in one chamber or the other, mostly B-4s and 2s.

"Like I said, the complex is enormous—spooky inside."

"Excellent," Capt. Stirling said. "A *big* bang. You shall not be disappointed, Colonel."

Ace guided Violet Patrol to the tiny oasis, used by the Italian Auto Sahara as a watering point. The place was a foul cluster of run-down mud huts in a small grove of wind-bitten date palms, with a few scrawny hens scratching here and there. A rheumy-eyed Bedouin sitting beside the miserable waterhole watched listlessly as the patrol pulled in.

"I prefer the pristine desert," Brandy said, "with no people polluting the view."

Zazerbo was a place time had forgotten. Heat. Flies. Sand-swept. Ugly. Diseased. Enveloped by deafening silence.

The munitions dump was on the outskirts at the edge of the sand dunes.

"Let's blow it," Lt. Col. Randal said, "then get the hell out of Dodge. I hate this place."

Ace led the way, followed by Capt. Stirling, Lt. Col. Randal, Brandy, Lt. Honeycutt-Parker and Mr. Treywick. They had to stoop down to go through the fissure at the mouth of the cave. Once inside, they found a massive cavern.

By the light of their flashlights, they saw tier upon tier of blue-black mines stacked to the ceiling. There were tens of thousands of them. Hard to imagine the Italians storing so much valuable war material in one place and then walking off and leaving it unguarded. But Lt. Col. Randal knew that the British did the same thing.

"What's the plan, Percy?" Lt. Col. Randal asked.

"A half-pound of 808 plastic high explosive should do the trick, Colonel," Capt. Stirling said. "I plan to use two pounds—half a pound in four different chambers—each with an individual fuse for redundancy. That way, if a fuse burns out, we will not have to come back and reset it."

"Once you light it off," Lt. Col. Randal said, "nobody's coming back here to see how it's going.

"Why don't you use three pounds?"

"Wilco."

Plastic 808 high explosive came packed in quarter-pound packages, wrapped in greaseproof paper. It had the consistency of cookie dough. Back at his jeep, Capt. Stirling only needed a few minutes to roll the toffee-colored explosives together and insert detonators, with the time fuses cut to a length of thirty minutes.

He and Mr. Treywick returned to the cave alone and placed the six rolls of 808 in individual chambers. Then, working from back to front, they lit them off.

When the two men returned, walking fast—the rule for demolitions is no running away from the charges—Violet Patrol drove a half mile away and circled up to watch the show. Then they waited.

And waited.

The dunes erupted in slow motion. The sky blurred. There was a muffled *CRAAAAK*, followed by a jolt that felt like an earthquake. Then smoke and sand billowed out in a thick, massive column climbing skyward, as a colossal, mushroom-shaped cloud formed. No one had ever seen anything like it—the visual impact of the blast was not anywhere near as spectacular as the unexpected fire volcano on OPERATION TOMCAT when the lighthouse blew. No one was taken by surprise or thought that the Nazis had attacked them with a wonder weapon.

But this explosion was even more impressive in its magnitude. The column of smoke kept climbing, miles high in the heavens. And the mushroom cloud kept growing, building on itself.

It seemed to be alive.

Violet Patrol stood, looking up in awe.

Debris in the form of jagged limestone boulders began raining down. Lt. Col. Randal dove under his command jeep. He found himself facing a wide-eyed Brandy Seaborn who had made it in from the far side ahead of him.

Nothing wrong with her survival instincts.

"Did we damage the planet," Brandy asked in a little-girl voice, "...blow up the world?"

"How the hell would I know?" Lt. Col. Randal said, as giant rocks pelted down like hailstones. "Anything's possible when Percy touches one off."

It sounded like the jeeps were being pounded into scrap metal.

"Take that, Rommel," Brandy laughed, as the debris continued to fall.

"I love *Fox* hunting."

27

DEATH OF POMPEII

COLONEL DUDLEY CLARKE AND JAMES "BALDIE" TAYLOR were in conference at A-Force HQ. Jim briefed Col. Clarke on the status of Raiding Forces Desert Squadron. Four patrols were in the field en route to their area of operations to support OPERATION BATTLEAX.

"When Bagnold was ordered to form the Long Range Desert Group, he launched his first patrol from scratch in six weeks," Jim said. "Randal matched his record, but he had the distinct advantage of having you and Lady Jane behind the scenes, paving the way."

"Correct. However, John has the disadvantage of not being a Fellow in the Royal Society for his achievements as a desert explorer," Col. Clarke said, "or, never having written a book entitled *"The Physics of Blown Sand and Desert Dunes*—a real yawner."

There was no love lost between Col. Clarke and Colonel Ralph Bagnold.

"Randal immediately recognized the opportunity presented by Afrika Korps' long line of communications along the Mediterranean Coast," Jim said.

"Not only from the sea, which no one in Middle East Command seems to grasp—but also from the trackless desert that flanks the Via Balbia landside.

"We know Raiding Forces can conduct pinprick amphibious raids—they pioneered the concept. Did extraordinarily well in Abyssinia leading native cavalry. Be interesting to see how they adapt to the desert environment," Col. Clarke said.

"Personally, I expect Randal to advance desert raiding to the next level: 'hitting and running' as he likes to put it."

"Count on it, Dudley," Jim said. "Bear in mind, it could take time."

"When John suggested the idea of small-scale 'guerrilla war from the sea', while we were in hospital having my wound dressed after the first Commando raid," Col. Clarke said, "I recognized that he understood the concept of economy of force in a way few officers do.

"Must be because he grew up in the American West, hearing stories about the Indian Wars, or maybe it was the experience he had in the jungle fighting Huks."

"I have been wondering," Jim asked, "why you had Randal form a Desert Squadron instead of simply increasing the size of the LRDG?

"Raiding Forces could have concentrated on amphibious pinprick raids along the Mediterranean coast—their specialty."

"The LRDG has a strategic reconnaissance mission, Baldie," Col. Clarke said. "Not organized, trained, or mentally geared to continuous raiding.

"Raiding Forces exists to do what its name implies."

While that was true, it was not the whole story. Jim did not have a "Need to Know" everything that Col. Clarke knew, and he did not know what he did not know.

That is how it works.

A closely guarded secret—only Field Marshal Sir Archibald Wavell knew—was the fact that Col. Clarke was using the LRDG as part of a deception. Middle East Command had a need for a lie to cover the truth. Or, in this case, a truth that was not exactly true to cover the truth—which must never be told.

GHQ knew the details of Afrika Korps' supply manifest, down to the last truckload, because of *Ultra* intercepts. This was a secret so precious that it had to be protected at all costs.

The LRDG conducted a Road Watch, monitoring enemy motor transport. The mission was hush-hush, classified "Most Secret, Need to Know." But every visiting dignitary to FM Wavell's headquarters was "privately" briefed on the details of the operation.

Photos of bearded desert operators wearing Arab headgear—sitting in their specially-modified Chevrolet 30-cwt gun trucks prior to a behind-the-lines Road Watch mission— "slipped past the censors" with appalling regularity and appeared in the press.

If the Road Watch was a genuine clandestine operation, none of that would have been happening.

The idea—cooked up by Col. Clarke—was to arrange for word of the LRDG, Wavell's "super-secret, deep-desert penetration reconnaissance unit commanded by the brainiest desert warrior to ever slit a throat," to filter back to the Germans.

That way, the Nazis would have no reason to suspect their Enigma code had been broken—*the most* important secret of the war.

Axis intelligence would believe that long-range reconnaissance operators conducting Road Watch were deep in the Western Desert, hiding behind every bush, spying out the information. And in fact, they were behind a lot of them.

The LRDG had no idea they were part of a deception.

Col. Clarke's A-Force was an organization set up to mystify and mislead the enemy. He was a master of military deception—the best in the business worldwide. Only *he* knew how all the pieces of the "great game" fit together. And he was always planning far into the future.

Creating unconventional military units was his passion. Col. Clarke named them, then helped them organize and train. Then, when they were turned loose to do their mischief, he arranged to maintain control of their operations covertly from the shadows, without anyone being the wiser.

Raiding Forces was one of his favorite creations.

In the case of the Long Range Desert Group, Col. Clarke had not been the creative force behind the unit—he had simply hijacked their mission. When it came to executing his deception plans, he was ruthless.

The commander of A-Force also had a fondness for beautiful women on his staff—called "Dudley's Duchesses." It was said that he collected them. One stuck her head in the door now. "Brigadier Davy on the telly for you, Colonel."

The conversation was brief.

"The Brigadier," Col. Clarke said, when he hung up the phone, "has reports from the Royal Air Force that their aircraft are observing a towering column of smoke arising out of the Libyan desert in the vicinity of these grid coordinates—a major explosion of some sort has occurred."

Jim took the slip of paper where Col. Clarke had jotted the numbers and went to the wall map in the office.

As he was looking at the vastness of the Western Desert, he could not help but think of the RFDS patrols. If they were posted on the map to scale, they would look like fleas.

"Violet Patrol—that's Randal's—has blown up something. Wonder what it was," Jim said, tracing the coordinates with his finger.

"The Oasis at Zazerbo…not a thing there that I know of."

"Whatever it was that you are not aware of must have been titanic," Col. Clarke said. "The RAF describes the smoke pillar as equivalent to what one might imagine at the 'death of Pompeii.'

"Definitely will attract Rommel's attention."

"Exactly what we wanted," Jim said. "Go, Johnny, go!"

***

LIEUTENANT COLONEL JOHN RANDAL surveyed Violet Patrol as the fitters went to work checking for damage. The five gun jeeps looked like wrecks you would find in a junkyard—headlamps shattered, fenders smashed, hoods dented, covered in dust. The exposed drum magazines on the Vickers Ks were all so banged up they had to be replaced.

Falling rocks had struck several of the men before they could reach cover. Fortunately, no one was seriously injured, but everyone was shaken.

The ominous mushroom-shaped cloud dominated the sky. It seemed impossible that they could have caused anything so fantastic. And, a little frightening to know they had.

"Let's roll," Lt. Col. Randal ordered. "We don't want to be hanging around here when someone shows up to investigate what happened."

Violet Patrol limped away from Zazerbo a lot worse for wear than when it drove in; however, there was no major damage.

Ace was riding in the jump seat behind Brandy. "There's a small Italian fort—about platoon strength—twenty-plus men, guarding a landing ground not far from here, Colonel.

"Might be possible to shoot up the airfield without attacking the garrison."

"How far?"

"Approximately fifty miles," Ace said.

"Give me an azimuth," Lt. Col. Randal said. "I'll crank it in the sun compass. Does this place have a name?"

"Fort Number Nine."

The run through the desert to the target was uneventful, but it was a subdued group of RFDS raiders that laagered at the base of an escarpment a mile from the Italian installation Ace had steered them to.

Lt. Col. Randal and Waldo climbed to the top of the limestone cliff to observe the fort. Since he was already familiar with the target, Ace began scratching out a model of the objective on a flat patch of sand so that they could use it to brief Violet Patrol on the plan of attack. The patrolmen cleaned their weapons and checked their personal equipment.

Everyone understood that action was imminent. For the Americans, this was to be their first taste of combat. They were impressed by how matter-of-fact the Raiding Forces veterans were at the prospects—business as usual. The new men did not feel that way. Not one little bit.

They were going to war—unreal.

When Lt. Col. Randal and Waldo reached the top of the ridge, they could see Fort No. 9.

The Italian position consisted of a tiny, walled mud fort surrounded by stunted acacia trees. The structure was two stories tall. A two-acre grove of date palms could be observed in the distance behind the walled structure.

There was a wood frame observation tower on top of the building, making it a total of three stories tall, with a limp Italian flag dangling from the flagpole. The tower was unmanned. The Italians in Fort No. 9 had nothing to fear. The nearest British troops were over 500 miles away.

Or so they thought.

About 400 yards to the left of the fort was the landing ground. A round-top hangar was located on the far side of the strip. The doors were open, and they could make out the silhouettes of three ancient Caproni 309 Ghibli bombers parked inside.

A 10-ton Lancia fuel tanker stood next to the hangar. On a pole, an air direction cone drooped as limp as the Italian flag over the fort. There were two unmanned antiaircraft machine gun positions—the gun barrels pointing to the sky.

A few men could be seen working in and around the hangar.

Lt. Col. Randal was clicked on, very relaxed. He felt the same out-of-body sensation that always occurred, even in training situations, when he laid eyes on the objective—a hypnotic state with a dose of clairvoyance.

In truth, what he was experiencing was a product of his training, experience, knowledge of tactics, the skill level of the troops he commanded, and an understanding of the capabilities of the weapons he had available. However, a bit of magic was in the mix—no amount of military schooling can teach it.

With no conscious thought, the mission played out effortlessly in his mind. The instant he saw the target, Lt. Col. Randal knew exactly what he was going to do and how he was going to go about it.

"Odds don't look real good, Colonel," Waldo said. "We only got fifteen men, plus two women, and there's a whole bunch a' bad guys. Ace says a platoon."

"We'll hit the hangar," Lt. Col. Randal said. "Destroy the bombers, and then see what happens."

"I was afraid you was goin' to say somethin' like that," Waldo said. "That 'see what happens' part is where we generally always get ourselves in some trouble."

"We have the element of surprise," Lt. Col. Randal said. "The Italians won't be expecting trouble."

"I thought the idea was for us to plink us some trucks on the coastal highway," Waldo said, "not be pickin' fights with forted-up Wops."

Lt. Col. Randal studied the enemy position through the Zeiss binoculars he had captured from a senior officer in the 10th Panzer Division at Calais.

"Mr. Treywick," Lt. Col. Randal said, "position your gun jeep and Lt. Kidd's on that little rise over to the far right of the fort, so that Frank can work it over with the Breda 20mm from there.

"Roy's coming with me, so you'll have the two gun jeeps to be in charge of. Ferguson can take the spare tripod-mounted Boys from my jeep and go with you too."

"Give the rest of us fire support when we make our assault. First, we'll take down the airstrip, then the hangar, then the fort.

"You get hit in the head by one a' them fallin' rocks, Colonel?" Waldo said. "You're plannin' to attack a fortified enemy position that knows you're a-comin'? Goin' across open ground with nine men?"

"Well, three of 'em will have to stay with the jeeps," Lt. Col. said, "so it'll be six. I'm only planning on using half of those for the final assault."

"Are you *crazy*?" Waldo said. "We're a long way from serious medical attention—anybody gets themselves nicked, they're in some real trouble."

"I'm counting on you to not let the Italians shoot at us, Mr. Treywick," Lt. Col. Randal said.

"Make sure they don't."

***

VIOLET PATROL WAS GATHERED in a semicircle around the sand table of the Italian installation Ace had constructed on the ground.

"SITUATION," Lieutenant Colonel John Randal said, holding a rifle cleaning rod to use as a pointer.

"The bad guys, in approximately platoon strength, are located in a small fort called Number Nine a mile over the escarpment to my immediate rear. There's a Regia Aeronautica landing ground next to it, with a hangar containing three Caproni Ghibli bombers inside. A Lancia fuel transporter is parked by the hangar."

"MISSION: Violet Patrol will assault the landing ground with three gun jeeps to destroy the hangar containing the enemy aircraft.

"EXECUTION: Mr. Treywick, with Lt. Kidd's jeep attached, will be in command of a two-vehicle fire support element and will take up positions here..." Lt. Col. Randal pointed to the sand table terrain map with the tip of the rod.

"Lovat Scouts Fenwick and Ferguson, armed with our two Boys .55 long range sniper rifles, will also be attached. Mrs. Seaborn will drive Mr. Treywick's jeep.

"Lt. Honeycutt-Parker will drive the twenty millimeter Breda gun jeep. Mr. Treywick's element will provide supporting fire to cover the assault on the airstrip.

"I'll lead the three remaining gun jeeps—the assault element with Lt. Kidd driving the command jeep down this road—and attack the airstrip from south to north.

"Capt. Stirling will be responsible for securing the fuel tanker parked next to the hangar.

"CONCEPT OF THE OPERATION: Violet Patrol will destroy the hangar and the three enemy aircraft inside.

"Capt. Stirling, after you secure the fuel tanker, move it to the hangar. Capt. McCloud, you will designate a driver to operate the Lancia for Capt. Stirling. Pump aviation fuel on the wooden structure, and on my command, light it off and burn it.

"At that point, stand by, prepared to develop the situation.

"Under no circumstances is anyone to fire on the fuel tanker at any time, regardless of the situation—is that clear?"

"CLEAR, SIR!" Violet Patrol chorused.

"COMMAND AND SIGNAL: The fire support element will engage the airstrip as soon as it arrives in position. When it commences firing, that's the signal for the three gun jeeps of Violet Patrol under my command to drive down the road to the airstrip. When the assault element reaches the runway, the fire support element will shift their fires to the fort.

"Mr. Treywick, in the event that the Italians in the fort attempt to interfere with Violet Patrol at the airstrip, be prepared to shift some of your fires to Fort Number Nine earlier.

"A green flare will be the signal to cease fire.

"ORDER OF MARCH: Command jeep, Capt. McCloud, followed by Capt. Stirling.

"What are your questions?"

There were no questions.

"In that case," Lt. Col. Randal said. "We're moving out in zero five."

***

BEFORE VIOLET PATROL CRANKED UP, LIEUTENANT COLONEL JOHN Randal had a brief conversation with Captain "Pyro" Percy Stirling.

28

DEVELOPING THE SITUATION

LIEUTENANT COLONEL JOHN RANDAL SAT in his command jeep, under the lip of the ridge. He was ready to lead his three-gun-jeep element to attack the Italian Landing Ground as soon as Mr. Treywick had his two-gun-jeep support element in place and had commenced firing.

King had cleaned Lt. Col. Randal's twin Vickers K.303 machine guns while he had been on his reconnaissance of the target. The machine guns would be his primary weapon on the initial assault. They were originally RAF air-to-air weapons modified for use on the gun jeeps.

The Vickers Ks produced a high volume of fire—so fast that it was not possible to distinguish individual rounds.

On the floorboard of the jeep, between his boots, was a pack containing forty 45mm rounds for his improvised Brixia shoulder-fired mortar. The stubby little sawed-off-shotgun-looking weapon was riding between his knees.

Strapped to the outside of the jeep, within easy reach, was a leather weapons case containing the exposed butt of his 9mm Beretta MAB-38 submachine gun.

"When I step out of the jeep at the airfield," Lt. Col. Randal said to Ace, "you move up and take over the Vickers Ks."

"My pleasure, Colonel."

***

WALDO TREYWICK SAID, "ANYTIME, MRS. SEABORN."

"Hang on, boys," Brandy said. She popped the clutch and the jeep roared over the top, out onto a faint hardscrabble road that led to the position where Lieutenant Colonel John Randal had indicated the support element should set up. Following close behind, with Lieutenant Penelope "Legs" Honeycutt-Parker at the wheel, was the gun jeep carrying ex-U.S. Marine Frank Polanski on the 20mm Breda.

"What is that?" Brandy asked, as the jeep skidded sideways into the first turn.

Up ahead, looking frantically over his shoulder and pedaling like mad, was an Italian on a bicycle. He was carrying a large, canvas satchel over his shoulder.

"Could be a postman," Waldo said. "Bring me alongside him, Mrs. Seaborn."

Bellowing limestone dust, the jeep quickly overtook the bicyclist. Waldo leaned out and butt-stroked the rider on the side of the head with his brand-new, best-grade Rigby magazine rifle—one of the first purchases with his newfound wealth. The Rigby seven-five-seven was a rifle he had fancied for years but could never afford.

The result was a spectacular pile-up.

"We'll get that satchel later," Waldo shouted over his shoulder as they raced past. "Ferguson—that's on you."

"Yes sir, Mr. Treywick."

Brandy turned off the road and headed toward the small rise that was the support element's assigned position to establish its base of fire. She pulled up on it and pointed the nose of her jeep directly at the Italian fort 300 yards away. That way, all the weapons mounted on the jeep—four Vickers Ks and the Boys .55 on the pedestal—could be brought to bear on target.

Ferguson bailed out of the jeep, set up the Omnibus General Purpose Tripod on the ground, mounted the spare scoped Boys .55, then settled into a cross-legged firing position, scoping for a target.

Lt. Honeycutt-Parker drove up beside.

Waldo shouted, "Fire 'em up, Frank."

The 20mm Breda opened immediately: *ponka ponka ponka.*

"Ain't no sense sittin' around waitin' for somebody to man 'em antiaircraft guns on the airfield and shoot at us," Waldo said to the Lovat Scout behind him on the pedestal-mounted Boys .55 sniper rifle.

"Take 'em out at the breech, Munro."

The Scout swung the scoped Boys .55 rifle mounted on the pedestal over to the airstrip and fired twice. Big solid steel slugs the size of cigars smacked into the two antiaircraft machine guns. They no longer posed a threat.

Inside the fort, the Italian soldiers were over the back wall at the first rattle of machine-gun fire, legging it for the date palm grove.

***

"LET'S GO, ROY," LIEUTENANT COLONEL JOHN RANDAL said when the support element engaged.

He had a thin cigar clinched between his front teeth.

"When we hit the airstrip, try to keep the hangar between us and the fort as much as possible."

The three-jeep assault element of Violet Patrol barreled over the top of the escarpment and headed straight for the west end of the landing ground— the farthest point away from the Italian fort. Lt. Col. Randal intended to roll the airfield up from left to right.

The nine machine guns of the support element were putting out a tremendous volume of fire, as much as a normal infantry battalion. Tracers vectored in on the fort—some glancing off and shooting sky-high. The Boys .55s were booming.

"King," Lt. Col. Randal said, when they were halfway to the target.

The merc, standing behind him on the pedestal-mounted Vickers Ks, commenced fire.

Lt. Col. Randal opened on the hangars with his pair of Vickers Ks. Lieutenant Roy Kidd had been instructed not to fire his guns until the command jeep reached the airstrip. His job was to concentrate on driving.

Behind the command jeep, the other two gun jeeps opened on the hangar area as their weapons came to bear.

When the range closed to 300 yards, Lt. Col. Randal brought up his shoulder-mounted Brixia M-35 and popped a round in the direction of the aircraft hangar, being careful to aim clear of the 10-ton Lancia fuel truck. He managed to reload and fire off a second round before the first one detonated.

Neither 45mm mortar shell hit the building, but the twin explosions had to give the defenders something to think about. There was no return fire. In fact, the Italians who had been working at the airfield seemed to have disappeared.

Lt. Kidd came racing up the airstrip with the two jeeps behind him in echelon, all guns blazing. Lt. Col. Randal blooped a .45mm round through the open doors of the hangar and got a resounding *KAAAABLAAAM*!

He could not determine the result.

The patrol roared up to the arch-roofed building. Captain "Pyro" Percy Stirling and ex-Captain Travis McCloud hopped out of their jeeps and ran to the fuel tanker. Ex-Capt. McCloud had designated himself to drive it.

Lt. Col. Randal grabbed his 9mm Beretta MAB-38 submachine gun and jumped out of the command jeep. He entered the hangar with the weapon at his shoulder. There was no one inside the building.

He ran back outside.

"Get these two jeeps up the strip," Lt. Col. Randal ordered, indicating his and ex-Capt. McCloud's vehicles.

"Fire up the fort.

"Roy, detail someone to help you search the hangar for anything of intelligence value."

"Ace," Lt. Kidd said, hopping out of the jeep, "you're on me."

The fuel tanker cranked to life. Ex-Capt. McCloud drove it up to the front of the hangar. Capt. Stirling was around back of the tanker.

This should have been a particularly vulnerable moment in the raid—only no one was shooting at them.

Lt. Kidd came out of the hangar carrying an armful of 9mm Beretta M-1918/30 submachine guns; he had several pistol belts slung over his shoulder. The Regia Aeronautica pilots had left them in the cockpits of their aircraft.

"Ace is bringing out a cardboard box of papers," Lt. Kidd said. "Not much else to be found, sir."

The fuel tanker pulled up, and Capt. Stirling brought the hose to the door of the hangar.

"Clear the area," Lt. Col. Randal commanded. "Soak it down, Percy."

"There's a stack of 100-pound fragmentation bombs on a pallet behind the hangar, sir," Capt. Stirling said as he began pumping high-octane aviation fuel inside the hangar. "Want me to blow them?"

"Have you got that other thing we talked about worked out?"

"Yes, sir," Capt. Stirling said.

"Put a charge with a ninety-second fuse on the pallet," Lt. Col. Randal said. "Order one of your people to be ready to ignite the fuse on my command—have your jeep standing by to pick him up.

"Is that clear?"

"Clear, sir!"

"When the fuse on the bomb is lit," Lt. Col. Randal said, "the fuel tanker needs to be ready to roll."

"Yes, sir."

After the floor of the hangar was doused in fuel, Lt. Col. Randal took out the Very pistol he had retrieved from his command jeep and plopped a flare round in the chamber. Then, from what he hoped was a safe distance, he fired it inside the open hangar doors. The flare glanced off the ground and ricocheted around inside.

WHOOOOOOOF. The building was engulfed in flames. The three obsolete Caproni 309 Ghibli bombers inside caught fire. Soon the rounds in their machine guns began cooking off, sounding like popcorn.

"McCloud, you driving the fuel tanker?" Lt. Col. Randal asked.

"Roger that, sir."

"Had much experience with big rigs?"

"Used to haul cattle for my father out of our ranch in northern New Mexico, sir, growing up."

"Saddle up, Percy," Lt. Col. Randal ordered. "Let's do this."

The Lancia's cab was a ragtop with only a pair of canvas safety straps for doors.

"Let's get this top off—don't bother snapping your strap," Lt. Col. Randal said, as he and ex-Capt. McCloud climbed up on the bench seat.

"We're not going far."

"You want to let me in on what we're doing, Colonel?"

"Light it off, Percy," Lt. Col. Randal ordered. "Bombs away."

"EXECUTE, EXECUTE, EXECUTE," Capt. Stirling yelled from where he was standing on the rear bumper of the tanker.

A jeep came tearing around the corner of the flaming hangar on two wheels. The men in it were hanging on to their grips of their Vickers Ks, blazing away at the fort as they drove past the fuel tanker.

"FIRE IN THE HOLE!"

"In about a minute, the pile of bombs behind the hangar is going to go up," Lt. Col. Randal said to ex-Capt. McCloud. He lit the cigar between his teeth with his beat-up, old U.S. 26th Cavalry Regiment Zippo.

"Colonel," ex-Capt. McCloud said, "we're sitting in a ten-ton fuel tanker that's almost completely full of highly-flammable liquid, and you're smoking a cigar…"

"There's a land mine strapped to the ass end of this truck," Lt. Col. Randal said. "Percy's got a five-second fuse igniter attached to it, but he's never been very precise with explosives.

"The plan is, Travis—you drive straight at the fort. When I give the word, 'Pyro' is going to pop the igniter; then we'll all bail out on the roll. Try to hit the gate."

"You're joking, aren't you, Colonel?"

"We're under thirty seconds," Lt. Col. Randal said, glancing at the lime green hands of his Rolex, "on those pallets of hundred-pounders going up.

"Better get a move on, McCloud."

***

BRANDY SEABORN WAS FIRING her pair of Vickers K machine guns at the fort in crisp, professional bursts of six. A hailstorm of suppressive fire was converging on the mud building, riddling the walls, pockmarking the visible parts of the upper structure. Mud chips were flying off.

There were ten machine guns in action mounted on the two gun-jeep support element, with sixteen more on the three assault element gun jeeps, all firing at the east end of the landing ground. Considering a standard line infantry rifle battalion had nine machine guns in its table of organization, Violet Patrol packed a massive amount of firepower.

And it was tightly concentrated.

"What is John doing?" Brandy called to Waldo Treywick, who was busy operating the pair of Vickers Ks in the passenger seat next to her. She had seen Lieutenant Colonel John Randal and ex-Captain Travis McCloud ripping the canvas top off the Lancia, then watched the 10-ton fuel tanker slowly pick up speed as it started to drive toward the fort.

"Developin' the situation," Waldo shouted back.

"If he develops it much more," Brandy said, "the three of them shall all be blown to smithereens."

At the wheel of the Lancia, ex-Capt. McCloud was having the exact same thought.

"You were an instructor at the Infantry School," Lt. Col. Randal said in a conversational tone, as the big tanker rumbled toward the Italian fort. "Know the different ways to detonate a landmine?"

Ex-Capt. McCloud glanced sideways to see if Lt. Col. Randal had gone off his rocker. Negative; cool as a cucumber.

Up ahead, a hailstorm of machine gun bullets was ripping into the fort.

"Electrical charge—remotely, you can rig a trip wire, or a time fuse like Capt. Stirling has in place back there, but the most common method is a pressure plate, sir."

"There's a pressure plate wired to our front bumper," Lt. Col. Randal said. "That's the primary detonator—the time fuse in the back is for redundancy.

"Make sure you don't bang into anything, Travis."

"Roger that, sir!"

Luckily there was nothing to run into—it was perfectly flat all the way to the fort. The distance was narrowing now at a good clip. Still, driving along in a 10-ton bomb was not for the faint-hearted.

One single incendiary round could send it up.

"Let me know," Lt. Col. Randal said, "when you have the wheels running true and think they'll hold."

Ex-Capt. McCloud took his hands off the steering wheel. The big heavy truck was rumbling along, steady. They were inside 200 yards and closing.

Lt. Col. Randal opened with his Brixia 45mm shoulder-fired mortar. The rounds arched toward the fort. He had three in the air before the first one exploded.

"Anytime, sir," ex-Capt. McCloud said. "We're good."

Lt. Col. Randal fired off two more rounds. The 45mm shells detonated with hollow *CRRRUUUUPHs*. The fort began to grow in size as the truck approached.

They were down to under a hundred yards.

"Light it off, Percy," Lt. Col. Randal shouted. "Time to go."

"FIRE IN THE HOLE!"

All three officers bailed off the rolling tanker. Being paratroopers, each instinctively performed a PLF—an ingrained habit executed by pure muscle memory from a million practice parachute landing falls.

Lt. Col. Randal landed on the right side of the road. Capt. Stirling and ex-Capt. McCloud ended up on the left.

"So, what's it like," ex-Capt. McCloud said, as the two rolled into the prone position beside the road, watching the fuel tanker continue on its way toward the fort. "Being a 'Death or Glory Boy'?"

"Spend an extraordinary amount of time," Capt. Stirling said, "scared out of one's bloody wits."

KAAAAAAABOOOOOM! The fragmentation bombs behind the burning hangar detonated—extremely loudly. The ground shook from the sharp explosion, and a shock wave rolled over them.

The Lancia rumbled toward the fort, straight at the gate. At the last second, it veered left and slammed into the wall.

Detonation was instantaneous. The blast was substantially softer than the fragmentation bombs going up, but the result was spectacular. The momentum of the truck sloshed the fuel in the tank forward when it impacted the wall.

The land mine strapped to the back of the tanker blew when the pressure plate on the front bumper made contact, the tank was ruptured, and the highly flammable fuel propelled up and out over the wall toward the Italian fort— nearly ten tons of it, on fire.

The front of the two-story building, and the observation tower on top, was engulfed in flaming aircraft fuel. The noxious smell was almost overpowering, even from a distance.

A white flag, a pillowcase tied to a broomstick, came out a window, but it caught fire.

The battle of Fort No. 9 was over.

The engagement had been almost bloodless. No one killed on either side.

The only combatant known to be physically wounded was ex-Capt. McCloud. Struck above his left eye by a tiny piece of shrapnel. The injury was not serious, but he was covered in blood—minor head wounds tend to be melodramatic.

As Lt. Penelope "Legs" Honeycutt-Parker was putting three stitches in the cut, Brandy said, "I will not hold your hand, Travis."

"I could be dying," ex-Capt. McCloud said.

"You merely look as if you are," Brandy giggled. "Now you will have a pretty scar to impress the girls."

Waldo said, "You ain't supposed to pull the pin on a grenade, throw it, then stick your head up to watch to see what happens, Cap'n—much less a bomb the size of a locomotive. You're lucky you didn't get your head blowed clean off.

"Didn't they teach you that at that big army school you worked at?"

"And I thought all along," ex-Capt. McCloud said, "that *Jump on Bela* was fiction."

"It was," Lt. Col. Randal said, "most of it."

"Maybe so, sir," ex-Capt. McCloud said. "Except, charging an enemy garrison in a ten-ton high-octane bomb—crazier than anything in your book.

"I don't believe we did it..."

"In case you're feelin' a little disorientated," Waldo said, "you've got yourself a head wound there, Travis.

"Colonel Randal here—he don't have no excuse."

***

THE BURNING FUEL PLASTERED on the mud fort quickly flamed out. But all the wooden trimmings, doors, window jams. etc. were flickering. On the roof, the observation tower was burning. The building was pockmarked with bullet holes—thousands of them.

The only Italians remaining inside were the commandant and his semi-hysterical mistress. All the enemy troops were ensconced in the date palm grove out back.

That was fine. They were harmless. Violet Patrol did not have room for—or an inclination to deal with—prisoners. Lieutenant Colonel John Randal blooped three 45mm rounds from his Brixia into the trees to let the soldiers hiding there know they had not been forgotten.

GG interviewed the Lieutenant, a plump Regia Aeronautica officer with a striking likeness to a young Mussolini. The man was distraught because he could not locate his gold braid-encrusted uniform hat. The Italian was not able to provide much information for the simple reason that he did not know anything of military value, isolated as he was out in the middle of nowhere.

The commandant of Fort No. 9 was not having a good day—one minute safe, 500 miles from the nearest known British position; the next minute, the fort he commanded was hammered by machine-gun fire, then slammed by a tidal wave of burning aviation fuel. His troops had deserted.

Scout Ferguson walked up, carrying the canvas satchel recovered from the bicycle rider, which did, in fact, turn out to be the mail. The bag might contain something of intelligence value. GG and Captain "Pyro" Percy Stirling, also fluent in Italian since he had been raised by an Italian nanny, could peruse the contents later.

Ace and King conducted a search of the premises. Lieutenant Roy Kidd, ever with an eye for weapons, confiscated the Italian officer's sidearm—a 9mm Beretta M-1923.

Not much else of interest was found.

"Pile up all the furniture in the rooms, then set the place on fire," Lt. Col. Randal ordered. "Turn the Lieutenant and his girlfriend loose as soon as we pull out.

"We're moving in ten minutes, people. Time to get the hell out of Dodge."

***

WHEN VIOLET PATROL DROVE OUT OF FORT NO. 9, the Americans were no longer "the new U.S. volunteers" or the "Yan*ks*." Now they were Pete, Joe and Harry—combat veterans.

29

KEYSTONE COPS

BRITISH ARMY MAPS OF THE WESTERN DESERT were divided into three classes that had once been described by Captain "Geronimo" Joe McKoy as "the good, the bad, and the ugly".

A small portion of the desert was well-mapped. A lot was poorly mapped. Some was mapped with nothing on the maps. And for other areas, no maps existed at all.

Captured Italian maps were pure fiction in part… as if drawn by crystal ball readers or possibly psychics.

The advantage that Raiding Forces Desert Squadron had, over even the Long Range Desert Group, was Mr. Zargo's intelligence network. The RFDS patrols had hard targets and reliable guides to lead them to their objectives. The combination of accurate intelligence and hit-and-run tactics, aggressively carried out by determined men who were highly mobile and heavily armed, was proving deadly.

Violet Patrol had been traversing the sand sea and fighting for 12 hours. Now in the evening, the desert sands were cooling quickly and the dunes casting long shadows. The troops needed to take a break, regroup, pull vehicle maintenance and clean their weapons. Ace led the jeeps to a wadi, where the patrol could laager for the evening meal and work out plans for the rest of the night's entertainment.

Lieutenant Colonel John Randal was beginning to develop a feel for the terrain, gain confidence in his ability to operate in a new, unfamiliar environment and get into the rhythm of desert patrolling. So far, results were better than anticipated.

He intended to keep up the tempo.

Violet Patrol was to continue operating through the night. The idea was to keep on until Ace ran out of targets…working under cover of darkness from now on. As soon as the sun came up, the Regna Aeronautica – and possibly the Luftwaffe – would be out in force looking for them.

The patrol would need to lay up under camouflage netting as much as possible while it was light.

Raiding Forces did not have to engage in big battles to be successful. RFDS patrols only had to appear out of nowhere, catch the enemy unaware, cause material damage and disappear. Then do it again at some other distant location.

A principal of guerrilla warfare, Lt. Col. Randal had learned long ago in operating against the Huks, is that at times it is just as effective to worry the enemy as it is to kill him…this was one of those times.

In an Area of Operations (AO) where it almost never rains, there are none of the restrictive topographical features found in a combat zone with normal climate…streams, lakes, forests, river valleys, etc. Or, any of the man-made structures like permanent villages, road networks, or canals, to channelize a traveler. The result of thousands of years of minimal rainfall had been to produce a barren, lunar landscape that allowed Violet Patrol's jeeps to strike out in virtually any direction at will – restricted only to a small degree by sheer escarpments or soft sand seas.

The Western Desert was a logistician's hell and a raider's paradise.

Lt. Col. Randal had thought that this might be so from studying the available maps, as bad as they were. The idea that the desert could turn out be a better theatre for guerrilla operations than the jungles of the Philippines or the mountains of Abyssinia had never occurred to him.

Now he realized that was going to be the case...the possibilities were unlimited.

***

ACE HAD TWO MORE TARGETS NEAR ENOUGH for Violet Patrol to raid that night. The first was a small fuel pumping station set up on one of the numerous dirt tracks that paralleled the hardball Via Balbia. It was located approximately 20 miles from the wadi.

A squad of Italian rear echelon support troops staffed the petrol station.

The other target was an aerial bomb cache located at a Regia Aeronautica emergency landing ground...LG 23, approximately 10 miles from the wadi. There were an estimated three to four hundred 100-pound bombs in the dump. In addition, a small amount of aviation fuel was stored at the site.

The landing ground was not guarded.

Both targets could be described as 'soft.'

Ace briefed Lieutenant Colonel John Randal. When he was finished, an officer's call was held. Waldo Treywick and Brandy Seaborn sat in.

"We have two objectives for tonight, a landing ground and a gas station," Lt. Col. Randal said. "Ace and I will escort Captain Stirling to LG 23 to blow the bomb dump located there. It's a small target and may be hard to find. Percy, swap out your jeep for the Phantom jeep tonight.

"Brandy, you travel with us to navigate."

Lt. Col. Randal was immediately rewarded with a beautiful, white-toothed smile.

"Love to."

"Travis...if you have recovered sufficiently, take the other three jeeps and attack the gas station. Parker, you go with McCloud as his navigator."

"Yes, sir," ex-Captain Travis McCloud said. "I'm fine."

"Here is where it's going to get a little tricky," Lt. Col. Randal said. "After you take down the refueling station, Travis...I want you to set up an ambush somewhere along the track, at a location of your own choosing. Ace says that the Italian trucks on the dirt tracts are traveling in ones and twos…no big convoys.

"Take GG along; we could use a prisoner who can provide us current information on enemy convoy procedures."

"Roger, sir."

"Now, your ambush will be conducted in broad daylight. Enemy air is going to be out looking for Violet Patrol at first light but the one place they will not be looking is *on* the Via Balbia road network."

"That's brilliant, Colonel," ex-Capt. McCloud said.

"We'll see," Lt. Col. Randal said.

"Mr. Treywick, after Travis executes his road ambush, I want you to take your jeep and break off with Fenwick and Ferguson. Set up the two Boys .55s somewhere else along the tract, at a point or points of your own choosing.

"Plink trucks or other thin-skinned vehicles, maximum effective range…you know the drill."

"Real long distance…'bout a mile," Waldo said. "We ain't gettin' close to *our* work. Not out here."

"Travis, you bring the remaining two jeeps back to the wadi. My element will have a patrol base established here," Lt. Col. Randal said. "In the event of an air attack on the return trip, go to ground and initiate standard operating camouflage procedures…link up after dark.

"Mr. Treywick, we won't expect you until tomorrow night. I'll put up a green flare every half hour after 2400 hours if you're not back by then."

"Brandy, you and Parker coordinate with Ace to plan the routes.

"Questions…?" Lt. Col. Randal said. "Travis, take charge of your element; move out when ready.

"OK, let's do this."

***

LIEUTENANT COLONEL JOHN RANDAL and ex-Captain Travis McCloud issued frag orders to their elements. The troops were tired from a long day but keyed up at the prospects of more action. Violet Patrol was ordered to complete their preparations, and then catch two hours' sleep.

At 2200 hours, Lt. Col. Randal's element pulled out. They had the longest distance to go and needed to be back at the wadi and under camouflage netting by daybreak. Capt. McCloud's element enjoyed the luxury of an additional hour's sleep.

The moon was out full. The desert was illuminated by pale yellow light. The two gun jeeps had no trouble averaging 10 miles an hour across the desert terrain, even driving with their lights out.

The patrol wound its way around boulders, patches of scrub brush, or the occasional stunted acacia tree. When the jeeps reached stretches of open going, Brandy gave Lt. Col. Randal directions to bring them back on the correct compass heading.

Few things are more exhilarating than a movement to contact...and tonight was no exception. Anticipation was running high. Lt. Col. Randal was clicked on.

"We should be there, John," Brandy announced.

Within minutes, the jeeps broke out of the patch of scrub brush the patrol was traveling through. They found themselves on an improved surface, which meant that it had been scraped. The Regia Aeronautica engineers mounted blades on their trucks and smoothed out the desert floor at the remote dirt landing grounds they constructed – it being not worth the effort to bring in bulldozers.

"Nice job, Brandy," Lt. Col. Randal said. "Bingo."

The patrol ran down the strip and hit the far end, which was easy to determine because the ground suddenly became rough. No joy. So, they turned around and drove back in the opposite direction and eventually came to a pole with a limp canvas aeronautical windsock hanging from it.

A single above-ground aviation fuel tank stood next to the wind direction device.

"Welcome to LG. 23," Ace said. "The munitions dump is 50 yards due north of the pole, Colonel. Off the runway."

The patrol rolled to a halt. Ace and Captain "Pyro" Percy Stirling dismounted from their jeeps and walked off in the dark to inspect the demo target.

It was always a thrill to be on an enemy installation behind the lines, even though there was no enemy present and none likely to show up. This is what Raiding Forces was originally formed to accomplish...slip in, do their business in the dark of night, and depart with nobody the wiser. Until, of course, the bad guys found the dead bodies, missing sentinels, or material damage the next day.

"Piece of cake, Colonel," Capt. Stirling reported when he and Ace returned.

"I've heard that before," Lt. Col. Randal said, taking out a thin cigar and sticking it between his teeth. "Tell me the plan."

"The bombs are buried underground, exactly as Ace described," Capt. Stirling reported. "All we have to do is open it up, place an explosive device on top, tamp it with sandbags to force the explosion straight down, light the time fuse off and this munitions dump is history, sir."

"What's it going to be like?"

"Make a huge hole, Colonel," Capt. Stirling said. "Other than that, not much. Most of the blast will be absorbed by the earth."

"Put a 30-minute fuse on it so that we can be a long way and gone when it goes up," Lt. Col. Randal said.

"Wilco," Capt. Stirling said. "I shall put a small charge on the aviation fuel storage tank at the same time. Like I said, sir, a piece of cake."

"I don't have that much confidence in your demolitions predictive abilities, Captain," Lt. Col. Randal said, "but you can sure blow the hell out of stuff."

"Do try," Brandy said, "not to damage the planet this time."

Twenty minutes later, Capt. Stirling and Ace reappeared. "Fire in the hole."

Lt. Col. Randal put the jeep in gear. He then deliberately drove over, rammed the pole holding the windsock, and knocked it down.

The two gun jeeps were driving slowly more than a mile away when the sky behind them glowed. Then in a few seconds, the patrol heard a muffled *WHUUUUUMPH!*

That was all.

Capt. Stirling was right. The explosion did not sound like much. However, Lt. Col. Randal knew it was the almost perfect small-scale raid.

The patrol had ingressed the target covertly, carried out their mission and departed with a minimum of effort, no casualties and were away – ready to do it again somewhere else.

"That was fun," Brandy said as the jeeps accelerated. "What's next, John?"

There were hundreds, if not thousands, of small targets like LG. 23 scattered across the vast Western Desert.

"I'm sure," Lt. Col. Randal said, "we'll think of something."

***

"CAPT. MCCLOUD COMING IN," KING ANNOUNCED. He and Lieutenant Colonel John Randal were the only two people awake in the wadi, on watch. Everyone else was racked out.

Two gun jeeps rolled up and carefully wound their way down into the Violet Patrol harbor. The crews immediately started putting up their camouflage netting.

Lieutenant Penelope "Legs" Honeycutt-Parker stepped out of her jeep, carrying her 9mm Beretta MAB-38 submachine gun in one hand.

"How did it go, Parker?" Lt. Col. Randal said.

"Brandy and I should be paying you, John," Lt. Honeycutt-Parker drawled, sounding drowsy. "We paid Bagnold bags of swag to ride around an empty desert, looking for a lost oasis. Nothing much ever happened.

"With you, it is a thrill-a-minute."

"I see," Lt. Col. Randal said, as she strolled past to where Brandy had prepared a camouflage net to screen their sleeping area, afraid to ask what she meant.

Ex-Captain Travis McCloud came over and took a seat in one of the folding canvas chairs with Lt. Col. Randal. His mouse-colored Stetson—with the little curled sterling silver U.S. Paratrooper jump wings pinned to the front of the hatband—was pushed down over his eyes. He had come to recount the details of his first combat patrol...a major milestone in any officer's career.

Ex-Capt. McCloud looked a little worse for wear.

"Give me a report, Travis," Lt. Col. Randal said, offering a cigarette from a pack of Camels out of the carton that ex-Capt. McCloud had given him prior to the patrol. He offered a light from his old beat-up Zippo, giving the young officer time to gather his thoughts.

"We rolled up on the Italian fueling point," ex-Capt. McCloud said, taking a drag on the cigarette. "Legs hit it right on the nose...beautiful piece of land navigation. No problem, everyone inside was asleep so we didn't disturb anybody.

"The gas storage tanks were above ground. Didn't require much effort to strap demolition charges on 'em, set time pencils, and move out to our next objective... ambushing the track.

"There was a Lanica parked next to the building. We hotwired it...thought an Italian truck might come in useful for the next phase of our operation, so brought it along – and it did.

"The gas station went up when we were rolling down the track. Lit up the sky briefly but no discernible sound. We saw an Italian camp off to the side of the road. There were 30 or 40 trucks parked haphazardly in the desert next to it.

"No one seemed to notice the explosion.

"We went on past the camp for a couple of miles, then I dismounted and did a foot reconnaissance to determine the best location to set up a cutting-out party to get you a prisoner, sir.

"My plan was to station two gun jeeps in concealment on commanding ground off the track, to provide cover with their machine guns. Stage a breakdown of the Lanica on the track to stop the first Italian truck that came by.

"'Legs' Parker's jeep was going to be parked close by, out of sight.

"We were driving up the track in the Lanica, with Legs following in the jeep, headed toward the enemy camp, dropping some 'specially doctored' boxes of German and Italian ammunition Percy had supplied me to help set up the fake breakdown and give the bad guys a little surprise later on when they tried to use it. Unfortunately, I failed to notice there was dead ground between the camp and the location where we were planning to establish the ambush.

"A small convoy of four or five Lanicas suddenly came into view, approximately 200 yards up the road, which meant we had to stage the breakdown then and there...on the fly.

"Of our crew, two men bent over the engine with the hood raised, another was on the pedestal-mounted machine gun off the jeep we had hidden under the tarpaulin in the back of the Lanica, and 'Legs' was alone in the jeep. We hoped the enemy would not be alarmed by it, having never seen one before.

"I had taken off my Stetson and was wearing the Italian Officer's hat Roy had swiped from the fat lieutenant at Fort No. 9...so, I stepped out in the road, held up my hand and the convoy stopped.

"Not giving the bad guys a chance to do much thinking, I walked up to the driver's door, reached up and jerked it open. Unfortunately, I was standing too close and the Wop was big...fell off his seat, grabbed my

Tommy Gun, which got tangled in my coat when I tried to bring it out. We went at it hand-to-hand.

"The son-of-a-bitch managed to jerk my Thompson out of my hands somehow and ran off with it. Meanwhile, the passenger bailed out, ran around the front of the truck and emptied his handgun at me until it clicked. And I mean from me to you, Colonel, point-blank.

"The slide locked back and he went to change magazines. Not a great feeling to be standing there empty-handed in the killing zone of an ambush..."

"What happened?" Lt. Col. Randal said. He had intended to allow ex-Capt. McCloud to make his report uninterrupted, but was unable to restrain himself.

"Legs shot him," ex-Capt. McCloud said. "Then, I got lucky with the grenade I threw at the guy who was running away with my weapon. Meanwhile, Waldo and Roy's jeeps were tearing up the convoy with their Vickers Ks and the Breda 20mm.

"Happily for us, none of the Italian trucks had machine guns mounted – but they had a lot of men on board with rifles. The action was fast and furious. Plus, the enemy camp could hear the firing and was bound to respond.

"The situation was deteriorating rapidly.

"So we drug a prisoner out from under the lead Italian truck, pitched a grenade in the cab, one in our Lanica, and piled into Parker's jeep and decided to call it a day.

Waldo and Roy turned the other trucks into junk metal...covering fire I'd rate textbook perfect, Colonel.

"Frank's an artist on that big Breda 20mm. Best heavy weapons man I've ever seen and that includes the demonstration teams at the Infantry School.

"After breaking contact, we looped out into the desert to throw off anyone following us but there was no pursuit.

"Where's the prisoner?"

"He didn't make it...captured a shot guy. It was that kind of day, sir."

***

WALDO ARRIVED AT THE WADI TWO HOURS AFTER DARK. He reported to Lieutenant Colonel John Randal.

"We set up on the track about 30 miles past Travis's ambush. He had himself a real Keystone Cops shoot-'em-up...guess you done heard. We found us a good hide position with excellent fields of fire. Didn't do much plinkin', though.

"By mid- morning, there was a flood of Italian vehicles headed back up the road away from Tobruk...way too many for us to take a chance sniping at.

"Then all of a sudden, the Germans come rolling down the other way, giant armored convoys – wall to wall – blowin' 'em Wops off the road runnin' hard *toward* Tobruk.

"We didn't shoot at them neither, those square-headed Nazi sauerkraut eaters was lookin' for somethin' to kill. Me, Frank and the Lovats wasn't gonna be it."

"What do you think it means, Mr. Treywick?" Lt. Col. Randal said.

"Colonel, I'd say the British attacked and now the Afrika Korps has done counterattacked...don't look real good."

"If you're right," Lt. Col. Randal said, "I fail to see how things could be any worse.

"Raiding Forces has found 'emselves a new home, Colonel," Waldo said. "It don't much matter to us what the big armies do one way or the other...we can operate out of the desert forever, fightin' our own private war.

"And that ain't bad."

"What are you doing here, Mr. Treywick?" Lt. Col. Randal said. "You're a millionaire, why not go someplace and enjoy it?

"I'm in the same boat as Rita and Lana, Colonel," Waldo said. "It's like the Chinese...save a man's life, and you're responsible for him forever. You capture a slave in Abyssinia, you own 'em. Should a' thought about that before you done freed us...now you've got obligations."

"This ain't China and you're not a Chinese," Lt. Col. Randal said. "We're not in Abyssinia anymore."

"Well, maybe I ain't a slave," Waldo said, "and you're right, I don't have to be here, but that don't keep me from wantin' to hang around just to see what you do next... beats poachin' ivory off the Port-chee-geeze any day.

"Can't really picture me a' gettin' a seat on the New York Stock Exchange...can you?

Intelligence Note Number 10

OPERATION BATTLEAX lasted 72 hours. The British Desert Force was defeated after the first 48 hours. Tobruk was not relieved. And now, at this moment in time, nothing stood between General Erwin Rommel and total victory in the Western Desert... which meant the war.

PRIVATE ARMY COMING 2015

About the Author

Phil Ward is a decorated combat veteran commissioned at age nineteen. A former instructor at the Army Ranger School, he has had a lifelong interest in small unit tactics and special operations. He lives on a mountain overlooking Lake Austin with his beautiful wife, Lindy, whose father was the lieutenant governor to both Ann Richards and George W. Bush.